I0671202

I knew they didn't it, but I couldn't let my friend ruin his life...

All the guys looked at each other, and without saying a word, we followed the jocks. Amanda and Roxie urged us not to do it. We ignored them. You didn't abandon your brother in his time of need.

"Time to make a final stand," Scuzz said.

The jocks approached Owen's red Jeep. Scuzz walked faster, so did we. He ran, we did too.

Scuzz slid a pistol from the front of his pants and sprinted.

"Shit," I whispered. I ran after Scuzz.

"What?" Mullie asked.

I ran, but Scuzz ran faster.

I shoved past people getting into cars. They yelled something, I didn't hear what. A truck nearly hit me. A horn blared, and some guy called me an asshole.

Scuzz gained on the jocks.

My heart raced. I breathed through my mouth.

Where the fuck were Mullie and Donnie?

Scuzz neared the jocks. They stood in front of the Jeep, talking to some tanned cheerleaders. All the guys had their backs turned. The girls didn't notice Scuzz.

This would be no duel.

I hated those guys too, but I had to stop it.

Scuzz raised his right hand.

I never ran so fast.

Almost there.

I gasped for air.

Almost there.

Scuzz's thumb cocked the hammer. "So you're a fucking god, huh?"

Almost there.

He raised the gun.

I tackled him. We hit the ground. Hard.

The gun went off.

Nick Karenka is lost in Sin City. His band's singer has navy SEAL aspirations, his dad's marrying a young stripper, and why does his girlfriend's family make such a big deal about eating with your elbows on the table? Nick holds LA as some sort of utopia, until a chance encounter with a kilt-wearing, hearse-driving drum-playing college freshman named Gremlin starts to bring out who Nick really is. They begin to explore the world beyond the desert island that is Las Vegas until they finally realize that their future isn't in Southern California, but with a bunch of lumberjack-dressing misfits in the Pacific Northwest...

KUDOS for *Bastards of Young*

In *Bastards of Young* by John Santana, Nick Karenka is a senior in high school in Las Vegas, Nevada. He has a band that he is desperately trying to keep together, but the band members are dropping like flies. Not only that, but his girlfriend, Amanda's, family thinks he's an uncouth jerk. To add icing on the cake, the high school jocks go out of their way to make his and his friends' lives miserable. With Nick's dad marrying a younger woman, a stripper, and his mom married to a Kenny Rogers wannabe, Nick is having an identity crises of major proportions. Can he keep it together long enough to graduate from high school and take his band on the road, or is he doomed to always be as invisible as he thinks he is? Santana has crafted a touching and poignant coming of age story that will make you laugh, make you cry, and warm your heart—a remarkable first novel, very well done. ~ *Taylor Jones, The Review Team of Taylor Jones & Regan Murphy*

Bastards of Young by John Santana is the story of a young man with dreams beyond his station. Nick Karenka is a senior in high school, the leader of a band, and a misfit at his high school in Las Vegas. With more determination than talent, Nick has managed to put together a four-piece band. But his other band members don't seem to share his dream of taking the band to LA after high school. War wants to become a SEAL, Micah is hooked on drugs and becoming violent, and Donnie has been kicked out by his grandparents and has nowhere to go. Nick's dad is marrying a stripper, his mom has married a man Nick can't stand, and his girlfriend's parents hate him. But it isn't until he meets Gremlin, a kilt-wearing drummer, that Nick's life really gets interesting. *Bastards of Young* is one of the most realistic representations of high school life that I have read in a long time. With a fast-paced and unpredictable plot, marvelous characters that you can't help but root for, and a ring of truth that borders on uncomfortable, this is one story you'll remember for some time to come. ~ *Regan Murphy, The Review Team of Taylor Jones & Regan Murphy*

ACKNOWLEDGMENTS

This novel would never have been completed without the input, friendship, and regular meeting schedule of a writing critique group that met every week at the Seattle home of Peter Kahle. In addition to Kahle, group members were Lyn McFarland, Sheri Short, Ingrid Scott, Kevin John Scott, Billie Escott, and Suzanne Brahm. They played a major role in shaping the book you now hold.

Thanks also to my wife, Trisha Santana, who, before we married, listened to me read an earlier draft manuscript, provided a lot of encouragement, and gave me the money to attend a writer's conference in Seattle.

BASTARDS

OF

YOUNG

JOHN SANTANA

A Black Opal Books Publication

Black Opal Books
BECAUSE SOME STORIES JUST HAVE TO BE TOLD

GENRE: HISTORICAL YA/NEW ADULT/COMING OF AGE

BASTARDS OF YOUNG
Copyright © 2018 by John Santana
Cover Design by Jackson Cover Designs
All cover art copyright © 2018
All Rights Reserved
Print ISBN: 978-1-626949-27-0

First Publication: MAY 2018

Published by Black Opal Books **http://www.blackopalbooks.com**

BASTARDS

OF

YOUNG

CHAPTER 1

February, 1988, Las Vegas, Nevada:

I kicked the door the way I should've kicked Owen Maywood's face.

Suspended. Me. For fighting. The jocks jumped *me*. But I didn't have a soccer or wrestling match coming up. Nothing for Fremont High to lose sending me home for a week.

"You're gonna learn to worship me. I am a god!" Owen yelled as he tried giving me cauliflower ear.

The door slammed into me the way James Janninks shoved me into my locker. I stumbled but didn't fall. I walked fast. I had to get outta there, even though I had to come back in an hour to get Amanda and take her home.

I wanted to key Owen's red Jeep. It was a few feet away, right in its own private parking space in that sea of newer cars that didn't have oxidized paint jobs and dirty carburetors.

Forget it. I would've stood out too much with my long hair, leather jacket, torn Levis, and scuffed combat boots. People get all paranoid when someone like me shows up. They see me doing something, and next thing you know, I'm off to juvee. Then what?

I parked across the street in a dirt lot, just like all my friends. Made washing my faded white 1971 Plymouth

Duster a waste. The winter desert wind kicked up and blew a dust devil right by my car when I got there. The pebbles struck my face and head. It felt like I got pelted by a semi-automatic BB gun.

After the twister moved on a voice said, "Hey, what's up, bro?" just as I unlocked my car.

On the passenger side was a thin, pale face with sunken cheeks and round brown eyes over a long, pointed nose. An over-sized gray sweatshirt hung off his coat hanger shoulders and stick-figure torso. His long, brown hair blew everywhere. He was barely five-and-a-half-feet tall, six inches shorter than me.

"*War,*" I said. "Where the hell you been?"

"Open the door. Fuckin' cold out here."

I got inside and let him in. He slammed the door behind him.

"You give me a ride?" he asked while putting on his seat belt.

I put the keys in the ignition and started the car. "Of course. Where you goin'?"

The 340 V-8 made a deep noise on startup, especially when I gunned the accelerator to keep the piece of shit from stalling.

"My dad's," War yelled.

I yelled, "Where's he live?"

War messed with the heater switch while I put on my seat belt. "Trailer park by the Strip. Go to Charleston, make a right."

I zipped the Duster out of the dirt lot just ahead of a lifted Chevy truck. The truck's driver honked. I flipped him off then stomped the gas pedal for a quick getaway, to avoid retaliation. "Dude, you never answered my question. Where you been?"

"At my dad's. Mom threw me out."

I glanced at him briefly as I turned onto Charleston, not even looking to see if any cars were coming. I sped to fifty in a forty-five. "You gonna tell me why?"

"Got in another fight with Marianne. Fat bitch kept sayin' it was my turn to do the dishes, so I grabbed a knife and said I was gonna cut her throat, shut her up for good. Mom saw the whole thing, freaked out, and started screamin' and shit." War shook his head and waited a few seconds before finishing his story. "She always freaks out over the stupidest shit."

A couple cars were ahead of me, slowing down. "Can you blame her?" I asked, thinking that his little stunt was easily the dumbest thing he ever did.

"I wasn't gonna do anything. I just wanted to get out of doing the dishes so I could watch TV."

I stopped for a red light at Jones Boulevard. The brakes squealed. "So you moved in with your dad?"

War turned on my radio. The station that called itself the "Rock of Las Vegas" played some damn Crosby, Stills, and Nash hippie crap. All treble, no bass, and some static came from cracked speakers. War turned it off the second the vocals came in.

"No. I've joined the navy. He's taking me to the airport tonight. Boot camp. San Diego."

The light turned green, but I didn't accelerate. I stared at him with a fallen jaw. "You what?" A horn blared. It pissed me off, so I floored it. Squealing tires, burning rubber, both of us thrown against the black vinyl bucket seats. "*You* joined the navy? What the fuck?"

"I'm gonna try out for the SEALs."

I laughed. "You? Try out for an elite commando unit? Right. You outta your fuckin' mind?" I laughed more, shaking my head. "Man, you've watched way too many Chuck Norris movies."

War shoved me in the shoulder. "Fuck you, Nick. This is my dream."

The car swerved violently into the center turn lane. "Don't ever fuckin' touch me when I'm drivin'," I yelled.

I straightened out the car, then I told War he was full of it about becoming a SEAL.

"I'm serious. I wanna blow shit up and kill people."

"I thought our dream was to graduate from that shithole, then take the band to LA."

"That's your dream. Not mine."

Wasn't he gonna say something like "Bless me, Father, for I have sinned"? Wasn't he gonna tell me he this was another one of his pranks? Join the navy. Right. He couldn't betray us.

"You don't get it, do you? I just wanted to have a good time. That's why I joined the band. We hung out, partied, got tore up, rocked out. I wasn't serious about it."

I sped as a yellow light turned red. "Sure acted like it."

I took out my anger on the 340. At least it quit hesitating. It revved at a steady fifteen-hundred RPMs.

"Man, slow the fuck down!" War shouted as I zoomed through the intersection with Valley View doing sixty-five, barely beating a red light. "Gonna get our asses pulled over."

"How the fuck can you say you weren't serious? We swore on our blood. Graduate, LA, place in Hollywood, gigs on the Sunset Strip. Remember? We swore it on our *blood*."

War laughed. He smacked the black, cracked dashboard. "Man, you better wake up. It ain't gonna happen."

I glared at him and asked what he meant.

"You and Donnie are the only guys that are any good. Micah sucks. Scuzz can't even fuckin' play."

I slammed the brakes as a red Pontiac Fiero cut me off. I wanted to remind War that he couldn't sing, when he swore he could. After every song he'd ask us if he sounded just like Steven Tyler of Aerosmith. *No, War, you don't sound like Steven Tyler*. I ignored him and kept the band focused. We moved on to the next song. Count off the tempo, and away we went. Good thing War was my friend. It was the only reason he ever got in. War was also right about Scuzz, but he's the only bass player I knew.

"So what're you sayin'?"

"Don't expect them to follow you."

How the fuck does he know? We're a serious heavy metal band. The music's us. We're committed.

"Turn here," War said.

He guided me into a dusty trailer park. I stopped in front of a single-wide that was white and faded green with brown dirt all over it, bent blinds in the front window, a rusting older green stepside Ford pickup in the driveway, and a carport protecting it from the sun.

War thanked me for the ride as he got out of the Duster, but I was pissed. I didn't tell him he was welcome.

"You ain't gonna make it as a SEAL."

"You ain't gonna make it as a fuckin' metal god, asshole," War yelled and slammed the door.

CHAPTER 2

Micah stamped out his cigarette in the overflowing glass ashtray. He poured the white powder on the small, wood-framed Van Halen mirror he won at the Jaycee State Fair a couple years ago. Then he pulled a razor blade out of the inner pocket of his black leather jacket.

"Dude." I shook my head. "Why'd you bring that shit to a jam session?"

Donnie passed what was left of the joint to Scuzz. Donnie stood up, coughed a few times, and slowly walked over to his Yamaha amp, his red Ibanez Roadster guitar leaning against it.

Imagine Ronald McDonald with whitish-blonde hair, no red makeup around the mouth, but the same kabuki grease-paint for a complexion. That's Donnie.

The living room of Scuzz's house always smelled like Marlboros, dirty clothes, and trash that needed to be taken out. Add to that what the guy behind 7/Eleven said was Acapulco Gold. The furniture looked like a trashed version of something off the set of *The Brady Bunch*. The carpet was covered with dirty clothes and ashes that spilled out of the casino ashtrays. Looked like a volcano erupted. If you thought that was bad, you should've seen and smelled the kitchen.

I tried ignoring my bandmates and tuned my Fender Stratocaster—a superior instrument, the axe of Hendrix and pretty much any guitarist that matters. Mine was a beaut, a body finish Dad described as Lake Placid Blue, with a white pick guard and a maple neck. It was light to play standing up and capable of all sorts of sounds from the three single-coil pickups with the flick of the five-way selector switch. And that was before you plugged it into an amp and any effects pedals. But I couldn't concentrate on tuning. I was worried about Micah. That and everyone's talking made it hard to pick out the subtleties in the tones that told you how out of tune your instrument was.

Micah's long brown hair obscured his thin face as he took the straw and snorted the lines. One by one, second by second, the white powder disappeared up his nose. He only stopped to breathe when he finished a line. When he finished the third one, he laughed. "Man, Nick, you should have some of this. A snort of this and you'll fuckin' nail *Master of Puppets*."

"Ain't you ever listened to the words?" I yelled. "'Chop your breakfast on a mirror.' It's about coke being your master and you being its puppet!"

Micah laughed louder. "Hey, Scuzz, where's your mom's Jack?"

Scuzz chugged whiskey. He held the bottle by its neck while sitting on his amp, his sunburst bass strapped on, seemingly ready to play. He burped, then exhaled like he was trying to cool his throat. "Right here, motherfucker." His voice was unnaturally raspy.

Scuzz capped the bottle and tossed it to Micah, who caught it, opened it, and took a swig. Then he screamed as loud as he can. "Let's fuckin' rock! I feel like a goddamn animal!" Micah threw his leather jacket off, his black Megadeth T-shirt hanging off his skinny frame. He walked to his blue drum kit and plopped on the stool, nearly falling backwards, then rocked forward, grabbed his drumsticks, tossed both of them in the air and caught neither of them as they fell to the brown carpeted floor. He kept laughing. "Hell, yeah," Donnie said, walking by me, going after the Jack Micah left behind. "Let's fuckin' play." I was stoned, but not like Micah. He mixed an insane cocktail of cocaine, pot, and whiskey. Only thing I had was pot and a swig of Jack. Too much booze and I couldn't play. I stumbled over chord changes, then I stumbled over my feet and nearly fell. But pot, especially a shared bowl, calmed me down. I lost fear. That was vital. And I wasn't about to shove Peruvian powder up my nose to try and conquer that anxiety. *Why make yourself more jittery? Just need a little something to take the edge off.* The music had its own edge, different from nerves. With War gone to boot camp, I became the singer. Didn't want to, but what choice did I have? And singing was my biggest musical fear.

Scuzz turned on his amp. Too fuckin' loud. Instant feedback on top of a steady, noisy hum. He staggered about, white stringy bowl cut, the epitome of a bad hair life, hanging in his pale face, the mop almost, but not quite, obscuring bulletproof bifocals. "Yeah," he yelled dragging it out as long as his lungs could pump air out.

I yelled, "Dude, turn your fuckin' amp down!" But I was ignored.

Micah banged his kick drum the way that rabbit thumps his foot in that Disney cartoon I can't remember the name of. He never kicked it so fast. Maybe he could nail *Master of Puppets*? But this steady, rapid bass beat wasn't musical. This was his heart rate. He slammed one stick into the snare and the other one into the tom-tom. He didn't hit drums— he punched them with the sticks—head bobbing, hair flying, the veins in his arms, hands and neck bulging.

Scuzz struck the E string on his bass with his pick. No rhythm. Nothing recognizable as a song, feedback blaring from his amp as much as his buzzing notes. And that idiot egged on Micah, who in turn egged on Scuzz. They screamed. The high-pitched squeal was the closest thing they had to being musical. At least the noises they shrieked were in sync.

Donnie turned on his amp and stomped on his distortion pedal. He slammed the same G power chord over and over. His hair bobbed, like he was in a video. He kept playing that fucking G chord, his fingering so sloppy that he got actual notes as often as not. Amazingly, Scuzz wasn't even hitting his bass in the same key.

What the hell came over those guys? Micah was the only one who did coke. Donnie and Scuzz didn't snort any. Never had. Was that horrific noise their idea of thrash metal? Was this what happened when you drank too much whiskey and got a contact high from a coke fiend?

I was so glad Amanda wasn't there to see that. She'd dump me for sure.

"C'mon, man," Donnie the hairball shouted. "Fuckin' rock, dude."

I tossed my guitar onto the faded green couch, plopped down on one of the sagging cushions, and gazed at the old dying TV. UNLV played a basketball game somewhere. I believed they were supposed to be at Cal-State Fullerton tonight, but I couldn't remember. Just wasn't as into the Rebels as last year, when they went to the Final Four and probably could've won the whole thing. But with Mark Wade; Freddie Banks; and The Hammer, Armon Gilliam, gone, this year's team isn't as good. Still, part of me wanted to watch the game. In a town like Vegas, where no one's actually *from* here, the UNLV Running Rebels were about the only thing that made this feel like a true community.

I could barely see the picture on snowy channel 21. Couldn't they get a damn UHF antenna? Maybe it was a good thing the TV reception was bad. The sound was down because all you heard was static. Not that it would've made a difference—you couldn't hear it anyway even if it was up all the way. Otherwise, I would've tried to escape their idiocy for another hour or two with some college hoops. I went through my usual warm-up routine for my hands—

shaking them, wiggling the fingers—to loosen up. Normally, I'd lead Donnie and Scuzz in those warm-ups, but not tonight. Then I grabbed the Strat again and began doing finger exercises to increase my speed and dexterity. This time, I went for speed. No matter how sloppy I was, I wouldn't hear it. The terrible noise of everyone else prevented that. And, while sitting there, I realized that what I told War about us being a serious band was pure bullshit.

CHAPTER 3

Rain every day this week. I couldn't remember when this had ever happened in Vegas. I once overheard on the local news that this hell on the Earth's surface averaged four inches of rain a year. I thought we were getting our year's worth of rain this week. It just wasn't right. My skin was feeling like it did back in Queens—that was, normal. Out here, the air was normally so damn dry that unless you drenched yourself in skin lotion every couple of hours, white lines appeared all over you because the air was sucking the moisture out of you. It was a vampire, wringing every last bit of water vapor from your body and whatever else it could find. I noticed it shortly after moving here. I ran through the sprinklers in the back yard then walked across the patio. I stopped an admired my wet footprints, only to see them disappear within a minute of me having made them. You could see the patio go from the dark gray of the wet footprint and watch the gray get lighter and the print shrink until there was no record of you having stepped there.

Living in the desert, you got used to water disappearing. You got used to constant thirst, even when you were not doing a damn thing. You got used to your skin feeling like a lizard when you touched it. Then along came a stretch like this, where a year's rainfall fell in a couple of days, and you

just didn't feel right. And adding to that was wondering if
everything was gonna float way. The ground here couldn't
handle a lot of water, so it gushed through the gutters. The
ground didn't absorb much of it, and as a result, the actual
desert became a muddy mess. If the rain fell too hard, the
once dry land turned into a gushing rapids that could—and
would—sweep you away. Happened all the time during the
summer flash floods. And you thought the occasional scorpion in the backyard or popping the hood to check the oil
and finding a rattler wrapped around your engine block was
terrifying.

In the desert, everything tried to kill you.

As I shut off my Plymouth Duster in the dirt parking lot
across from Fremont High School, I wondered if the damn
thing would still be here after school, or if it would be
swept away in a torrent of water and tumbleweeds and con-
struction debris from some new subdivision. It was bad
enough knowing my shoes and jeans were gonna be soaked
with mud by the time I got inside.

The lot was yet another way this school segregates people. The seniors from families with money—and juniors
with the right connections—got to rent their own paved
parking space, while the rest of us lowlife scum had to park
across the street in a dirt lot. But that's not the only sign of
class segregation at this place. The football, baseball and
softball fields were immaculate, their grass green even during the blazing summer heat, not a speck of litter to be
found. The rest of the school had broken glass and dead
grass, the building a big, gray concrete box with no windows. *Welcome to Fremont High School ~ Home of the Pi-
oneers* painted in brown letters with yellow trim across the
roofline, facing the dirt parking lot.

I got out of the Duster at the same time Donnie emerged
from his dented and scratched red Baja, a Volkswagen bug
converted for off-road driving. He got out and pulled his
leather jacket over his head.

"Donnie!" I yelled as I got out of the car.

He stopped running. "Hurry up. It's fuckin' pouring."

We sprinted indoors to discover a new smell: musty rain. Everyone was soaked. There were wet footprints everywhere. Muddy shoe prints littered the tan carpeting. This smell and images of muddy footprints would be engraved into our collective brains. Maybe in twenty years everyone else can look back and laugh.

In the halls packed with idiots in wet coats, I saw Amanda, and everything was right. Nothing mattered except seeing her face and smile. It was the only thing that thawed my icy emotions, although I made sure nobody saw or knew what I felt.

Amanda wasn't gonna be prom queen. She was pale, almost anorexic. She had no tits; skinny legs; a pointed nose; narrow, pink lips; and thin, but long, blonde hair. I thought she was the hottest fuckin' thing around. She had really hot green eyes and a crooked smile that dragged a grin out of my constant frown. She moved to Vegas from Denver last summer when her dad's job transferred him.

First time I saw Amanda was after school in October, outside Mad Dogs, which has the best chili-cheese fries. She was with her mom, walking one way, me and Micah the other. Me and her saw each other and stared. I didn't know what it was, but I was hooked. I turned and slowly walked backward, staring at her. She glanced at me over her shoulder, her mouth open, like she couldn't breathe. Then I walked into a stucco beam, hit my head, and yelled, "Oh fuck!"

Micah laughed. Amanda giggled as she got into the front passenger seat of a minivan, still looking at me.

The next day, I noticed she was in my English class, sitting next to me. How did I not see her before? Had she noticed me at all? We never spoke. I'd look at her, she'd turn away. I was afraid to talk to her, I found her that attractive. Finally, on the last day before Christmas break and after class, I asked her to go with me. She accepted.

Her crooked smile when she saw me was the same as

when I first asked her. A tote bag was slung over her shoulder. She wore jeans and a black button-up sweater that made her pale face and thin, white neck stand out. I loved her skin, and her neck. Turned me on.

"Hi," she said.

Me and Donnie walked up to her. I smiled, put my right arm around her waist, pulled her close, and kissed her. "Good morning."

We walked with our arms around each other's waist to where me and Donnie had our lockers. It was there that we met up with Scuzz and Micah.

"Hey, guys," Donnie said. "Geez, Scuzz, you're soaked."

If there was one good thing about the rain, it was that Scuzz got a bath and his clothes got washed. His 1975 Ford Ranchero had a flat, so he was walking to school. His white hair was soaked, drops all over his face and glasses. He smelled like a wet dog. It was actually an improvement.

"So, we gonna jam tonight?" I asked enthusiastically at the thought of playing music. "Maybe this weekend?"

Donnie dug through his locker in search of some textbook. "Thought you said we needed a singer."

I turned the combination on my locker, amazed that Donnie remembered anything from our jam-session-turned-stoned-noise. "Well...I don't know. Maybe. Doesn't mean we can't jam."

"Oh look, it's a wet stoner," Jeff Day said and shoved Scuzz into the lockers.

Scuzz's glasses hit the tan steel. It was how his glasses got bent in the first place, only *that* body slam was courtesy of James, captain of the football and wrestling teams.

Jeff and Owen continued walking, laughing and high-fiving each other. Jeff turned to us. "We're gonna finish you fuckin' filthy hippies off!"

I yelled, "Try it now, fucker?"

They kept walking.

Owen turned to us. "Clean up your act and worship us. We are gods!"

Donnie shook his head. "Typical."

Scuzz grimaced. He almost grabbed his right shoulder with his left arm but stopped as his hand got about halfway there.

"You all right?" I asked gently as I got my locker open.

Amanda bent down to help him up, but Scuzz ignored her.

Once he was standing, Scuzz adjusted his glasses. "Yeah, I'm fine."

Donnie slammed his locker shut. "Fuckin' pussies."

"How long is it 'til graduation?" Scuzz asked, glancing at the floor, getting no reply. He bent down to get the folders and spiral notebook he dropped.

Micah adjusted his backpack on his shoulder. "Why they call us stoners when they're taking steroids?"

"What's with the whole they're gods thing, anyway?" Donnie asked.

"I think it's something coach whats-his-name been drilling into them," I replied.

Damn jocks. They had it all. Names in the papers, cheerleader chick girlfriends, their pictures all over the damn yearbook, new fancy cars. Yuppie bitches would consider James and Owen good looking. They got their muscles, tanned faces, neatly trimmed hair, brown in Owen's case, blond in James's case. Perfect Hitler youth. Jeff, though, had a bunch of zits all over his face and a brown peach fuzz mustache. I swore the dude would've been a joke if he wasn't good at sports and had small arms. He also frequently wore a T-shirt that said *AIDS kills fags dead* under his letterman's jacket. He got away with wearing that, and we had gotten lectured by the principal about wearing T-shirts that "promote Satan and devil worship." Of course, we thought the shirts were promoting Ozzy, Metallica, Led Zeppelin, and Judas Priest.

During sophomore year, Fremont's football team was

the worst in Vegas, and probably the worst in Nevada. The last two years they won the state championship with most of the same players and all the same coaches. And guys like Owen, James, and Jeff all came back to school in August of last year a helluva lot bigger than they were in June. For a while, we made fun of Jeff—behind his back, of course— about how he suddenly had more zits than in junior high. Classic sign of steroid use, I heard. So was the fact those motherfuckers got even more aggressive toward us.

So there they were, calling us "stoners," when they too were using illegal drugs. The one I liked to smoke—the only one I dared touch—was a plant that grew in the wild, not something created in some lab.

I closed my locker and reached for Amanda's hand, partly out of love, partly to keep calm while I faced what I knew was inevitable. "Tell you what. Why don't we jam tomorrow night and write a song? Somethin' about anybody who plays sports is an asshole."

"Why don't we just forget about playing and just hang out, have a good time, party?" Micah looked away from me as he said that.

Donnie, meanwhile, stared at a chubby redhead he'd had his eye on all senior year. He hadn't met or approached her, and I knew he wouldn't. He'd need help meeting her.

"Yeah, why don't we just let go on the weekend for once?"

The redhead Donnie gawked at passed out of view. I knew this because Donnie glanced at me when he complained, "Let's just forget about it."

I spoke slowly. "We can't forget about it, cuz if we're gonna go to LA, *we gotta get better*. And we need some real material."

"We got plenty of time to write songs," Micah said as the bell for first period rang. "Hey, let's get some peyote from Sonny. Let's get fucked up."

"Uh, guys," I said, "we were just called stoners."

"Yeah, whatever." Donnie headed toward his first period class in the opposite direction from us.

"Well?" I asked Scuzz.

"I need to get away, Nick. I'm gonna hang out with Micah and Donnie."

I closed my eyes, slowly shook my head side to side. I knew this was coming, but that didn't make it easier. I began getting the sense that music was insignificant to those guys. I looked at Amanda, my last hope to avoid spending a weekend with my parents, alone.

"And you're goin' out to dinner with your parents tonight?" I solemnly asked.

She pouted. "Yeah, sorry."

"All right. Guess I'll see ya in English class." I kissed her hand and headed to chemistry. I walked past Scuzz, gave him a dirty look, and didn't say a thing to him.

CHAPTER 4

Instead of taking notes on chemical reactions in first period, on psychology in second period, and the three branches of government in third, complete with all sorts of idealistic crap about how wonderful it all was, I scribbled and erased lyrics for a song about assholes who played sports. I hunched over my spiral notebook so no one could see what I was doing. The best part—the teachers thought you were busy taking notes.

The first lyrics I came up with were:

You think you're so great
Playing football and lifting weights.

That was in chemistry class after a lot of thought. What a bunch of crap. Granted, it was early in the morning, and I wasn't a morning person. I drew a single line through the words. Still, it was a start.

In psychology class, I scribbled:

I can't catch a pass
But I ain't slappin' guys on the ass.

I crossed that out too, but I liked something about it.

Then I came up with a title: *Jock Itch.* Should I put a B in front of itch? Radio and MTV play depended on that kind of crap. That and nearly naked chicks in your video humping a sports car hood. Maybe cheerleaders spreading wide on those Acuras in the paved parking lot. We could do the video here, have a bunch of Lita Ford-wannabes kick the cheerleaders off the hoods and then get all slinky while wearing faded blue denim skirts, black spike heels, and glittery tube tops, slamming guitars through the windshields. Then cut to show a bunch of stoners beating the jocks at baseball, hitting home runs with their guitars while the jocks had dumb expressions on their faces while the heshers gave the finger to the buzz-cut steroid boys during the home run trots.

Daydreaming in class. Gotta love it.

After coming up with the title, a wide, slick grin appeared. My face tired quickly from rarely used muscles. I muted a laugh so Mr. Markhart wouldn't embarrass me in front of the whole class.

And in government class, I couldn't find a word that rhymed with steroids.

Mongoloids?

Freakazoids?

Anything at allazoids?

It ain't easy writing the "Stairway To Heaven" of teen misfit angst.

And when Mr. Jenkins stood in the front of the class, in the kind of leisure suit my dad got rid of eight years ago, and talked about the supreme court's role in watching the president and congress, I tried coming up with something that rhymed with assholes. Buttholes was the best I could do. But I knew the music had to be three or four power chords, played really fast. It *had* to sound pissed. It had to be raw and aggressive.

Once the bell ended government class, Mullie came up to me. He was like everyone I knew. He was the aftermath of a nuclear family that detonated into two parts in its own blast, and he'd lived in an endless winter ever since. He was the kind of guy you wouldn't even notice, unless you were a jock looking like someone to pick on. He looked like the ninety-eight-pound weakling but dressed like a buff surfer. His baggy clothes threatened to consume him.

But Mullie could draw. He gave the best Christmas cards. The one he gave me last month had a guy who pulled his heart out with knives on his fingers and handed the beating organ to a horrified girl. The guy bled all over the place, tongue waggling out of his mouth, eyes looking up. On the inside, the card read, *This Christmas, give a little of yourself.*

He asked if the band was jamming or if me and Amanda were doing anything. Nope.

"Wanna hang out? I stole a twelve-pack of Moosehead," Mullie asked as we walked into the halls.

Nothing like proving some people correct. What the hell. I took peyote last year with Sonny and War, and we all puked. Drinking never did that to me, unless I downed a fifth by myself. I agreed to hang out with Mullie. It beat hanging out with Mom and her new husband, Rick, a Kenny-Rogers-looking, country- music-loving Teamsters fork lift operator. We didn't get along. In fact, I hated him the first time I heard his gruff voice. I walked into the house, and Rick, watching pro basketball on our TV, blurted, "Boy, the Lakers sure got a lot of niggers on them."

I took an instant dislike to the guy. And it only went downhill.

He got on me about mowing and watering the lawn, all while he bitched about the water bill and the fact my showers took more than two minutes. My comeback was that watering the front yard to have a lawn was a waste of water. We never spent any time out there, and besides, this was one of the driest deserts on the planet. They didn't tell you that in the schools here, and if you brought it up anywhere in this place, you got dirty looks from people. *Do not ask questions. Do not think. Why waste water on something you do not use? If you wanna cut back on the damn water bill, cut back on what uses the most water. Sounds reasonable, right?*

And get this, even though I had a solid argument, a plan to help our "family" save money, I lost the argument. *Of course, that's what being a redneck fascist who's got my mom wrapped around his finger gets you.*

So yeah, hanging out with Mullie sure beat hanging out with the water-wasting KKK guy.

❧❧❧

Shortly before Mullie arrived, I had my weekly phone call with Dad. I told him how and why I was a lead singer.

"Oh, that's cool," Dad replied. "Man, it's easier to get laid when you sing and play guitar. Don't tell your mom, but there was one time she wasn't around, and I was singing 'People Get Ready' at a club in Greenwich Village, and this black chick with a huge afro started running her hands right by my nuts, and then…"

Mullie's car, a faded black 1975 Firebird, pulled up in front of the house.

"Dad, I gotta go." I hung up before he could tell me something I didn't need to know.

I grabbed my leather biker jacket, said bye to Mom and Rick, ran outside, and only slowed down to open the passenger-side door.

"Where you wanna go?" Mullie asked as I slid into his car, "Guns 'N Roses" playing at low volume from his cassette deck.

The rain had stopped, the stars again visible, but barely thanks in part to the city's gaudy neon lights on the Strip. "How about Lone Mountain?"

Mullie's foot slammed the accelerator. With squealing tires and G-forces throwing us farther into the tan bucket seats, we rushed to leave my neighborhood of small, old houses and dead lawns. He turned his stereo as high as it could go. Volume, no bass, plenty of treble. The gunning motor mixed with Axl Rose's voice and Slash's guitars in a scene that wasn't repeated much, if at all, in our yuppie high school.

Lone Mountain was where we took girls to fuck, or get drunk or stoned with nobody around. The road that passed in front of the mountain was where one could get *the* view of the growing city, the orange glow of the distant street lights shimmering. The Strip was visible, but from twenty miles away, the lights were just a faint glow.

I grabbed two Mooseheads and used the opener Mullie kept in the glove compartment to pop them open. We put the beers between our legs when were weren't drinking. A few minutes after leaving my house, Mullie was doing seventy on a fifty-five freeway.

"Remember how Mr. Barrato would start driver's ed class by yelling, 'Fourteen people a day—'" I copied the teacher's fist-pounding technique on the tan dashboard. "'—are killed, in drunk driving accidents.'"

Mullie chuckled. "You think he was telling the truth?"

"I don't know. Maybe it's a Trivial Pursuit answer."

Mullie looked at me, smiling, both hands grasping the steering wheel. "Maybe we'll be numbers fifteen and sixteen."

"The only problem with death is that it only happens once."

And death approached from behind in the side view mirror with flashing lights.

"Oh shit! Mullie, slow the fuck down! It's the cops."

"The cops? Where?" He looked at his rear view mirror. "*Ffffuck.*" He let off the gas.

"Keep the beer down," I yelled. "Fuck, man, we're dead."

The flashing lights drew near.

We tried starting straight on. Mullie turned his stereo down. My heart wanted to break out of my rib cage. I heard Mullie's breathing. He bit his lower lip.

The siren got louder. Mullie tapped the breaks.

My palms sweated.

The siren overpowered the stereo.

I imagined Mom yelling at me. That'd be a shame. She was such a sweet, quiet woman with brown eyes that Dad said looked like a koala bear, and it turned out that "compliment" always pissed her off. I always was nicer to her than Dad. Wasn't sayin' much, but still. He cheated on her, beat her whenever he got drunk, and, best I could tell, hardly ever told the truth. Why she stayed with him all those years was beyond me. Letting her down was, in the back of my mind, my biggest disappointment, and now, I was on the verge of being hauled in by the cops, the biggest disappointment of all. Then again, she did marry a Kenny Rogers wannabe. This could be my revenge for letting that jerk shack up with us and use my deodorant a couple of times without even asking me first.

The pigs didn't trail us for long. They pulled alongside almost as fast as they snuck up on our asses. We stared at the road.

I'm gonna hyperventilate. Mullie's breathing's loud.

And the cops breezed by. They merged back into our lane after passing us. Didn't even use their turn fuckin' signal.

Mullie and I looked at each other and exhaled.

"Let's wait 'til we get there before takin' another sip," he said.

"Yeah." I turned up the volume on the tape deck. "And lay off the gas, will ya?"

℘ℐ℘

A few minutes later, we arrived at Lone Mountain. We pulled off the two-lane road and parked the Firebird facing the valley. We sat on the hood for warmth. My black leather biker jacket was unzipped, my tattered blue flannel shirt unbuttoned, and a purple T-shirt with the words *Group Therapy* scribbled on it with a cartoon of a massive orgy featuring people and animals. Mullie wore a faded black leather bomber jacket and a white long-sleeved T-shirt that could've used some bleach.

It was cold, dark, and windy.

Then Mullie had to ask about the fucking band and who was singing with War gone. I told him I was because...

a) Nobody wanted it cuz they were too chicken shit; and
b) Scuzz and Micah figured I could help them get chicks.

"So, you like being a singer?"

"Shit, I could barely handle backing vocals without screwing up a riff. You do the math."

"So you suck?"

I smiled and chuckled. "Yeah, I suck. Wanna sing?"

He looked at me, and, even through the darkness, I saw he was blushing. "Me? You nuts?" Mullie turned away, took a swig, and let out a deep long burp that echoed.

"Bless you."

"Thanks."

All he needed to do was say yes, and the job was his. I might have been the type to ask the other guys what they thought in terms of some band decisions, but this was a problem that could only be solved by Nazi-ass tactics.

The strong wind pointed our hair south as we took another drink from our beers.

"You know, I don't think these guys're serious anyway. I think they just like being in a band just to try and get laid."

"Can't be working for Scuzz."

I laughed. "Scuzz could go to the Chicken Ranch with a wad of hundreds and wouldn't be able to buy a hand job."

Mullie sighed. "My dad says he's gonna take me there when I turn eighteen next month."

"Yeah. So?"

Mullie finished a sip. "Well, it was...just...*weird*, you know? When you don't hear from your dad for five years and then you finally do, you don't expect him to announce he's gonna take you to a whorehouse. Sorry," he quietly said. "Shouldn't've said anything."

"Don't worry about it, bro."

In a long swig, I finished my fourth Moosehead. I threw the bottle into the darkness after sliding off the hood. The bottle must've been caught by the sagebrush. We didn't hear it break.

"War said he was never really into it," I said, after sitting on the hood again. I belched, but not nearly as loud as Mullie's a minute earlier. He never blessed me. Not that it mattered.

"He used to brag about it so much, bein' in your band."

I turned toward him. "Exactly. That's what I don't understand. All of 'em seem to like being in a band and talkin' about goin' to LA after we graduate, but they don't wanna practice or write songs or anything." I leaned toward Mullie. "You know what they wanted to do tonight? Get peyote from Sonny. Didn't even wanna play."

I folded my arms in front of my chest, trying to keep warm in the subfreezing wind chill, totally forgetting I could've zipped up my jacket or buttoned the flannel. Mullie got two more beers. He returned and slid onto the hood, handing me a bottle.

"Guys got any gigs coming up?" Mullie brought the bottle to his lips to have a swig.

I sarcastically laughed. "Where we gonna play? A fuckin' casino lounge?"

"Why not have a party, invite some people and jam."

Why didn't I think of that? Maybe I could assess the band. Maybe the guys would wanna practice. Maybe we'd write songs. Maybe Amanda would put out, and if not her, maybe some other girl or two would show up and prove Dad's theory of singing and playing guitar.

Ah hell, it's supposed to be about the music, ain't it?

Mullie said he'd show up. I now had my first fan on my way to someday standing atop an arena stage, Stratocaster in hand, preaching my yet-to-be-written, middle-finger electric gospel before tens of thousands of disciples each night in city after city all over the world.

"That's fuckin' brilliant, man." I tapped his arm. "Hey, why don't you design a flyer for us."

"Me?"

"Yeah, you draw great."

"Thank you."

"Yeah, just draw whatever you want."

Mullie agreed, and, with that taken care of, I just had to get the rest of that concert organized—after we finished off the stolen brews and avoided becoming a Mr. Baratto statistic.

CHAPTER 5

Y ou want to have a party *here*?" asked Donnie's grandfather, a guy nearly seven feet tall and had to weigh more than three-fifty.

It was obvious who Donnie got his height from. The old man had a gray flattop and tanned arms covered with military tattoos. He watched a war movie on TV, gunfire and shouting coming from it loud and clear. His wife, a frail woman barely five feet tall, with a wrinkled face and thinned gray hair, sat in another chair, knitting. She always knitted but never seemed to finish anything.

Donnie leaned against the white living room wall. "Please, Grandfather. We're gonna play our music for some friends from school."

How Donnie could look at that guy, I didn't know. Dude was gross to look at. He sat in a tan recliner, a can of Bud clutched in his oversized right hand. He wore a white V-neck T-shirt that had yellow stains on the armpits and allowed his abundant gray body hair to stick out from whatever opening it could find. His gut was so huge the shirt couldn't cover it.

Grandfather stared at that box that emanated horrible sounds of death while he thought about Donnie's request. Me, Scuzz, and Micah stood out of his grandparents' view in the dark hallway.

"I don't know about that, Donald," his grandfather said, folding his arms and resting them on his belly. He never took his eye off the movie.

"Oh, c'mon, Grandfather, please. We've been practicing for years and have never played in front of anybody. Please, Grandfather. We just wanna play in front of people."

"With the way you boys sound, you shouldn't play in front of anybody. That shit sounds like something those North Korean Commies I used to kill back in the war would listen to."

Donnie's grandmother looked up from her knitting, but kept going, as if she was running on instinct. "Your grandfather's right, Donald. Why don't you boys play some nice music, like Pat Boone?"

Me, Micah, and Scuzz looked at each other, wondering who the hell she was talking about.

"No. No way, Donald." His sagging jaw skin flopped around like a goldfish on a floor.

Donnie's grandmother stopped knitting. "Elmer, let the boys have their little fun. Besides, we haven't gone to see the *Folies Bergere* in a couple of years. Let's make a night of it."

"Think the showgirls wear pasties?" Scuzz whispered.

"For that old fart's sake, I hope not," I replied.

While Grandmother, as Donnie called her, showed a yellowed gap-toothed smile, Elmer gruffly mumbled something and unfolded his arms before turning to his grandson, pointing at him. "All right, Donald, you can have your little party. But on one condition—no drugs, no booze, everyone you invite is out of here by midnight, none of that weird sex or Satanic rituals, and you and your friends clean up this place when you're done."

"That's five conditions," Scuzz whispered. Micah and I shushed him.

This was probably as good a time as any to get something off my chest. I was really sick of practically everybody thinking that just because you listened to heavy metal, that you were some sort of Satan-worshipping, cat-killing antichrist. None of us were anything like that. We didn't believe in Satan. I didn't believe in God, and I'd never asked Micah, Donnie, or Scuzz if they dis. If these idiots who believed everything some televangelist told them actually looked at the lyrics, they might realize that most of the bands we listened to weren't anything like their preconceived notions.

Jury was still out on Slayer, however.

"Okay, Grandfather. Thank you," Donnie said. He jogged to the hallway and joined us. "All right, guys," he whispered, smiling, "We got it. Let's jam."

Only reason we chose Donnie's was that most of us thought Scuzz's house was too filthy. Rick and Mom killed the idea of having it at home, and Donnie volunteered to ask before Micah did. So we had our guitars, Micah his drums, only we had to play in Donnie's bedroom. With the drums, it became cramped, meaning me and Donnie had to share an amp. Good thing his Yamaha had two input jacks.

Donnie's room was black-lit. It smelled of incense and had walls covered with magazine pictures of metal bands and *Sports Illustrated* swimsuit pics above two antique-looking dressers. Hanging on the ceiling, covering the hanging light fixture, was a green Jimi Hendrix tapestry. Donnie slept on a pull-out sofa. It felt more like a studio apartment than a bedroom.

I told Micah my idea for the drum part for "Jock Itch," then we played the song. I kept the lyrics I wrote in class, but didn't come up with any more.

Everyone liked the lyrics, but no one cared for the music, even though Donnie and Scuzz nailed their parts on the first try. No wonder. It was only three power chords, three bass notes, and the progressions were pretty much repeated for two minutes. Didn't require a lot of thought to play.

"Keep that shit down," Elmer shouted from the living room after we finished the song. We quietly laughed it off. At least me, Donnie, and Scuzz could turn down the volume on our guitars or amps. There wasn't no quiet way to play drums.

We decided not to push Elmer any more. We shut off our amps, and Donnie put Motley Crue's "Girls, Girls, Girls" on his turntable, the volume low so his grandfather wouldn't get pissed off. At least me and the old man had one thing in common—we both thought the Crue sucked.

Scuzz reached into a pocket inside his faded blue denim jacket and broke out a fifth of unopened peppermint schnapps he said he found walking behind a grocery store the other night. Suddenly, the night became much better.

Me and Donnie sat on the sofa bed, Scuzz on the floor, Micah on his drum stool. We passed around the bottle, taking big swigs before handing it off. The candy-flavored sauce didn't even burn going down my throat.

"Let's have a toast." Scuzz picked his nose. "To the band and our first gig."

Donnie changed the toast to include me going with Amanda.

I smiled at the thought of Amanda while trying not to laugh about Scuzz digging for gold. "I'm all for that."

"So, Nick, you gonna write a love song for Amanda?" Scuzz's crooked, chipped yellowed teeth flashed through his smile. He wiped a booger on the carpet.

"Uh, no. And, besides, Boston had that song 'Amanda' last year, remember?"

"Actually, I was trying to forget that song," Donnie said.

"Yeah, me too," I replied.

Scuzz leaned back against one of the dressers. "You mean you and her haven't slow danced to that song."

Donnie handed me the schnaps.

"Hell. no. Song sucks," I said.

"So have you fucked her yet?" Micah asked sarcastically.

I glared at Micah, eyes narrowed. It was my pissed off gaze.

"You haven't even fucked her yet?" Micah asked. "You pussy."

I took a drink and handed the booze to Scuzz. "Dude, she told me she ain't ready yet."

Micah tossed a drum stick in the air. It spun a few times before it came down. and he caught it. "Since when've you decided to *wait* for a chick?"

"This is different than with Michelle or Tina. Just is."

Donnie changed the subject. He must've guessed how pissed I was getting at Micah. "So, how we gonna get people to this 'gig'?" Donnie asked.

I leaned back on the sofa. "Mullie's gonna do some flyers for us, and we'll hand them out to people we wanna invite."

"Mullie?" Donnie asked. "Why?"

"Ever see any of his drawings?"

Donnie and Scuzz shook their heads. Micah said no before taking a drink.

"He's good. I've seen his stuff, so I invited him to do it."

"I didn't know he drew," Scuzz said.

Micah handed the schnaps to Donnie. "What's the flyer gonna look like?"

"I don't know. Just gonna let him do his thing."

We spent the next ten minutes finishing off the bottle. Micah and Scuzz planned to crash there. I didn't. I told Mom I'd be home later.

"I'm gonna head out, see if Amanda's still alone tonight." I invited her to Donnie's to watch us play, but she had to baby-sit her younger brother while her parents went out.

"Gonna fuck her, finally?" Micah asked.

I glared at him and left Donnie's room, even though I wanted to break Micah's face.

Turns out schnapps was deceptive. Its proof was about half that of Bacardi or Southern Comfort, but that didn't mean it failed to pack a punch. It did—about a minute after I drove away from Donnie's. It was a light kind of drunk, not like prior blackouts I had from stronger booze.

I still saw the straight lines of the divided lanes—
somewhat.

One good thing about driving drunk was you concentrat-
ed more on maintaining the speed limit than usual, and you
were more careful to use your signals. It was the only time I
drove with both hands on the wheel and the radio off.

Okay, so it was a week earlier that me and Mullie nearly
shit our pants when a pig pulled up behind the Firebird.
That was different. We had *beer* in the car. But if I got
pulled over, I might've been able to get out of it. One of the
first things me and Donnie did when we got our licenses
was practice walking in a straight line and touching our fingertips to our noses while drunk or stoned. We got pretty
good at it too. Never thought about how to evade a breath or
piss test.

I sped into the driveway of Amanda's two-story house,
stopping just in time to avoid turning that one-car garage
into a second carport. I had to piss. The living room lights
were on. After staggering to the door, I struggled to find the
doorbell before buzzing it. And buzzing it again. And again.
And again.

When the door opened, I pulled my finger off the doorbell. What a beautiful sight. Amanda stood in front of me
only wearing her pajamas, a long blue T-shirt that draped
her shapeless body. It made her milky skin stand out. Her
ghost-colored legs looked good. Her blonde bangs hung in
her eyes. I wanted to do her right there. Just grab her hips,
lift her up, put her against the wall, spread those lean,
milky-white thighs, and start banging away. And I'd do the
same thing to her twin sister. Twin sister? Whatever. It'd
been so long I thought I regained my virginity.

A great thing about being seventeen was you could get a
boner even though you need to pee.

"Come on, my parents might be home any minute now,"
she said as I put my arms around her waist and began moving my right hand from her lower back to her ass. Figured

that way would be more...*romantic*...*y*eah, that was it, than what I thought about a minute earlier.

"Stop it," she whispered, shoving me away. "My brother's sitting right over there."

So much for a quick one while they were away.

"But—it's—uh—ain't it midnight, or some'in'? What's he doin' up?

"We're playing 'Risk.' "

I gave her and her twin a look that was meant to show I wasn't impressed.

"You smell like peppermint candy."

Now what? Admit I'm drunk? Could they tell? I did something with my face, moving my eyelids, my mouth, crinkling my nose.

Amanda sighed. "Look, my parents might be home soon, and if they meet you when you're like this, they'll never let me see you again." Then her voice turned happy. "But come over tomorrow night for dinner. I want you to meet them."

It's amazing what peppermint schnapps will make you say yes to.

CHAPTER 6

I went to bed a drunk seventeen-year-old and woke up in a middle-aged body. My neck ached. So did my back. It must've been the way I slept. Every time I passed out on my stomach, I bent my spine all screwy. I sweated from the heat of the waterbed, the covers, and Boss, my fat tan cocker spaniel, using my back as a bed.

Damn peppermint schnapps.

I gently rolled over, waking Boss and tossing him onto a wavy mattress. Facing the ceiling, I reluctantly opened my eyes. We both yawned, and I patted his head.

Boss was my brother, my lone cousin. He' was a grandparent, uncle, and aunt. Why? Ain't got the real thing anymore. He also was a friend I took for special trips during the blistering summer. Sometimes, just to get the hell away from everybody, he and I would hop into the Duster with the windows down, make a high-speed run through the desert, and go to the high country of Mount Charleston, where we'd breathe cooler air, walk among tall pine trees, and realize that there were places in Nevada that weren't totally ugly. And our high-speed runs allowed me to act out a childhood desire: To be Han Solo. The Duster became the Millennium Falcon, and Boss, of course, was Chewbacca. Ever since we moved here, this place had been Luke Skywalker's home planet of Tatooine. How much? Whenever Boss and I returned from a trip to the mountains, and Vegas came into view as we sped along US 95, I recited Obi Wan Kenobi's warning to Luke: "'Mos Eisley spaceport. You will never find a more wretched hive of scum and villainy.'"

And on that grim Sunday morning, a road escape from ugly reality would've been nice.

"You got it so easy, Boss." I closed my eyes. "All you have to do is eat, sleep, bark, and shit. Me? I get to meet Amanda's parents tonight. They're not gonna like me boy. Nobody ever does."

Boss rested his chin on my ribs with a moan. I continued petting him.

"I don't wanna meet her parents." I put my other hand across my forehead. "Especially feelin' like this. And what am I gonna wear? I ain't got any good clothes."

I rolled over to check my digital alarm clock.

"C'mon, boy, let's get up." I sat up, getting hit with a rush of dizziness that almost knocked me down. "It's half past noon." Then I got out of bed, opened the curtains, and peered through the blinds to see what was going on outside. I closed my eyes and turned away. It was too damn bright. Every day when I stepped outside or looked outside the window, I saw the sun ninety-nine percent of the time and groaned, "Dammit. Sunny again. That just ain't natural."

I did a lot that day, mainly to avoid showing I was hung over. I did a load of whites so I could wear clean underpants and socks. I tried not to let on to Mom and Rick that I was hung over. I was thirsty all day, but didn't drink a six-pack of Mountain Dew. Stayed in my room mostly, listening to, *Strange Days* by the Doors, an album I stole from Dad, over and over again.

"We want the world, and we want it now."

I wanted to scream like Jim Morrison right after those lyrics.

After listening to that album so much that Mom

might've thought I was a Vietnam vet with a Fu Manchu about to have a flashback, I showered, but didn't shave the three or four bits of stubble I had. Lately, I had turned into Scuzz and left clothes on the floor in my room. I grabbed a T-shirt from the pile and my blue flannel.

When it came time to leave, I felt better, but I wasn't ready. I never met a girl's parents before. But as I left the house, I realized my best bet was to keep quiet.

I walked the mile from my house to theirs. Every place in their neighborhood had tan stucco exterior walls with red Spanish tile roofs, trimmed green lawns, and young trees. The garages were out front, houses in the back. All the yards were rimmed by gray cinder block walls that were taller in the backyard than out front. My territory was a bunch of faded and cracked aluminum siding and regular shingles. Yards were full of grass, weeds, dirt, and older vehicles parked on the dead front lawn. Chain-link fences and sun-bleached wooden fences defined everybody's backyards.

Amanda's house differed some from the others on her circle. It was made of stucco and Spanish tile, but the garage was next to the front door. It also had a carport, and behind a gate was a burgundy minivan. In front of the garage was a light blue 300ZX.

The house, the neighborhood shouldn't have been intimidating, but it was, for some reason. I stood at the door and thought about turning around. I could go home, call Amanda, and tell her I was sick. It'd be a half-truth, but still a truth. But I told Mom and Rick that I was having dinner here. I rang the doorbell, looking at the red tile I stood on, hands in front pockets of my faded Levis. At least I was smart enough to not to wear a pair of pants with holes in them.

I thought the Lee Iacocca dude from those TV car commercials opened the door. It wasn't. It was Amanda's dad, Thomas. He reached out to shake my hand after introducing himself. He wore glasses, blue sweatpants, and an orange

Denver Broncos T-shirt. He dressed like one of Dad's cab driver buddies.

"Come on in." Thomas swept his left hand to show me inside.

I was sure he did that to dry that hand from my sweaty palms.

It was a typical new Vegas house—white walls, but the ugliest blue carpet that wasn't the shaggy variety seen in my usual haunts. That painting with the melting clocks hung on one wall, a stone fireplace next to it. I knew it was a copy of a famous painting and was about to judge them for having it. Then I remembered that all my band did was copy others. *Who knows?* If they could relate to pirated art, maybe we could relate to each other. And, besides, that picture gave the house some color. In that respect, it was no different than any other house in this town. Here, in the land where going outside could make you a redskin, the houses reflected the ideal. And, on the floor, laying on his stomach in front of a fireplace, a fat brown-haired little kid wearing blue sweatpants and an orange T-shirt read a comic book.

"This is our son, Jimmy."

He looked up long enough to say and wave hi before he resumed reading. I nodded.

"I hope you like spaghetti and meatballs. That's what we're having tonight," Thomas said as he escorted me into the kitchen, where Amanda and her mom prepared dinner.

"Oh, I do. A lot."

"And this is Amanda's mother, Vera."

Vera greeted me with vibrant blue eyes, a bright smile, a brown-colored hairdo that looked like the top of a mushroom cloud, and an enthusiastic hello. And, man, did she have huge tits! They stuck out nicely through the same orange Denver Broncos T-shirt that Thomas wore. She also wore blue sweatpants.

The excitement over Vera's tits passed quickly. First of all, she was kinda old. And Amanda seemed like a misfit in her own family. Was she the only blonde? Was Thomas's

slicked gray hair once blond? Her entire family was tanned,
she was pasty. While everybody else celebrated the Denver
Broncos, she wore faded Levis and an Aerosmith black-
sleeved baseball jersey. What was with all the Broncos shit,
anyway? Ain't football season over with?

Thomas hung my leather jacket in a closet, leaving me in
a current-looking kitchen with white appliances. They had a
dishwasher, something no house I ever lived in had. The
kitchen smelled of frying ground beef, garlic, peppers, and
spaghetti sauce that was cooking in a pot and not in a microwave. Bet the sauce came from a jar and not a can.

Amanda left the meatball fryer and greeted me with a
hug and crooked smile. She placed her hands on my shoulders, mine wrapped around her waist. She kissed me on the
lips.

"I'm so glad you could make it."

I groaned. "Thanks."

She stopped smiling. "You feeling okay?"

"Yeah." I looked at her sneaker-clad feet. "I just slept
wrong, that's all."

Amanda pouted when I looked up. It was an unrehearsed
act to hide the truth from her, even though I was sure she
knew I was hung over. "Well, I gotta get back to the meatballs." She tapped my shoulder and smiled. "Sit down and
relax."

I sat on a chair that was part of their dining room set.
The table was a rectangular glass-top that had six chairs
with blue cushions.

Thomas came and sat in a similar chair facing me. "So
you and Amanda are in the same English class?"

I nodded.

"Are you from here?"

Damn, now I had to talk. "Nah. I'm from New York.
The city."

Vera and Amanda got the food ready to take to the dinner table. Thomas seemed relaxed, but I felt like I was on
trial.

"So how long you been here?" he asked.

"About ten years."

This was strange, eating at a dining room table. My family never did it. Same went for everyone I knew. Dinner was eaten in front of the TV. But Amanda's family wasn't too weird—the way they sat at the table gave them a view of the TV in the living room. I sat with my back to it. I saw their big, grassy backyard and swimming pool through a picture window. The yard was floodlit, which turned the window into a mirror. I looked like I had bags under my eyes.

There was a blue paper napkin with silverware on it next to my plate of spaghetti, meatballs, and garlic bread Vera said was homemade. They served me Pepsi with ice in a Denver Broncos glass that smelled like phony lemons. Guess you could use glasses when you had a dishwasher. I mean, why not just drink it out of the bottle?

Then Vera led us in saying something called grace. I got through it, imitating them—head down, palms together.

Thomas, who sat across from me, used the remote to turn on *60 Minutes* but a commercial came on. "You're Amanda's first boyfriend," Thomas told me. "Did you know that?"

"Dad, Todd was my boyfriend back in Denver, remember?"

Thomas hadn't even touched his food yet. "Well, we never met Todd."

Jimmy stuck out his tongue at his sister. "Yeah, how do we know he exists?"

"Well he does, Jimmy." Amanda had sounded that snippy after I copped a feel last night.

I ignored the family drama just enough to eat. "Mmmm. This is very good," I said.

"You like it?" The best way to describe Vera's eyes, although it was a cliché, was that they sparkled.

I nodded and smiled.

Vera clapped her hands. "Oh good!"

Here I was afraid of meeting them, and it seemed like they were seeking my approval.

"Do you like Teenage Mutant Ninja Turtles?" Jimmy asked.

"What're they, a band?" I got a good look at Jimmy's moon face. It was tanned with red freckled cheeks. His hair looked like something off one of dad's Beatles albums.

"No, it's a comic book." Jimmy stared at me, making me more uncomfortable than I already was.

I looked at my plate and spun spaghetti on my fork. "I don't read comic books."

"Why not?"

I was about to take a bite. "Never got into them." I shrugged, annoyed by his questions.

"Please don't put your elbows on the table," Vera said, "So I removed them.

Thomas held a slice of garlic bread like some people would hold a cigar. "Well, Amanda hasn't stopped talking about you the last few weeks. It's always this and that about you and this band you have—"

Jimmy interrupted. "She says you have the jaw line of Jon Bon Jovi."

Amanda dropped her fork into her spaghetti. "Are you ever gonna stop eavesdropping when I'm on the phone?"

Thomas and Vera laughed. "Okay, that's enough," Thomas said, and his two kids went right back to eating. Amanda's normally peaceful eyes gave Jimmy an evil glare.

Then Jimmy sang, "Amanda's in love. Amanda's in love."

She slammed a palm on the table. "Jimmy, knock it off!"

"I said that's enough!" Thomas declared.

I looked at my plate, then I glanced at Amanda, who also stared at her food, twirling spaghetti on her fork, but not lifting it. The tops of her cheeks were red. She was embarrassed, but why? It wasn't not like I didn't already know she worshiped me. Still, sitting at that table, while this stupid non-drama took place, I felt like an extra in a lame sitcom. The jawline of Jon Bon Jovi? Couldn't she at least say I resembled somebody whose music didn't suck ass?

I ate a couple more bites when Thomas asked about my family. So I told them about my divorced parents, being an only child, and a collection of dead relatives. We died in almost any way you could think of: Car wreck, lung cancer, heart attack, OD on heroin, the Vietcong, suicide, industrial accident. And none of those relatives gave me cousins.

"Oh, my God." Vera touched her cheek after I explained why my family should've been declared an endangered species. And Thomas, Vera, and Amanda expressed their sorrows for a bunch of people they'd never know and I never knew.

"Oh, it ain't no big deal," I cheerfully said. "I have a dog."

"Please don't talk with your mouth full," Vera said.

And once I swallowed, I told them about Boss.

My dinner was getting cold, and I had barely touched it. Everyone else's pasta mountains were gradually being eaten, creating eroded foothills.

"Well, Nick, we're very proud of Amanda," Thomas said. "She's going to college next year. She'll be the first in our family."

I smiled, nodded, and smacked my lips.

"Please don't do that at the table." Vera's tone changed from polite to losing patience.

"Amanda's going to major in physics." Thomas sipped cola from his Denver Broncos glass. "She's good in science. She's getting A's in her physics class."

Now, I didn't know if I could look at Amanda or not. These people were creeping me out, dressing alike and worshiping some damn football team. And Thomas kept looking at me, sizing me up, I guessed, probably deciding if I was proper enough to give him grandchildren or whatever it was people like him thought about in these situations. Still, I wanted to see if Amanda liked her dad's idea, so I turned to the right to crack my back. Amanda wore a big-ass frown.

Vera sighed. "Come on, please don't do that at the table."

"Do you plan to go to college?" Thomas asked.

I shook my head and ate garlic bread, trying not to smack my lips, keep my elbows off the table, not crack my back, and not chew with my mouth open. How the hell was I supposed to eat and think, think and eat at the same time?

"So what are you going to do after high school?" Thomas had mastered the art of not talking with a full mouth.

After making sure I could follow all their damn rules, I talked enthusiastically for the first time that night. I told them about the band and how we were gonna move to LA and how we were having a party soon to jam in front of some people. I was trying to write songs to play at the party. It was gonna be our first gig, and—

And then Jimmy interrupted. "Ewwwww! Dad, his shirt has people doing the nasty on it!"

No wonder Jimmy kept staring. I knew I should've done more laundry than just whites. I grabbed the Group Therapy T-shirt that had the orgy picture on it.

And to think, I could've stayed home getting the hang of rhythm guitar and singing and writing more lyrics for "Jock Itch."

"Let me see that shirt," Thomas demanded while I stared at my cooling dinner, twirling spaghetti with my fork, sipping watered-down Pepsi. I pushed my chair back and stood. I grabbed the flannel and showed them my shirt.

"Oh, my God, that's disgusting." Vera made a cross on her huge tits, lowered her head, clasped her hands ,and started mumbling to herself.

Then I burped, but I kept my mouth closed.

"Pig!" Jimmy shouted.

"For the love of God, don't you have any manners?" Thomas asked.

I glanced at Amanda.

"Excuse yourself," she said.

Excuse myself? What the fuck's that?

"What makes you think you can wear a shirt like that around here?" Thomas yelled. "Don't you have any respect for people?"

You know how sometimes you speak first and think later? "Oh c'mon, man, it's just a fuckin' shirt."

Open mouth, insert foot.

"Nick!" Amanda screamed.

Vera gasped, clasped her hands together, bowed her head, and whispered to her imaginary friend.

"He said a naughty word." Jimmy stuck his tongue at me and slowly shook his head.

I wanted to punch that little shit. And I wasn't gonna apologize. That ain't me. I got nothing to apologize for. Couldn't they tell I ain't from their world? I didn't bother explaining my shirt. I really felt like I hadn't done anything wrong.

Thomas stared at me, mouth open. "Get out of my house! Now!" He pointed at the door.

Guess it's too late to try and bond over that painting in the living room. Which is fine. They want me gone, I'll leave. I pushed the chair away and went to get my jacket.

"Nick! Wait," Amanda yelled.

"Amanda, you are not to see that boy again!" Thomas yelled.

"But, Dad—"

"And you are not going to see this…band of his play."

Amanda must've begun getting up from her chair.

"Sit down!" Thomas screamed.

"But, Dad, please give Nick another chance. He's really a sweet guy."

Yeah, right.

"Amanda," Vera ordered, "Pray to Saint Jude for that boy before you go to bed tonight,"

I opened the front door and slammed it behind me. Their nagging pissed me off.

And as I walked home, I realized I failed the audition and didn't even bring my guitar.

CHAPTER 7

Should've done a load of darks. As I got dressed for school, I grabbed my Judas Priest baseball shirt from their 1984 Defenders of the Faith world tour. It was a warm February morning, so I didn't wear a jacket or flannel. Since I woke up late, I took the Duster and didn't bother cruising by Amanda's to see if she needed a ride. Besides, I wouldn't have been surprised if her goddamn parents got her a police escort to school.

It was in the dirt parking lot at school that I discovered I was having a bad shirt week.

Scuzz got that flat fixed on his Ranchero, and he celebrated by wearing the same shirt I was.

Vegas hesher culture worked like this—Go to concert, get shirt, wear it the next school day. So here it was almost four years after we saw Judas Priest and suddenly it was the morning after. I ducked behind the Duster so Scuzz wouldn't see me. I waited for him to cross the street.

Donnie's truck parked next to the Duster. Donnie wore a faded black long-sleeved T-shirt from Motley Crue's Shout at the Devil tour, also from 1984.

I high-fived him after he closed the door. "Hey, you wanna trade shirts today?"

Donnie laughed. I knew it was coming, but I at least had to try. "Dude, you fuckin' hate Crue, and besides, Scuzz's wearing that shirt."

Then as I jogged to chemistry class, Micah saw me in the halls, just as the bell for first period rang. "Hey, ain't Scuzz wearing that shirt today?"

"Yeah, thanks for reminding me."

In second period, as I entered the classroom, some girl who wore pancake makeup and was a member of the drill team pointed. "That guy who, like, smells real bad is, like, wearing that shirt today," she said.

I ignored her. She had now gotten even for that time when Mr. Markhart interviewed her in front of the entire class and I embarrassed the shit outta her. When he asked who her best friend was, I blurted out "Max Factor."

It's better to be a smart ass than a dumb bunny.

Mullie was already seated when I walked into government class for third period. He wore a dark blue Ocean Pacific T-shirt.

"Hey. You wanna trade shirts the rest of the day?"

"No. Scuzz is wearing that shirt."

I guess it could've been worse. I could've worn a Poison T-shirt like all the little freshmen pukes did. Would've had to go see them first. And compared to that, listening to my dad tell…or make up?…stories about his days in a band would've been better.

After class, Mullie gave me twenty copies of the flier he drew to promote our concert. He even did a logo for us.

"Since you guys're called the Tuff Boyz, I figured something that looks like spray paint would work."

About time that damn name was good for something, aside from making me feel like a goddamn idiot.

Mullie drew the four of us, interpreting what we looked like. He drew them like four police mug shots plastered on a brick wall. He drew Scuzz without glasses and longer hair that curled at the shoulders and the eyebrows. He looked like a genuine tough guy. Micah's face was extensively shaded. He looked unhealthy and sick. Donnie's hair was drawn not quite as wavy as it really was. The way Mullie shaded the picture made Donnie look like an angel. Mullie softened Donnie's eyes and lips, which almost gave the impression that whatever crime Donnie was accused of, he was innocent. Mine seemed odd. He emphasized the firmness of my jaw, the darkness of my eyebrows. He drew my bangs touching my eyes, hair wavy in the back. He gave me pouty lips and captured my tanned face.

I smiled as I looked the fliers over, amazed at how professional they looked. "Dude, this is fuckin' great."

And it was Mullie's turn to beam. "Really?"

"Yeah, man, these are perfect."

"Why, thank you."

"I owe you one."

Donnie and Micah wanted to go off-campus for lunch, so we got into Micah's tan Ford Escort wagon and drove to a nearby pizza place. I got stuck in the back seat with my fashion twin. Our shirts were each four years old and his smelled like it had never been washed.

"Dude, we're wearing the same shirt." Scuzz smiled and bobbed his head along to the beat of the Deep Purple song "Perfect Strangers" that played on the cassette deck.

I looked out the window I opened so I wouldn't have to breathe BO. "Yeah, I know."

Micah and Donnie chuckled.

As we sat down to eat, I handed out the fliers. We each got five.

"Invite whoever you want," I said, "But no jocks or cheerleaders or anyone like that."

"Don't worry about that." Scuzz took a bite of his supreme slice.

The guys scanned the fliers while eating. Scuzz and Donnie seemed impressed. Micah scowled the more and more he stared at them.

"How come he made you two look like pretty boys?" Micah asked me and Donnie.

Scuzz chuckled. "Maybe Mullie's got a crush on you guys."

"Geez, maybe Mullie's a fag," Micah added.

I came to Mullie's defense while eating. Vera would've had a fit if she saw me doing that. "C'mon, guys. Who cares? Besides, he did this for us for free." I bit into my pepperoni slice, the hot, orange grease trickling down my forearm toward my elbow. "I think the least we can do for him is get him a bowl or some beer."

Everyone was cool with that.

As I walked into fifth period English class, I finally saw Amanda. I said hi to her, and she ignored me.

I'm screwed.

As Mrs. Smith began talking about *Beowulf*, a piece of lined paper was placed atop my unopened notebook.

Here it goes. Dumped in a note. Ouch. Could be worse. She could do it in front of all my friends. Maybe she was doing me a favor.

And the handwritten note said, in really big printed letters, probably to make her point real clear. *I'm mad at you.*

Gee, what a surprise that wasn't. But she didn't write that we were through.

Even though I figured I knew why she was pissed, I wrote *why?* on the paper—in small print—and handed it to Amanda, who was seated to my right. I made the hand off as low as I could so Mrs. Smith wouldn't notice.

A couple minutes later, a new sheet of paper reappeared on my notebook.

Because you're an insensitive, inconsiderate jerk and a slob who can't even apologize when he screws up. And you didn't even bother to come over this morning to see if maybe, just maybe, I'd want to walk with you today. Do you even love me? Do you even care about me? Or is it all about you and your stupid overblown ego?

Did you know you can write first and think later? I wrote *Yeah, and...?* and handed it to Miss Manners. Wrong move.

I curled my lips inward and closed my eyes in disgust. I just did myself in with the girl I'm all hot for.

Amanda didn't respond. She stared at Mrs. Smith and took notes. At times during the rest of class, I glanced at her. She seemed prettier than usual. She did something different with her bangs, for her eyes stood out more. It was the first time I noticed how deep green they were, the almond shape they had. Her hair wasn't curled as usual, just flowing midway down her back and wavy. Even her ski slope nose and thin lips looked gorgeous. And her legs looked damn hot in the short denim skirt she wore with panty hose and pink high heels. She had on a pink cotton top with sleeves that hugged her thin arms right to the elbows, which weren't resting on the desk.

Turned out I liked Amanda more than I let on. All I could think about was spending time with her, playing records, talking music, holding her soft, bony hands, caressing her long, thin fingers, kissing her all over, and doing so without a damn curfew or parents or cops or teachers around to ruin everything.

All through class, Amanda did everything she could to keep from looking at me.

Toward the end of class, I opened my spiral notebook and wrote something. I carefully and slowly tore it out so Mrs. Smith wouldn't hear it and slipped it on Amanda's desk when the teacher turned her back and wrote something on the chalkboard.

The note said: *I'm sorry. Forgive me?*

I glanced at her again. She looked at me and smiled, biting her lower lip. She lowered her head flirtatiously and lipped, "I forgive you."

After class at her locker, we kissed and made up. And a black kid I knew from junior year American history class walked by when we finished kissing.

"Hey, isn't that smelly guy wearing that same shirt?" he asked.

CHAPTER 8

Fists punched the air as we thrashed through the end of *Master of Puppets*. There was plenty of shouting, even though our covers weren't perfect. We sounded like four guys playing instruments at the same time. But the twenty or so people who crammed into Donnie's house loved us. We got a standing ovation. Granted, there was almost nowhere to sit, but we got a standing ovation. Some people shouted, "Yeah" as the sound of our distorted guitars sustained through the amps. Mullie and Amanda were among them.

Amanda stood in front of me as I jammed. She smiled. Between songs, I winked at her, even blew her a kiss. She wore her Aerosmith shirt, but her faded jeans were so tight I saw the slight curves of her slender hips. Awesome.

Two blondes were next to Amanda. They tried dancing like strippers, totally out of tempo with the songs we played. Only person I made eye contact with while singing was Amanda, but the two dancers tried getting my attention.

But why bother with Michelle and Tina, my ex-girlfriends?

Michelle was a short, chubby platinum bleach blonde with a fake-and-bake tan. Her hair was long and feathered, and she wore a tight one-piece pink dress and pink heels. Tina was a shapeless stick with shoulder-length blonde hair curled in the bangs. She wore eye shadow so thick and black the Indy 500 could be run around her eyes. Tina wore tight black jeans, black spiked heels, and a black glittery tube top that showed off her deep natural tan and a collarbone that threatened to break out of her skin.

Why were they here? I didn't talk to either of them. We weren't in any classes. I didn't invite them.

I invited the fair-skinned, long-haired curvy redhead Donnie had his eye on. Her name was Roxie. After our first set, Roxie talked to Donnie right by his amp. I strolled by, an open can of Bud in my hand, and me and her said "hi" to each other. The first Van Halen album played in the background.

I talked like a radio DJ taking a phone call during a rate-a-record thing. "So. What'd you think?"

Roxie stared at Donnie, her white smile flashing. "You guys sound pretty good."

"Thanks." I put my beer-free hand on Donnie's shoulder. "This guy's a good guitarist. He's on tonight." Roxie giggled. I tapped Donnie on the shoulder and left.

The goal wasn't just to jam but to get some too. It was all up to Donnie now. I did my part. Now to go work my charm on Amanda.

But Tina cut me off. "Hey you," she said. Tina leaned her head against her hand, which rested on the door frame.

I wasn't enthusiastic to see her. I wanted to get to the kitchen, where Micah was talking to Amanda. I limped out a "Hi" to Tina. Amanda looked over and turned away, disgusted. Micah kept talking to her, but she didn't seem too interested in whatever he was saying.

Tina slowly licked her lips. "You have gotten so*ooo* much better on that guitar."

Then Michelle came by and gave Tina a playful shove.

"Hey, Tina, don't you hog him." They giggled.

Something's going on. This *had* to be rehearsed. This shit didn't happen for real, only in pornos, right?

"Since you got to play rock star, why don't we play backstage?" Michelle said then.

Both girls giggled and batted their thick, long eyelashes.

So Dad's theory about playing guitar and singing was apparently true. Or not. All I knew was that Micah better get the hell away from Amanda, or I was gonna shove his drumsticks up his ass.

Besides, I'd already had Tina and Michelle. Dad said a dog always returned to his vomit. I might be a dog, but I sure didn't wanna return to my vomit.

"Look, I...uh...I gotta go. All right?" I shoved my way past Tina and Michelle.

Micah stood close to Amanda, who gazed at the floor. I elbowed him in the shoulder to get to my girlfriend. "Hi, Amanda."

Micah shoved back. "What the fuck, Nick?"

I ignored him.

Amanda walked away.

"Hey, where you going?"

I followed her and caught up with her in the empty hallway, the only light coming from the living room. I cut her off and lightly touched her shoulder. "Hey, what's the matter?"

Amanda looked at the floor. "I have to go to the bathroom."

I grabbed her arm as she tried going around me to go into the bathroom. "What's bothering you?"

She started crying. "Why'd you invite all your ex-girlfriends? I don't want to know who you used to fuck."

Amanda? Cursing? What the—Invite Tina and Michelle? She's joking, right?

"I didn't invite those two blondes. I invited a redhead Donnie likes. That's it."

"Micah said you invited those dancing sluts."

If I were a Bugs Bunny cartoon, my eyes would've popped out of my head as an old car horn blared.

"He said you wanted to have a four-way with those two sluts and me." Then Amanda yelled, "What kind of a girl do you think I am?"

I felt fingers shoved in between the buttons of my jeans.

"Hey, sexy, I got a joint." Tina ran her tongue over my earlobe—and Amanda turned around and saw the whole thing. Did she see my boner? "Let's go in the backyard and relive some old times?" Tina continued.

Amanda shoved Tina. "You bitch!"

My ex slammed into the wall. I lost my balance. Amanda rapid-fire slapped Tina with both her hands. Tina ducked and covered her face.

Everyone rushed into the hallway. A couple of guys yelled "Catfight!"

Amanda's blonde hair flailed wildly from side to side as she slapped Tina, yelling, "I hate you, I hate you, I hate you, I hate you—"

I put Amanda into a bear hug and pulled her away. "Amanda! Calm down!"

Tina kicked Amanda's shins with her spike heels. "Don't you fuckin' slap me, you little cunt!"

I spun Amanda around so she wouldn't get hit. I yelled, "Tina, get the fuck outta here!"

"Nice psycho girlfriend you have." Tina walked toward the living room and hopefully anywhere else. The crowd left.

Me and Amanda struggled to catch our breath. I whispered, "You okay, sweetie?"

"I want to go home," Amanda cried.

"Hey, c'mon, stay for our second set. It's all right. She's gone."

"I said I want to go home." She shoved me aside and headed for the front door.

I chased after her. "Amanda. Amanda, come back. Don't go. Please?"

But she kept walking, crying, arms at her side swinging wildly.

I followed her outside. "Amanda, c'mon, don't do this."

She stopped and looked at me. Amanda's face had mascara pinstripes all over it. "I have put up with so much garbage from you. You disrespect my parents, embarrass me in front of them, and now this? You haven't even tried to make up with my parents yet!"

Crap. She had a point there.

"Do you realize I snuck out of my house to come and see you play? Do you?" I barely made out what she yelled because she was crying. "My parents think I went to bed early because I was tired. I had to crawl out a second story window and try not to be seen, and then I rode my bike here, Nick. I rode my bike here. I risked getting grounded just to see you play, and this is what you do to me?"

"Amanda. C'mon," I begged. "I didn't *invite* them. And a four-way? I don't know what the fuck Micah's talkin' about."

Amanda pulled her blue ten-speed out of the bushes, getting ready to leave. She calmly said, "Sometimes I think the only reason you're going with me is you're just waiting for me to put out."

I looked everywhere but at her. "Well…Sure…I like you a lot and…yeah, I would like to eventually have sex with you, but—"

"Pervert!" She cried more, turned her bike around, and rode over the lawn as fast as she could. "Don't ever talk to me again!"

I ran after her, but there was no way I could catch her. I rode here with Scuzz, and by the time I got his keys, who knows where she'd be? I could try and meet up with her at her house, but just me being there would get her in trouble. I didn't want that.

My stomach sank to my ankles. But I quickly decided my best bet was to try and make up with her tomorrow. I'd have to face her parents, apologize for what happened at dinner. Let her cool off tonight.

I went back inside and slammed the door. I ignored everybody and walked into the dark hallway. At the end of the hall, by Donnie's room, my head sank onto the wall. I wanted to be alone, which was probably a bad move. Serious rage toward Micah built up.

"Nick," Michelle softly said, "You okay?"

"No."

She sighed. "You really like that girl, don't you?"

I didn't turn around. "Why do you care?"

"I just wanted to tell you I'm sorry."

"For what?"

"Micah wanted me to come on to you 'cause he wants that scrawny geek chick." A lighter clicked. Cigarette smoke began filling the hallway. "I mean, no offense, but she's built like a pencil. I don't why anybody'd wanna stick their dick in her."

I sighed. "So why'd you do it?"

Michelle took another drag. "Micah gave me some shit. You can have it if you want."

I didn't want any drugs, just Amanda back. "Did he offer Tina some too?"

"I guess."

She exhaled and put one of her hands on my back and rubbed it up and down. It was the closest thing to a sincere gesture she ever made. "You gonna be all right?"

It took everything I had to sound calm. "Yeah. Just leave me alone, okay?"

She patted my back and went to the bathroom.

I stormed out of the hallway. I found Micah in the kitchen getting something out of the fridge. When Micah closed the door, his ear met my fist.

"Fuck you tryin' to do? Huh?" I yelled. Micah nearly fell. I shoved him into the counter. I pointed and walked toward him. "You're fuckin' dead."

A right hook hit his head. Micah tackled me. Punched me in the chest.

Somebody pulled Micah off me. I jumped up and was held back. "What the fuck, Nick?" Donnie yelled.

I breathed fast. "Ask that motherfucker. Fuck you doin', puttin' the moves on my girlfriend?"

Scuzz held Micah's arms. The drummer glared at me like he wanted to kill me.

"You know I wanted her, asshole. Fuckin' told you that at Mad Dogs," Micah yelled.

I brashly replied, "Yeah, well, you had your chance. You blew it."

"You stole her!"

"I didn't steal her. She don't even like your sorry ass."

"She don't like you anymore either, fuckhead." Micah swung his right arm to free himself. He gave me a dirty look as he walked past me and Donnie. I wanted to break free and beat the shit of Micah. I squirmed and squirmed, but Donnie had a strong grip.

"This party sucks. Let's go," said some chick in the background said.

As Micah disappeared into another room, I yelled, "I'm gettin' her back. And you better fuckin' stay away from her, or I'll kick your ass."

No response.

Donnie let go. He stepped in front of me and slammed a finger into my chest. "If all this bullshit fucks up my chances with Roxie, I'm gonna kick all your asses." He left.

Mullie came up to me. "You all right?"

I caught my breath before answering. "Guess so."

"Did Amanda leave?"

I looked across the living room, where other people were drinking beer and talking. There was no music playing. "Yeah. She's probably gone for good. This band's probably done. Fuckin' Micah. That goddamn son-of-a-bitch." I turned to face Mullie. "I thought everything was gonna go so well tonight. But no, right down the fuckin' toilet."

Mullie put a hand on my shoulder. "Hey, c'mon, Nick. So tonight went wrong. Don't give up yet. You don't think every band's had a disastrous gig? They all have 'em, but they keep goin'."

I thought about what he said for a second then grinned and nodded. "Yeah, I guess you're right, Mullie. Don't worry, I won't give up. Thanks, bro. You gonna hang around?"

"No. I'm taking off. I'll see you at school Monday."

And, with that, Mullie left, and I went into the living room. I sat on the couch, not wanting to talk to anybody, just think things over. About what, exactly, I wasn't sure. I just wanted the answers to come from somewhere. The party was still on, and we were supposed to play again. But I didn't wanna play, not with a traitor on drums.

People came by and tried talking to me, but I was such a fog that I ignored them. I wondered if I could get Amanda back, if I could patch things up with Micah, if I should even bother with him.

Then Mullie opened the front door. "Hey, you guys better come outside," he shouted.

I sighed because my concentration was broken, then yelled, "What now?"

"You guys better come outside. I'm serious."

Scuzz and I were first out the door, after Mullie. Donnie and Micah followed. So did a few other people, including Roxie.

The Beastie Boys song "Fight for Your Right to Party" filled the air. The front of Donnie's house was turned into an omelet. Egg shells were in the dead grass and on the house, eggs splattered on the walls and windows near the front door.

Jeff and James were in Owen's red Jeep.

"Sorry to break up your little party, you fuckin' stoners," Jeff yelled.

The other jocks laughed.

"See what's on the wall. That's your brain on drugs," Owen shouted. "Next time it's gonna be your blood."

"We're gonna fuckin' kill you, goddamn stoners," Jeff added before Owen shifted into drive, squealed the tires, and sped away.

CHAPTER 9

D onnie stared at the egg-stained front wall of his house and feared for his life. "We better clean this up or Grandfather's gonna kill me," he whispered.

I calmly asked, "Don't you got a rake in the garage? We can clean up the eggshells pretty quick."

Donnie nodded, and I left to get a rake. It was hung on the wall next to the door to the house. When I came back, Donnie had grabbed a hose and rinsed the egg and dirt off the front of the house.

"Funny thing is, the house'll probably look better than it did earlier," Donnie said.

As I raked in the dark, the only faint light came from a small fixture by the front door, pieces of egg shell broke into smaller pieces that disappeared into the high green grass and weeds. While I raked, a bunch of dead grass was rounded up and put into plastic garbage bags by Scuzz, Mullie, and Roxie. Scuzz took the bags and put them in the bed of his Ranchero. Cleaning the house seemed to calm us. It gave us a way to release our tension and allowed us to think.

How'd the jocks find out about the party? Donnie didn't give a flier to anybody who liked them. Neither did me or Scuzz. We couldn't figure it out. Maybe someone dropped a flier, and a jock found it? Maybe they overheard someone else talking about it? Maybe they were driving by, recognized our cars, and decided to buy some eggs?

Who knows? Who cares?

But where was Micah? How come he wasn't helping us? Was he somehow responsible for the jocks showing up? People left in droves, but Micah wasn't one of them. We were so concerned about getting the house cleaned up that no one bothered to check where he went.

Micah showed up just as we finished cleaning. He walked toward his Escort, drums in hand.

"What the hell're you doing?" Donnie asked.

"Getting out of here," he said as he put his drums in the car.

Then an old, faded gray, dented four-door Cadillac with one working headlight sped into the driveway and stopped before hitting the garage door. The brakes squealed. The engine sputtered, then seemed to stall out.

"*Oh*, shit," Donnie whispered.

His grandparents weren't supposed to be home for another hour and a half.

"Relax, man, the house looks fine," Scuzz said.

"Ain't there still beer in the fridge?" I asked.

"Why you think I said oh shit."

I slapped Scuzz's arm. "C'mon, let's hide that beer."

Me and Scuzz ran into the house. Mullie followed. "What're we gonna do with it?" he asked as he slammed the front door behind him.

"I don't know, hide it in Donnie's room." I opened the fridge.

"Good idea." Scuzz grabbed a couple of six-packs. So did I. That was all the beer we thought had left in there.

We emptied the fridge with one run to Donnie's room. Micah calmly removed the rest of his drum set while we were busy saving all our asses.

We left Donnie's room just as he and his grandparents entered the house. We heard a car start...Micah's Escort?...and then leave. Donnie's grandfather was unhappy about what had happened to the house, even though we cleaned it up. But he noticed the garbage can near the front door and let his grandson hear about it.

"I don't care, Donald. We trusted you with this house, and you broke that promise."

"I understand, Grandfather, but we weren't doing anything wrong—"

"I smell cigarettes," his grandfather said as he entered the house. "I smell marijuana."

Donnie snuck into the hallway where me, Mullie, and Scuzz were. "Get out now," he whispered as he passed us, on his way to his room.

I whispered, "Donnie. Don't go in your room."

The voice boomed from the giant as he came down the hallway. "Donald, where the hell did you go? Donald!"

The door to Donnie's room quietly shut. His grandmother, still in the living room, meekly said, "Elmer, please. They're just boys."

The house had iron bars on all the windows to prevent burglaries. I just hoped Donnie figured out how to open them and get away, since there was no lock on the door to his room. Roxie joined me, Mullie, and Scuzz in the hallway as Elmer opened the door and disappeared into the darkness of Donnie's room.

"Goddammit, Donald. I thought I told you no smoking and no drugs in this household."

A fist pounded the wall.

"Grandfather, please! I'm sorry! I really am!" Donnie sounded like someone in one of those *Friday the 13th* movies pleading for their life just before Jason slashed them to death. Donnie's grandmother joined us in the hall. She had a sad look on her wrinkled face, sporting a black eye that wasn't there when they left to go see the Folies Bergere at the Tropicana earlier. "He's in a bad mood," she said.

"Grandfather. Please don't!"

A slap.

Donnie's grandmother stood next to us. Me, Mullie,

Scuzz, and Roxie turned away, but we didn't leave. We also didn't go into the room. *What do I do? What can I do?*

"You can't do a fuckin' thing right, can you?"

It sounded like Donnie got shoved into some furniture.

"You're just like your goddamn mother, her and her fuckin' drugs."

A punch.

"Grandfather! Please! I'll never do it again!"

"I knew I should've shoved a coat hanger up your mother's cunt and aborted you, you fuckin' worthless piece of shit!"

I cringed.

"Oh my God," Mullie whispered.

Roxie ran into the bathroom and threw up. We heard more punches and slaps.

"This happens all the time around here," Donnie's grandmother told us calmly.

Then it got worse.

"Is that beer?"

My stomach sank.

"You little fucker." A punch. Another one. And another. It sounded like Mike Tyson was going for a first-round knockout. Donnie's breathing was erratic. He sniffled.

Then, silence. For a moment.

"Get out of this house now! I don't ever wanna see you again. You hear me?"

"But, Grandfather—"

"No, Donald. I'm tired of you. I'm tired of that fuckin' crap you listen to, I'm tired of that fuckin' guitar. I'm tired of looking at you and your girl hair, I'm tired of your fuckin' foul language. I'm tired of your stupid friends. Just get the fuck out of here. Go find your mother downtown and smoke crack with her."

Another punch. Then more silence.

"Clean up that blood," his grandfather said with all the warmth of a drill sergeant.

Elmer stormed out of Donnie's room and saw the

stunned faces of me, Mullie, Scuzz, and the seen-this-before face of his beaten wife.

"Why don't you kids go join the army and kill some Commies? Make something of yourself instead of that crap you call music. Better yet, maybe you'll all get fuckin' killed."

Donnie's grandmother reluctantly followed Elmer into the living room. Once she was gone, me, Mullie, and Scuzz entered Donnie's room.

The dresser was toppled. Donnie sat in a corner, arms wrapped around bent knees, his breathing fast and erratic. He sniffled. The tan carpet was stained red. His black Ozzy T-shirt was soaked with blood that dripped from his nose and lips.

Three chins dropped to the floor.

"Oh, my God," Mullie whispered.

We rushed to Donnie. I wanted to ask him if he was okay, even though it would've been the dumbest question ever asked. Instead, I put an arm around him. Mullie did the same after sitting to Donnie's right. Scuzz sat in front of him and put his hands on Donnie's trembling shoulders.

"Where's Roxie?"

"She's in the bathroom," I whispered. "She got sick."

Donnie lowered his head and cried. I pulled myself closer to him. Mullie and Scuzz did the same. And all the frustrations of our lives gushed out as tears.

CHAPTER 10

The house smelled like frying eggs when I came out of my bedroom. Boss rushed past me and went straight for the kitchen. I was barely awake, staggering through the hallway barefoot, in torn jeans, no shirt, bed hair going any way it wanted.

The living room was too damn bright. All the blinds were up and the windows open. For February, it felt warm. The heater wasn't going. If it were, I'd hear it. Thing was old and noisy. Instead, there was the sound of birds chirping and traffic coming into the house.

Someone must've thought the sunshine made it a beautiful morning. The hell it was.

Country music played from a small portable radio. Mom stood at the stove, Boss sat nearby, begging.

"Hi," Mom said in her usual soft voice. "You want some eggs, sweetie? I can scramble them for you." For morning, she sure sounded alive.

The living dead slowly uttered, "Uh, no thanks." Instead, I got a box of Crunch Berries out of the cabinet.

Mom didn't look like somebody who had a seventeen-year-old son. She didn't have any wrinkles. The only sign of her being in her mid-thirties was the gray streak in her curly brown hair. She regained some the weight Dad forced her to lose a few years ago, when he got tired of her being what he called fat. The white T-shirt she wore was tighter around the waist than it was the last time I saw her wearing it. Rick, though, never made an issue about her weight. It was one thing I liked about him. Probably the only thing I liked about him.

And whenever I began liking the bastard, the feeling was short-lived.

"When're you gonna clean up after that fuckin' dog?" Rick yelled from the backyard in his gruff voice.

I hadn't noticed the sliding glass door was open.

I sighed as I grabbed a gallon of milk from the fridge. "I'll do it after I eat."

"Forget it, you lazy shit," Rick yelled.

Then he went into something about me not mowing the lawn and, because of that, I disrespected my mom. I tuned him out. I didn't need somebody else telling me how worthless I was.

I slowly ate about two spoonfuls of cereal when Mom and Rick joined me at our round wooden dining room table. Why was I sitting there in the first place? I fuckin' *hated* country music. Why didn't I just go to my bedroom and turn on the TV, maybe listen to that Doors album?

I was so not awake.

"So how was your party last night?" Mom asked.

"Fine." Another good thing about Mom: She never bitched about me talking with food in my mouth.

Mom didn't ask any more questions. She knew she couldn't get any info out of me. "Fine" was my stock answer. It was nice, neutral, and implied that nothing bad happened. That was good enough for most people. And another benefit of being so direct was something I learned from government class—anything you say can, and will, be used against you. I knew it was meant for dealing with cops, but it was also useful in dealing with pretty much anyone.

I was also trying to hide what actually happened. Too much shit. Too much to do now. Step one: Get Amanda back. Step two: Go to Scuzz's house, see how Donnie was doing, and figure out what to do with Micah. Getting Amanda back would be the toughest part. Best to get that out of the way. Normally, I'd avoid doing something, anything, that was really hard, but what the hell? Her house was on the way.

Once I was done eating, I showered and read a letter from War that came in the mail. He was trying to make boot camp seem like fun. Instead of talking about getting up at hours one should go to bed at, running several miles a day, and having some cranky spit-talking drill sergeant yell at you all the time, all War wrote about was getting "liberty," going to Tijuana, getting plastered on rum because the drinking age in Mexico was eighteen, and getting a fourteen-year-old hooker for two bucks an hour.

YOU GOTTA COME DOWN HERE. WE'LL PARTY, he wrote in small black, all caps print on lined white notebook paper. Never knew how immaculate his handwriting was.

I planned to bring the letter to Scuzz's place and let Donnie read it. Anything to cheer the guy up. Maybe he'd wanna take a road trip? Get in the Duster and make a high-speed run through five hours of desert to get to San Diego. Park the car on the beach and walk across the border to Tijuana. A shitload of booze and no parents, cops, or teachers to stop us. Walk from bar to bar, eating cheap tacos and downing shot after shot, music coming out of every place we pass, hoping to stumble on a place cranking out Metallica and Ozzy. Get ripped on tequila, talk and try to score with every girl we see. Four wild boys turned loose south of the border. Drink all night and pass out on the beach as the sun rose to our backs, the early morning light reflecting off the Pacific Ocean. Then, as a joke, try and cross back into the US like an illegal alien. Okay, maybe not that last part.

But that daydream passed quickly. More practical, less-fun stuff to take care of first.

I chose the clothes I'd wear to Amanda's a bit more carefully. I opted for a plain white T-shirt. When I threw on my leather jacket and looked in the bathroom mirror, I

looked like James Dean with a 1970s haircut and no cigarette.

I drove to Amanda's, arriving right when they got home
from church. They walked into their house as I neared the
driveway. I saw Thomas the clearest. He was in a dark suit.
Before I rang the doorbell, I stood, looking at the tile.
There was still time to get back in the Duster and flee to
Scuzz's house. Man, that was tempting. I'd entered fights
where I knew I was gonna get my ass kicked easier than this.
This would dig deep into who I was where I was going in
life. A simple "I'm sorry" wasn't gonna cut it. They were
the type of people who would lecture me about everything,
from manners to proper dress and probably even voting.

Apologizing. For my very nature. Just not natural. If I
was still on good terms with Amanda, I wouldn't even
bother doing this, but after Micah's stunt, this was the only
way to get her back.

Enough. Just ring the damn doorbell already.

Thomas opened the door, still in his dark suit, his thick
tie knot loosened some.

"Hello." He didn't sound enthusiastic to see me.

Do what you need to do. "Hi, Thomas. How're you?"

"Fine."

I wavered between looking him in the eye and letting my
head roam around my surroundings as I talked. "Look,
I…I…um…just wanted to…uh, apologize…for the…way I,
um, acted…when I had dinner here."

Thomas stood firm, eyes unflinching, arms folded in
front of his chest. Vera came by and stood behind him. She
didn't seem happy to see me either.

Jesus, this is intimidating.

"What you did that night was disgusting, and it deeply
offended us," Thomas said. "And I cannot believe that you
would not only wear a disgusting shirt like that but that
your parents would *let* you wear something like that."

Should I tell them the Group Therapy T-shirt was actually a hand-me-down from my dad? Or did I just steal it from

him? Whatever. Probably not a good idea. Skip that.

Should I mention that belching after a meal is considered a compliment in Italy, and doing so means you enjoyed the meal? It was true. Our Italian neighbors in Queens told me that. Or maybe they just said that to get away with it. *I better not. Thomas and Vera ain't gonna go for that. Hell with it. Suck it up. Admit to them I ain't perfect, even though I am.* "I didn't mean no disrespect. I'm just...not used to...um, eating formally."

Couldn't Thomas at least unfold his arms? Couldn't Vera quit scowling? When I met them, they were smiling and friendly, but now, my god, I was talking to two living, breathing antarcticas.

"Look, really, I'm sorry." *Wow. That came out easy.*

Thomas sighed. He kept looking at me. He didn't blink, smile. No clue that he was gonna give me another shot.

"How do we know you're sincere?" Thomas asked. "I've read about kids like you. You have no respect for parents or authority, do you?"

Well, yeah, no shit, but I can't say that. I respect Mom, but Dad, Rick? Teachers? School administrators? Cops? Fuck no. Especially on that last one. "No, sir, I do, really." *Sir? I'm saying sir? What the fuck? I am that desperate to get Amanda back?*

"Well, if you do have respect for people, you do not show it at all," Thomas said.

"We're very easy people to get along with, Nick," Vera said slowly. "We've never become so upset over a house guest in our twenty-two years of marriage as we did with you."

Wow. Is that right? Sweet. I'll put that in my mental trophy case. Brag about it to the guys next time we hang out. Then we'll mock their perfect middle class uptight asses. We'll have a hell of a laugh. Now back to our regularly scheduled sincerity. "Look, you gotta understand, I wasn't trying to make you guys mad. I was really nervous. I...I really like your daughter, a lot. She's a wonderful girl, and I was totally scared about meeting you guys. It's not something I've done before, and, well, I guess I can't do much worse, can I?"

Don't these two have a sense of humor? They ain't smiling. Almost reminds me of Grandma and Grandpa on Dad's side of the family. All Vera and Thomas needed were Russian accents, and the flashbacks would truly begin.

Thomas looked at Vera.

"It's up to you," she said.

Did he ask her something? If so, I didn't hear it.

"So if we let you have dinner here again, you are going to act like a civilized human being and not like a slob?"

It was a question worded like a command.

Then Vera jumped in. "And you better not to wear that disgusting shirt again."

I rarely cracked my back. No prob. Not wearing Group Therapy? Easy. Not smacking my lips, slurping soda, putting elbows on the table, or burping? Shit. That was gonna take some practice.

Getting Amanda back is gonna be a lot of work. "Sure."

"Do you promise?" Vera still stood behind her husband.

Geez, how tough were they gonna make this? How binding was a promise?

Just do as they're asking, already. "Yeah. I promise."

Thomas slowly dropped his arms from his chest. "All right. You get one more chance." He turned and walked into the house, throwing his sports coat on the couch.

Then Vera asked if I wanted to talk to Amanda.

"She's in a bad mood today, I don't know why. She hasn't said a thing all day," Thomas said, taking off his tie. He sat down, grabbed the remote, and turned on the TV to one of those televangelists begging for money.

Great. And it didn't help my nerves any that I saw Jimmy sticking his tongue out at me. It should've given me a twisted desire to pull the little shit's tongue out with a clothespin and dump a bottle of Tabasco sauce all over it.

Vera yelled for Amanda, who was in her bedroom. Within seconds, she appeared. She came down the stairs, still in her church dress. It was a black and white one that went to her knees and hung off her body like a baggy shirt on a wire hanger, a thick black belt around her slender waist giving the dress some shape. Her hair was really curly. She moved like a model as she walked down the stairs with her right hand sliding on the wooden railing.

Her voice was cold. "Hi."

I should've taken off my leather jacket. I was starting to sweat. That's what happened when I got nervous. Or go outside. Or wear a leather biker jacket inside a house.

"Hi. Can we talk?"

"What for?"

Man, she sure could be icy when she wanted to.

"Amanda, please. Just let me talk to you?" Okay, that too came out effortlessly.

She hesitated and looked at the floor. "Sure."

She walked into the living room, acting like I wasn't there. "Dad, can we go out by the pool and talk?"

"Go right ahead, sweetie."

The patio next to the pool was shaded by a wood patio cover that created plenty of shadows. The picture windows allowed the rest of her family to spy on us, if they wanted, but at least they wouldn't be able to hear us, unless Amanda went apeshit and started yelling.

Amanda folded her arms in front of her chest, a perfect mirror of her father just a few minutes earlier. "Well?" She tapped her black high heels on the patio. It sounded like a fast-paced metronome.

I put my hands in the front pockets of my faded jeans. I swung my shoulders side to side, twisting at the waist, trying to look at her angry face but having a hard time doing so.

"I'm sorry about last night." Did I look at her?

"Yeah, sure you are. Did you have your little group therapy with those two sluts?"

That shirt was becoming more trouble than it was worth.

"No, I did not do anything with those chicks. Remember? Tina left right before you did, then everybody else left."

Amanda's arms didn't move. Her face didn't change expressions. There was no sign of weakening in her. Her metronome foot was still at it. "Oh, really?"

The last time I heard anyone sound so unconvinced of something, my parents were watching a presidential debate in which Reagan promised to help the lower middle class. "Yeah, everybody left. And Michelle told me that Micah gave her some shit to try and turn you against me."

Amanda scoffed and looked away. "You expect me to believe that?"

"And you believe what Micah tells you? You're the one who said one day he'd act all nice to you, and the next he'd seem like he was on some weird drug. You told me that he'd call after nine on school nights, trying to get you to go with him to Lone Mountain. Remember?"

Amanda looked at the brown wooden beams that shaded the patio. "I don't know who or what to believe any more. Micah says one thing, you say another."

"You wanna know what happened after you left?"

"Not really."

"Micah and I got into a fight after Michelle told me what he did."

She looked right at me. I sensed she didn't believe me, even though she interrupted me. "Really?" Her skepticism flowed through her words. "I'm supposed to believe *you*?"

I pointed at the house. "We can go inside right now, I'll call Scuzz and Donnie, and they'll tell you the same thing."

The metronome shoe stopped. She looked at her feet. "So did you guys settle it?"

Should I tell her everything? The truth might seem like the biggest bunch of crap she might've ever heard. "Yeah, pretty much." I didn't want to talk about last night. I came here to make things right. "Amanda," I reached for her hand, but she didn't grab mine back. "When we were in the hall, and you said I should've apologized to your parents, you were right. I really should've. And I did just now."

She looked surprised as she looked at me, but her voice sounded skeptical. "You did?"

"Yeah." I sighed, let go of her hand, and resumed fidgeting. Her parents watched us through the window like scientists studying two lab rats. "I told them I was wrong, and that I'd be more respectful when I'm over here."

Amanda unfolded her arms. She put her hands on her hips instead. Was that a good sign?

"I apologized, and they...well, I guess they accepted. I'm back here talking to you now."

"They forgave you?"

"Well, I don't know, but they did let me in here to talk to you." Time to make my move. I should've taken off this jacket. A full summer-like sweat came on. It poured from my temples, behind my ears, from the bridge of my nose, down my face and neck. My body tensed. Hands shook, even though they were in my jeans' pockets. I breathed faster. "Look, I—I know you're not like those girls I used to go out with, and that's what I like about you. You're like no one I've ever met before."

Amanda stared at me. I moved close enough to whisper to her.

"I just think you're so pretty, and...I really like you, a lot."

Amanda lowered her blushing head. "I'm not pretty," she whispered.

I slowly put my hands on her shoulders and caressed them. "I think so."

"Yeah, sure."

My hands cradled her cheeks. "No. I really mean it, Amanda. To me, you're the prettiest girl I've ever seen. I'll take you over anybody."

Amanda stared at me. "You mean that?"

"Yes."

And let's just say that some of that stuff you'd read about in a romance novel, yeah, it happened. With her parents watching.

CHAPTER 11

Donnie looked terrible. He spent Sunday at Scuzz's house with bags of ice on his face. The swelling and bruising went down quickly, but he still looked alien, especially around his eyes. Try a raccoon to the tenth power.

He didn't go to school on Monday, and I didn't blame him. Donnie wasn't about to give the jocks any ammo by showing up beaten up.

Donnie was so confused that he asked us to empty his locker and bring his school books to Scuzz's house, where he was staying. He even asked Roxie to bring any assignments from government class.

You know your life's a wreck when you turn to school-work to ease your pain.

And when I ran into Micah in the halls at Fremont before first period on Monday, I had to deliver a couple of messages.

"Everybody's gonna do their own thing for lunch," I said as the class bell rang. I didn't mention that Donnie wasn't around. As Micah turned to go to class, I called to him. Time to deliver the second message. "Lone Mountain. Today. Three o'clock. Be there."

CHAPTER 12

No one said a word as the Duster sped toward Lone Mountain. The radio was off. The sounds of wind and the freeway zipping by at seventy accompanied us. Donnie was in the back seat hiding his beaten face behind dark sunglasses, looking out the side window. Scuzz sat next to me, eyes fixed straight ahead, the wind that came through the open window blowing about his increasingly longer hair.

We weren't enthusiastic about what we had to do, but Micah had to go. That, we agreed on. And this sucked. As I drove, I thought about how Micah and I became friends in fifth grade. He had just moved from Pittsburgh. The teacher asked Owen Maywood to show him around, but he refused, pawning Micah off on me. During recess, I introduced Micah to Donnie and War.

I thought about going with Micah and his parents to the Colorado River, Lake Mead, and Mount Charleston a couple of times. I thought about how me, him, and Donnie used to race our BMX bikes in the desert. I thought about the early jam sessions we had, back when War was still in the band. We thought we sounded great, but we sucked. None of us had a clue about musical scales. I barely knew any chords. Donnie didn't know any. Micah hit whatever drum he felt like. No sense of tempo or structure. Just five tone-deaf boys having a blast ,making a bunch of noise, practicing their faith, emulating their gods.

It was all so simple before high school, girls, and hard drugs got in the way.

"Think he'll show?" Scuzz asked as I turned off the freeway and onto the two-lane road that went to Lone Mountain.

"He'll show," I replied.

"Think he'll be high?" Donnie asked.

"Probably."

Scuzz looked out the window. "And we ain't got any weapons."

"Think we're gonna need some?" I asked.

"Depends on what you told him," Scuzz replied.

Then I had a feeling telling Micah to come out to Lone Mountain, the way I did sounded like a threat. "Think I was a little too blunt."

Scuzz looked at me. "What'd you say to him?"

"I told him to be at Lone Mountain today at three. That's it."

"Shit, he's gonna expect a fight," Donnie said.

"Look in the glove compartment. I got a couple screwdrivers in there."

Scuzz grabbed the flat head and Phillips head I kept with me in case the Duster broke down. Scuzz closed the glove compartment and held the tools tapping them against his thigh like drum sticks. Those things had yet to save my ass because whenever the car broke down, I needed sockets and wrenches.

As we pulled up, we saw Micah leaning against the hood of his Escort wagon smoking a cigarette, his long, straight brown hair blowing about. I parked the Duster facing him, but several feet away.

A gravel truck, coming from a nearby pit, roared by, a few loose pebbles hitting the already dented and partly rusted fender of the Duster.

"Take the flat head," I told Scuzz as I grabbed the Phillips head from him and put it in my back pocket. "Hope we don't need 'em."

"I'm with you," Scuzz said.

"Amen to that," Donnie added.

We exited the car, walking toward Micah, me out in front. We decided I would do the talking. Micah stamped out his cigarette on his car's hood and threw it into the sagebrush. He walked toward us. The wind kicked up a bunch of dirt that got into our eyes and ears. I had to squint out of one eye and close the other. It was the only way to keep the eyes from tearing up. No way could I let Micah think I was crying.

"Can't do it on your own, can you?" Micah was fidgety and nervous. He sniffled some. "You had to bring backup, huh? *Huh?*" His breath raced. His eyes were wild, bloodshot. Hands trembled, twitched. "So it's gonna take three of you to kick my ass, huh?"

I faked being calm. "We ain't here to fight you."

Micah laughed. He sounded sinister. "Yeah, sure. Then why'd you call me out here? Huh?"

"'Cause we didn't wanna do this in school."

"Dude, be careful," Donnie whispered to me. "He's high."

Micah pulled a chrome butterfly knife out of his back pocket. It seemed like he had practiced breaking it out and flipping it open, his wrists and fingers limber as the knife opened with a dramatic flourish.

Knew I should've taken a different approach to get him out here.

"I wanna piece of you, motherfucker." Micah held the knife at waist level, the right arm that clutched it pointed right at me, trembling. "I wanna cut your goddamn throat!"

Micah began walking in a circle. Veins bulged out of his thin, pale neck. Sweat trickled from his temples.

"Christ, Micah," Scuzz said.

I also walked in a circle. I wanted to keep a distance of a few feet from Micah and his paranoid, bloodshot eyes, which I kept my gaze fixed on. After a knife had been pulled on you a few times, you'd think you'd know how to handle it. Nope.

"Micah, what the fuck you doin'?" There was no way to fake it. I was nervous, and he knew it. He saw me sweat, breathe through the mouth, hands that trembled so much, the screwdriver could fall to the ground at any second.

He smiled. We continued pacing. He lunged toward me with the knife drawn. I jumped back. He laughed and lunged again. Then again. I backed away. Donnie and Scuzz yelled things as me and Micah made this potentially deadly dance.

I pointed at Micah. "Put the goddamn knife down."

He continued laughing. "Scared, aincha?"

"I ain't scared."

We continued facing each other down making our circle in the dirt.

"I don't want you doin' something you're gonna regret."

Micah kept laughing. "Oh, I ain't gonna regret it. I ain't gonna regret it. I ain't gonna fuckin' regret it, man. I've been wanting this ever since you stole Amanda from me."

My jaw fell open. "*I* stole Amanda from *you*? Are you out of your fuckin' mind? You drove her away. She told me she kinda liked you at first, but then you'd start acting all weird an' shit, and she wanted no part of that."

Call him out.

"You get like this every time you do coke. That's why Amanda didn't want anything to do with you. Cuz you acted like this around her. And let me tell you something, man, her parents would not go for this kinda crap at all. Trust me."

"Bullshit," Micah snarled. "Coke makes me feel good. Makes me feel *invincible*!"

"That shit'll kill you, man!"

"This ain't about coke." Then Micah began screaming, his voice echoing off the nearby foothills. "This is about

how much you've fucked me over, man! You always fuck
me over!"

With one hand, I pointed at my own chest. I didn't know
whether to have my other hand ready to grab the screwdriver. "*I* fucked you over? *I* fucked you over?" I pointed at him.
"No, Micah, you did yourself in. You did yourself in with
Amanda, and you did yourself in with us. That's why
you're out. That's why we called you up here. We came
here to tell you you're out of the band, and maybe get your
ass to clean up. We ain't here for a fight!"

Micah's face went from angry to a mask of confusion.

"Dude, we're tired of you acting all weird one minute
and normal the next," Scuzz said. "You walked out on us
the other night when we needed you, when Donnie needed
you, that was it, man. You made the decision for us."

Micah ground his teeth. His jaw tightened. He screamed
and lunged at me, the knife raised above his head. I grabbed
the screwdriver. I fell to the ground and rolled out of the
way. Donnie and Scuzz ran next to me. Scuzz had the flat
head drawn.

Micah stood a few feet away. He kept laughing. He
looked like those pictures of Charles Manson. This was a
side of Micah we never saw before and never wanted to see
again.

"So you're all in on this, huh? Huh? Huh?"

"Yeah, we're all in on this," Scuzz said. "We decided
yesterday that you're out."

Micah's chest rose and sank with each breath. He sweated. He showed his clenched teeth. He laughed. He shook his
head, slowly at first, gaining speed with each passing second. "Oh, no. No, I'm not. You need me. You fuckin' need
me. *You fuckin' need me!*"

"You're out, Micah," Donnie said softly.

Micah began crying. Veins bulged from his neck and the
forearm and hand that held the knife. I wanted to feel bad
for him, but couldn't. What would he do next? Throw the

blade at me like a freak at a carnival sideshow? Go into a wild rage, slashing the knife about like a medieval sword?

Micah's shaking head slowed. It went from side-to-side. "No."

I slowly nodded and replied, "Yes."

Micah shook as if he was having a seizure. "No."

"Dude, go home," Donnie urged.

"Yeah, get your shit together," I said, Phillips head drawn like a gun.

"We need to get the fuck out of here first chance we get," Scuzz whispered in my ear.

"Yeah. When I yell 'now,' make a line for the Duster," I whispered.

"Got it," Donnie said.

Micah kept shaking. He cried. Face red. "No. No. No, no, no, no! *Nooo!*"

He ran at us, the knife raised above his head. He screamed, and spit flew from his mouth. As he got near, we leapt whichever way we could. I got a leg out and tripped Micah. He hit the ground and dropped the knife.

"Now!"

Me, Donnie, and Scuzz got up and ran for the Duster. Donnie dove in through the open driver's side window. Scuzz got in through the passenger side door. I got in and slammed the door.

Donnie's foot hit me in the head as he crawled into the back seat. Good thing I left the keys in the ignition. Something told me to do that.

I started the car, shifting into reverse as soon as the engine turned over. Micah ran to his Escort. The tires squealed as I whipped a one-eighty. Micah started his car. I shifted into drive, gunned the accelerator, and not much happened.

"Floor it," Donnie shouted.

"I am! Fuckin' car's hesitatin'! Knew I shoulda cleaned the carburetor."

Micah was gaining. Was he gonna try and run us off the road, rear-end us? Force us into a wash?

The Duster lurched forward. The gas gauge moved toward E, the speedometer jumped toward forty.

A few seconds later, the car hesitated again.

"Dammit!"

"Of all the times for your car to crap out." Scuzz sounded calm.

"No shit!"

Then horsepower kicked in again. And a few seconds later, it would hesitate.

Donnie shouted in my ear, "We get out of this alive, you better fix—"

"Yeah, I hear ya, all right! Shit, you don't need to yell in my fuckin' ear!"

Think fast. I wasn't gonna ditch him on a straightaway. I turned off the road. Right into the desert.

"What the hell are you *doing*?" Donnie shouted.

"Somebody's gotta save our ass!"

Once, the jocks chased after me out near Red Rock Canyon. Going into the desert ended it. Guess James didn't wanna scratch his brand new Acura.

Sagebrush scraped at the Duster's sides, crunched under the tires, scratched the underside, even though the back of the car was lifted. I dodged a couple of Joshua trees, flattened a few creosote bushes. *Better not get a flat from all these thorns.*

Scuzz rolled up his window. "Hope you know what you're doing."

"He'd be crazy to follow us."

"He's followin' us," Donnie added. "Right on your ass."

A shallow, dry riverbed was dead ahead. I barely saw it. I spun the wheel quickly to the left. Dirt flew everywhere, getting into the car, blinding the view from the windshield, pebbles, no doubt, further scratching the windshield, already pockmarked from previous dust storms.

Scuzz flung his arms in front of his face. "Jesus!"

The accelerator kicked in. We bounced on the rocky terrain, throwing us against the doors and each other, bouncing us against the headliner. The violent side-to-side movement of the car made it almost impossible for me to hold on to the wheel, but I did. I held it so tight my hands threatened to cramp up. But I had to grip that wheel with every muscle and tendon in my hands. The nervous, soaking sweat would've made my grip disappear.

I looked in the rear view. Micah was gone. His Escort went into the wash. Did he smash in his front end? Or was he in a sandy embankment? I couldn't tell. I let off the accelerator. We quit bouncing about. The needle quit moving toward E. I let out a heavy sigh and let the car coast, lightly applying the brakes to ease to a stop. No point advertising that we were stopping. Never know what someone in a madman state might do. Must approach with caution.

"He's in the wash," I said, shifting into park.

All three of us turned to look back once I stopped.

"Think we oughta help him?" Donnie asked.

I sighed again. "I'd love to, but—"

"Fucker'd probably try and stab us," Scuzz interrupted. "Or run our asses over."

"We can't leave him out here!" I yelled. "We're miles away from anywhere."

I turned around to look in the rearview. Scuzz and Donnie scanned through the back window.

"See anything?" Donnie asked.

I didn't see anything at first.

"Wait a sec."

Micah got out. He walked to the front of his car, looked at the front end, and screamed. He slammed his hand into the hood. He did it again and again and kept screaming. Couldn't make out any words, just a raw, angry vocals, rawer than anything heard on a great song, but more like a toddler in the midst of a tantrum over his bedtime. Was he crying? Who could tell? But no matter. It was a pathetic sight. A once good friend now alone in a wash in the middle of a desert wasteland, abandoned by his only friends. A high school drug casualty on a trajectory to oblivion.

"What do you wanna do?" Donnie asked.

"Let's see if he can at least start his car."

Scuzz turned to me. "You crazy? Let's get the hell out of here now, while we know we can."

I looked at Scuzz. "We can't leave him out here."

"Dude, if his car's broken down there's *no one to help him*," Donnie added.

"He pulled a fuckin' knife on us!"

I shouted, "God dammit, it's the middle of the fuckin' desert! We can't leave him out here! He'll die of dehydration, trying to walk to the highway!" Then I quietly said, "Jus' wait a minute, all right?"

Micah got back into the Escort. Took a while for the engine to kick over, but it started. The tires flung a bunch of dirt in the air, and he drove slowly down the wash. He wanted to speed off, you could tell by the sand being flung from his tires, but the sand slowed him down. He cruised away, seemingly not even looking for a way to get out. Luckily for him, the sky was clear. On a cloudy day, the threat of a thunderstorm and a flash flood made what he was doing a suicide trip. Maybe he wanted the sky to darken, the air to rumble, and the thick curtain of rain to quickly turn that barren wash into a Grand Canyon rapids, taking his Escort downstream, bouncing off boulders, threatening to overturn him. To drown him in an angry, high-speed torrent of mud. Let nature do quickly what the drugs would do slowly.

But none of that would happen, at least not today. He seemed uninterested in finding us and continuing the fight. The Duster kicked over, and we drove off, relieved, but very, very shaken.

CHAPTER 13

Amanda leaned her head against my chest, arms wrapped around my waist, mine around hers. "Do you have to leave? Why don't you stay? We're gonna play Monopoly."

We stood outside her front door. I had just successfully eaten with her family. I wore a blue New York Mets T-shirt. *Yes, I am aware of the irony of being a baseball fan while simultaneously hating high school jocks.* I didn't burp, crack my back, fart, curse, slurp my soda, or commit any other mortal sin. Vera gently reminded me to take my elbows off the table and not chew with my mouth open. She only made each of those requests once.

Now her family was gonna play a board game. It was something they said they enjoy, although Amanda and Jimmy hated that Thomas always played the same Chuck Mangione record. Amanda said Chuck Mangione was some 1970s jazz trumpet player. No wonder I never heard of him.

Besides, I wouldn't be able to play Monopoly my way. With my exes, I always "negotiated" the rent. I'd scoot my chair next to theirs, put my arm around their shoulder, and gently caress their arms with my fingertips, hoping that I gave them the sensation that I was feeling.

I'd lean over and whisper in their ear, "You don't wanna charge that, do you?" I'd kiss their earlobe then work slowly down their neck toward their shoulders. They'd moan their pleasure. And that was when I knew I had already won. All it was now was just wait for was the signal. And as soon as they said they wouldn't charge me anything, I stopped kissing their neck and shoulders. No more caressing their arm. I moved my chair away from them. A toss of the dice, and calmly, coldly saying "Your turn."

Oh, the things they said. I was a cheater, a tease, a conman. Yup. But a deal's a deal.

Seriously, think Thomas and Vera'd go for that? Imagine the look on their Middle-American faces as I seduced their pure, virgin daughter, giving her sensations she had never before experienced? At least I'd like to think that. Yeah, I don't think they'd go for that.

And I'd never tried my "strategy" on any guys, nor was I about to. No wonder the only time I "won" was when I played one-on-one with a girlfriend. Besides, I had plans for this night.

"Sounds great. But I wanna talk to Sonny and see if he wants to join the band."

"So who is this Sonny? You didn't say much about him at dinner."

I said Sonny was a friend who played drums and went to another school. The drums part was right, but the second half was pure bullshit. He dropped out of Fremont over the summer, and frankly, the school was probably better off without him. Not that he was always in class, but when he was there, you could feel the tension in the classroom rise. No one seemingly felt safe around him. He had the aura of menace. Pure danger. But what did you expect from someone who was probably on the Medellin payroll.

Not that me, Donnie, or Scuzz was interested, or could afford cocaine, but he was always able to get us a bowl if we ventured into Bum City, where he lived. Rumor had it that he was named after the founder of the Oakland Hell's Angels. Another rumor was that he was the son of the founder of the Oakland Hell's Angels.

Donnie and Scuzz thought I was nuts for extending an invitation. Maybe. But I didn't want the band to die because we didn't have a drummer.

"Well, babe, I don't wanna talk too much about him. Might make it seem like he's in, you know. Might not wanna join."

"You could have told us a little more about him."

"Ain't much to say. He's a metal drummer, goes to another school, known him a few years. Good guy."

Amanda kissed me. "Well, good luck."

I grinned. "Thanks."

She smiled. "Guess what?"

"What."

"I love you."

Without going into detail about all the mushy-type feelings that happened after someone you liked said those words to you for the first time, I'd just say I had all those mushy-type feelings.

But now what? I never said those words to anyone, not even Mom, I think. I can't say those words. I'm tough. I'm a guy. I'm—

"I…I, uh…well, um…I, uh…yeah…" *I'm an idiot.*

"Just say it." Her beautiful, warm smile was hiding a threat. *Say those three words or else!*

"I know."

"You know?"

"It's what Han Solo told Princess Leia before he got frozen in carbonite in *The Empire Strikes Back.*"

"Fine, Han. Go find Lando Calrissian."

We kissed again, longer this time. Amanda pulled away before it turned into a public make-out session.

"See you later."

Amanda stood, seemingly hugging herself. Her smile stretched wider than ever as I started the Duster and slowly backed out of her driveway. I waved. She waved back.

Ain't it said that love is a pretty splendid thing, or something like that?

ɞɷɞ

It was dark when I got to Bum City. Street lamps, hung from scattered telephone poles, spread soft white light. On the sides of the aging two-story apartments of sun-bleached white paint and gang graffiti were a few flood lights that drew plenty of moths.

The alley and parking spaces between the apartments were filled with older cars. I found a dimly lit space near Sonny's apartment. Right in front of the car, on the apartment wall, was graffiti that said *Tom suck*. I stared at it after shutting off the car. What did it mean? Was it supposed to read *Tom sucks*, or did someone forget or not have a chance to add *dick* or *cock* to the wall? And why the fuck was I so interested in graffiti anyway? Did I miss Queens that much?

I got out of the car and walked to a dark courtyard. Dead grass crunched underneath my Air Jordans. Which apartment was Sonny's? Was it on the first or second floor? *That's right, first floor. Now which one?* Was it that one in the corner, the one with no light outside the door turned on? I walked over there.

Yup. That's it. Hit the doorbell. Didn't work. I knocked. No answer. I knocked again. Wait.

A tall, ghostly stick figure answered the door abruptly. Surprised me. A jet black afro framed his freckled face. He wore a faded black sleeveless T-shirt that read, in pink cursive lettering, *Death before disco*. The shirt was cut off above the belly button. He wore tight, faded blue jeans. His forearms were covered with needle marks. His hands resembled boat paddles. If the cliché about eyes being the windows to the soul was true, Sonny's showcased a twisted world of sadistic volatility.

"Fuck you want?"

"Sonny, what's up, man?"

He suspiciously checked me out, trying to remember who I was. Just part of the game when dealing with drug people. "Oh, hey, man, what's up?" He leaned out the door, checking both directions. "Any pigs with you?"

"'Course not."

"Get the fuck in here."

The dimly-lit living room smelled like pot, body odor, incense, and dirty clothes. Laundry was everywhere, even on Sonny's red drum kit in front of the sliding glass door and the blinds that hid it. Crushed beer cans and cigarette ashes littered the floor and coffee table. A pizza box filled with uneaten crusts took up part of the old sofa. The white walls had plenty of holes punched in them. Candle wax dripped over empty booze bottles. Some song called "Snorting Whiskey and Drinking Cocaine" was playing. It was Sonny's favorite.

I followed Sonny into the kitchen. The sink overflowed with dirty dishes. A flower-patterned dinette set rested against one wall, a bong and ashtray teeming with cigarette butts atop it. A pistol sat next to the ashtray. He opened the refrigerator and grabbed a half-gallon of milk. The kitchen reeked of rotten food and cat piss.

This apartment made Scuzz's house seem like a Caesars Palace penthouse suite.

"So, how you been?" I asked.

Sonny drank from the carton then spat it back into the fridge. "This fuckin' milk is spoiled."

He threw the carton against the wall. Milk went everywhere, even on my arms, shirt, and hair.

Sonny dug through the fridge, tossing rotten and moldy food over his shoulder. I dodged beer cans and rotting fruits and vegetables, leaning one way, then the other, depending on where stuff was flung. I wished I had a camcorder so I could tape this and show Vera that my table "manners" really weren't that bad. 'Course, I'd probably get eighty-sixed from their house cuz I knew this guy.

Sonny grabbed a jar. He opened it, dipped his fingers in it, and put a wad of peanut butter in his mouth. It was the first time I'd ever seen him eat something.

He smacked his lips. "So what's up, man? Need some
pot? Acid? H? Got some skag. I even got some crack.
Oughta try that, man. Shit the niggers around here get off
on. Give you a free hit."

Then I heard screaming.

"Get these goddamn leeches off me!"

What the fuck was Micah doing here?

I started backing out of the kitchen. "Uh, well, you know,
Sonny, I—"

Something bumped into me from behind. Stunned, I
turned around and saw a scrawny middle-aged woman
wearing a stained white T-shirt and nothing else. She had
stringy, whitish blonde hair. Her skin was yellow. She
smiled, and a few teeth were missing. The ones that were
there were yellow, and partly eaten food was stuck between
some of them.

She checked me out. Micah screamed about getting
away from the leeches that were crawling up his legs.

"Well, well, what've we got here?" she asked.

Her breath, ugh—fish would've been an improvement.

The skank put her arms around my neck and smiled.
"You're so beautiful. I'd fuck and suck you dry for free."

"Hey, we're paying for you." Sonny threw the jar to the
floor and grabbed her arm from my neck. He yanked her
toward him. They kissed.

Do not throw up. Do not throw up. Do not throw up.

Sonny is *not* gonna be the next drummer in the Tuff
Boyz.

When I turned to leave, a shirtless Micah ran into the
kitchen. He was covered with bruises. "The fuck you doing
here?" His body trembled. He turned to look behind him.

I smiled nervously, hopefully genuine in appearance.
"Hey, Micah." I waved at him, nodding. "How you doin'?"

He came closer, stopping just inches from my face. His
bloodshot eyes bulged. He kept looking around and behind
him. "You got a lot of nerve showing your goddamn face

around here." He twitched, eyeballs drifting all over the ceiling, keeping tabs on his hallucination.

"Look, Micah, I'm—"

"Hey, Sonny, take out this son-of-a-bitch."

What the—

What did he mean by that? My heart beat faster, body warmed up, knees tensed. I wanted to move but was frozen in place. I could've easily pushed past Micah and run to the door. Why didn't I? Why wouldn't I run from two volatile, stoned freaks and a stoned whore who wanted to infect me with every disease they told us about in health class?

Sonny quit making out with the whore and walked next to Micah. "What for?" he asked. "What'd he do?"

Micah glared at me, wanting revenge. Guess the leeches were gone.

He wasn't really like that. Sober, he was calm and cool to be around, sometimes funny. *Why, Micah, why?*

"Stole my girlfriend, threw me out of my band, made me wreck my car. Fuckin' ruined my life."

Micah used to be an honest person.

Sonny's boat paddle hands clutched my T-shirt and my throat. He lifted me off the floor with one arm. I got slammed into a wall.

Then I deep throated that pistol.

Chips of teeth went down my throat. I peed. It gushed down both legs, soaking my jeans. Blood drained into my throat. My heart beat so fast, it felt like it was wrapping around my ribs, threatening to consume them, before exploding. I gagged, but the gun was in place. Dinner wanted to come up.

"You're a real motherfucker, ain't you," Sonny snarled, teeth grinding, eyes bulging.

I couldn't move. Fear. Sonny's fingernails razored their way into my neck. I sweated.

The skank slowly said, "Whoa, man, things are getting heavy in here,"

"Shut the fuck up!" Sonny yelled, "

Sonny leaned in. I stared into his bloodshot eyes that were so dark, they looked black.

He pulled the trigger.

The gun wasn't loaded.

Sonny let go. He laughed sadistically. I fell, legs too weak to stand. I gasped.

You know how people say they had the shit scared out of them? This was real.

Sonny struck me with the pistol's barrel. Right above my ear. My head hit the wall.

"Let's smoke some more in my room," Sonny said.

They walked away. A few seconds later, a door slammed. I got up. I ran toward the front door. I opened and didn't close the door. I keeled over and threw up into dead bushes. It came out of my mouth and nose, an awful burning sensation that would linger for hours, a constant reminder with every breath of what I just went through.

I tried regaining my breath after a couple dry heaves. I cried. What the fuck had Micah turned into? Why didn't I listen to Scuzz and Donnie? Why was I so desperate to keep the band going? Maybe War was right. Maybe it was a crazy dream.

Better yet, why couldn't I be at Amanda's playing Monopoly? I'd even play fair. Why couldn't I just be holding Amanda? Hold me, run those long, slender fingers through my hair, tell me everything's gonna be all right. Amanda. What would I do without you?

What if Sonny or Micah came outside? The door was still open.

I ran. It felt like that nightmare where you're being chased, and you can't get away. You know, where you're in slow motion and the bastards aren't, and they're gaining on you, and just to go faster you get down on all fours and crawl, but even that doesn't work.

I slammed the car door, fumbled for the keys, started the Duster. The 340 sounded strong.

I sped out of the parking space in reverse. I shifted into drive while still going backward. Squealing, burning rubber, I gunned it. Speed bumps launched me out of the front seat. I forgot to put on the seat belt. I felt wet splatter as I landed. I dry heaved.

Rubber burned as I left the alley and turned recklessly onto a street. A car honked.

Go to Scuzz's house. Get out of these clothes. Hell, borrow some from Scuzz. Take a shower. And tell Scuzz and Donnie they were right about Sonny.

CHAPTER 14

Finally! Me and Amanda, alone in her room! I held and played with something I loved. Amanda lay on her bed, and I saw every little curve of her body, the way her jeans hugged her ass. Her socks and shoes were already off. And while I played, my hands gracefully moved about, making beautiful sounds come out of her.

Too bad the playing and beautiful sounds were coming from my Strat.

I sat on her just-vacuumed floor playing my guitar, my back leaning against Amanda's bed. She was laying on her stomach, looking at college brochures and admissions applications. In between playing notes and chords, I checked out her room. White walls with some girly posters on it, you know, Def Leppard and Billy Squier, and crap like that. She had an antique dresser that I'm sure Mom would love to have. But Dad and I hated antique furniture. He called it junk. I hated antiques too. Why? Guess who always had to move Mom's antique junk? That shit was too damn heavy.

So yeah, my first time alone in her room wasn't all that good.

Her parents watched TV downstairs, and they demanded the bedroom door stay wide open. Across the hall in his room, Jimmy played a game on his computer, and I was certain that he was acting as the spy for her parents, so I forgot even trying to kiss her. If I tried it, he'd burst in, yell "Eww" as loud as his fat little cheeks could, and, before you know it, the Puritan parents would be upstairs. Thomas would grab my sleeve and drag me downstairs and out the front door while Vera would lecture Amanda about how she was gonna get AIDS from kissing someone Saint Jude couldn't help.

Aerosmith's *Permanent Vacation* played on her turntable. I tinkered with the main riff to an older Aerosmith song, "Walk This Way." At least that song had some filth to it. Almost everything in this shit decade was too smooth, too polished. Hardly anything was real anymore. It all sounded too mechanical. I read somewhere that so many of these albums now were recorded digitally, and some said the stuff sounded cold. Maybe. But it just seemed like no one was taking chances anymore. Take the new Aerosmith and that *Permanent Vacation* album. "Dude Looks Like A Lady?" *Jesus, even a song about meeting a tranny seems safe enough to play around your parents.*

"Oh, my God, how gross."

"What?" I calmly asked.

"This college is asking girls about their periods on their applications."

I stopped playing. "You're kidding?"

"No."

"What college is that?"

She crumpled the application and threw it toward her metal Garfield garbage can. "Some college in New Mexico."

The wad hit the rim and dropped to the floor. Amanda left it there with a few other crumpled college applications. Other than her makeup atop her dresser, it was the only sign of a mess in an otherwise perfect little room.

I went back to playing whatever I felt like, but with no excitement. My technique was good, but the feeling from my playing was gone. Guitar just wasn't the same since my run-in with Sonny and Micah. I rarely jammed with Donnie and Scuzz. Donnie hung around Roxie a lot, and when me and Donnie got together, our girls were with us.

Hell, why lie? The little excitement I felt from life was gone. I didn't wanna die. I just wanted to cruise along on autopilot until it was time to land—or crash and burn.

I picked at some random notes. "So where you thinking of going?"

"I don't know. I really don't wanna go to UNLV or UNR."

So Amanda didn't want to stay in Nevada. Another thing we had in common.

"You really wanna go back to Colorado, don't you?" I hit a note and bent the string.

Amanda looked my way. She sounded excited. "Oh, you should see it there. It's so beautiful. The mountains, the trees, the seasons, the snow." She rolled onto her back and looked at the ceiling. "God, it's so gorgeous." She rolled back over onto her stomach and opened a brochure. Her voice soured. "So unlike here."

I stared at that Def Leppard poster hanging next to her bed. I sighed. "You got your heart set on going back there, don't you?"

She closed the booklet and rolled over on her side. "Hey, come on, sweetie. Don't be sad. I applied at Colorado and Colorado State before I met you. Besides, I got accepted at other schools. I'm gonna check out the University of Washington in Seattle this weekend." She leaned forward. "I love you. I want to stay with you. Hey, why don't you come with me and take some classes?"

I had this look I always gave people when I was convinced they were full of it. I cocked my left eyebrow upward, tilted my head some, and sneered.

She must've known what that look meant. "I'm serious. You're smart. You're really are."

"Yeah, right." After a while, when people told you how stupid and worthless you were, you believed them. "How can you tell?"

"I can just see it in your eyes."

Sounded like something a chick would say. "What're you talking about?"

"You have intelligent eyes. I don't know how to explain it. I mean, I just look at you, and I can tell you're smart."

I sighed and plucked a few notes. The strings buzzed, from me not pushing down hard enough with my fingers. "You sound like my mom and the teachers at school."

"See, I'm not the only one who sees it. You are smart—"

"Amanda," I loudly interrupted. "I ain't college material. I get Cs, I'm not in advanced classes, I don't come from a rich family, I ain't a jock. Hell, no one in my family's ever been to college."

She got off the bed and stood up, facing me. She pointed at her chest. "Uh, yoo-hoo. We're not rich either. I don't play sports, my parents didn't go to college and—"

"Oh, c'mon. You got this big new house, fancy cars, fancy clothes—"

Amanda's face got red. "A minivan isn't a fancy car. And I wear Levis, just like you do. Those aren't fancy—"

"Yeah, well, yours ain't torn and faded like mine."

I set the guitar on her bed and got up. I walked toward her mirrored closet doors. I saw her reflection, but I didn't look at it. I folded my arms and stared at the carpet.

"What are you going to do after graduation?" Amanda softly asked.

I knew that question was coming, and I thought I knew the answer. Thought it was coming together.

I spoke meekly. "Play music."

"Where, on a street corner? You don't even have a band."

I turned around. "I do so have a band."

Amanda's face seemed to be pleading with me. "Nick, you don't even have a drummer. How can you have a band without a drummer? You haven't even tried looking for one ever since Sonny told you he didn't want to join. What are you going to do? Your mom won't pay for car insurance forever, you know. She won't give you money to do things forever. At some point, you're going to have to support yourself."

Amanda was right, and I didn't wanna admit it. Pride. Dad said Mom was never right about anything, whether it was about his gambling, drinking, or going to titty bars. Dad said gambling was how we were able to afford a house. Mom said gambling kept us out of better neighborhoods. Whatever. All I learned from Dad was that men were always right. And I was starting to learn that Dad was dead wrong, but I wasn't gonna admit it.

"Look, I know what I'm doing."

Her jaw fell. She laughed. "That is such a lie, Nick. What's your plan now, go somewhere in your car, sleep in an alley, and try to find a band that needs a guitar player?"

Wow. What a smart girl Amanda was. I hadn't thought of that, but that was a good plan if Donnie and Scuzz were no longer serious about making it. I wasn't being sarcastic here. "If I have to, then yeah, I'll do that."

"Where?"

I hesitated, trying to say something to avoid this argument getting worse. "Anywhere with you."

Amanda's eyes got that familiar icy look. "Then you better get yourself together."

Get myself together? I have it together. I know what I'm gonna do. I'm gonna play music. So after thinking those thoughts, I shared them with her.

She sat down on her bed and glared at me. "Don't you want to have something to fall back on? Don't you at least want some stability in your life?"

Stability? What the fuck's that? Queens to Vegas, this uncharted desert isle, then Mom and Dad split up, and Kenny Rogers moves in? Instability? It ain't so bad. "Oh, gimmie a goddamn break, will you, Amanda? What're you, my mother, or my girlfriend?"

"I'm not your mother and, if you snap at me like that again, I won't be your girlfriend either!"

Way to go, dumb ass. And she says I'm smart? "Amanda—"

"Don't Amanda me." She lay down on her stomach and opened another brochure. "Get out of here!"

"What's going on up there?" Vera shouted from downstairs.

"Nothing, Mom. We're okay." Then Amanda whispered, "See what you did?"

I pointed at my chest. "What I did?"

"You're the one who yelled."

I pointed at her. "You started it."

"Don't point at me. It's rude."

What is it with this family and all these fuckin' manners? I hate arguments. Leave now, hope for a cool down later. I grabbed my Strat, opened the case, put it in there, and snapped the case shut. I grabbed the suitcase-like handle and started walking out. I stopped at the door. "Whatever. Call me when you get back from your ritzy college tour next week."

How the hell did this thing get to this point, anyway?

Amanda's voice boomed behind me as I walked down the stairs. "I will if you get your act together!"

CHAPTER 15

With Amanda checking out some faraway college while pissed at me and Donnie probably getting laid, that left me no choice but to hang out with Scuzz. My life had plunged to new lows.

We visited a new record store I saw when me and Mom went grocery shopping the other night. Reclamation Records was next to that grocery store in one of many shopping centers that littered this city. If nothing else, maybe looking at albums would at least make Scuzz wanna play.

Scuzz parked his Ranchero next to a faded black four-door Cadillac hearse that was parked backward. It had no hubcaps, a bunch of dents, and several scratches. It had big bumpers, a front grille, and bumpers of tarnished chrome, and even tailfins. It also was caked in desert sand. Whoever owned this thing thought the same thing I did: *Why bother washing your car when the wind would kick up sand anyway?* Judging by the body type, headlights, and front grille, it was new probably around the time the first James Bond movie was made. But all those details weren't what made this thing stand out. *Deathmobile* was spray-painted in red over the two doors on the passenger side.

I tapped Scuzz on the shoulder while he shifted into park. "Take a look at this thing you parked next to."

Scuzz leaned over after shutting the Ranchero off. "What the—"

I laughed. "Somebody's seen *Animal House* waaay too many times."

Then I saw something else after getting out of Scuzz's Ranchero. "Hey, check this out."

Scuzz came by and we looked at a white skull and crossbones painted on the hood of the Deathmobile. The paint was streaked, like it was put on with a brush.

"Whoever drives this car is a real freak, man," Scuzz said.

I laughed. "Yeah, no shit."

A loud blast of punk rock and air conditioning hit when we walked into the store. A singer screamed about a holiday in Cambodia, where people dressed in black. I kinda liked it. The store's walls were covered in posters, nearly all of them for bands I never heard of. Scuzz and I were the only customers in the place.

A stocky guy with a short, red mohawk, red 1970s porn mustache, and three silver hoop earrings in his left ear sat behind the register. He read a magazine and bobbed his head fast to the music's beat. He wore a white T-shirt that said *Minor Threat* that had a picture of a black sheep running away from a flock of white sheep.

"What's up?" he asked, never bothering to look up from his magazine.

"Nothing," I said. "Just looking."

"Cool. Need help, just ask."

We found the rather small inventory they had of metal records. Scuzz flipped through Black Sabbath albums when I tapped him on the shoulder. "That guy seem familiar to you?"

Scuzz turned toward the counter. "No. Why? You know him?"

"Think he went to our school last year."

"Hmm." Scuzz picked up a worn copy of "Paranoid."

The guy behind the counter kept singing, in tune with the

song, "Pol. Pot. Pol. Pot. Pol Pot Pol Pot Pol Pot…"

I flipped through records as the song came to an end. The next song was a cover of "Viva Las Vegas." Not what I wanted to hear. Never been any sort of Elvis fan, but the impersonators, especially the fat ones, in their high-colored jumpsuits, sequins, playing a casino lounge, were cool as shit. Actually, so was this cover version. I quickly abandoned the metal section and looked through the many bins labeled "punk." This place had a hell of a lot more punk records than you'd ever find at Warehouse Records in the Meadows Mall. *Come to think of it, I don't think Warehouse has a punk section.*

After the song ended, the clerk put on another record. This one opened with cops raiding a party. A pig said, "This is the Minneapolis police, the party is over." A voice in the background yelled, "Hey, fuck you, man!"

"Sounds like some parties we've been to," I said.

Scuzz chuckled and put back the album he was checking out. "Yeah, no shit."

The fast music kicked in. Then I remembered there was a guy in my auto shop class last year who looked like that clerk. I left the record stacks and went over to the counter.

The fast song that was playing sounded a bit like "Jock Itch."

The guy was still reading his magazine. "Hey, didn't you go to Fremont?"

He looked up. His face was freckled, eyebrows red. "Yeah, I used to go to that shithole. Graduated last year. You used to go there?"

"Still do. I'm a senior. So's my friend over there."

He tossed the magazine onto the counter. "Got less than three months to do, and you're out, eh?"

"Yeah. Can't wait. So what, you just work here?"

"No, I go to UNLV, got a full class load. Sixteen credits. DJ at the campus radio station."

"UNLV has a radio station?"

"Yeah, KREB. Ninety-one FM on the left of your dial.

Doesn't come in all that good on this side of town, though. I work once a week during the Rock Avenue show. You've never listened to it?"

"No. Never even heard of it." Listening to his voice, I knew who this guy was. "Hey, aren't you Steve—"

"The name's Gremlin."

I paused to think about what he said. "Gremlin?"

"Yeah."

"Like that ugly-ass seventies car you used to bring to auto shop?"

"Hey, I liked that thing 'til the motor died."

"You named yourself after your shit-ass car?"

He got off the chair. "Always reinvent yourself after high school."

"So why Gremlin?"

"Because it's a small, ugly thing that causes trouble."

He walked from behind the counter. He wore a knee-length red and green plaid skirt with scuffed combat boots exactly like mine. He was a few inches shorter than me and had thick, muscular legs. His T-shirt was tucked into the skirt, a silver studded belt holding it in place. "Besides, you don't wanna be the same guy six months from now, do you?"

This was a lot for two minutes. An ex-classmate names himself after a lemon, grows a 1970s porn 'stache, gets a spiky mohawk and starts dressing in drag? *Now what, comment on the skirt?* Gremlin never wore skirts at Fremont, and he didn't have a mohawk or a porno mustache. His hair was side parted when he was in high school, and he usually wore green camouflage pants.

Scuzz saw Gremlin's clothes and laughed. "What the fuck? What's up with the skirt?"

Gremlin turned toward Scuzz and, with a fake Scottish accent angrily, said, "It's a kilt, not a skirt."

"A kilt?" I asked.

"It's the traditional garment of Scotland," he said, talking like an American again.

"You Scottish?" I asked.

"No."

"So why do you wear a…kilt?" Scuzz asked.

"Either of you guys eat Chinese or Mexican food?"

"Yeah," I said. "I eat both."

"Hell yeah," Scuzz said. "I love Taco Bell."

"Either of you Chinese or Mexican?"

It took a second for me to realize, but he had a point there. And his point was that some things belong to everybody, not just one group of people. I agreed with him—to a point. Tacos and General Tso's chicken were one thing, but a skirt—er—kilt?

Meanwhile, Scuzz didn't grasp this concept. The sound vibrations went in one ear and out the other. He wanted to make a clever reply but, apparently, couldn't think of a damn thing to say, clever or otherwise.

One thing was clear: Even though Gremlin seemed totally whacked, he was going to be himself, no matter what. He came across as the kind of kind of guy who not only said he didn't care what other people thought, but genuinely didn't give a shit. He had freed himself from high school and the pressure to conform to the majority. Of course, it helped to actually *be* out of high school.

All this became obvious as me and Gremlin talked while Scuzz looked around the store. In the background, the album he played went from song to song. The only interruption came when Gremlin went to flip the record over to side two. It was a fantastic album. Short, three chord songs, fast tempo, and relevant lyrics. One song was called "Fuck School." Another one was called "Goddamn Job." Other songs were called "White and Lazy," "Gimmie Noise," "Kids Don't Follow" and "Dope Smokin' Moron." This was my life pressed onto vinyl.

I asked, "Who are these guys?"

"The Replacements, from Minneapolis. White and talentless, but none of that playing makeup, wearing guitar

like so many bands. Spokesmen of our generation and nobody knows it."

I chuckled. "All those kids at school think it's Bon Jovi."

Gremlin took a couple of steps away from me. He began
mocking Bon Jovi, doing a bad impersonation of how he
sings. "'Whoa, we're halfway there. Whoa! Livin' on big
hair!" Then he stopped singing and said, "What a bunch of
slick, hyper-processed garbage. Or better yet, if you're talking spokesperson of our generation, how about Madonna
and all that bragging about being a materialistic, selfish
bitch, eh?"

"Well, it's true. Everyone is a materialistic—"

Gremlin began walking around the store, flailing his
arms about. "Atypical of Reagan! Greed is good! It's all
about me, me, me! Kill, kill, kill, kill the poor. AIDS'll kill
all the fags and the junkies slowly dying in the dank urban
alleyways. It's genocide, eh? Defense budget is beyond the
Space Shuttle's reach, and no one cares. More bombs to
blow the planet to bits after we've *already* blown the plan-
ets to bits. Can't let them damn Ruskies get the last shot!
Stock market crashes but what the hell, eh? Reagan, he's a
fuckin' God! He stands up to the Commies all around the
world, and that's all that matters. Fuck the Salvadorans! Let
the death squads exterminate 'em before they come crossin'
the Rio Grande. We love Ronnie, eh? The plastic president.
The image king. The Nazi who makes you feel good while
he fucks you over, especially if you're an air traffic control-
ler. Trickle-down economics, eh? How about that? Anything trickle down to you? Only thing that's trickled down
to me during his seven years of shit is the jizz from the Man
jerking his money off."

Scuzz's face was a mask of confusion. I was amazed and
impressed that this guy had some seriously strong opinions.
It was like he read newspapers or always watched TV news
or something. He was clearly not as dumb as he looked.

"Casper Weinberger, Ed Meese, George Bush, Alexan-
der Haig, Ollie North. Republican Nazis, all of them! Kill

the Palestinians who had their land robbed, but kiss the Saudis' ass 'cause they give us oil. We kill the Sandinistas in Nicaragua 'cause we don't agree with their ideology! Fuck 'em all. We're the big dog. Central America's the tree where we lift our leg and mark our territory."

Gremlin weaved his way back to where we were. By now The Replacements record stopped. He grabbed my plain black T-shirt. His eyes were wild and trembling, but not in any sort of drug-induced stupor. His anger was from within, genuine.

"We support those death squads, invade Grenada as a 'Nam rebound. We're the other empire. The Soviets are the evil empire, and so are we!"

It seemed like he was a criminal defense attorney making an over-the-top impassioned plea before the jury.

"And it's all going down. It's all going down. And Ronnie's leading us to mutually-assured destruction. We're all gonna fuckin' die an atomic death so the Moral Majority and Jim and Tammy Fae can have their make-believe second coming of Jesus."

Gremlin let go of my shirt, walked behind the counter, removed The Replacements record, put it back in its jacket and didn't put on another album. He grabbed his magazine and sat in his chair. He started to read.

"Need help, just ask," he said calmly.

Scuzz elbowed me in the arm. "Dude, he's the guy who needs help," he whispered. "He's a fuckin' nut job. Let's get the hell outta here."

"No, no. Hang on. I think this guy's a drummer."

Scuzz leaned in toward my face. "Are you nuts, man? We'd be better off bringing back Micah instead of this freak. We'd be better off with Sonny."

When the hell was the last time Scuzz brushed his teeth? "You wanna deal with a psychotic cokehead or get a gun shoved in your mouth and lose a tooth, go right ahead. I wanna talk to this guy. He's got something going on."

"Yeah, insanity."

"No, no, no, man. This guy's got it all together. And brush your teeth, will ya?"

I walked toward the counter. Gremlin was still reading.

"Hey, don't you play drums?"

He didn't look up. His voice lacked the passion and intensity he had during his rant. "Yeah."

"You in a band?"

"Used to be."

"What happened?"

Gremlin looked up from his magazine and told me about once being in a punk group called Projectile Vomit. He was the drummer, wrote some lyrics, and his own drum parts, based on the style of his idol, Keith Moon, who he perfectly described as, "That dead guy from The Who." Gremlin said his girlfriend dumped him for the band's singer, Bobby Barfo. And Gremlin got kicked out, mainly because, as he put it, he was pissed that his girlfriend cheated on him with Bobby Barfo.

Bobby Barfo?

"Turns out she was fuckin' everybody in the band 'cept me," Gremlin said loudly. Then he talked like a normal human being. "That's why they threw me out. They figured me and my three-inch dick was *way* too much a threat."

"I didn't need to know that."

"Sorry."

"It's all right. So that's the only reason they booted you out?"

"I guess."

"You're not into any hard drugs?"

"I'm straight edge."

"What's that?"

"Don't drink, don't smoke, don't do drugs, abstain from sex."

"Oh, no fuckin' way, man," Scuzz yelled.

"I get high playing the drums, cranking music, driving fast in my hearse, that kinda shit."

I quickly looked out the windows at the front of the store and then looked back at Gremlin. "That thing called the Deathmobile is *yours*?"

A huge grin appeared his freckled face. He nodded. "Yeah, that's mine. Got it for three fifty from a junkyard when the AMC's engine blew up. Pretty sweet ride, eh?"

I didn't answer his question, even though I did think the hearse was pretty cool. I wanted to ask him how the hell a car in Vegas's climate could rust, but that thought quickly passed. I could tell this guy wasn't like us, but he was like me in ways I didn't know I was. I always assumed I thought for myself, but all I was doing was just following everyone I knew. He was free. I wasn't. I was a prisoner to peer pressure.

Gremlin gave no sign of being like this in auto shop, but we never talked to each other in that class unless we were actually in the garage trying to tune a Chevy Citation engine. An impossible task. If a pro mechanic couldn't get that piece of shit in tune, what chance did a pair of high school upperclassmen have? But something in him changed when he left Fremont. Or maybe not. Maybe he was repressed, just like me.

And it was all my fault. I let this happen. I let everyone else dictate how I presented myself to the world, even the kind of person I was. Yeah, I liked *some* metal. I liked Metallica's *Master of Puppets*, some Ozzy, some Slayer, but that wasn't all I liked. All the guys knew I liked The Doors, but that was about as far as it went. For reasons, I didn't quite understand, you could listen to The Doors and still be considered cool in the metal crowd, even though the only obvious listeners of The Doors at Fremont were the goth kids with their long black bangs and their anti-desert pasty complexions.

What nobody else knew was, thanks to my dad and the albums he played when I was little, and we lived in Queens, that I was also a huge Beatles fan. Some of my earliest memories from my life were playing on the floor of our place in Queens, and either the White Album, *Sergeant Pepper*, *Abbey Road* or *A Hard Day's Night* was on Dad's turntable.

One of my favorite things to do during those years was to look through Dad's albums and gaze at the covers. I was amazed by the colors of the psychedelic records, by the stark covers of the White Album and *Who's Next*. And I used to get a kick out of the afros on his soul and funk albums.

That was another thing I had to keep secret: My love of 1970s funk. Those records were at Dad's house. All I had was one funky 45 from childhood, a song called "Love Rollercoaster" by the Ohilo Players. Of course, my so-called "friends"—and Amanda—had no idea that I still had several Elton John 45s from when I was a little kid. Sometimes at night, I'd put on the headphones and pop on "Benny and the Jets." But the guys would really laugh at me if they knew I once had, let alone still have, the 45 for the Bay City Rollers "Saturday Night." Yes, I liked that song when I was five instead of something by Alice Cooper or KISS or Black Sabbath. So what? And so what if, every once in a while, I still put on that record. I kept the volume low. "S-A-T-U-R-D-A-Y NIGHT!" That opening refrain still gave one of the few warm and fuzzy moments I ever had. These were my secrets. I even had a place where I kept those of old 45s. If anyone found out, I would be instantly uncool. I would go from having enough friends to count with the fingers on my left hand to none.

So not only did I deviate from the top forty and poodle hair rock category, but also the mandatory metal mentality. And not only that, but I wanted to hear something new. I wanted new sounds, new songs, something that deviated from the verse/chorus/verse/chorus/guitar solo formula. Was a guitar solo really required? I had this need for new—to me—music that this record store and Gremlin's radio show could meet. But even then, if I made tremendous discoveries and new possibilities, I was gonna risk pissing eve-

ryone else off or becoming a laughing stock if I tried to get
them to listen to it. After all, it might be different than both
kinds of "acceptable" music: heavy and metal.
And you know what else pissed me off? The way so
many people at school treated kids who were fat or gay. We
didn't have anyone at school who was gay, but was it really
necessary to call them faggots? Or as the jocks called them,
likely encouraged by their coaches, "fuckin' faggots"?
Those T-shirts they wore that said *AIDS kills fags dead*
were, to me, far more repulsive and disgusting than Group
Therapy. And what was the point of poking fun at someone
who was fat? So what? Why did guys poke fun at fat girls?
Why did anyone poke fun at anybody? And, as for fat girls,
some of them were pretty. In freshman year, I even had a
crush on one but didn't act out on it. I never even talked to
her. Why? Because I was afraid of being made fun of.
Whenever she smiled at me, I turned away. It wasn't out of
shyness, but because I wanted her to think I was too good
for her.
Gremlin was right. I didn't wanna be who I am now in
six months. And the change started now.
"Tell you what, I'll take that Replacements album you
played earlier, and uh, you wanna join a band?"

CHAPTER 16

I discovered "The Replacements Stink," which officially became the Greatest Album Ever Made, even though it barely lasted fifteen minutes. Even though I learned how to play and sing every song on it in a matter of a few hours. Even though my band might get back on track thanks to this strange new drummer who called himself Gremlin, these great things were nothing but diversions. All I thought about that weekend was Amanda. Were we still on? What was happening when she was in Seattle? Was she staring at other guys? Were other guys hitting on her? Was my escape from my shitty life escaping me?

Things were so much easier when I was aloof and used Tina and Michelle for getting off. I had no use for love. What the hell did love have to do with fucking anyway? Now I loved Amanda, who looked like one of us but really wasn't, and I hadn't screwed her yet? What was wrong with me? Why was I still with her? Why was she with me in the first place? I found it hard to believe she couldn't do better.

When I came by her house that Monday morning to walk with her, she was gone. At school, I didn't see her in the halls, she didn't come by my locker, and since we had different lunch periods…well, I didn't see her then either. And when I walked into English class just as the bell rang, she acted like she didn't see me.

Amanda must've been serious when she said she wanted me to get my act together.

I opened my notebook and scribbled a note: *Wanna go to Mad Dogs after school so we can talk?* I handed Amanda the note when Mrs. Smith wrote something on the chalkboard. Amanda ignored it. It sat on her desk, atop her spiral notebook. The paper I wrote the note on unfolded some on its own, but she never touched it. Probably didn't even look at it. *C'mon Amanda, I drew a smiling heart on it. You know, to show you that when I think of you, my heart smiles. Doesn't that matter to you?*

And while I sat and stewed, Amanda took lots of notes on whatever Mrs. Smith was talking about, ignoring the one I handed her.

My angst went on for the next forty-five minutes.

The bell rang, ending class. Amanda looked at the heart I drew and didn't smile. She opened the note, grabbed her books, and looked at me coldly. "Sure. We'll walk over to Mad Dogs."

ↄﾉↄﾉↄ

Amanda held her collection of textbooks and notebooks close to her chest as we walked. Her pink purse hung off her shoulder. She looked straight ahead. The afternoon sun forced her eyes into a squint. I had on black Wayfarer sunglasses pushed so far back on my nose that my eyelashes rubbed against the tinted lenses.

"So how was your visit to the University of Washington?"

"Fine."

"That's good. Is Seattle nice?"

"Yeah."

"Cool. Does that college have what you want to study?"

"Maybe."

"So you think you're gonna go there?"

"Perhaps."

"Well, that's good. I'm happy for you."

She didn't say a thing the remaining half block to Mad Dogs. I didn't ask any more questions. I figured I'd wait until we sat down. I didn't feel any better when she thanked me for opening and holding the door open for her. Her response was cold. She had gotten on my case before to be more chivalrous, some word from the Middle Ages she had to explain to me. So now I acted like Sir Galahad, and she was still pissed?

It appeared I had used up the ninth life of our relationship. Maybe she was trying to control me. Dad said women did that. Said they'd nag on you like crazy trying to change you, like what Mom did to him. "Never let a woman walk all over you," he'd told me again and again. Was Amanda trying to trample on me?

Amanda sat at a booth while I ordered and paid for chili cheese fries and two Pepsis. I sat across from her and tossed my sunglasses on the table. I smiled at her and stared into a pair of glacier eyes and flatlined lips.

She tapped her red fingernails on the table, creating a steady, up-tempo beat. "Well?"

"Amanda, I'm sorry about the other night. I really am."

She curled her bottom lip inward. "Why do you always snap at me? I don't like it."

"It's something' I learned from my dad. He does that all the time."

Her fingernails continued the steady beat. "You need to stop."

"I'm trying."

"Don't try to stop. Do it."

Just then an overweight, middle aged waitress brought our order along with some utensils and plates, but neither of us dug into the steaming chili cheese fries right away. I put a straw into my drink.

"So can you tell me a little more about your trip…um, please?"

"It was cool. The campus is in a great neighborhood, and it's near a huge lake, lots of trees." She grabbed a fry and ate it before continuing. "And a lot of really hot guys, too." I nearly choked on my soda. "Say what?"

"There's a lot of guys up there who look like you. Long hair, flannels, T-shirts, torn jeans, clunky boots. They were pretty hot. Mmm, mmm."

Amanda reached into her purse, got out a slip of paper, and put it in front of me. A phone number with the 206 area code was on it. Vegas's area code was 702.

I was ready to panic. "Stone? That's a guy's name?"

She smirked. "Yeah. He's hot. I met him in a record store near the university."

Great. I go to a record store and meet a skirt-wearing, hearse-driving freak and discover the Replacements, and Amanda's in another state, probably wearing a skirt, at a record store, meeting my replacement, and sends our relationship away in a hearse.

While Amanda ate some fries, I lost my appetite. I began to dwell on the three bucks I lost buying this snack, and, more importantly, the first girl I fell in love with. I was jealous of some guy in another state with a fucked up sounding name he probably made up just to seem cool to chicks.

I wanted to yell, but I couldn't. I wanted to hit something, but that was out of the question. I had to come up with the right response, with the right voice tone, for the moment, if there was to be any hope of keeping this thing going. Be calm, dude.

"So what? Is—is he—is he calling you?"

Amanda didn't look at me and somehow spoke without food in her mouth. "No. My dad would have no part of that. I might sneak out to a pay phone and call him later. He seemed real nice. He plays guitar too."

I felt like my blood gushed from slit wrists. "So what're you saying, we're done?"

"Well, let's see. You don't seem to care about me, you

don't care about yourself, and Stone seemed sincerely pleased that I was considering the U-Dub, and my parents can't stand you. So, yeah, right now, it doesn't look good for you."

Amanda ate, and I felt like she blew a hole in me with a shotgun. I fell in love with a girl and failed worse than I did in algebra in freshman year. And just like algebra, I failed because I failed to pay attention.

My stomach felt like a dumbbell in quicksand. "Amanda, give me another chance."

"Why? And can't you say please?"

Even though her insistence on proper manners irritated me, I slowly reached for and grabbed her hand. It sat limp in mine, which sweated. I stumbled while trying to speak, but finally got some thoughts together. "I did a lot of thinking this weekend, and I'm trying to figure out what to do after graduation. Other than not staying here."

"Wow," she said, cold. "We have something in common."

"C'mon, Amanda, I love you."

She stopped eating and looked at me. Her eyes seemed to soften. I breathed like I was running laps. *What did I just say? Did I actually say those three words I've been reluctant to say to her? It seemed so easy to say, and now I'm terrified.*

"Do you really?" Her voice said she didn't believe me.

"Yes, I do. I really, really do. I just…I guess I just don't know how to show it."

"No, you don't," she snapped.

"I'll try," I pleaded, before realizing my mistake. "No, no. I will. I'll—I will show you I love you."

"Will you respect me?"

"Of course."

"Will you respect my family?"

"I won't be a slob anymore. And I'll try not to curse. Promise."

"Will you respect yourself?"

I didn't quite know what she meant, but I promised I would.

Amanda glanced up at the ceiling. A hint of a smile began to appear. "Are you going to take any college courses?" *Damn. She's tough. Guess this is what Dad talked about, that whole controlling and trying to change you thing.* "Amanda, my grades ain't any good. I'm just a C student."

"You could go to a community college and take some music classes. As long as you graduate, a community college will take you."

I glanced at a Chicago Bears pennant on the wall and sighed. Dad also said women always had an answer for everything. Maybe that asshole was smarter than I thought. "Amanda, I can't even read music. I don't even know scales or the names of most of the chords I play, or even if they're real chords."

"They have introductory classes where they'll teach you to read music and all that stuff, and then you can take other, more advanced classes. They even have classes on guitar."

Okay, Dad might be right about them always having an answer, but Amanda must've looked into this stuff. So maybe "Stone" wasn't my replacement. Maybe she wasn't ready to quit on us.

My appetite returned. I put some of the chili cheese fries on my plate—using a fork and butter knife instead of my hands— and thought about what Amanda said while she sipped soda.

Was she really telling the truth? Could I go to school and study guitar? It would keep me with Amanda, and who knew, I might actually learn something new and be able to explain it, although hopefully not in some fancy-ass terminology. Something grittier, more street. "You think I'd have to take any other classes?"

"If you wanted to go for a degree, you would. It wouldn't hurt you. And you can get loans or grants to pay for it."

"You ain't tryin' to bullshit me, are ya?"

"Nick. Why would I do something like that?"

"All right, all right. So where can I find out more about this?"

Amanda reached into her school pile, pulled out a catalog, and pushed it toward me.

"Seattle Central Community College?" I asked.

"Yeah. I got a few other catalogs for other community colleges in Seattle."

"Why just Seattle?"

Amanda took another sip even though the cup was little more than ice. "Because I've decided I'm going to attend the University of Washington."

"Really?"

"Yeah. It is so cool there. I couldn't believe all the music I heard around the campus and in the surrounding neighborhood. They have tons of bands there, a total scene. You guys would totally fit in. Well, maybe not Donnie with that hair, but you and Scuzz, oh my god, you guys would *so* fit in. It had such a cool vibe."

I never thought Seattle was that kind of place. I assumed that since it was near Oregon that all anyone did up there was cut down trees.

"I was touring the dorms, and I walked by this one room, and the girl in there was playing this awesome record. Funny thing is, it sounded like that song about the jocks that your band played, which made me mad because you were the last person I wanted to think about, but the song was so good."

"So what was it called?"

"You ready for this? It was called 'Nothing to Do.' Is that us or what? It was by one of their local bands called Green River, so I went to a record store and bought the album, and that's when Stone started flirting with me. He even tried to claim that it was his band." She rolled her eyes. "Yeah, sure."

"You're gonna bring that guy up every chance you get, aincha?"

"Why not? It's kind of fun to watch you squirm." She giggled.

I couldn't. I was still pissed off at this Stone guy. I wanted to kick his ass, and for all I know, she could've made the whole thing up just to piss me off, even have some random chick write down a phone number just to fuck with me. *Well, it worked. I mean, listen to the name: Stone, Stone, Stone.* How could I compete with a guy with a name like that?

"Relax, okay? He's a little old for me. He wanted me to go to some bar with him. If my dad saw him hitting on me, he would've killed him, and, God, Dad would've grounded me."

I would've preferred Thomas to take care of Stone for me. And my stomach felt like it had that guy's namesake sitting in there. "Well, I think your parents are over-protective of you."

"Oh, they are. Even now, they still treat me like a little girl. They give Jimmy more leeway, and he's in fifth grade. I get so tired of that. My mom found a deck of those naked lady playing cards in his room a couple months ago, and my parents were almost joking about it, but I try to kiss you when you come over, and I get yelled at. I mean, hello, I'm almost eighteen."

I stroked her hand. "Hey, c'mon, don't think about that now. We ain't got long to go before this is all over. So tell me about that record you bought."

"Well last night, after Dad and I got back from the airport, I listened to that album, and it is so good." Amanda ate some of her fries. Then she talked with her mouth full. "It is so much better than that new Aerosmith album I tortured you with."

Two thoughts came to mind: *Amanda must really like this band if she says they're better than the new Aerosmith album. Granted, that doesn't say much for Green River, but still. And she talked with her mouth full! I knew she had it in her.*

I then told her about going to Reclamation Records, finding Gremlin—but nothing about his kilt—him agreeing to join the band, buying that Replacements album, and how great I thought it was. We agreed to record copies of our new albums for each other.

"So are you going to go to Seattle with me and take some classes at one of the community colleges? If you do good there, you can transfer to the U-Dub with me!"

"Geez, put me on the spot, why doncha? You ain't even told me anything else about the place. I mean, you're asking me to make a pretty big decision."

Amanda said Seattle was the total opposite of Vegas. She said it ain't sunny all that often, it rains a lot, doesn't get very warm, and she said the people seemed friendly. "But they drink a lot of coffee, though. Anyway, I brought a camera and took pictures. I should get them back later this week."

Hmm, let's see. Go to LA with a bunch of guys who may or may not be committed to music, and jump into a music scene that seems about as plastic as the dashboard in Dad's car, or go to Seattle with the love of my life and jump into a music scene where I might actually fit in. I could reinvent myself, just like Gremlin suggested. Hell, maybe he'd come along. And I won't have to get up in the morning, look out the window, see the sun and think "Huh. Sunny again" all grumpy and shit. What the hell? I agreed to go. Amanda's eyes went from icy to flirtatious.

Then I told her Gremlin would jam with us on Saturday at Scuzz's house. "Roxie's coming. Why don't you come along too?"

She accepted.

"I will warn you, though, this Gremlin guy who's our new drummer, he's a bit...different."

She didn't respond right away, which I thought was odd. I was getting concerned again.

She reached for my hands, leaned toward me, licked her lips, and said something I didn't expect. "The time's right. Keep Friday night open."

CHAPTER 17

During junior year, Mullie got into a lot of trouble with Fremont's administrators for designing an ad campaign for a marketing class project. He drew a cartoon condom that looked like Bill from *Schoolhouse Rock* making a thumbs-up sign, and a caption that read, "Wrap that rascal." He got suspended for a week because the administrators accused him of undermining "good moral values." This coming from a bunch of assholes that looked the other way when their athletes beat up people like me.

I took Mullie's advice and bought some rubbers at Sav-On. When you were seventeen, there was no easy way to buy those things. I tried so damn hard not to have a huge smile on my face when the white-haired, stiff-lipped bitch rang up my purchase. I also bought a Mountain Dew and a Snickers to cover up what I was really buying. That, of course, after I walked up and down every aisle of the store twice, smiling, proudly showing off that I was buying condoms, hoping someone from school would see me there and know that I was about to get some. Didn't think about what would happen if either mine or Amanda's parents walked in and saw me with a package of Trojans.

Amanda told her parents, and I told my mom and Rick that we were going to a movie. We said we'd decide what we were gonna see when we got to the Cinedome.

"Do you think our indecision on a movie will blow our cover?" Amanda nervously asked as I drove the speed limit on the freeway toward Lone Mountain. A copy of Green River's *Dry As A Bone,* the album Amanda bought in Seattle, played on the cassette deck.

"We'll be okay."

"But what if they go by the Cinedome and don't see your car there?"

"Then we tell 'em we decided to cruise the Strip. That's all." I grabbed her hand. I had to reassure her that we'd be okay. I knew that if we were questioned, I could talk my way out of it. Done it before.

Then Amanda flashed that crooked smile. "I'm so excited!" She let go of my hand and turned up my cheap-ass stereo as loud as it could go. She rolled down her window. "Floor it."

"What?"

"Floor it!"

"You hate when I drive fast."

"I said floor it!"

I slammed the accelerator and got nothing. Two seconds later, the 340 and the Holley four-barrel kicked in. Fifty-five to ninety in three-point-five seconds. We were briefly slammed against the bucket seats. I weaved around boxy Buicks and old farts in Oldsmobiles as Amanda undid her seat belt, stuck her head out the window, and with her long, blonde hair blowing about, screamed at the top of her lungs. "Fuck you, Mom and Dad!"

I loved that girl.

⌒⌒⌒

For my seventeenth birthday, Dad gave me the only book he ever bought for me. It was a baseball stats book that had the numbers for every guy who played in the Majors from 1900 through the 1986 season.

"Memorize that book," he said as we had dinner at the Palace Station Casino's coffee shop. "Those stats'll come in handy when you need to stop yourself from coming too soon. Let me tell you, son, it works great. Whenever I was about to blow a wad into your mother before I wanted to, I just thought of Joe Pepitone's career stats. Worked every time."

Nothing like knowing that the likely reason for your existence was because your dad didn't think of Joe Pepitone. Who the fuck was Joe Pepitone anyway?

I did glance through the book a few times, studying the numbers for some Mets and Yankees. The book was filled with all sorts of oddball stats that were never on the back of baseball cards. On base percentage? Okay, that made sense. But there were others that simply didn't make sense to me. I did look up Joe Pepitone to satisfy my curiosity. He wasn't half bad, but I wasn't about to memorize his home run totals. Last thing I needed to do was think of him during those moments, which would probably lead me to think of Dad. And by the way, my dad had Pepitone's home run total wrong. Dad memorized Pepitone's home run numbers with the Yankees.

The book went in the closet and out came the shoe box of baseball cards I kept hidden away from everybody. I found the cards of my favorite players from childhood and read the stat lines like I never had before. I studied them the way I should've studied the vocabulary for government class.

At my birthday dinner, Dad looked like a reject from the set of *Magnum P.I.* He wore white slacks, a blue Hawaiian shirt, white topsiders, and no socks. All that kept him from looking like Tom Selleck's TV character was a bushy mustache and a Detroit Tigers cap on top of his Huey Lewis hairdo.

While he ate a T-bone steak dinner with a Coors chaser and I ate a cheeseburger with fries, Dad gave me a play-by-play of how to get my rocks off with a girl. He led off by talking about foreplay. "It's supposed to be like stretching before you lift weights, like a warm up. Just get it over with as fast as you can. Get to the good stuff."

Then Dad proceeded to tell me, in as crude detail as he could get, about all kinds of stuff they never told us about in health class. How embarrassing. I mean, it was one thing to talk about that stuff with your buddies out in the desert, when you were buzzed from drinking warm beer that the creepy dude in the beat-up muscle car bought for you, but to hear it from your loudmouthed dad who's dressed like a human peacock in a crowded casino coffee shop? With old ladies glaring at him?

As I finished the last bite of my hamburger, Dad said, "And beware of the afterglow. That's after you blow your load. They're gonna wanna talk, snuggle. Then they're gonna get all emotional on you. Your mother did that all the time. God, I fuckin' hated that shit. You can stall 'em by saying you gotta go to bathroom, even if you don't hafta take a shit or a piss, although you'll probably hafta pee. And it's good for you too. Keep ya from getting' the clap."

That wasn't what I heard in health class. There, it was all about abstinence until marriage, over and over again, as the best way the avoid venereal disease and especially AIDS.

Then Dad's face got serious. "You can do whatever and whoever you want, but whatever you do, don't make me a grandfather before I'm forty."

The amazing thing was, Dad wondered why I couldn't look at him while he shared this so-called wisdom.

"Son, are you listening to me?"

"Yeah, Dad."

He frowned and looked away. Guess I didn't convince him. He flagged down the cocktail waitress and ordered another Coors, his fourth of the night, this time with a side shot of Southern Comfort. I looked at the keno board, wondering if the numbers six, nine, thirteen, and sixty-nine would come up, killing time until Dad dropped me off back at Mom's place.

That entire night I thought of what a moron Dad was. We should've had that talk for my fifteenth birthday.

കൗൈ

Getting laid in the backseat of a car was real weird. My Duster was spacious compared to Tina's Chevette. Me and her always folded down her back seat, and even though she was barely five feet tall, we never had enough room to do much of anything. Same with the Duster. That, and in the back of a car, you could never get a girl naked. Tina always had to keep her skirt on and her bra lowered, even though her top was off. I had to keep my shoes on and my pants and underpants around my ankles in case a pig showed up. How did they make screwing in a back seat look so easy in Dad's porno mags?

Me and Amanda were in the back of the Duster. I had all but torn open her white button-up blouse and was fumbling trying to unsnap her bra. Why didn't Dad explain how to do that? I'd never been able to unsnap a bra. Girls had it easy. We didn't wear bras. Amanda took my T-shirt off with no problem.

Then I unsnapped her bra. How I did it, I didn't know and didn't care. I'd worry about that next time.

Reggie Jackson hit five home runs and drove in eight during the 1977 World Series.

Then something strange happened. I didn't reach for her nipples. I slowly caressed her back. I felt every curve and bone of her spine, and something about it felt different. I never thought of caressing Michelle or Tina, especially their back. With them it was straight for the tits.

Then there was the kissing. Amanda and I were doing it slow, almost tender. She moaned. So did I. Eventually, my hands and lips worked their way to her chest, but at an unusually slow speed. Must've been five minutes. And I didn't grab them in my usual aggressive manner. I was gentle.

Was this that making love stuff they talk about in all those songs from the 1970s?

And what did Dad mean about get to the good stuff, anyway? All this slow kissing and touching and feeling up was pretty damn good. Why would I wanna rush through that?

Amanda stopped kissing me and lifted up her knee-length denim skirt. She had on tan thigh-highs and a white lace garter belt. She pulled her white lace panties aside and whispered, "I'm ready."

Don Mattingly hit .352 with thirty-one homers and 113 RBIs two years ago.

I barely got my pants and underpants lowered and the condom on. Only reason I did was that Keith Hernandez's career batting average was .302.

Amanda smiled. She breathed heavy. "I love you so much."

"I love you, too."

And when Amanda climbed on top of me, the moment I had waited for ever since I met her in December, all I could think about was that Dwight Gooden went twenty-four and four in 1985 for the Mets.

I wasn't always thinking of baseball stats. Sometimes I got into it, gently kissing and caressing her wherever I could. I also wondered if I put the emergency brake on, if the shocks were gonna hold up from all this bouncing, if Amanda was gonna hit her head, and if I should've rolled the windows up. Then I remembered we were at Lone Mountain. Only thing that was gonna hear us was a rattlesnake.

Then Amanda began screaming "Oh, God" repeatedly.

And I thought, *She thinks I'm God. Fuck, yeah!*

Ron Guidry won twenty-seven games for the Yankees in 1978. Or was it 1977? Did he ever win twenty-seven games?

That worked—for a few seconds. Good thing I wore that condom.

After we were done, Amanda breathed harder than I've ever heard her. She climbed off and sat next to me. I breathed like I had just finished a lap around the school track. We were both sweaty. The windows were fogged up—not an easy thing to do in a dry climate. After my head quit spinning, I leaned toward her and kissed her some more, both of us still gasping for air. My jeans and underpants were around my ankles. I hadn't even taken the condom off.

Amanda pushed me away. "We have to stop."

"Why?"

She was regaining her breath. "Because we're all sweaty and your car, oh my God, it smells like—"

"It smells great in here."

Amanda grabbed her bra and out it back on. Then she quickly pulled down her skirt. "Yeah, and that's why we need to stop. If my parents find out about what we just did, they'll kill me, and my dad will probably come after you too. If I walk in smelling like this, I'll be grounded until after graduation and have to say forty Hail Marys every day. I'll have to have weekly meetings with a priest to repent, and him to remind me that sex without procreation is a mortal sin, and I'll have to wear the rosary everywhere, probably two or three of them. Oh my God, do I even *mention* this at confession?"

Well, Dad was right about one thing: The afterglow sucks.

Amanda buttoned her blouse. "Besides, we can't be out too late, or our parents will know we were doing something."

I got dressed, throwing the condom out the window and making sure I wouldn't drip anything onto me or the backseat. Sweat made my legs and back feel like they were stuck to the black vinyl.

"Maybe we should stop at a McDonald's so we can wash some of this smell off of us," Amanda suggested.

"Sure. There's one on the way back to your place."

After I was dressed, Amanda leaned in, and we kissed slowly. Then she pulled away, looking into my eyes, running her fingers through my sweat-moistened hair. "I never dreamed our first time would be that amazing."

CHAPTER 18

Gremlin walked into the living room at Scuzz's house and drew amazed stares from everybody but me. Our new drummer wore his red tartan kilt, combat boots, and a faded black sleeveless T-shirt that said *The Clash* on it. He carried some of his drum kit in his hands.

Gremlin looked around the room, a huge toothy grin on his face, his head nodding. He talked like an Australian. "G'day, mates."

He and I high-fived. I turned to face the guys. "Donnie, this is Gremlin, our new drummer. Gremlin, that's Donnie, guitar. You already know Scuzz."

Then Gremlin talked normal. "Who are the ladies?"

"Oh, the redhead's Roxie. She's Donnie's girlfriend. Amanda's the blonde. She's the love of my life."

Gremlin, smiling, nodded, and said, this time with a fake British accent, "Top o' the evenin' to ya, ladies."

The girls, who sat on dinette set chairs, said hi to him and waved slowly. Then they looked at each other like they couldn't believe what just walked in the door.

Neither could Donnie. "Can I talk to you?"

We walked into the hallway while Gremlin started setting up his drum kit and talking to our girlfriends. Donnie leaned against the wall. "You brought in a drag queen to be our new drummer?"

"He's wearing a kilt."

"Whatever," Donnie snapped. "I ain't playin' in a band with a guy who wears a skirt."

"Relax. I think it's a skirt too," I lied. "But will ya jus' give him a shot? Maybe he's a damn good drummer. We need somebody right now."

Donnie laughed. "You ain't even heard this fuckin' guy play? How the fuck do we know he's any good?"

"C'mon, Donnie, we ain't exactly the greatest either, all right? Look, I just have a hunch about this guy. I can't explain it. I think he'll be good. Hell, he's got a kit. That's a good start. And if he don't fit, he don't fit."

Donnie walked toward the bathroom. "I can tell you right now, he don't fit." He slammed the door behind him.

No surprise. Scuzz felt the same way when I invited Gremlin to join. It was funny how these guys bitched about how the jocks and preppies give them shit for the way they look, but I bring in somebody who looked truly weird, they went and freaked out. Whatever.

Gremlin had his kit set up and ready to go within a few minutes. It was a nice looking set, about as big as the ones Micah and Sonny had, a standard rig, with a red sparkly finish. He sat down on his drum stool, holding his two sticks, still grinning, tuning his bass drum. "So, what do you guys want to jam on first?"

I stood with the other guys near the drums. Donnie and Scuzz looked like Olympic gymnastics judges: arms folded, no smiles on their faces. My hands rested in my front pockets. Gremlin tuned his snare. Tuning drums was something Micah never did. That alone impressed me.

"The other guys wanna hear you play a little bit," I calmly said.

"Play what?"

I looked at Donnie and Scuzz. They didn't say anything. Just shrugged their shoulders. I turned to Gremlin. "Just whatever you want, I guess."

Donnie, however, spoke with a voice loaded with hostility. "Show us what you got."

Why can't Gremlin stop smiling? He wasn't like this at the record store. Ever since he walked in the door, he's worn this gigantic grin like it's one of those earrings he wears.

"All right." He began tapping the foot cymbal and started a rhythm with the hi-hat. Then he struck a tom-tom drum. I imagined the sound a bug would hear as it got squashed under a human foot sounded like that. His other foot kicked at the bass drum. Then he launched into a mid-tempo roll on the snare. And all the while, he kept the smile on his face. It looked like he bounced up and down on his drum stool.

Didn't take long before Gremlin showed he was clearly a better drummer than Micah ever was. Gremlin could play. He was cool back there, totally in control. Then he went berserk.

He picked up the speed, playing at seemingly an impossible tempo. Each one of his limbs flailed about the drum kit, free of each other, striking whatever drum or cymbal Gremlin wanted them to, yet he never lost the rhythm he played. He looked like he swatted away a swarm of wasps, yet his face had the grin of an evil scientist who had just brought his monster to life. His shoulders were hunched, neck jutting forward, veins bulging out of his neck like ropes against a tree, head and neck perfectly stiff, all while his limbs flew in every which direction.

We had seen stuff like this before, but that was at concerts in the Thomas & Mack Center. That was several dozen rows away from us, not right in our faces. Those guys on the stage seemed mythical. But Gremlin was right here, auditioning for *my* band. And when I looked at Scuzz and Donnie, it was clear they had the same feeling I had.

Donnie's mouth was so wide open, jaw just hanging, that a navy ship could've dry docked. Scuzz's eyelids were raised underneath his long bangs. And with each passing second, as Gremlin played even faster and not losing the beat at all, a sly grin appeared on my face. *Question my gut feeling, eh?*

Then I realized Gremlin was the musical partner I'd wanted ever since I first started this band in junior high. But the grin was a cover-up. Were we good enough to play with this guy? Sure, Donnie had gotten better, and I'd become used to singing and playing rhythm. But Scuzz seemingly hadn't improved since he took up the bass. If I showed any lack of confidence in our abilities, would Gremlin bail? What if we sucked as bad as when Micah was still with us? Would Gremlin say 'screw this' and bolt?

Why the hell was I so surprised that Gremlin was this good? I looked him up in last year's yearbook and next to his name in the senior class portraits was all the musical background he had. Jazz band, junior and senior year. Marching band, sophomore through senior year. Orchestra, all four years. This guy had to know how to read music. He probably knew the difference between major keys, minor keys, scales, time signatures, and all sorts of stuff I read about the guitar magazines I read every once in a while. To him, a coda was more than just an album of Led Zeppelin leftovers. Hell, he probably knew about music theory, whatever that was. Whenever that was mentioned in some guitar magazine, I got bored and went straight to the song transcriptions, which thankfully were done in something called tablature. Basically, it was sheet music for people who can't read sheet music.

Then again, we played metal, not Beethoven.

With a flurry of drum rolls and cymbal crashes, the flashy drumming display ended. Gremlin sat on his stool, sweat pouring from everywhere on his body, chest rising and falling with each breath, drumsticks resting on his kilt-clad legs. "Well?"

I looked at Scuzz then Donnie then the girls. My mind was made up. He was in. But I wanted these guys to vindicate me, to tell me that I was a genius for finding this odd-looking God of Thunder. The girls both looked amazed at what they just saw.

"Welcome aboard," Donnie eked out. Then he exhaled, his eyes propped wide in disbelief, as if he had just watched an aboveground nuclear bomb test. "Wow. Fuckin' incredible."

I turned to Scuzz to see what he'd say. Not that it mattered. A majority already wanted Gremlin in.

"Yeah, man, I guess you're in," Scuzz quietly said.

CHAPTER 19

Gremlin rested his sticks on his snare drum, clapped his hands once, then rubbed them together. He kept grinning. "All right then. Let's hear what you got."

I had just turned on my amplifier and began tuning my Stratocaster. "What?"

"Show me what you got."

"But we're the band," I said.

"You laid down the gauntlet for me. Now I'm laying it down for you guys."

Donnie tuned his red Ibanez Roadster. "Why?"

"How do I know if I want to join you guys? You might totally suck."

Shit. After hearing him play, this was what I was afraid of. What to play? I was great with simple, basic chords and riffs, and could play pretty fast. Donnie was pretty good too. But Scuzz? *Shit. He's gonna fuck it all up. And will we sound together? And isn't it supposed to be a one-way audition? You know, the guy trying out all but begs to be in the band? He's supposed to be telling us how badly he wants to join us, how great we are, maybe bring a bottle or a chick we can pass around. That is how it's supposed to work, right? Or are those magazine stories just a bunch of crap?*

"What, you don't think we're good?" I asked.

Gremlin laughed and clapped his hands once. "You

don't honestly think I'm dumb enough to just join you guys outright, do you?"

Do you know how tempting it is to tell Mr. Skirt to go fuck himself?

"'Course not," I said, thinking Donnie—and especially Scuzz—had better be up to this. "We kick ass." Then I told the guys, "Let's play 'Jock Itch.' We'll show this guy we're legit."

Scuzz turned on his amp. A low, steady hum came from the amplifiers, filling the living room. "Without a drummer?" Scuzz asked as strapped on his bass.

"Yeah, without a drummer," Donnie snapped while stepping on his distortion pedal, turning it on.

"Guys, ready?" I asked. Donnie and Scuzz nodded. Fast, I yelled, "One, two, three, four!"

We launched into the song, all seventy seconds of it. Donnie and I were dead on, in perfect sync. I even nailed the few vocal parts, not missing a single power chord. Scuzz wasn't quite keeping up, just a bit behind me and Donnie, but somehow, it worked. Would've helped if he could tune his bass right.

After we finished the song, Gremlin sat at his kit. He didn't smile. Then he folded his arms. He shook his head.

"What?" I asked defensively. He was not going to tell me he thought that was shit, right?

Gremlin stopped shaking his head. He smiled. "I like it. Good stuff."

"You fuckin' bastard," Donnie said, flinging his pick toward Gremlin. "I thought you were gonna say we sucked. I was gonna kick your ass."

Gremlin laughed. "You do it to me, I do it to you."

"So you in?" I asked.

"Sure. I'll give you little high school kiddies a shot."

Me, Donnie, and Scuzz protested the little high school kiddies bit, but Gremlin quickly reminded us that he was just giving us shit. I knew that. I really did.

Then we got to talking about our one song. Gremlin asked me, "You need to flesh out the lyrics a little more, eh?"

"Wouldn't hurt. I sorta know what I wanna say, I'm just having a tough time getting it out."

"Well, we can work on the lyrics later. I got an idea for a drum part, maybe speed up the tempo a little bit. Tell me what you think."

Gremlin launched into another high-speed drum part that took advantage of his entire drum set, even though most of the time he only used the kick drum, the snare, and a cymbal. It sounded perfect. So after telling him that, we played "Jock Itch" again. We sounded like a real band. Now if only we could get Scuzz to somehow learn to play the bass, we'd probably become the best band in Vegas that wasn't wearing tuxedos and playing Sinatra tunes in a lounge on the Strip. A few more lyrics and we had our first true original song.

After we finished "Jock Itch," we didn't know what to play next.

"I got a couple songs," Gremlin said.

"Yeah?" I asked. "Let's hear 'em."

"Sure. I got the drum part, and that's it. Can you set up the microphone by the drums so you can hear my words?"

It took a couple of minutes of adjusting the location of the amplifier and my mike stand so our new drummer could sing his song. "I wrote this about my girlfriend after I found out she was cheating on me." Gremlin started playing hyperactive, again using every piece of his drum kit. Then he sang:

"I want her to get cancer.
Yeah, I want her to die.
I want it to be goddamn painful
like a needle in the eye.
But I'm not bitter about the way we ended.
I just hope she gets—beheaded."

Then he stopped playing. His drumming was great. His singing was terrible. Off every key known to music, I think. His nasaly tone and high pitch had a real nails-on-chalkboard quality to it. It made me cringe, hunch, tighten my shoulders, and covered me in goosebumps The fact this guy could sing and play the drums and keep the rhythm was damn impressive. But I wasn't judging his singing. I was listening to the words. After getting over the nails-on-chalkboard quality of his singing, I laughed. So did Donnie, Scuzz, Roxie, and Amanda after they got over the same feeling.

"That's good, real funny," I said. "What do you call that?"

"Marie Antoinette."

Donnie and I laughed even harder, so did the girls. Clever. Mom always said world history class in freshman year would come in handy someday. She was right. Never thought it would be in a jam session with a borderline drag queen, though.

"Your ex-girlfriend's name is Marie Antoinette?" Scuzz asked.

Gremlin thankfully explained it to him while the girls laughed at Scuzz. They kept whispering in each other's ear, and I'm sure they talked about how dumb Scuzz was. *Yeah, he may not be the brightest guy in the world, but it ain't cool to make of him for it.*

After Gremlin finished his French history lesson, he said, "So anyway, I got this other song, right, it's pretty cool. I wanted to write a song about me and my kilt, so I came up with some lyrics, and, well, I never presented this to the guys in Projectile Vomit, but, well…anyway."

Gremlin began playing a solid, straight ahead, up-tempo beat, using less of his drum kit, mostly snare and bass. Then Gremlin hit a cymbal and sang, alternating between sounding like Iron Maiden and that Tom Jones guy who plays at the MGM Grand.

"I'm going commando. I'm running free*ee*.
I'm going commando baby. I'm running free*ee*, yeah.
Ain't got no skidmarks baby, I'm running free*ee*.
I ain't got no skidmarks, fuck yeah, I'm running free.
I'm letting it all hang out, now. I'm running free.
Yes, I'm letting it all hang out, baby, I'm running free, yeah.
Cuz, I'm going. I'm going. I'm going commando!"

Then he stopped drumming. "And that's it."
Donnie and Scuzz laughed so hard that Donnie keeled
over. Roxie and Amanda both went "eww" again and declared that the new drummer was "gross."
Gremlin had that big, wicked grin of his. I stared at my
band's lunatic drummer, my face blank, my teeth about to
make my lower lip bleed. I wanted to laugh but knew I
couldn't.
*Cannot give this guy any encouragement. What other
songs would he write then? Making out in the back of his
hearse? Or maybe something called "Ride the 'stache, get a
pussy rash?"*
"We are not doing a song about not wearing any underpants," I said, doing a rotten job of not laughing out loud.
Gremlin tilted his head and spoke in an English accent.
"Oh, please?"
"Are you sayin' you honestly don't wear any underwear
underneath that…that…kilt—"
"Oh, c'mon, Scuzz," I loudly interrupted. "Do we really
need to know that?"
Scuzz thought about it for a second. "Good point."
Donnie leaned his guitar against his amp and walked
down the hall, laughing. Gremlin's face scanned each of us,
trying to read our thoughts. "Well?"
I had my arms folded in front of my chest. "You know,
with that whole running free bit, you're totally rippin' off
Iron Maiden."
"So. You've used chords that other people have used."
He had a point there, and I wasn't gonna argue about po-

tential plagiarism. I had another goal in mind. "I ain't singin' that."

Gremlin said, "Fine. I'll sing it."

Donnie returned to the living room, still laughing. "Dude, let him. It is pretty funny."

Funny? What the hell is Donnie thinking? That song was probably the dumbest thing I ever heard. Yeah, even dumber then the crap Motley Crue and Poison put out. I wasn't about to let the band play something that retarded, no matter how funny it was.

"I don't think so, Donnie. We play that, and no one's gonna take us seriously."

Gremlin tossed his drum sticks into the air. He got up and walked toward me. His drumsticks fell to the floor and bounced around, the sound muffled by the carpet. "Oh really? You wanna play a song called 'Jock Itch' and you still want people to take you seriously?" He talked louder. "Gimmie a break, you pretentious asshole. This isn't art, this is rock-n-roll! It's supposed to be fun! You wanna purge your pain, release your emotions? Go see a goddamn shrink." He walked into the kitchen. "Why did you form a band anyway, eh? You didn't do it to express your feelings. You did it to have fun and get laid."

"He's right," Donnie said as he grabbed his guitar. He smiled and winked at Roxie.

"Fuck yeah!" Scuzz yelled. "So when am I gonna get laid?"

Gremlin returned to the living room, carrying a glass of tap water with no ice in it. He pointed at Scuzz. "You, never." Then he turned to me. "So, Mister Serious, what is the name of this band you want to make deeply profound artistic statements about high school jocks?"

"Tuff Boyz," I said seriously, hiding what I really felt. "T, U, double F, boys with a z."

Gremlin stood still for a second then erupted into over-blown laughter. He tossed the glass of water into the air, spilling all the contents. The glass didn't break when it hit the carpet. Then Gremlin sang. "Tuff Boyz are gonna be tough, yeah!" He made a fist and pouted his lips. "The Tuff Boyz are gonna rock!" Then he shoved one fist skyward. He kept laughing. "So, where's the umulat? Over the U or the O?" After he caught his breath, he yelled, "Come on. What the hell you think you are, one of those makeup-wearing poodle rockers on the Sunset Strip? You guys don't even wear codpieces and spandex. At least, I hope you don't."

Thank you, Gremlin. I hated that name. Friggin' embarrassing. It was voted in when War and Micah were still in the band. I was the only one who didn't like it. The name stuck because I didn't have anything else to offer that they would accept, other than not adding umulats over the U and the O. Damn Motley Crue fans. I mean, what was so bad about Roadkill Cannibals? Bathroom Stall Poets? I thought—and still think—those were pretty cool band names.

And Gremlin's little impersonation was pretty damn funny. Amanda and Roxie didn't think so. They both looked worried. Amanda must've thought I was gonna kick Gremlin's ass, but she didn't know I hated the name. Both of them also protested Gremlin's makeup-wearing poodle rocker comment. A pretty funny comment coming from a guy in a dress.

"So why the hell you with us, then?" Donnie asked Gremlin. "Didn't you know we're a metal band?"

"Metal?" Gremlin shouted. "You call that metal? That jock itch song, metal? Man, are you in denial or what? That song is punk as fuck."

"Punk as fuck?" Scuzz asked.

"Fuck yeah. Punk as fuck. Sounds totally Ramones, Johnny Thunders. You guys sound and look like total garage rockers."

"What're you talking about?" I asked.

"Stooges. Replacements. MC5. Dead Boys. True underground bands. Outsider art. Art for people who hate art. Full of spirit and energy, low on talent. Bands that play just to play. No costumes, makeup, hairspray, just the clothes on your back and basic, primal rock-n-roll."

Gremlin had the right idea.

"Well, other than the Replacements, I ain't heard of any of those bands," I said. "I don't think anyone else has either." I glanced at everyone else. "See, told ya."

"Well then, you guys're just gonna have to come with me to the station when I'm doing my totally-rockin', asskickin' show. Either that, or I can get you guys hired at the record store. We're adding some people."

"Sounds good to me," Donnie said. "I should get a job."

I looked at Amanda, who was planning to look for a job in a couple of weeks. She smiled and nodded. I always wanted to visit a radio station. I also didn't wanna a job, but at a record store? Cool. It would get Mom and Rick off my ass and start making good on that promise I made to Amanda. Sure would beat slingin' burgers at Wendy's or bagging groceries.

"So what do we hafta do?" I asked.

"Well, if you wanna work at the store, just come in, get an application and give them to me after spring break. I'll put in the good word for you. The station, just come there with me."

"I'm in," Donnie said.

"Yeah, we'll do it," I added.

Scuzz didn't say a word. He showed no interest in Gremlin's offer of a possible job at the record store, and, oddly, he didn't seem interested in visiting a radio station.

"So what, you guys want to change our band name?" Scuzz asked. He sounded bummed.

"I don't mind," Donnie announced.

"To be honest," I said, "I don't like it. Never have. I think it's fuckin' stupid. I wanna change it, but right now, let's just jam."

We spent the next hour playing songs off *The Replacements Stink*. Scuzz sounded better than ever on bass. Somehow, his total lack of talent fit perfectly with those songs. He was just slightly behind the beat, just enough to give the songs the sort of sloppy feel that was captured on the record. Then Gremlin and Donnie talked me into writing some music for "Going Commando." We came up with a simple metal riff—at least we thought it was metal—that somehow fit in with the goofy vocal style Gremlin came up with. When we finished writing the song, I realized we wrote a borderline metal song that poked fun at all things heavy metal.

We ended at almost midnight, deciding to end on a high note and not get a visit from the cops. I was elated. Best jam session ever.

"Man, that was awesome," Donnie said as he wound up his guitar cable. "We gonna do this again?"

I unplugged my amplifier. "Yeah, let's jam on Friday."

Gremlin was tearing down his kit. "Sorry. Can't."

"Why?" I asked.

"Going to Havasu for spring break."

Donnie put his guitar in its case. "So when can we jam again?"

"Two weeks, after I get back." Gremlin pointed at me. "I'll call you when I'm back in town."

A few minutes later, Gremlin put his drums in the Deathmobile and was gone. It was only us high schoolers in Scuzz's house. I had a constant buzzing in my ears, and all the sounds I heard were muted. It was just like how everything sounded after a concert, and I was so stoked that I flashed back to the best concerts I'd ever seen: Priest, Maiden, Van Halen—with David Lee Roth, not Sammy Hagar. It was a pumped up feeling, of electricity running through your body, but your mind and heart were still with the music.

Amanda and I kissed. "What'd you think, babe?"

She put her arms around my neck. "You guys sounded great, and you don't need to yell." Me and her kept looking into each other's eyes, and her comment made us laugh. "But Gremlin has a funny-looking car."

I barely heard Roxie say, "You guys did sound great, and I'm with you, Amanda. That car gives me the creeps. I mean, what is he, a Herman Munster wannabe?"

Only Scuzz didn't laugh. He put on the TV and quietly sat on the couch.

"I gotta hand it to you, bro," Donnie yelled. "Gremlin's a strange lookin' dude, and that hearse—" He laughed. "Oh jeez. But, man, he kicks ass on the drums."

"He ain't gonna be back," Scuzz yelled. "We'll be right back where we were last week."

"You think?" I asked.

Scuzz got off the couch and walked into the kitchen. "He's in college. He ain't gonna hang around us. I'm tellin' you guys, don't get your hopes up."

CHAPTER 20

The weather was as gorgeous as it could get in Vegas—sunny, dry, slow breezes, about seventy-two degrees. It screamed at us to get outside, and since it was spring break, we didn't have to wait for the weekend or ditch school. So me, Amanda, Donnie, and Roxie got into the Duster, and Mullie and Scuzz got into the Ranchero, and we headed to Calico Basin in Red Rock Canyon. I took Boss's Frisbee, and we put together a picnic with lunch meat, white bread, packs of mayonnaise Scuzz stole from a Jack-In-The-Box, and Mountain Dew that we put in a cooler I borrowed from Mom and Rick. I also borrowed a blanket for us to sit on.

We parked at the end of a road and went to a box canyon rather than the nearby picnic area. We were all alone there. We played Frisbee, ate, talked. Sometimes me and Amanda would kiss, or Donnie and Roxie would kiss.

It was everything that not only high school, but life, should be.

"Hey, Mullie, let's go climb that rock, do some exploring," Scuzz said. "Leave the lovebirds alone."

"Okay." Mullie turned and pointed at us. "Remember, wrap that rascal."

"Yeah, yeah. Have fun, you guys," Donnie said.

With the single guys off to explore, the rest of us lay on

the blanket, watching the cloudless sky, letting the sun warm our faces and bodies. Amanda had put on some coconut-scented sunscreen. Her head rested on my chest, my arm cradling her against me. Her face glistened from the warmth of the sun.

"It's so gorgeous out here," Roxie said. "It makes me think about riding a horse. That's what I want more than anything, a horse of my own—go riding, be in nature, surrounded by all this peace and quiet."

Amanda rubbed my chest. "Mmmmm. It is pretty out here."

I ran my fingers over her hair, which was sticky with hairspray. "Yeah, not everything around here is ugly."

"What do you guys dream of?" Roxie asked.

Then I learned something about Donnie I had no prior clue about. "I want kids. I wanna have a family, raise kids right, try my hardest to insulate them from everything I've seen growing up here."

"What's wrong with how we've grown up?" I asked.

"Dude, we've had it pretty hard."

I hadn't thought of my life that way. I actually thought I had it easy. I mean, I'd been healthy, and even though I didn't live in a rich house, I wasn't poor. I always had food to eat, a roof over my head. So what about my divorced parents, dead relatives, and all that shit. Weren't the basics all you needed?

"You say so," I said.

"I want a family too," Amanda added. "But I want to get my life and career started first. I'm in no hurry to have kids."

"You ain't even decided what you wanna major in," I said.

Amanda kissed my lips. "Yeah, but I have a year or so to decide."

The sun moved almost directly above us. I squinted. Since everyone else was talking about the future, I figured I'd jump in. "I wanna change the world."

"Really?" Amanda asked, gazing into my eyes. "How?"

I stared at the sky. "I want people to realize that just 'cause someone doesn't think like 'em, dress like 'em, listen to their same music, that they ain't some kind of freak. I think following the rest of the pack is pretty weird—and damn safe. I'd rather be my own person, think for myself, dress the way I want, look the way I want, not the way I'm expected to."

"Wow. That's pretty deep," Roxie said.

Amanda smiled at me. "So how do you intend to do that?"

"Probably through music. I still think it can change the world."

Silence. Guess everybody else was thinking about what I said. I thought about what the hell I just said. Just came out. Wasn't something I had thought about.

And what, exactly, did I mean by "change the world'? Change the whole damn thing, or just part of it? Was I becoming one of those people who'd tell everyone how to act? Maybe Gremlin was right. Maybe I should just go back to having fun, being stupid, and making noise. Be young while I still was.

Then Mullie screamed, "Help us!"

Me and Amanda turned to where Mullie's voice came from. He struggled down the red slick rock. Scuzz was leaning on Mullie, both of them with an arm slung over each other's shoulders. Scuzz's head was slumped down. He struggled to walk.

Me and Donnie got up and ran to where Mullie was approaching with Scuzz. Our bassist had bruises on his face and arms. His glasses were broken. Blood that came from his nose was starting to dry on his swollen lips and his T-shirt. Only constant sniffling kept more blood from pouring out. He had trouble breathing. It came erratically from his mouth and nose.

"What happened?" I asked. "Did he fall?"

"The jocks are here," Scuzz eked out.

Me, Donnie and Mullie looked at each other. "Which ones?" Donnie asked.

Scuzz tried standing on his own, but he couldn't put any weight on his right ankle. "Jeff Day and Owen Maywood."

"Just those two?" I asked.

Scuzz screamed in pain while trying to stand on his own. He leaned on Mullie to keep himself upright. "Only voices I heard—They were—pounding my face into the rock. They jumped me—when I went—off—on a—different trail— then Mullie—"

"Mullie, you and the girls let Scuzz lay down. Use a napkin and stop that bleeding. Donnie, let's find those motherfuckers."

We ran up the rocky hillside. Time to make a stand. I wanted to send them a message. Fuck with us, they were gonna pay. They'd feel my revenge one punch, one kick, one slammed face into the rock, their blood adding to the red in Red Rock Canyon.

And why were these guys giving us shit? Because Donnie hung out with Scuzz? Because they started making fun of me after I arrived from New York, calling me a retard because of my thick accent? And then because I became friends with Scuzz? And then because none of us knew the Fremont High School fight song? Were those valid reasons to make someone's life hell whenever you felt like it? Were there any legit reasons for that?

Every time I thought they'd grown up and decided to let us be, like they had for the last few weeks, they went and did something like this.

Fine. You wanna fuck with us? Now we'll settle this like men. At school, we were always outnumbered. Us against the football team, the soccer team, the deans, the principal. But out here, it was like those Clint Eastwood movies Rick liked to watch. A gunfight played out with fists. Four men. Two against two. The odds were even.

We quickly reached a fork in the trail. We stopped running. We breathed heavily through our mouths. My thighs and calves burned, and we were drenched in sweat. Donnie bent down and put his hands on his denim-covered knees, trying to regain his breath.

"What should we do?" Donnie asked, still breathing hard. "Split up?"

I checked out the surroundings, including a huge red and black boulder right next to us, my hands on my waist. I couldn't see anybody. "No. That's what they'll want."

Donnie, hands still on knees, looked at the orange dirt and rocks. I looked out over the canyon, my back to the boulder.

Someone grabbed my neck, dragged me to the ground. My left knee hit a rock. A fist grabbed my hair, smacked me into the rock. I tasted sand.

"Looks like you've smoked your last joint, you fuckin' drug addict," Jeff Day's voice boomed from behind me.

Pain shot through me. Punches to my neck, my head. He screamed, "You better learn to worship me, because I am a god!"

I rolled over, flung Jeff off me. I leaped onto him. My knees hit his thighs. More pain. I ignored it. Sweat poured. So did blood. From my nose, it ran onto my shirt. My red badge of courage.

Seventeen-and-a-half years of rage. It came out in a punch to the chest, then a punch to his mouth, and one to his nose. He covered his face.

Another punch to his chest. His throat? Narrowly missed it.

Then I was knocked to the ground. Jeff fled. Owen was with him.

I got up and looked all around. Where the fuck was Jeff? They ran away.

"C'mon back here, you chickenshit wimps," Donnie yelled. "You goddamn pussies!"

I trembled, my breathing erratic. "I thought you were a god," I yelled.

I looked at Donnie. His face was bruising, skin red. Blood trickled from his lip.

"He said that to you too?" Donnie asked.

"He did. Think we showed 'em?" I asked, almost out of breath.

Donnie's chest rose and sank with each word he spoke. "Gave 'em something to think about."

I smiled, still breathing through my mouth. "Let's go see if Scuzz is all right."

We ran down the same way we came up. It was the opposite direction of the jocks. But I still made sure we wouldn't get ambushed again. One second, I looked at the narrow path we weaved through cactuses and Joshua trees, another I'd glance at my surroundings, making sure we were in the clear. All the while, me and Donnie were on the verge of skidding down the slick trail. The sand gave way from the soles of our sneakers. I nearly twisted my ankles about a dozen times.

Amanda and Roxie ran toward me and Donnie when they saw us coming down the hillside. We got huge hugs from them when we met up.

"What happened?" Amanda asked, her face worried while her hands gently touched the damage my face suffered.

"Fuckers jumped us, but we fought 'em off. We got 'em good."

"What happened?" Roxie asked.

"They ran off," Donnie added. "Gutless pansies."

"C'mon, let's check on Scuzz," I said.

We ran to where Scuzz lay on the blanket. Red and white napkins were shoved up his nose. His face was bruised. He wasn't moaning any more.

"How is he?" I asked.

"We should get him to a hospital," Mullie said. "Says he's got a lot of pain in the ribs."

"Well, let's get him there," I said. "Let's carry him to his car."

Donnie and Mullie each grabbed one of Scuzz's legs. I carried him under his arms, his back resting against my chest. For such a skinny guy, Scuzz sure felt like he weighed a lot. With each step we took, breath was sucked from all our lungs, leaving us gasping while Scuzz groaned in agony. Slowly, we got him to his Ranchero. Donnie got the passenger side door open, and slowly, we got him in the car. Somehow we didn't bang his head, thank goodness. As I lowered him into the car, my lower back tightened. Dad always said to lift with your knees, not with your back, but I ignored him.

After Donnie put the seat belt on Scuzz, I gave Mullie an order.

"Take him to UMC and we'll meetcha there later. The rest of us are going to the cops. We're gonna put an end to this shit."

CHAPTER 21

This one-story brown brick building was the police headquarters for all of northwest Vegas? Impossible. Couldn't be any bigger than my tiny, dumpy house. Didn't anybody know how much this damn place was growing? They were building houses within a few miles of Lone Mountain. Was anyone even thinking of putting in a larger police station anywhere in this part of town?

That's right, me, who's been calling cops "pigs" his whole life was suddenly Mister I-Love-Law-Enforcement. It was like having a rival hit man take out the boss of another crime family just to save your own ass.

The front area of the county sheriff's office substation was painted turquoise, with a few brown chairs. Photo portraits of all the sheriffs, some in color, others in black and white, hung on the wall. The room reeked of cigarettes and bleach, both smells so strong they'd stick in your nose for hours, coming back with every breath to remind you of the damn place. The smell turned my stomach. A female uniformed oinker sat behind a window.

She sounded like someone working a McDonald's drive-thru. "Can I help you?"

I came to the window. "Yeah, we need to report an assault that took place at Red Rock Canyon."

"I'll have you talk with an officer. Come with me."

A loud buzzing sound filled the reception area. My heart skipped a beat. Amanda put her hand on her chest. Donnie cringed, Roxie quickly shrugged her shoulders. The woman opened the door to let us in. The station was busy. Some uniformed cops were typing, others on the phone. There were men in dress shirts and ties walking around. The room was filled with metal gray desks that were crammed together and was lit by a few fluorescent bulbs in the ceiling and some sunlight that came in through the rectangular windows.

Me and Amanda held hands. We both had sweaty palms. I was surprised I wasn't wearing handcuffs. I assumed that'd be how I'd see the inside of one of these places. Donnie and Roxie also held hands, their fear evident. A few officers and detectives gave us casual glances as they walked past us. These faces were supposed to help us?

We were led into a tiny, windowless gray room where the air conditioning was set on blizzard mode. It was the coldest room in the joint. The steel door closed behind us and the sound echoed through the square room. The only furniture was a scratched, gray plastic table and a few brown metal folding chairs. There weren't even enough of them for us to sit on, so me and Donnie stood, hands on our girlfriend's shoulders, rubbing them in an effort to keep them warm, but also to keep our nerves from getting to us. Amanda had buttoned up her white top, but she shivered. Goose bumps rose on my arms, and my nipples got stiff.

A pig walked in a few minutes later. He had short, close-ly-cropped brown hair, a thick mustache that obscured his upper lip and a muscular physique. He wore a short sleeved brown uniform and had way too much arm hair. He had brown eyes and a pointed nose. The door echoed again as it closed on its own.

My shoulders were tense. Nerves raged, palms sweaty even though goose bumps appeared on my arms. I had to pee. Just the presence of this cop was intimidating. He walked like a jock, with his arms flared out to make himself look more muscular. This guy should be on our side, but is he?

"I understand that you kids are here to report an assault and battery." His voice boomed with well-honed authority.

We all looked at each other. Donnie looked more afraid then when we went off to confront Owen and Jeff. The girls also looked scared. Apparently, we had the same thoughts. No one said anything. All four of us nodded our heads.

"So what happened?"

It took me and Donnie a while to work up the guts to tell something you'd think would come easy. You'd think our anger would carry us through this, but it didn't. I hadn't been that scared since Sonny shoved the gun in my throat. What was poor Amanda going through? She looked as uncomfortable as me. And why were *we* scared?

Finally, me and Donnie got enough nerve to recall what happened. It went surprisingly quick. If one of us left out something, the other would add it in to complete the tale. Donnie remembered that Scuzz was eighteen and shared that with the officer, who asked the rest of us our ages. Donnie was eighteen, so was Roxie. Me and Amanda were both still seventeen.

"Well, since two of the victims are legally adults, this probably won't be a juvenile court matter," the cop said, not looking up from the notes he took in his slim, hand-held spiral notebook. "If that's the case, it would be tried in district court, and we would refer the case to the county prosecutor's office, not the juvenile prosecutor."

"Is that good?" I asked.

The cop shrugged his shoulders. He quit taking notes. "Well, your assailants could face…oh, I don't know, maybe a year in prison, depending on whether or not they have a prior record. If one or both of your attackers are eighteen, then they'll face charges of assaulting a minor, which is more serious. Of course, this depends on whether or not you two and your friend want to press charges."

Me and Donnie both nodded. I said, "Oh yeah. We wanna press charges."

"It means you will both have to testify in court if the case goes to trial."

Court and trial. Frightening words. But me and Donnie told the officer we'd put ourselves on the witness stand.

The cop's face softened as we talked. Maybe he felt empathy for us? Maybe I'd been wrong calling cops pigs all these years? Maybe Dad was wrong?

"Can you give me the names of the suspects?"

This was my moment, my time to confidently end the suffering of me and my closest friends.

"Jeff Day and Owen Maywood. They're seniors at Fremont High School."

The officer didn't take notes right away. The empathy I thought he might've felt must've disappeared. His face went blank, and he sighed. After a few silent seconds, he asked for our phone numbers so he could contact us later. We gave them to him.

The cop walked toward the door. "I'll get someone on this right away," he said in a flat tone. He wasn't looking at us. "You kids are free to go. We'll have someone get in touch with you soon."

Then he left and let the door close behind him.

None of us got up right away to leave. Were we frozen by the air conditioning or by fear? You'd think all four of us would've jumped at the chance to get the hell out of this depressing echo chamber in this pathetic building, but we didn't.

"Think he's telling the truth?" Donnie asked.

I broke the few seconds of silence that followed. "No."

"Why not?" Roxie asked.

I wanted to kick something, punch the wall. That's how pissed off I was. I sighed. "I saw his name tag after we gave him our phone numbers. We're dealing with Officer Owen Maywood."

CHAPTER 22

We were at the hospital for a few hours when someone unexpected arrived.

The woman who stood in the doorway had light-socket white hair, a bunch of wrinkles on her orange face, a beer gut, and bags under her eyes big enough to pack a week's supplies of groceries.

"Is that a homeless person?" Amanda whispered to me.

And Scuzz, with no enthusiasm, said, "Hi, Mom."

That was his mother? I looked at Donnie, and he shrugged his shoulders. I guess he couldn't believe it either. That said a lot about this thing, since Donnie had been living with Scuzz ever since his grandfather kicked him out.

So this woman was the thing we had never met before, even though we knew Scuzz for ten years and hung out at his house a lot? At first glance, she didn't even look like him. And I sure as hell wasn't gonna look at her to find some resemblance.

Mullie, Amanda, and Roxie all had the same horrified looks on their faces that I was sure I had.

No one spoke as his mom walked in the room and acted like we didn't exist.

She had a slight limp and smelled like cigarettes, body odor, and stale beer. And I complained about my parents? Amanda's parents? Rick? At least they didn't smell.

Scuzz's mom looked at her beaten son and saw his cracked glasses and black eye underneath his long, stringy white hair. "Guess I'm gonna have to buy you some new glasses." She had the raspiest voice I ever heard. She also didn't sound terribly sad. Her face seemed blank.

Scuzz stared at the TV. "You mean you'd actually leave the casino to get me something other than TV dinners?"

About time Scuzz stood up for himself. It must've surprised his mom. She didn't reply.

"What're you doing here?" Scuzz asked.

"I got a call at work that you were hurt, so I came down here as soon as my shift was over." She reached into her purse and grabbed a cigarette and a lighter, then threw it back in her purse. "Shit. This is a goddamn hospital, ain't it?"

"You waited until your shift was over before coming down here?" Scuzz asked, amazed.

"My boss wouldn't let me leave."

From what I knew about how casinos treated their employees, what she said was believable. I just hoped she didn't work in the El Rancho with my mom.

His mom got a cigarette from her purse, but didn't light it. She fumbled with it nervously between her fingers. She looked at her son, and he continued watching TV. Amanda reached for my hand, probably more frightened than that time we watched "Nightmare on Elm Street" on the VCR.

"You gonna need me to pick you up when you're all better," Scuzz's mom asked, "or will one of your friends get you?"

"I'm being released tomorrow. My car's here."

The sound of a TV commercial filled the room. His mom glanced at those of us huddled around Scuzz's bed. She tried sounding happy. "You must be popular at school. You sure have a lot of friends."

How out of touch is this woman? She doesn't recognize Donnie, who's sleeping in her house? Eating their TV dinners? Actually using their shower? Where is this woman at all the time? I'd heard Scuzz mention that his mom was always in the casinos or some bar, but I thought it was an excuse. Was he telling the truth all these years?

And just because there were five of us in the room, that led her to believe that her son was popular at school? She didn't realize we were the only five people in the world who gave a shit about her son.

Scuzz sighed. "Mom, just go."

"What, you don't wanna see me? It's been a while."

Scuzz closed his eyes. His jaw tightened. "Mom, get the hell outta here." He sounded like he was ready to jump out of bed and start beating on her the way he should've beaten the jocks.

Scuzz's mom threw the unlit cigarette into her purse. "Fine. Be that way, you ungrateful little shit." Her voice gradually got louder as she spoke. "I gave you life, give you a home, provide you clothes and food, and this is how you treat me? Fine. If I ever hit the Megabucks at the Gold Coast, I won't even split the goddamn jackpot with you!"

"Dammit, Mom," Scuzz yelled. "You don't get it, do you? You can't just make a payment once a month, put a bunch of TV dinners and sodas in the fridge every couple of weeks, and expect me to be fine!"

What's gotten into Scuzz? It was the first time I heard him admit to having emotional needs, needs that could only be fulfilled by a loving parent and clearly weren't being fulfilled.

His mom grabbed another cigarette out of her purse. "You should be happy," she yelled. "You have things I never had growing up."

"Well, I could use someone who cares about me!"

What he said was jolting. Then I realized that you could know someone for ten years and never really let them know you cared about them.

Scuzz's mom stormed out of the room just as a nurse walked by our door. "Everything all right?"

"You oughta let that ungrateful little fucker in there die..." Scuzz's mom yelled. Her voice trailed off as she went away.

The nurse looked in the room. "Everything okay?"

No one spoke. Then Scuzz, his voice low but seething with anger, said, "Yeah. Everything's fine."

The nurse left. Scuzz pulled the yellow blanket over his head. He wasn't crying. He was getting angrier. I felt it. I heard his breathing slowly get deeper, more intense.

How did you console someone who could not be consoled? Was anybody else in the room as confused as I was? I didn't check the looks on anybody else's face, just stared at the lump underneath the blanket.

Then a cold female voice came over the intercom informing us that visiting hours were over. This was not the time to abandon a friend. But what could we do to make him feel better? Donnie put a hand on one of Scuzz's blanket-covered shoulders. Mullie tapped Scuzz's thigh. I let go of Amanda's hand and leaned against the chrome railing of the bed, wanting to say something, but couldn't come up with anything. I glanced at Amanda and Roxie. Both of them started to cry. If only Scuzz would pull the blanket off his head and see that he had at least one part of his wish— he had people who cared about him.

A different nurse, this one Asian, peered her head into the room a few minutes later. "Let's go, kids," she said with all the warmth of an ice cube. "Visiting hours are over."

Donnie, Roxie, and Mullie all wished Scuzz a good night and then left the room. I held Amanda's hand while looking at Scuzz, who was still underneath the blanket, still breathing hard.

"You gonna be all right?" I asked.

Slowly, a muffled angry voice spoke. "Ain't got a choice, do I?"

CHAPTER 23

Scuzz grabbed the bottle of Yukon Jack from my hand and chugged the whiskey. His Adam's apple moved four times, one for each swallow. He pulled the bottle away from his lips and handed it to me. He exhaled, as if he was cooling the burning the whiskey put in his chest and throat. He shook his head. "Can't believe that bitch," he said with a new, raspy voice.

We sat on the roof of his Ranchero at Lone Mountain, facing the yellowish streetlights of the Las Vegas Valley, our feet resting in the truck's bed. His face and arms were bruised, his left eye black, and a rib fractured. Should've been on painkillers, but his mom wouldn't pay for them. He tried numbing his pain with the booze.

It should've been a nice night. The air was cool, still, and dry. It had a sweet smell thanks to flowers blooming on the sagebrush.

I took a drink, but that shit was so harsh that I had to swirl it in my mouth before swallowing. "Amanda thought she was a homeless person when she walked in."

"Might as well be." Scuzz took another swig after I handed him the bottle. "We always get calls about late house payments. Bill collectors're always calling. Seems like the power or the water's always getting turned off."

I still cringed from my last drink. "You serious?"

Scuzz looked me in the eye and I saw a face filled with shame because of something that wasn't his fault. "Why do you think I hardly ever shower or have clean clothes?" I looked away. My head dropped. "Was that why you keep us away for days at a time?"

"Yeah."

"And why you ignore us sometimes?"

He sighed. "Yeah."

"Why didn't you say anything?"

"What, and end up a foster child in some other school?"

"Bullshit," I declared. "One of us would've helped ya."

His voice got louder. "How? How would you, or Donnie, or War, or anybody have helped me? Huh?"

The attack at Calico Ridge unleashed something in Scuzz. This wasn't the guy I knew. Not the roll-over-and-hope-I'm-forgotten guy. First, his mom gets it, then me. I could understand lashing out at her. "Dude, why you fuckin' yellin' at me?"

Scuzz slammed the bottle against the steel roof of the Ranchero's cab. "What the fuck would anyone do? Huh?" He turned away, folded his arms. His breath was fast. I could hear it. Scuzz screamed, "I hate that fuckin' bitch! Fuckin' hate her! I fuckin' hate you, Mom!"

I knew it was true. But I felt like I had to find out otherwise. "You really mean that?"

"Yeah, I fuckin' mean that."

I patted my left hand on Scuzz's shoulder and handed him the bottle.

"Ow! Don't fuckin' do that!" He reached for his ribs. He curled forward, gritted his teeth, and winced.

"Sorry."

No matter what I did or said, he was making me feel wrong. *Why didn't I go to Amanda's for game night? Why'd I have to cave in when he begged me to hang out with him? So I tell Amanda I'm not coming over so I can hang out with Scuzz, and this how he repays me? Why am I getting mad at him? I'd be pissed too. And I thought my life was fucked up.*

This must be why Donnie opted to go to Roxie's. Maybe he didn't wanna face the new Scuzz.

Scuzz took a huge drink. I asked, "Where'd you get that bottle?"

"Mom's stash." He held the bottle between his open legs. "I wanna get even with her."

I sighed. "This cuz of what happened at the hospital?"

"No."

I grabbed the whiskey from him. "So what, you've let this build up all these years?"

His voice quivered while I drank.

"All I wanted was to be a good son, have what everybody else has, and I've got the most fucked up family."

The booze sent chills through my body. I shook. "Hey, c'mon, man," I said. "You ain't the only one from a broken home. My parents're divorced, Mullie's parents, Micah's. Donnie don't even know who his father is. Least you know who yours is. Shit, Donnie's mom's a junkie. And he's livin' with you!"

Scuzz stared at the city. From what I could see of his face, he looked emotionless.

I wanted to pat him on his shoulder, but pulled away before I did. No point giving pain when all I wanted to give was reassurance. "All I'm tryin' to say is you ain't the only one."

Scuzz grabbed the bottle from me and took a huge swig. He had to be getting seriously bombed. He drank that shit faster than me. "So you went to the pigs?"

"Yeah."

His voice became raspy. "They didn't do shit?"

"Got the call today. 'Insufficient evidence.'"

"They never talked to me."

"They didn't talk to nobody. Guess who we talked to."

"Who?" Scuzz asked.

"Officer Owen Maywood."

He slammed the bottle against the car's roof so hard it sounded like a BB gun. "You're shitting me! His dad's a fuckin' pig?"

"Honestly, you surprised?"

Scuzz drank three shots at once. He shook his head. "Fuck no."

We sat and stared at the city for a few minutes. I felt lightheaded.

My gums and lips went numb. I decided we were gonna have to crash there. No way in hell we're leaving. DUI? No way. Good thing Mom thought I was spending the night at Scuzz's.

The anger left Scuzz's voice. "Ever wonder what your life would be like if you weren't here?"

I sighed. "Every. Fuckin'. Day."

"I wonder what Mom'd be like if there were no casinos." I glanced at him. "Why?"

"She might be home, instead of sitting in front of some goddamn slot machine, suckin' on Marlboros." He took another drink. "Might make dinner, wash clothes, clean the fuckin' house." His voice got louder. "Act like I fuckin exist! Like I fuckin' matter!" Scuzz trembled. He punched the roof of his car. The whole thing shook. Doing that seemed to calm him. "Ever tell you why my dad's in prison?"

I shook my head.

"Armed robbery," Scuzz said in a flat voice. "Murder. Kept holding up Seven/Elevens to get money to pay off his gambling. Then he shot and killed a clerk. Said it was an accident. Judge didn't believe him."

For some reason, I was shocked and not surprised. "When was this?" I asked.

"Twelve years ago," Scuzz said, then he sighed and chuckled. "I remember Mom walked in my room, I was playing with a G.I. Joe, having him run over the covers on my bed like it was real dirt. She came in and told me, 'Daddy ain't ever coming back.'"

I thought about what he said. I wanted to ask him what he did after that, but couldn't do it. Instead, I asked, "He's doing life?"

"I guess," Scuzz said. Then he chuckled. "Don't even care."

Each of us had another drink. The bottle was almost empty.

"Sick of those assholes giving me shit," Scuzz said.

"The jocks?"

"Yeah."

My head spun. "Been giving me shit ever since we moved out here."

Scuzz spoke with the seething anger he showed in the hospital. "Been getting it since fuckin' kindergarten."

I couldn't feel my gums or lips anymore. "Really? Why?"

"Didn't like the way I looked." More Yukon Jack went into Scuzz. "You?"

He handed me the bottle, but I didn't drink. "Didn't like my New York accent."

"Jesus fuckin' Christ," Scuzz said.

I poured whiskey into my mouth. I spilled some on my shirt. Most of it went into my mouth. I could barely swallow. My voice went raspy. "Said I sounded like a retard. A fuckin' retard, man. You believe that shit?"

"We're gotta take care of this," Scuzz said.

We didn't say anything for about a minute. We took shots, passing the bottle back and forth. I hadn't been that drunk in weeks. My stomach felt queasy.

"I know how we can get even," Scuzz said.

"What?"

"My mom's got a bunch of guns. She's got ammo too. Cops didn't take all of Dad's guns when he was arrested."

I looked at the blurry lights of the valley. "I know. Saw one in your mom's room once."

Scuzz's voice perked up. Clearly, he was fortified by the whiskey. "I got everything we need. We can do this Monday, man. Those motherfuckers'll never fuck with us again after we put a bullet in 'em."

"Serious?" I couldn't tell if he was messing with me or not.

Was Scuzz smiling? "Fuck, yeah." He spoke with a brashness I hadn't heard from him in weeks.

"Think everybody'll leave our asses alone?"

Scuzz laughed the way Micah did when we confronted him, and he was high on coke. "Dude, they'll so respect us." He grabbed my shirt and got in my face. "They'll be so afraid of our asses that we'll be able to get away with anything, man." Then he screamed in my face, "Fuckin' anything!" His breath smelled like a full shot glass. He let go of my shirt and laughed. "Just like the motherfuckin' jocks."

The lights of the valley were blurry. The numbness was spreading to my hands. I smiled. Nodded my head. Then I laughed the way Micah had, too.

"You're on."

CHAPTER 24

Fremont's main doors burst open. We stormed in, clad neck to toe in black—combat pants, combat boots, turtlenecks, leather gloves, Wayfarer sunglasses. Multiple holsters adorned our skinny bodies. Every one of us carried a semiautomatic rifle in our hands. One by one we filed through the doors. Then we got into the formation we scripted and practiced. Sequential, two in front, side-by-side, two in back, same formation. A paramilitary unit in perfect sync.

Scuzz led us. I was next to him. Behind us were Mullie and Donnie.

All morning conversations stopped. Everyone in the crowded corridors gazed at us. Like, what's going on?

"Time to unleash The Plan," Scuzz calmly said. Then he yelled, "Spread out!"

Mullie and Donnie fanned out from their positions. We made a triangle formation. We raised our M-16s, our faces stone.

"Now!"

The victims scattered. Screams everywhere. Chaos. Gunfire randomly scattered about as we forged a path of blood.

I saw Jeff Day and his letterman's jacket within arms' reach. I pulled a large hunting knife out of its holster on my belt. I swung it with my right hand. Blood gushed from his throat, a perfect slice. My expression never changed, my eyes focused on what was ahead. I had no emotion. No anger. No remorse. No smile. No frown. Nothing. *This isn't me. This can't be me. I am this cold? No way. What about Amanda? Where is she? I'm not gonna kill her, am I?*

None of us uttered a sound as we made our way around the school. We were immune to the screams and panic of the corpses-in-waiting. We spread out, each to fulfill our role in The Plan.

"Go that way!" Scuzz ordered Donnie and Mullie.

They went down one hall, clearing a path of death as they moved. Gunfire continued nonstop. Me and Scuzz went down another hall. We sprayed gunfire through the corridor, clearing a maroon path. Bodies of classmates current and former fell to the ground. The lives of other kids we had never seen or met, or maybe just passed by, also ended.

Was this really happening? Did everyone need to die? Did anyone need to die? Did everyone need to pay for the sins of a few? There were far more innocent than guilty.

We kicked open classroom doors and fired at will. Did we kill any teachers? Who knew? Who cared?

Wait, I didn't hate the teachers, did I? What'd they do to me? They ignored me. Is that punishable by death?

When we used up the M-16 clips, we cast them aside, grabbing a new, different gun from the arsenal we had so quickly assembled. Semiautomatic pistols, AK-47s. One clip at a time, just hold the trigger and maximize the kill count.

This can't be happening.
I can't put a stop to this. Not now.
But I wanted to. Stop! Please!

The assault continued for only a few more minutes. The Plan was a success. Untold casualties. Dozens? Hundreds? Let the stupid newspapers and TV stations add it up.

Amanda wasn't there, was she? What about Roxie? Where was she? Please tell me they stayed home.

Revenge was ours. In pairs, we regrouped in the outdoor patio area, the gray concrete of two stories rising around us as the bright sun made its way through the square opening. As we regathered, Scuzz pushed the remote control he had in one pocket, setting off a homemade pipe bomb planted the night before. The cafeteria picture window exploded. Glass everywhere. A last call of destruction, a final terrorist act against everything that terrorized us.

We high-fived and hugged each other. Congratulations all around.

"Mission accomplished!" Scuzz yelled.

The Plan had an exclamation point.

"Pair up!" Scuzz ordered.

We chose different partners than during the invasion. Me and Scuzz on one side, Donnie and Mullie in front of us. Two lines. Perfect little soldiers. One by one, we raised our pistols, laughing. The pistols, still hot from discharged bullets, went into each other's mouths, charring everything the barrels came in contact with.

No. No. Not this. Not like this.

Police sirens blared in the background, getting louder as the pigs approached.

"The Plan needs to end. Now." Whose voice was that?

Did it really have to end like this? What did we gain? What will we lose?

Mullie pulled the trigger. So did Scuzz at the same time. Mullie fell back into a torrent of his own blood. Scuzz stood for a second. Shock. His laughter stopped. He collapsed to the side. Another pool of blood formed.

I'm gonna be sick.

Me and Donnie stood in the red sea. We looked at each other. Demonic laughter emanated from our mouths. Our joy continued. Donnie cocked his nine millimeter. I did the same with my .38. The guns rose as the sirens got louder.

Slowly, firearms touched teeth. My tongue burned from
the heat of the nine millimeter. The skin of my lips peeled
off as quickly as the heat of the barrel touched my mouth.
Donnie breathed the smoke from the .38, burn blisters instantly forming around his mouth. We too would go down
laughing.

CHAPTER 25

That was the worst nightmare I ever had. I sat up and rubbed my eyes.

It should've been a gorgeous sunrise, but it was a backdrop to ugliness.

I wanted so bad to stop the uncontrollable sickness, but even though I kept trying to think about other things instead of the queasiness in my stomach, the body was more powerful than the mind.

My throat burned. I moaned with every heave. Then, almost as suddenly as the sickness came, it stopped. My stomach still tried purging itself, but there was nothing left in there.

The taste, that acidic burn, was going to linger in my throat and nose until I could brush my teeth and rinse with some mouthwash. And even then, it wouldn't go away.

"You all right?"

"Yeah, I'm fine."

I took some deep breaths. I had an awful headache. My head felt like it was wobbling from side-to-side, even though I could see straight. "Think I got some on the paint. Sorry about that."

Scuzz ignored me. I went from being slumped over the truck bed to lying flat in it. I banged my head on the scratched steel. My stomach felt like I just did a thousand sit-ups.

The empty fifth of Yukon Jack sat upright between me and Scuzz, as if I needed another reminder of the angry night that turned into that terrible nightmare and became a horrific hangover.

The morning sky looked calm. It looked so different in the middle of the desert. The sky seemed so clear, unlike the brown haze of dust and smog that hung over the city all through the winter.

"Can't believe we drank that fifth," I moaned. "Think I'd learn after that fifth of Bacardi me and Micah drank last summer."

"And you couldn't keep it down, just like that night."

I mumbled, "Don't even try to tell me you're fine. You drank more of that shit than I did."

"Fuck, dude, I ache all over. Still feel dizzy. Fuckin' rib's killing me." Scuzz took a couple of deep breaths. "We should've passed out on the dirt."

My voice got more intense. "We should've been in the hospital. We should've had our stomachs pumped. We could've fuckin' died."

"Yeah, well, we're still alive." Scuzz didn't sound enthusiastic.

We stared at the sky. I remembered the dream. Scary. Vivid. I felt like I lived The Plan.

I took a deep breath to calm myself, but I still trembled. Was I cold or just scared? My voice quivered. "I had a nightmare that we shot up everybody, the jocks, the teachers, everyone in school." I had to catch my breath. "Then we killed ourselves."

Scuzz sighed. "Why can't I have that dream?"

I sat up, looked at him, and yelled, "You wouldn't be saying that if you had it."

Scuzz lay motionless on his back, eyes closed, arms folded over his chest as if he was in a casket ready for a viewing. "How do you know?"

"Man, you're freakin' me out." I ran fingers through my moist hair. I must've sweat during the night. It was a chilly morning for a Vegas spring.

Then I saw what the city looked like from Lone Mountain during the day. Was this the same place we always come to? It looked so much more built up. Seemed to go in every direction. Even now, after all these years, I was still unsure if this was home. It was like I was waiting for me and Dad to hop on the subway to Shea and catch the Mets, or go to Coney and ride the Cyclone.

As the sun rose and temperatures quickly warmed, my mind drifted back to more serious concerns, despite my hangover, although breathing the clean morning air made me feel better.

I glanced at Scuzz and asked, "Were you serious last night?"

"'Bout what?"

"Shooting the jocks."

Scuzz thought about it for a moment. "I talked about shooting the jocks?"

"Yeah, you did. Said your mom's got guns, ammo, the works."

Scuzz opened his eyes wide. "You sure?"

"Dude, I may be hung over, but my memory ain't gone. You talked about shootin' the jocks at school."

Scuzz closed his eyes again. "Would be nice."

"You fuckin' crazy? We only got a few weeks to go, and we're outta there." I figured calling the rest of our public school sentence as weeks rather than two months would sound more appealing.

Scuzz groaned. "Oh, like you don't wanna do it." He sat up and yelled. "You want those motherfuckers dead just as much as I do."

"I don't wanna kill 'em."

Scuzz lay down again. He banged his head on the truck bed.

"I don't get you," I said. "You bitch about your dad being in the pen, you say you don't wanna be anything like him, then you wanna turn around and do somethin' that's gonna make you his roommate for the rest of your life? Fuck's your problem? I paused to let him think about my words. "You honestly think those guys're worth it?"

Scuzz kept his eyes shut, folded his arms across his chest dead person style. But he breathed. I saw his chest slowly rise and fall.

"We can't shoot the jocks."

Scuzz moaned again. "Why not?"

"Why not?" I yelled. "Don't you realize, for the first time we got a future? We can get jobs. In a record store! A freakin' record store! We got a kick-ass new drummer—"

Scuzz opened his eyes but kept them squinted. "C'mon," he interrupted. "You honestly think he's gonna jam with us again?"

"Yeah."

"He's in fuckin' college and a punker. We're nothin' but a bunch of high school head bangin' losers."

I surprised myself. "You're only a loser if you think you are."

Then Scuzz surprised me. "Dude, I totally suck on bass, and you know it. I got no talent at all."

"Hell you talkin' about?"

"I can't fuckin' play bass."

"Bullshit," I yelled. "You sounded great last time we jammed. Your style fit in with what we were playing. We found something the other night. We found ourselves!" *Did I actually say what I just said? Did I believe that, or was I making shit up to keep Scuzz in the band? Hangover ramblings seem deep and intellectual until true sobriety kicks in.* "Well, I think we got something here."

Scuzz sighed. "I'm holding you and Donnie back."

"Well, if that's what you think, then why don't you let my Dad give ya some lessons? He's offered to show you some stuff."

Scuzz lay motionless. I couldn't read his face. Was he

asleep? Thinking about what I was saying? Awake but otherwise ignoring me?'

"You know, he taught me and Donnie how to play guitar."

No reply.

"Hey, you listenin' to me?"

His voice was flatter than a note played on an old, dirty string. "Yeah."

I lay back down and closed my eyes to shield them from the high morning sun. "This is all cuz of the jocks, ain't it?" I asked.

"What're you talkin' about?"

"All this 'woe is me' crap," I said. "The way you're talkin', you wanna piss away our whole future cuz of three shitheads."

"Yeah, well look at your life compared to mine!" Scuzz screamed, still lying down. "You got a girlfriend who's in love with you, you got a dog, you got two parents!" He sat up and talked quieter. "Compared to me, you got everything."

Damn. He's right. He's got it worse than everybody. At least Donnie has Roxie. "Look, bro, don't give up. Not yet. We ain't got long to go. Then, who knows?"

Scuzz lay back down. "You sound like one of those happy people."

"Somethin' tells me it's gonna get better."

"Can't get any worse," Scuzz said.

I chuckled. "Well, there you go. Nowhere to go but up." I sat up and stared at the city, I squinted my eyes. My stomach growled. "You hungry?"

Scuzz moaned. "Yeah. Thirsty too."

"How you feeling?"

"Like shit. You?"

"Starting to feel better, actually. Head's sorta spinning a bit, body's weak, but I don't feel all that bad. Fuckin' weird, ain't it?"

Scuzz arched his back and groaned. "It's amazin' what a good puking'll do for ya."

I grabbed my wallet out of my back pocket and saw I had a few crinkled dollar bills. That should be enough to get something to eat at McDonald's. "Let's go get some breakfast. I'll buy. I'll drive if you want."

Scuzz reached into his pocket and tossed me the keys. They rattled when they hit my hand.

With a sudden burst of energy, I leaped out of the truck bed. "C'mon, dude. Let's get outta here and forget about all the shit."

CHAPTER 26

I pushed the cold stainless steel bar that opened one of the front doors to Fremont and got hit with a blast of air that resembled a heated oven. It was the first day back from spring break, and it felt like the first day of school in late August.

"Damn," I said, squinting my eyes to shield them from the blinding sun. "We gotta stop leaving our sunglasses in the car."

"God, no kidding," added Roxie, holding some books and notebooks against her chest. "You'd think after eighteen years here, I'd learn."

Walking from the school to the dirt parking lot, we heard some otherwise white yuppie types talk about tanning. As if their brown and orange skin wasn't already dark enough. Wouldn't be long before they developed brown spots and deep wrinkles on the top of those tans. Yuck.

I looked at Amanda, who was the total opposite. She shielded her squinting eyes with her right hand, a backpack slung over her shoulders. She looked like she was saluting a general.

"So this is what we have to look forward to," she said, not excited at all.

I put an arm around her waist. "Relax, babe. It's only gonna be like this for the next six months."

"Hey, Nick," Donnie said, "don't hide your enthusiasm."

I smiled. "Ever know me to do that?"

Scuzz, Donnie, and Mullie all said, "No," at the same time. Everybody laughed.

The four of us had parked our cars next to each other in the dirt lot. The air was full of dust from cars and a slight breeze. We were just about to cross the street when Scuzz get shoved into the pavement.

"What the fuck are you doing back in here, you filthy stoner?" Jeff said. "Thought your filthy ass wouldn't come back after last week." Then he walked away. Owen and James were with him, all three of them in fancy acid-washed jeans and short-sleeved pastel polo shirts, all laughing and high-fiving each other.

"Gonna run off again, you pansies?" Donnie yelled.

No reply. They kept on walking.

"Forget about 'em," I said. "Hit and run. Typical chicken-shit tactic."

Scuzz sat on the asphalt, head down.

"You okay?" I asked.

"Yeah."

"Need a hand?" Donnie asked.

"No." As Scuzz stood up, he coldly said, "Let's teach 'em a lesson."

All the guys looked at each other, and without saying a word, we followed the jocks. Amanda and Roxie urged us not to do it. We ignored them. You didn't abandon your brother in his time of need.

"Time to make a final stand," Scuzz said.

The jocks approached Owen's red Jeep. Scuzz walked faster, so did we. He ran, we did too.

Scuzz slid a pistol from the front of his pants and sprinted.

"Shit," I whispered. I ran after Scuzz.

"What?" Mullie asked.

I ran, but Scuzz ran faster.

I shoved past people getting into cars. They yelled something, I didn't hear what. A truck nearly hit me. A horn blared, and some guy called me an asshole.

Scuzz gained on the jocks.

My heart raced. I breathed through my mouth.

Where the fuck were Mullie and Donnie?

Scuzz neared the jocks. They stood in front of the Jeep, talking to some tanned cheerleaders. All the guys had their backs turned. The girls didn't notice Scuzz.

This would be no duel.

I hated those guys too, but I had to stop it.

Scuzz raised his right hand.

I never ran so fast.

Almost there.

I gasped for air.

Almost there.

Scuzz's thumb cocked the hammer. "So you're a fucking god, huh?"

Almost there.

He raised the gun.

I tackled him. We hit the ground. Hard.

The gun went off.

CHAPTER 27

I always thought my first taste of the county jail wouldn't be walking through the main entrance. Try the back of a cop car.

The county jail was only a few blocks away from Fremont Street and Glitter Gulch. If I wanted to, and if I was old enough—or had a fake ID—I could've walked a few blocks to the Horseshoe, the Four Queens, or the Union Plaza and play some blackjack or slots, get an eighty-eight cent shrimp cocktail—like I'd ever actually eat one of those things—maybe buy a dice clock in a tacky souvenir shop.

I walked in the door and decided I never wanted to come into this kind of joint again. Even though I was gonna home later, sleep in my bed, I didn't feel like I was free. I felt like I was in a cell block. There was a bunch of signs telling you what you couldn't bring in there. They tell you what you *couldn't* do. No sign of what you *could* do or *could* bring in. Probably nothing.

There was drab gray everywhere, the walls, the tile. There was a line to get in. I passed through a metal detector and got patted down by some sleepy-eyed black chick dressed as a cop. I was guilty before being proved innocent. I had no weapons, no drugs on me. I wasn't that stupid. And what a tense atmosphere. Never saw so many unhappy faces in my life, and that included the staff.

Do you have to be sour-faced to work here? Is that part of the job interview?

Are you always bitchy and crabby and depressed?

Yes, sir.

Are you incredibly unfriendly, prone to making people feel hostile?

All the time, sir.

Congratulations. You're hired. When can you start?

I passed through security with no problems. I wore my red and white Air Jordans instead of my combat boots to get through the checkpoint quicker. Mom warned me about the metal detectors. Guess she visited Dad in here before. I showed my driver's license to a short-haired stone-faced woman in a tan uniform. She looked at my license and typed something into a computer. *Guess she's seeing if I'm wanted. Is this what life's like in the Soviet Union? East Germany?*

When I passed that checkpoint, I was led to the visitor's area. It was a long, windowless gray room. Hard plastic gray chairs, the same kind we had at school, were for visitors to sit on. The chairs were in areas set off by small blue walls. There were a lot of women and a few men in there, almost all of them black, some Mexican. Several of them cried.

Some yelled at the guys they talked to on a telephone behind clear plastic. I couldn't hear what anyone said, with all the crying and the yelling going on in there. Someone must've just cleaned the room. Like the cop station, it had that bleach smell that burned into your nose and stayed there for the next few hours.

I slowly sat on a chair. Seemed harder than anything in any classroom I'd ever been in. I couldn't get comfortable. Nervous, scared, fidgety. Kept cracking my knuckles, biting off and chewing on fingernails, then spitting them onto the floor like a baseball player spitting sunflower seeds. Felt like going for a run just to get rid of the tension.

Waiting. Forever, I think. If I had a watch, I would've looked at it. Not that I had anywhere else to go, but that was not where I wanted to be. *How long 'til Scuzz gets here?*

A few minutes later, an officer brought Scuzz in. He wore a red two-piece, short-sleeved V-necked outfit. His face looked like it was getting a permanent frown. He sat down and slowly reached for the phone. He didn't look up from the shelf he put his elbows on as he pulled the receiver to his head.

"Hey," I said.

It took him a while to respond. "Hey."

What next? Ask how you doin'? That'd be the dumbest question ever. Should I ask him what's up? Nah, that'd be pretty stupid too. I fell silent.

It sounded like I was talking to Scuzz on the phone from my house. "It sucks in here."

"I bet."

"Food here's fuckin' terrible. Makes the school cafeteria seem like Taco Bell."

Was he was trying to be funny? I didn't laugh or smile. "That bad, huh?"

"Lunch today was supposed to be a hamburger. I think was a ground-up scorpion."

So much for hitting the McDonald's drive-thru once I got out of here.

"So when's the trial?"

Scuzz mumbled. "Ain't gonna be one."

"Why?"

"Pleading guilty to all charges."

I was stunned. "What're the charges?"

Scuzz was monotone. "Attempted murder, reckless endangerment, illegal possession of a firearm. Shit like that. I'm eighteen, so I'm being tried as an adult. That's why I'm here and not in juvee."

"Why ain't you gonna at least go to trial?" I asked. "Ain't you got a lawyer?"

"Court-appointed one."

"So why ain't you fightin' this?"

Scuzz sighed. "Get real. She's just like my mom. She don't give a fuck about me. She just wants to get me through the system so she can get on to the next case."

"How can you tell?"

"When no one's given a shit about you your whole life, you just know."

I exhaled deeply and put my head in the palm of my hand. "C'mon, don't give up. We'll help ya, man, testify for ya. Maybe you can get off easy. Maybe we can get ya another lawyer."

"With what money?"

Good point. "Look, we don't wanna let you go that easy," I said. "We can bring up all the shit those guys've done. Maybe we can get you some sympathy from a jury or something."

Then he sounded like he had truly given up. "I don't wanna burden everybody with a trial. Just get this over with, let everybody get on with their lives."

"I don't get it. You seemed so feisty in the hospital, so willing to fight. Now you just wanna give up without even defending yourself?"

His head fell and hit the counter. "Yeah."

"Why?"

"Guess who the district attorney is."

"Who?"

"Jeff Day's father."

I sank in my chair. I looked at the gray ceiling. I could and could not believe what Scuzz said. I took a deep breath. "Lovely. Owen's dad's a pig, Jeff's dad's the DA."

"System's totally stacked against us."

"So what're you facin'?" I asked.

"Twenty years. Maximum sentence for every offense."

I spoke louder. "But this is your first offense. You've never done anything wrong. Well, never been caught, anyway."

Scuzz finally looked me in the eye. He looked terrible. His cheeks and eyes were more sunken than ever and bloodshot. He had bags under his eyes that resembled his mom's. His eyes were almost completely red. Was he sleeping? I figured he was barely eating.

"Dude, go to trial. I'll testify for ya. Donnie'll testify. So will Mullie and—"

"Oh, cut the shit," Scuzz yelled. "You know every damn jock and cheerleader and coach in school'll be called as witnesses. Probably even the teachers too. Nobody there gives a shit about us. They just wanna get rid of us any way they can." Then his voice was flat. "It's okay. By the time I get out of here, I'll be thirty-eight. Plenty of time to live after that."

Did he want me to laugh? Was he trying to be funny? I didn't laugh. "What were you gonna do?"

"With what?"

"The gun."

Scuzz looked down again. He sighed long, spoke slowly. "I was gonna shoot him and turn the gun on myself."

I closed my eyes. I wanted to cry. Scuzz wanted to commit suicide? I thought I was the only one who had those thoughts. I thought I helped Scuzz. I tried reassuring him things would be fine. I tried telling him things had to get better.

And I failed. Did I try hard enough?

I couldn't cry. Not in jail. Who cared if other people talking to prisoners were crying? I must remain tough. Why? Good question. Wish I knew the answer.

"Dude, we were all right behind you. Didn't you think we were gonna stop you?"

"When you want the end to come, you don't think of those things."

It was then I realized that Scuzz was more depressed than he ever let on. All the jokes, the smiles, the laughter, were just a cover-up.

"You know what really sucks?" Scuzz asked. "Now that I'm here, I totally wish I had never brought my mom's gun to school. Now that I'm here I don't wanna die." Then a tear went down his cheek. "My cell faces west. I can see the mountains, Red Rock Canyon. I can see the sunset every night." He sniffled. "You ever look at the sunset?"

"No."

Scuzz's face fell into his right hand, his left holding the phone. He took off his glasses and put them on the shelf in front of him. He struggled to talk. "They're so pretty. I've hated this fuckin' place my whole life, but watching the sunsets, man, every night I see the sun go down over the mountains, and I just want outta here."

I tried being numb. I felt like I needed to be strong for my friend.

"Now I'm gonna end up in the pen with my dad. And I never wanted to see that motherfucker ever again!"

"Hey, Scuzz—"

He slammed his hand on the shelf. "Don't fuckin' call me that anymore! I don't wanna be Scuzz anymore. I just wanna be Chris Scozzoli. That's all. Next time I get out of here, if I ever get out of here, I'm gonna be Chris Scozzoli, ex-fuckin' con."

I nodded slowly. Then I remembered that I'd all but forgotten that his real name was Chris. It had been such a long time that we had called him "Scuzz" that it became his identity.

We spent the next few minutes talking about Donnie and how he didn't know where he was gonna live. We also talked about the band and what would become of it. I told him we planned to get another bass player, although I might take over that instrument in the meantime. I could always borrow Dad's Rickenbacker, I told Chris.

And just when I thought I could leave that depressing lockup having brightened Chris's day, his face went sour again. "Guess what. Micah's dead."

CHAPTER 28

What a lousy time for War to come back to Vegas on leave. We didn't give him much of a welcome home. No party, nothing. But we were glad to see him. It's just that nobody was in the mood to party.

We had something more important to do. We had to scatter Micah's ashes.

Micah OD'd on heroin that Sonny injected him with. Chris told me Sonny was in the county jail, facing murder charges, and went around the yard bragging about killing Micah.

"Like he's proud of it," Chris told me.

Micah's parents reluctantly let us take him. That was the hardest phone call I ever made. His poor mother was so heartbroken, his dad so pissed. They spent half the time on the phone with me talking about how guilty they felt for doing coke. Losing their marriage because of drugs was one thing, losing their son to drugs was worse, they said. And when we went to get Micah one day after school, I was the only one who went to the door at his house to get him. Donnie and Mullie couldn't do it. War didn't want to.

Micah's house was surprisingly nice. Looked pretty new with a green lawn, perfectly mowed and edged, a Mercedes in the driveway, a big bay window facing the street, and a fireplace. How did he get mixed up with us? The house looked like he should've been a preppie. It certainly looked like they could afford all those brand-name clothes at the mall. Of course, anybody driving a new-looking Mercedes could also afford to buy coke. I remembered he told me they used to work all the time. Guess coke was one way he could feel closer to them.

Maybe Scuzz wasn't the only one with parents who didn't give a fuck.

 espes

When one of the double doors opened, I couldn't look at his mom. I gazed at the ground and asked for Micah. Whoever it was that brought him to me said nothing and closed the door.

I never did ask his parents why they never told us what happened.

The five of us crammed into Donnie's Datsun King Cab. War and Mullie were in the tiny back seats. I had my seat all the way forward so War could have some room back there. I held the cardboard box containing Micah's remains, and my knees were maybe two inches away from the glove compartment.

We were doing about seventy on a narrow, bumpy two-lane road headed toward Nelson's Landing, south of Vegas. The worn suspension and sagging seats made me feel the road's every bump, and there were plenty of those to be felt. Dry wind blasted through the open windows. The sun and heat were at their late afternoon intensity. It had to be over ninety. The radio was tuned to the Rock of Las Vegas, but the signal cut in and out as we wound deeper into the canyon. Static mixed with "Ballroom Blitz," the wrong song for the moment. I turned it off and heard no complaints.

The pavement ended at a viewpoint overlooking the Colorado River and the mountains on the Arizona side. A dirt road went down a steep slope to the river's edge. A few bumpy minutes later, we parked near a bunch of mesquite trees. A metal sign in front of us said *Warning: Flash Flood Area*, since we were in a deep, wide wash. But we were in no danger. Not a single cloud had passed that way for a month.

The mesquite tree branches hung low, forcing us to walk bent over. I pushed away branches with one hand while holding Micah under my other arm.

Once at the river's edge, we stood, looking everywhere but at each other. Only thing I heard was ringing in my ears. No wind. No boaters. No cliff-jumpers. Total isolation.

"Well?" Donnie asked.

"Might as well get this over with," I said.

We didn't have a plan, but it seemed like we did. Everyone did the same thing. We took off our shoes and socks and rolled up our jeans above our calves. Then we went into the frigid river about two feet deep, the four of us making a straight line. Everybody shivered. I handed Micah to Donnie, reached into my back pocket, and grabbed a picture.

"Remember this?" I handed Donnie a pic of me, him, and Micah, all of us fourteen, all with our shirts off, sunburned, and smiling. Me and Donnie had put a towel over Micah's head to make him look like an Arab.

Donnie smiled. "Where was this taken?"

"Rogers Spring, I think. Yeah...Yeah, Rogers Spring."

"He always loved coming out to the lake."

I got used to the cool water, but it didn't cool my temper. I ground my teeth and tensed up, like I was ready to fight. *Hell if I'm gonna cry.*

The pic was passed around.

"He let the drugs get out of control," War said.

"Didn't listen to us," Donnie said.

Donnie handed me the pic and I put it in my back pocket. "I think we should share a memory of Micah before we scatter him."

About a minute passed before Donnie ended the silence. "Maybe it's just that picture, but now I remember all the times we came to the lake with his parents, before they broke up, and your parents—" Donnie pointed at me. "—before they broke up. I remember how much fun we used to have, splashing each other, laughing."

Donnie sniffled and gazed at the water.

"He was pretty smart," Mullie said. "I sat next to him in a few classes, and he used to get pretty decent grades."

I put Micah under my other arm. "Until his parents split up and he got into the drugs. He changed. He really did."

Donnie sighed. "We did that peyote and acid, and, fuckin' a, he wanted to do more of that."

"Scared the shit out of me," I said.

Donnie stared downriver. "Then he found his mom's coke."

I couldn't look at anybody. My head was down, gazing at the lazy river.

War sighed. "Remember in seventh grade, Micah wrote for the yearbook that his name was Alex Van Halen?"

Donnie chuckled. "Yeah. He tried to get all of us to put down that our names were someone from Van Halen."

"He was the only one who did that, wasn't he?" I asked.

"Yeah," Donnie said. "He thought he was so cool, but everybody thought he was a dork."

And we laughed.

"He was so pissed off at us for not doing that," War said.

Then I said, "Remember we were fifteen, sitting in the desert behind Donnie's house, drinking warm beer in that abandoned camper shell? And I said that, by the time I was twenty-one, I'd either be dead or in prison?"

No replies.

"Here it is not even three years later, and one of us is dead and another one's heading to prison."

Donnie exhaled. "Jesus Christ."

War and Mullie didn't speak.

"We gotta keep ourselves alive and out of prison," I said. "We can't just go away that easy."

"I don't wanna die," Donnie whispered, "or go to prison."

"Me too," Mullie added.

"Well, I can't guarantee that," War boasted. "I'm gonna be going on dangerous missions."

I chuckled. "You're talkin' like you're already a SEAL."

"I'm gonna make it."

"Yeah, right," I replied. "Let's put it this way. How about we not die of drug overdoses and not pull any guns on people?"

Everybody agreed on the drugs, and Donnie and Mullie agreed about the guns. But not War. "I'm gonna be trained in using all kinds of weapons and hand-to-hand combat—"

"Dude, what the fuck?" I yelled. "We're scattering Micah, and you're talkin' all violent and shit."

"Nick, I'm in the military, and if it means giving my life or taking someone else's to do the job, it means giving my life or killing someone. You guys need to realize that."

I glared at War. "Listen, dumb ass, we knew that when you went in. This ain't the time to be talkin' like that."

"I'm being honest."

"You're bein' a fuckin' asshole."

Then War came toward me. We stared each other down. His arms went out from his body, like an old west gunfighter ready to draw. I glanced at his shaved head, tanned face and arms, broad shoulders, and that he was looking me straight on, since he grew a few inches while in boot camp. It was clear the War I knew was gone forever. A few months ago, War was just his initials. Now, it's what he's all about.

But I wasn't intimidated. I knew he wouldn't start a fight. Not with me holding Micah and Donnie and Mullie ready to break us up. That and I kicked War's ass plenty of times when we used to fight for fun when we had nothing better to do.

"Guys, let's just scatter Micah," Donnie said.

I never took my eyes off War as I opened the box. He walked next to me and stared at Arizona. Then I looked into the box. What was left of Micah was in a clear bag. I put the box under my arm and tore a hole in it. It was filled with what looked like small pieces of gray and white rock and fine gray dust. Were the white pieces unburned bone? I breathed deeply. I trembled from seeing for the first time what human remains looked like. This was Micah? My friend who used to smile and laugh and buy weed and who could barely hold a steady beat?

Donnie noticed I was disturbed. "You okay?"

"I'm all right. You guys wanna take a look at this?"

No one wanted to.

I couldn't take my eyes off of what was once my friend. Donnie sniffled repeatedly. Then I forgave Micah. I forgave him for everything. For trying to steal Amanda. For pulling a knife on me. For dying. He had his own pain and hid behind a bunch of illegal substances that became him.

No point carrying one more grudge.

I wanted to say something, but couldn't come up with anything. So I tilted the box and poured the contents. A slight breeze arose, blowing some of Micah onto all our jeans. Most of him went into the river. Clumps of his remains lingered against our legs. It was like Micah was clinging to the only people who understood him.

We watched Micah slowly drift south toward Lake Mojave. Donnie kept sniffling, War and Mullie stood quietly. I was pissed and sad. I wanted to hit something, but I also wanted to let go and cry. I knew I had it in me, but somehow, for some reason, I couldn't do it. I'd feel tears well up inside, but it was like there was a wall between there and my eyes.

I ground my teeth, hunched my shoulders. This was about more than losing Micah. This was also about losing Chris, and about Donnie getting beaten up by his grandfather. This was about being sick and tired of being on the losing side, and, standing in that cool water watching Micah's remains drift away, I vowed that I would never be defeated.

CHAPTER 29

I hated visiting Dad. That was why I always told him I had something going on. Sometimes I even claimed I had too much homework or a test to study for. Made him think I was trying in school. And just to drive that point home, I'd actually do homework. If he'd insisted I drop by more often, I'd probably be a straight-A student.

But suddenly things were different. Not even War being in town could change Dad's mind. He insisted I come over. "Homework can wait until after you get home."

Dad and his girlfriend, Lilly, lived in a townhouse near Mom's place. They'd been dating all of five months. They'd only been seeing each other for two weeks when they shacked up. Lilly was fuckin' hot, belonged in *Playboy,* and was twenty-two years old. Dad met her at her job—at the Palomino Club in Northtown. *That's right, Dad's dating a stripper thirteen years younger than he is.* I didn't know whether to be jealous of the asshole or just sickened by my father, a cab driver, fucking a stripper.

Mom marries a poor man's Kenny Rogers, Dad hooks up with Miss July. Dad 1, Mom 0.

First time I saw her, we were all gonna meet up for dinner. She stepped out of her black Trans Am—and holy shit! She wore a short, tight black skirt and black stiletto heels that showed off her long, toned, white legs. Her tight black long-sleeved turtle neck showed her flat stomach and every curve of her tits. Then she noticed I had a hard-on and told Dad. I was so damn embarrassed. *And no, I have not told Amanda about Lilly.* Like everyone else in Vegas, Lilly wasn't from here. Dad said she was from LA and used to be a dental assistant. But she had some dream of being a showgirl and came up here to become a dancer in the *Folies Bergere* or the *Lido* at the Stardust. She didn't make it, or didn't or wouldn't blow the right guy, so she ended up hugging a pole at the Palomino, wearing nothing but stilettos and having dollar bills thrown at her by jerks like my dad. A wonderful story. Made me all depressed when he told it to me.

A stripper from LA, hot as hell? She'd be perfect for my music video.

But when I came over, Lilly dressed modestly. Her uncurled red hair was in a ponytail. She wore gray sweatpants and a gray oversized sweatshirt that hung off her shoulder, no socks, or shoes. She sat on a white sofa they just recently got.

She keeps dressing this normally, and I'll never come over again.

Dad cooked dinner while me and Lilly watched a *M*A*S*H** rerun. Not that Dad was some sort of chef. He made Frito chili pie, and he used canned chili and packaged shredded cheddar cheese at that. But he actually used a pot on the stove, not in some Tupperware in the microwave. Guess that counted as cooking to Dad.

I sat as far away from Lilly as possible, on the other end of the sofa. Any closer and I'd be at full mast. I snuck glances at her bright red toenails and white, slender feet, wishing she had those stripper shoes on. Who would've thought that feet could make you breathe harder?

"Do you like *MASH*?" Lilly asked during a commercial.

"No."

"Why not?"

"It's a show for parents."

"What shows do you like?"

Normally, I would think of that as flirting. I assumed she wasn't, but then again, in Vegas, who knows? "Nothing really."

"You don't watch TV?"

"No."

"Wow. That's pretty impressive," she said, and my other brain sprang to life. I wasn't about to admit I watched *Star Trek* reruns every once in a while. That fear of being ridiculed just wouldn't go away.

"You know, your dad talks about you all the time," Lilly said. "He says you're really smart, and quite the guitar player."

That came out of Dad's mouth? Never told me that. "That's nice," I said, as bland as I could.

Then Dad called from the kitchen. "Hey, dinner's ready."

Lilly reached for the remote and turned the volume up. Then she went to their new glass-top dining room table. *Guess we're eating there. That's a new one. We never did that when my parents were still together.*

This would be convenient. I could practice proper table manners in the front of the guy who taught me by example how not to have any.

Dad dished out my Frito chili pie in a white ceramic bowl and put the pot containing the rest of it on a green oven mitt. He arranged yellow paper napkins and some plastic forks on the table.

He even got me a bottle of Mountain Dew and a glass of ice to pour it into. Lilly got herself a salad and a Diet Pepsi out of the fridge and sat next to him.

Dad spoke with his mouth full. "So how you doin', son?"

M*A*S*H* suddenly didn't seem so bad. Watching it kept me from looking at him, and he sat right across from me. It also kept me from looking at his hot-ass girlfriend. So all I said was "Fine."

"You dealing okay with what happened to your friend, what was his name?"

"Chris."

"Chris?"

"Remember, we called him Scuzz?"

"Was that the smelly kid?"

What an asshole. I began to move past such superficial crap to actually look at people for their personalities and how they treated me, and my father was still shallower than a dry lake bed. I glared at him. "Yeah, Dad, the smelly kid."

"Hey. Where'd you get this little smart-ass attitude from?"

"Oh, I don't know. Probably my dad who always mouthed off to my mom whenever she'd ask where he'd been all night."

"Hey, c'mon, guys," Lilly urged, sounding tough. "Can we please have a nice dinner?"

Dad took a few more bites. Then he asked me, "How's school?"

"Fine."

"How's your girlfriend?"

"Fine."

"Have you talked to that friend of yours, what's his name, Micah?"

Was he that out of touch that he had no clue Micah's dead?

"No."

Dad sighed. I didn't take my eyes off the TV, even though the end credits were on and the *M*A*S*H** theme song played. I heard Lilly kiss him. She asked if he was okay. I guess he nodded.

Dad put on his tender voice. "So is there anything going on in your life you care to share with me?"

I was never so interested to watch a commercial for a used car lot in my life, but I figured I'd better make it seem like I wanted to talk to dad. "Got a job."

Dad's voice perked up. "Oh, yeah? You working at a burger joint again?"

"No. A used record store near the Albertson's by mom's house."

Dad and Lilly said to each other that maybe I could get them discounts on records. While that was going on, I saw their white sofa and their dining room set on a commercial for a rent-to-own place.

"Hey, son, think you can get me some Springsteen albums?"

I kept looking at the TV. "Doubt it."

"Why?"

"Store mostly carries underground stuff."

"Like what?"

Time to go for the generation gap thing. "Dead Kennedys. Suicidal Tendencies."

"What the—What kind of fuckin' music you kids listening to? Lilly, you shoulda heard this Jewish Priests album he has. It has this song where the singer's going 'I love dykes. I love dykes.'"

I glared at dad. "The band's Judas Priest and the song's called '*Love Bites*', Dad."

"Whatever. Your stuff is shit. You should listen to Springsteen. He's The Boss."

I shook my head. "Yeah, thanks for naming my dog after him."

Then Lilly interrupted, probably to keep me and dad from getting into an argument, "So does your store carry Madonna?"

What a stupid fuckin' question, I thought. *Let's see, Madonna's so popular, so generic and seemingly has a general overall appeal that she might as well be called McDonna. Of course, the store carries Madonna.* But that wasn't how I worded it to Lilly. "Yeah, but not much," I said nicely.

"Well, I'm proud of you, son." His voice tone wasn't convincing. "So how'd you get the job?"

Happy Days was starting. I hated that show, so I actually looked at my father. I wanted to tell the truth—I filled out an application and passed a brief interview with the store owner, but I knew Dad would accuse me of being a smart ass, and then we'd be in another argument. "My band's new drummer works there. He told me and Donnie about the openings. We're both gonna be working there."

"Your new drummer? Tell me about him."

I twirled my spoon in my bowl. "Uh, can I finish eating? My dinner's getting cold."

That worked in not only letting me eat food that was gonna make me fart, but also in giving me a few minutes of relative silence. I took seconds, even though I was full. I took small bites and chewed slowly. It was the only way I could digest that gassy, greasy nightmare. After dinner, we went back to rent-a-sofa, and Dad put on another channel. *The Cosby Show* was on.

Then came the first commercial break. "Son, Lilly and I have great news."

"Your dad and I are getting married."

I kept looking at TV commercials. I was not happy to hear this, even though I expected it the minute they moved in together. "Congratulations."

Dad sighed again. "Son, I don't want this to be like when your mom married Rick, and you didn't go to the wedding. I want you there, I really do. It means a lot to me."

Refusing to go to a quickie wedding in a chapel on the Strip got me the third degree from just about everybody, even Dad, which I found strange, since he was pretty jealous of Mom remarrying so quickly after finally throwing him out and filing for divorce. But I didn't like Rick. I didn't like the way he talked about blacks and Mexicans, the way he talked down to me, and I fucking hated his goddamn Oak Ridge Boys tapes.

"Sure, Dad," I put on a fake happy voice. "I'll be there."

"All right." Dad smiled and clapped his hands once. "That's great, son. I was hoping you'd say that, because we want to ask you to have a big role in our wedding."

Oh shit. Dad wants me to be his best man.

"Me and Lilly would be thrilled if your band can play at the reception."

I gave dad my 'you gotta be kidding me' look. "You want *my* band to play at *your* wedding?"

"Yeah. I figure it'll be fun for you. You can have your buddies with you, you guys can hang out, have a good time."

"Yeah," Lilly said, "I'd love to hear your band. What's your band called? What kind of music do you guys play?"

Oh please, please become our, I mean, my groupie. Please. Please! "Some metal, punk," I said. "We don't have a name right now."

"Only thing I ask," Dad said, "is that you play something from the sixties or early seventies, like Mungo Jerry."

"Uh…sure, Dad."

Mungo what? Even Lilly looked at him funny.

After getting past that off-the-wall request, I asked, "Hey, Dad, can we borrow your bass and amp?"

"My Rickenbacker?"

"Yeah. Mullie's joining us, but he ain't got a bass."

Dad looked away from me and at the TV. "No."

"Why not?" I calmly asked.

"Son, I'm already letting you use my Strat. If you wanna use my bass, I'll let *you*, but you gotta gimmie back my Strat. I ain't lettin' one of your buddies touch my instruments."

"Can't Mullie borrow it at least until after the wedding?"

Dad pointed at me. "Do you have any fuckin' idea how valuable my instruments are? Huh? I trust you, but I don't really know this…Mullie."

"Dad, if you're that worried about it, I'll hold on to it, and let Mullie use it when we're jamming."

"No."

"Well, what if me and him came over here, you gave him lessons, and we borrowed it for when we're practicing and for the wedding?"

"I said no—" He pointed at me. "—and that's final."

"How you expect my band to play at your wedding reception if our bass player ain't got a bass?"

Dad gave me the face he always made before he slapped me and reminded me that he brought me into this world, he could take me out of it. "Why don't you try getting one on your own? You're a smart kid, come up with something."

"Fine," I snapped. I folded my arms, flopped back on the sofa, and turned to watch TV. "I'll come up with something."

CHAPTER 30

"Can't believe we're doin' this."

"Shut up an' drive," War demanded.

"Dude, I was jokin'," I said calmly.

I let up on the accelerator as the Duster neared a cul-de-sac. The street was dark and had a backed up sewer.

"Sounded serious," War replied.

I drove slowly. "Breaking and entering into Scuzz's house ain't my idea of keepin' the band goin'."

"Shut up, Nick. You know this is the quickest way to get Mullie a bass."

I coasted into the driveway of the house Chris used to live at and shifted into park after the car came to a stop. "It's also the quickest goddamn way to land us in county with Scuzz and Sonny."

War removed his seat belt while I shut the engine off. "What're you worried about?" he asked. "I'm goin' in. You're just sittin' out here."

I chuckled. "Hello. I'm drivin' the fuckin' getaway car."

War opened the squeaky passenger side door. "Shut up and be cool. We'll be outta here in a few minutes, okay? Relax, I have military training."

I shook my head. "Training? You're trained to march in a straight line, do push-ups, and make your bed."

When I glanced at War, he had the nastiest look he'd ever given me. "Goddammit, I am trained by the United States Navy—"

"Just shut the fuck up and get this over with, will ya?"

War got out of the car, slowly closed the door, and walked toward the cinderblock wall next to the garage. He pulled himself over easily and disappeared into the night. It was easy to do at this house. The yard was a mix of tall, dead grass and weeds, bushes that hadn't been trimmed in who knows how long, and trees that needed to be pruned. With all the lights off and no car in the driveway, you could easily think this was an abandoned house.

Maybe this'll turn out fine. My car's no stranger to this driveway. None of the neighbors should get suspicious.

It seemed like War was in that house for an hour. I couldn't relax. I sat low in the car. I needed to take a piss. Why didn't I just lie to Dad and tell him I'd play his bass, then "forget" to give him his Strat back, then come up with another story if he asked?

Then I wondered why I kept taking those stupid-ass risks. I had a great thing going with Amanda, even a job. And what about what I decided at Nelson's Landing about never being defeated? This could destroy everything I'd dreamed of.

Then I wondered why the hell War was in on this. Jail wasn't where he wanted to go. This could fuck up his so-called dream of becoming a SEAL.

Then again, maybe he wanted to prove he could break into and get out of places. Maybe he thought it'd help him get into the SEALs. Never had been the smartest guy.

All I knew for sure was that, if Amanda found out about this, even if me and War didn't get caught, she'd dump my ass. This was the band's secret.

Relax dammit. We've had ten years to case this joint.

Then I saw headlights in the rearview mirror.

I slid down, hoping I couldn't be seen. My neck pressed against the vinyl seat, back lying on the bottom cushion, legs and feet crammed.

Please tell me Chris's mom did not actually decide to spend a night at home.

Then I made that crossing gesture I'd seen Amanda and her family do at the dinner table before eating. Believing in an invisible man who lived in the sky didn't seem so stupid at that moment.

The lights disappeared. I crept up slowly and saw that the car pulled into another driveway. Whoever was in that car went inside the house.

War came out through the front door as if he lived there. He had all the gear with him, the bass, amp, cables, strap. He was totally relaxed as he closed the door behind him. You'd think he lived there, and I came over to pick him up. I turned the ignition as soon as he opened the passenger side door and began loading the gear into the back seat.

He got in the car. "Told you this was nothing."

"We ain't in the clear yet."

"Just fuckin' drive. Normally," he said, getting in and closing the door. "Not like a goddamn maniac like you usually do."

I backed out of the driveway. "Fuck off. I drive fine. Least I got my license."

And I drove a whopping two blocks away from the house at the speed limit—twenty-five miles an hour—when I saw red flashing lights in my rearview mirror.

CHAPTER 31

One phone call. That would solve everything. Just call work, tell them what happened, and ask if I could have a payday advance.

That would be Dad's advice, Mom's too. Since I had a job, they figured I could afford to pay my way out of whatever mess I got into.

When we got pulled over, I nearly pissed my pants. I imagined ending up in the slammer and Amanda telling me to fuck off, my mom telling me to fuck off, and Dad telling me how not to become some black dude's bitch.

I hoped the cop pulling us over wasn't Owen's dad. But it wasn't him walking to the car. It was a muscular guy in a short-sleeved tan uniform, tan pants, and black knee-high boots. Reminded me of a Nazi from some World War II movie.

The cop shined a flashlight into my car, making me squint. He was clearly on the lookout for some reason to haul our asses in. His radio crackled with all kinds of cop talk.

I wanted to kill War for letting us go through with this. I wanted to kill myself for not having the guts to stand up to a guy I never had a problem standing up to in the past.

Glad me and War were smart enough to wear our seat belts.

When I calmed down and my eyes adjusted to the blinding light, I saw a typical cop face—square-jawed, cold eyes, thick mustache, and heard a typical cold cop voice.

"License, registration, and insurance."

Think Thomas, Vera, and Amanda would give this guy shit for not saying please?

I stayed calm as I handed the pig what he demanded. You had to do it calmly, so you didn't get a Nazi cop suspicious. Otherwise, they'd suspect something, ask you to step out of the car, pretend to search it, but actually plant coke or pot or heroin, then arrest you on bullshit drug possession charges with intent to sell. Least that's what Dad said.

"What seems to be the problem, Officer?" I had put on my perfectly-rehearsed little innocent teenager voice.

"Are you aware that you have a taillight that isn't functioning?"

"Oh, I'm sorry, Officer. I wasn't even aware of that." That, actually, was the truth.

The cop shined his flashlight into the back seat. "Is that your guitar equipment in the back seat?"

I told War to let me do all the talking and quickly rehearsed an answer. I knew this question was coming. Kept me calm. "Why, yes, it is."

"Are you boys in a band?"

"Yes, sir. We're on our way to a practice." I pointed at War. "He's the singer."

Then the cop turned to War. "Can I see some ID?"

War calmly reached into his wallet and got something out. "United States military," he said.

The cop glanced over the ID, which, when War showed us, made us laugh. The shape of his head, combined with the buzz cut, made him look like a tennis ball. I wanted to change his nickname to Wimbledon, but no one would have any part of that. His hair had grown out some since the pic was taken, but his hair was still pretty damn short. Looked like just-cut grass, only brown. But all I was thinking of at that moment was a twist in my story that might be believable. Thought I had it all figured out.

"Where you stationed?"

"San Diego."

"And you're in a band with this guy?"

I was about to interrupt, but War had a quick answer. "Yeah. When I'm on leave, I come here and jam with his band, just like before I enlisted."

Way to go, bro. That's exactly what I was thinking. You might just redeem yourself.

"Wait right here." The cop left, taking both our IDs, and my car's insurance and registration with him.

I looked forward, hands gripping my steering wheel. I had to remember to loosen the grip when the cop returned. We didn't say anything for several minutes while the Nazi looked for a reason to haul us in.

I breathed deep through my nose, trying to stay calm. "Hope he buys that story."

"Yeah, well," War urged, "Just be cool. Story's true."

"I'm cool, you just be cool. But whatever you do, don't look back."

So we both turned around at the same time to see what the cop was doing. He was getting out of his car.

"Shit," I said. "What'd you look back for?"

"You looked back too. Here he comes. Be cool."

He stopped alongside my window, his flashlight on but tucked under his armpit. He just stood there. Didn't do anything, and his face had the same blank expression it did when he pulled us over. He gave me back all the stuff he demanded, even War's Navy ID. But he also handed me something else.

"Drive safe." Then he walked away.

I got a citation for faulty equipment.

Faulty equipment? That's it? I nearly shit myself for a faulty equipment citation? I thought that pig was gonna bust our asses and haul us in.

The cop went back to his car, got in, and left. I exhaled

and restarted the Duster after he was gone. Then I punched War in the arm.

"Ouch," he yelled. "Fuck's that for?"

I looked at my confused buddy as I shifted into drive. "You know what it's for." I steered the car back onto the road and gently hit the accelerator. "Let's get to Mullie's and get rid of that goddamn bass."

CHAPTER 32

Rebel Subs was in a shopping center right across from the UNLV campus, a good fifteen miles from my house, but Gremlin insisted me and Donnie meet him there after his sociology class. He promised to buy dinner, and considering Mom now made her chicken fricassee with onions only because Rick liked them, I just couldn't eat something I once loved.

Gremlin heard about the shooting at Fremont from his two roommates after he got back from Havasu. Guess it was all over the newspapers and the TV, because it turned out Jeff Day and James Janninks had committed to play football at a couple of California colleges next year. I wondered why there were all those TV cameras at school that day in November.

I found Donnie at Roxie's and told him Gremlin demanded we meet up with him. Donnie only agreed to go when I told him Gremlin would buy us dinner.

We walked in the door to a sandwich shop that had white walls with two thin red and silver stripes, matching UNLV's school colors. The place was pretty empty. Only a few students were eating, all while intently gazing at their textbooks.

A Janet Jackson song at a low volume gave background noise.

Gremlin got up from the chair he sat in and walked toward us as soon as we were in the door. He wore blue surfer shorts, flip-flops, and his white Minor Threat T-shirt. He looked concerned. He then put an arm around Donnie and hugged him.

Donnie didn't know what to do. He had only met Gremlin once, at our one jam session nearly two weeks ago. Then Gremlin tried hugging me and, putting my hands in front of me, I said, "Uh, don't."

He shook his head. "Oooh. The two bad asses. Too tough to hug. Cuz you're Tuff Boyz!" he said sarcastically.

Yeah, he's right, but still, a hug? C'mon. I don't even hug my parents, and I only hug Amanda to get my hands on her body.

After ordering our sandwiches and sodas, we sat at a table in the back of the shop.

"So what's up?" I asked, unwrapping my sandwich. "Why'd you call us down here?"

Gremlin looked worried. "How're you guys holding up?"

I took a bite and looked at Donnie, who dug into his sandwich. He looked at me. We were both thinking whether we should tell Gremlin the truth. I took the lead. I told Gremlin, with my mouth full, "We're fine."

"Bullshit."

Donnie chuckled after he swallowed. His voice became tense, trying to emphasize his point. "Yeah, we are."

Gremlin, who hadn't even unwrapped his sandwich, slumped in his chair. "No, you're not. After what happened to Scuzz, *your* friend of I don't know how many years, and *our* bass player, you two are gonna sit there and tell *me* that you guys are just fine."

I stared at Gremlin briefly, not eating. "I thought you meant right now."

Gremlin began unwrapping his sandwich. "Dude, weak. You know exactly what I'm talking about."

"You're right," Donnie said, and I knew just what he was talking about. "Just been trying to forget that ever happened. That and Micah dying."

Gremlin asked who Micah was, so I filled him in on all the details. As we talked, Donnie wolfed down his sandwich and I ate mine in spurts, talking with my mouth full, all while Gremlin sat there, his face showing he was amazed at what we were telling him. He barely touched his sandwich or soda and hardly said a word. And all along, me or Donnie would chuckle here and there as we told our grim tale, going all the way back to the attack at Calico Ridge.

After I finished the story and half my sandwich, Gremlin again slumped in his chair. He slowly shook his head. "Incredible," he uttered. "I *knew* something like that was gonna happen at that school someday."

Donnie had finished eating and wiped his hands with a paper napkin as he asked, "What do you mean?"

Gremlin still slowly shook his head. He crinkled his nose. "I used to get all kinds of shit from John Janninks."

"James's older brother?" I asked.

"Yeah." Then Gremlin's voice sounded bitter, a side of him I hadn't seen before. "One day, I was walking home, since I didn't have a car then, and all of a sudden a PVC pipe hits me right here." He smacked his hand on his left shoulder. "I looked up, and there was John fuckin' Janninks, headed to USC on a football scholarship, just staring at me out of the window of a fuckin' BMW, looking like he wanted to kill me, and I never knew why. I never did *anything* to him. Never."

"So what happened?" Donnie asked.

Gremlin's deeply exhaled, then continued. "I called the cops on him, filed a report, and we were all set to go to court on the charges when I learned they were dropped. I didn't even get a fuckin' reason why from anybody. And for the rest of my senior year, I had to listen as that asshole bragged about how that little Partridge Family-looking faggot told on him. Him, the fucking football star. I'll never forget when he said I should worship him because he's a god. Exact words."

"They're still saying that shit," I replied.

"Well," Gremlin said, a smirk on his face. "Glad to know some things don't change."

The story dug up memories that I tried to bury alive. One of them was James Janninks doing the same thing to me and Chris last year—Gremlin's senior year. Only James rode in Owen Maywood's red Jeep, and we never filed a police report. We figured, why bother? The pigs weren't gonna do shit, we thought at the time. So nice of the LVPD to prove us right.

And that's when Gremlin joining us made sense. Even though we looked and dressed different than him, he knew that deep down, even with our different musical roots, we were all the same. I sensed it when I ran into him at Reclamation Records, and this monologue proved me right.

"And it was about this time last year that another drummer in the orchestra told me that he was getting the same shit from John," Gremlin continued. "and he talked about shooting that asshole one day at a track meet. At first, I wanted to do it. I mean, I used to come to school wearing a cup because I feared the jocks would beat me up. But then I realized that music was what I wanted to do, and I didn't want to give that up, not over some shithead like John fucking Janninks."

Donnie put his face into his hands. I asked, with my voice soft despite the seemingly loud rap music that was playing, "So what happened?"

"Me and Rico talked each other out of it. We realized it was stupid, but, boy, did we wanna do it." The anger seethed in his voice, which crept through his clenched teeth. "We wanted to *bury* that motherfucker."

"I did the same thing," I said, shaking. "I tried to talk Chris out of bringing the gun to school." I got goose bumps on my arms and back of my neck even though I felt like I

was gonna start sweating. "I tried, guys. I really tried."
Then my voice cracked. "And I failed. I totally failed."

Donnie put his hand on my back. My breathing was un-
steady. Gremlin reached out and grabbed one of my wrists.

"Nick," Gremlin said, "if he was totally set on doing it,
there's nothing anybody could've done. Not you or Donnie
or anybody."

I closed my eyes. I wanted to stay tough, especially in
public, even though a cold sweat came on. "I'm so damn
pissed off at myself for not being able to stop it."

I heard Donnie sniffle. Gremlin said, "Nick, don't beat
yourself up over it."

"I wanted to stop him. I tried, man, I really tried. He
fired the gun when I tackled him."

I tensed my jaw and shoulders. I shook. I made my neck
twitch. I wanted to hit the table, unleash some of the anger
that grew day by day, minute by minute, second by second.

"Nick," Donnie said. "You saved Chris's life. You don't
know that, but you did. If he'd shot and killed Jeff Day,
he'd be facing a murder rap, probably the gas chamber. You
saved two lives."

"Too bad one of them was Jeff Day," I said coldly. "He
belongs in prison, not Chris. All those guys belong in prison.
What the jocks do to us is no different then what the KKK
did to black people."

At first, I got pissed. Then I quietly laughed at the
thought of saving Jeff Day. I saved the life of one of my
worst enemies, all while trying to save the life of one of my
best friends. I was even trying to save the band and my
dream of getting out of Vegas and into the music biz. But
Gremlin wasn't here to talk about breaking up the band. I
realized that by him calling us here, he was trying to *save*
the band. Like me, he somehow saw our seemingly unlikely
partnership as a way to reach his musical dreams. He felt
something, as did I. I didn't think either one of us could explain it, but we *felt* it. We *knew* it.

Then Gremlin asked how Donnie was doing, and Donnie said he was still living in Chris's house, even though he never saw Chris's mom. Donnie also talked about how his grandfather threw him out, he didn't know who his father was, and that his mom was a drug addict probably living on the streets downtown.

"You're moving in with me," Gremlin said.

"What?" Donnie asked.

"We got a room available at the house. I'll hold it for you. Nobody should be homeless."

Donnie smiled bigger than the first time he kissed Roxie. It seemed like Donnie wanted to tell Gremlin he loved him for the gesture, but he didn't say it. I saw it in his face. I felt bad that I didn't think of asking Mom and Rick if Donnie could move in. I assumed, since there wasn't an extra bedroom in the house and Rick didn't like me, that he'd just say no. But if Gremlin and Donnie wanted me to stop beating myself up over Chris, I knew I should've quit doing the same about not asking if Donnie could move in with me. Of course, actually succeeding in *not* beating myself up mentally would be the real challenge.

"Dude, that's real nice of you," I said.

Gremlin assured Donnie that he could make the cheap rent of a hundred bucks a month, saying that Donnie could take on more hours at the record store, maybe work twenty hours a week instead of fifteen. I offered to give Donnie one of my days so he could make the rent.

Donnie smiled, sniffled, and tried not to cry out of happiness. I was just happy for him that things truly looked like they were going his way. If anybody I knew deserved something to go right, after his grandfather's abuse and everything that'd happened since, it was Donnie.

Then Gremlin turned to me. "Hey, Nick. Forget about what I said at our first jam session. Write about your feelings, okay? Write about what you feel about those guys and the jocks. Make them into songs. That's what Rites of Spring did."

"Who?"

"Rites of Spring. Punk band out of DC. Only made one album, but it's pretty powerful. Instead of writing about politics or the social order, they wrote about their feelings. Let me tell you, they had great lyrics. I think we have a copy at the store, if you wanna check it out."

"So we should write something about Chris and Micah?" I asked.

Gremlin slowly nodded. "Absolutely."

CHAPTER 33

Donnie and Gremlin's two roommates were gone, so the house was ours for our first jam session since spring break. And what a prison-like house it was. The outside was tan painted cinderblock with black metal bars over the windows. A lot of places in less-than-perfect neighborhoods in Vegas had houses with those bars, and this neighborhood fit that description. I think everyplace had those damn bars over the windows. And the home's interior wasn't much better. White painted cinderblock, brown wood paneling, Venetian blinds underneath sun-blocking curtains to keep out the desert sun.

But the metal bars weren't the only reminder of a prison. The cinderblock brought forth similar memories, in the form of the first school I attended after we moved here. It was a place called a "sixth grade center," a school that only housed kids in grade six. It was the school district's pathetic attempt to even out the impact of bussing. For eleven out of twelve years, black kids got bussed from their neighborhoods to schools in mostly white areas. To even things up, for one year, sixth grade, the white kids were bussed into the black neighborhoods of the West Side.

My first day was really memorable. Black kids shouting at us "Who's the nigger now, honkie?" as we rode in on the buses that were not air conditioned, even though it was already ninety degrees, and barbed wire ringing the school grounds, and, of course, cinderblock buildings.

When we'd arrived in town a week earlier after leaving Queens, my parents tried telling me that Vegas was gonna be better than Queens. Bullshit. No school in Queens had barbed wire surrounding cinderblock cellblocks.

Nonetheless, Gremlin, Donnie, and their roommates tried to make the place a decent place to live. A poster in the living room said, *Say No To Crack* with a black and white picture of a fat guy, sitting on a cooler, showing his ass. It was enough to make you go on a hunger strike. But at least there was a pinball machine in the dining area. And Missile Command! Yes, an arcade relic of the early 1980s, quarter slots and all, sitting in the area most people would've put some dinette set. I didn't think anyplace in town carried that game after Ted, Ned, and Fred's closed down a couple years ago.

Bye-bye to the pair of quarters in my wallet.

After all of my cities were quickly nuked—I was seriously rusty—Gremlin came into the living room wearing a black Dead Kennedys T-shirt and the camouflage pants he used to wear at Fremont all the time.

"Wow," I said. "You mean you actually dress like a guy sometimes and wear pants?"

Gremlin smiled and gave me the finger, which he had shoved up a nostril.

We also settled on a new name for the band—The Subterraneans. It was the title of a book and a name Gremlin said was a hidden gem.

"Is it your favorite book?" I once asked him.

He smiled. "Never read it."

Still, we all liked it and agreed with him. I realized that, at some point, we better read that damn novel. Imagine getting interviewed by *Hit Parader* and them asking about the name and us having no fucking clue about the novel. It would either be seriously embarrassing or a great little PR stunt. *But why take chances? Read it, one of these years.*

While we debated the new name, we set up our gear and tuned our instruments. We showed Mullie how to play the few original songs we had, and to everyone's surprise, Mullie nailed them right away. It was not like the songs are hard, but still...

After we finished our three tunes, I said, "Hey, I gotta new song I've been working on. This is one of the guitar parts." I played a slow arpeggio in a minor key, the notes ringing clean from my amplifier. Then I stopped and said, "After I play that run three times, the second guitar comes in like this," and I kicked on my distortion pedal and played a simple power chord riff low on the neck.

Me and Donnie decided who'd play what and we started over again. After Donnie had played the power chord run once, Gremlin came in on the drums. Then Mullie came in on the bass and surprised me with how simple and perfect, single note bass line he came up with. It fit, and fit well, but it would need some variety. Hell, I didn't even know what key this song was in.

We had our fourth original, "Fallen," a song about Micah and Chris.

"Good song," Gremlin said after we ran through the tune a couple of times.

"Yeah," Donnie added. "Totally unlike our other songs."

"Yeah, but I can't come up with any words," I said. "Just can't."

"Relax," Gremlin said. "It'll come. One of you guys has the words in you."

How Gremlin knew how to say the right thing at the right time was beyond me. But I took that advice and decided to move on to the other big announcement. "By the way, my dad's marrying a hot-ass stripper next weekend," I said, "and he wants *us* to play at the reception."

"Is that the Lilly chick you were talkin' about?" Donnie asked.

"Yeah." I took off the guitar and leaned it against my still buzzing amp. "But he asked if we could play something from the sixties or early seventies, and he suggested playing something by some dude I've never heard of. I think his name Gary Mungro." I stared at three puzzled faces. "Or maybe it's Mungro Gary."

"You mean Mungo Jerry?" Gremlin asked.

"Yeah, that's it. How the hell you know that?"

Gremlin played a bum-bum-pah fill that followed a 1950s comedian's punchline. "My hippie uncle Dave liked that music. It sucked."

"Well," Donnie asked, "What kind of music is it?"

"It's shit." Gremlin tossed a drumstick and caught it. "That's all you need to know."

"Well, Dad did say play something from that era, so we could play some Beatles," I said.

Gremlin nodded, seemingly in agreement.

"The Beatles?" asked Mullie. "Seriously?"

"Yeah."

"Why?" Donnie asked.

"Cuz I like 'em, that's why."

"You do?"

"Yeah, I do. Always have. My whole life. Got a problem with that?"

"Man, I never knew that," Donnie complained. "Why would you like them?"

"Because it's good music, that's why." He was really starting to piss me off now.

"I ain't playing any fuckin' Beatles." Then Donnie sang mockingly, "She loves you, yeah, yeah, yeah."

"Whadda you wanna play, then?" I asked Donnie sarcastically. "She got the looks that kill?"

"It's better than all this stuff you've been listening to ever since he joined up. This stuff doesn't even have a guitar solo."

"Yeah, and?"

"It's like you've been a goddamn poser for all these years, either that or a serious bandwagon jumper."

"You callin' me a fuckin' poser?" I yelled at Donnie. "What, you wanna go around wearing spandex, mascara, and pucker up your lips oh-so-cutely for the camera?"

Donnie shoved me, and I nearly fell. Gremlin jumped in between us. "Calm the fuck down. Penalty box, two minutes by yourself. Both you guys."

I ignored Gremlin's hockey reference. "You don't like the direction we're going, leave," I said. "That simple."

Couldn't see if Donnie was considering my offer, I was that pissed. And it was not like he was truly essential to our music anymore. I wasn't writing in a spot for a guitar solo on my lyrics anymore, so why bother? I could handle all the rhythm parts myself.

Still, I didn't want Donnie to go. Just wouldn't be right without him. Not with all we'd been through.

"I don't need two minutes," I said quietly.

"Yeah, what are you, our mother?" Donnie asked, the hockey reference sailing high over his head.

Gremlin, meanwhile, acted as if nothing happened. "We can do this wedding gig and play something everybody's cool with." He walked toward a brown bookcase filled with albums. "Hey, Nick, does your dad like The Who?"

"Yeah. He's got *Tommy* and that album where they pissed on a concrete slab for the cover."

"*Who's Next*," he replied.

"Yeah, that's it."

Gremlin pulled an album out of the bookcase, went to the stereo, put the record on the turntable, and dropped the needle, and within seconds "I Can't Explain" filled the living room. Our debate continued. Clearly, the Beatles were out. Gremlin added the no play tally to three by refusing to play anything by Zeppelin or Sabbath, even though I made it clear that Dad probably wouldn't be too happy if we played, say *Sabbath, Bloody Sabbath* at his wedding. And Donnie was clearly pissed that Gremlin refused to play anything by two bands he held as sacred.

Before our debate escalated into full-on violence, a song came on that caught my attention. It started with a slightly overdriven guitar playing power chords. Sounded cool, but it was the chorus that really sucked me in, talking about pictures that made his life so wonderful and helped him sleep at night.

"Hey Gremlin, this song called 'Pictures of Lilly'?" I asked.

"Yeah."

"What's it about?"

"Jacking off to nudie pictures."

My sly grin appeared. I nodded slowly. "We're playing this."

Gremlin smiled too. He understood. Mullie and Donnie looked stunned.

"Are you crazy?" Donnie asked. "Your dad'll kick the shit outta you."

"Yeah, well, fuck him." I walked toward my amp to grab my guitar. "Start that song over again, Gremlin." I pointed at the stereo. "We gotta learn it by next Saturday."

CHAPTER 34

Being forced to dress up like your dad's clone totally sucked. What was with his white suit, white belt, pink T-shirt, white topsiders, and no socks? And why did he have to get me a matching outfit? He even wanted me to get the Huey Lewis haircut he had.

Uh, no.

And there was no fuckin' way in hell I was gonna wear a pink T-shirt. I wore my plain black one with my white suit. I also wore my black scuffed combat boots—with white socks.

Besides, black was the color associated with death. Dad said a wedding was a bachelor's funeral. I was just trying to get into the spirit of the thing.

But I didn't know who was dressed worse: Me, Dad, or Gremlin. That drummer wore a powder blue tuxedo jacket and matching bell-bottoms, and both were too small. The pants were so short that he was showing two inches of ankle. And he was at best five and half feet tall. He was ready for a flash flood, but how the hell did he find such a tux so short?

But the tux wasn't the only bad part of his outfit. He also wore red Converse All-Star high-tops, a white tuxedo shirt with ruffles, and a plaid bow tie that was so big, I thought he stole a propeller off a Grand Canyon tour plane. He also didn't wear his red hair in a mohawk. Instead, he had it slicked down to look like he had a comb-over.

Me and him sat next to each other waiting for the ceremony to begin. "Where'd you get that tux?" I asked. "It's awful."

"Deseret Industries Thrift Store. It's amazing the crap those Mormons have in there. What, you don't like it?"

"Hell no. What'd you pay for it?"

"Five bucks for everything but the shoes." Gremlin flashed a toothy smile and gave two thumbs-up.

I laughed. "You got ripped off."

Gremlin picked his teeth with a toothpick. "Did I? Well you look like a *Miami Vice* reject."

I smiled. He was so right. "Yeah? You wear a suit like that downtown and John, Three Sixteen Cook'll give ya a bowl of soup."

"Ooh, good one," Gremlin replied. "Mister, Mister called. They want you to become their new guitarist."

I nodded. "Yeah, well, Joan Rivers called. She wants to marry you. Right after my dad's outta here."

And Gremlin just had to ruin everything by saying, "Sweet," followed by a smile and two thumbs up. "Maybe we can tag-team the old bag."

"Let's not and say we did."

Twisted bastard. No wonder I liked him.

Gremlin wasn't the only badly-dressed person in the chapel. Most of them were Dad's fellow cabbies. A bunch of balding middle-aged guys in cheap slacks and shirts that were so short, they showed off the bottom of their hairy, heaving bellies. Dad's buddies from the gym were dressed normally. Same for Donnie and Mullie. They wore black jeans and white long-sleeved dress shirts.

"Seriously, why'd you dress like that?" I asked Gremlin.

"We're playing the Strip. Gotta look the part."

"We're playing a wedding reception in a conference room at the Riv, not the lounge."

"It's still the Riv, baby."

I sat back, put an arm around Amanda, who was seated between me and the aisle, kissed her cheek, and waited for the ceremony to begin. We were in Vegas's most famous wedding chapel, The Little Chapel of the West. And for a place that was such a big deal, it actually looked kinda pathetic. It was a small brown building that looked like a church you'd see in some photo of Vermont. It was right next to the Riviera, on the other side of the street. After the wedding, one of Dad's cabbie buddies was gonna drive him and Lilly across the street to the reception—in Dad's old white Cadillac convertible. A bunch of empty Bud Light cans were attached to the back bumper. *And Dad wonders why I don't wanna be anywhere near him.*

But at least me, Amanda, and my band rode down here in the Deathmobile. She thought it was terrible that we drove a *hearse* to a *wedding*, but we tried telling her it was the best way to get our gear to the gig. I wasn't about to tell her Dad's bachelor death idea. Still, it sure beat riding around in that aircraft carrier Dad drove, especially with him looking like he did.

Amanda looked hot in her white lace one-piece dress, but she was in a pissy mood. Across the aisle were all of Lilly's friends from the Palomino Club, a bunch of young, hard-bodied babes in short, tight skirts and tight-fitting tops. It wasn't fair. Gremlin and Mullie could gawk all they want. So could Donnie, since Roxie wasn't there.

I tried glancing over carefully and tried showing Amanda I was indeed happy to be with her. I rubbed her knee, which was covered by tan pantyhose, and just the texture of the pantyhose on her bony knee made my heart beat faster and my dick rise. But she shoved my hand away when I touched her. Then she caught me checking out a seriously leggy blonde and punched me in the balls. Nearly pissed my pants. Her jealous sneer showed that I was not to look toward the other side of the chapel. If this was one of those power struggles Dad said happened with women, she was gonna win. I didn't need my nuts crushed. And not bringing

her was not an option. Me, like an idiot, told her when we
first started dating that my dad was dating a stripper. So
thanks to that bit of unnecessary information, I *had* to bring
Amanda. And yeah, go ahead and laugh at me for not thinking ahead, but how the hell was I to know that Lilly would
actually wanna marry my idiot father? I figured they'd be
done within a few weeks.

Gremlin, meanwhile, flirted with plenty of Lilly's
friends. He stuck that toothpick between his two front teeth,
would point at one of the girls, and make a clicking sound
with his mouth. The strippers giggled and waved back at
him.

As if the fact this wedding was taking place wasn't
enough, the reactions Gremlin provoked further proved that
hot chicks went for dorky-looking guys.

"Hey, Nick," he asked. "You think one of those girls're
gonna wanna 'ride the 'stache and get a pussy rash'?"

"They're laughing at you, not with you."

"What?"

"Said your hair looked nice."

He patted his comb-over. "Why, thank you."

Dad and his best man, a beer-bellied, sagging-joweled,
balding cabbie named Frank, stood by the altar when Lilly
walked up the aisle in a tight-fitting white wedding dress.
The cut on it showed almost all of one her toned, milky legs,
while the cloth on the other side almost went all the way to
the floor. Guess what side we got to see up close? The leg.
All of it. And some hip too. Was she wearing panties?

Oh. My. God.

And she wore white spiked heels. Her red hair was up in
a loose bun, with curled strands coming down, lightly
touching her shoulders. And I got so stiff I could've tried
out for a porno.

"Damn," Donnie whispered, "she's fuckin' *hot*."

I slowly nodded, and Amanda shoved me in the shoulder.
She had her arms folded, her jaw locked, her thin eyebrows
lowered. *This day is gonna suck.*

"I am so gonna hafta masturbate in a few minutes," Gremlin said, "and it's gonna last a few seconds."

"I wanna lap dance," Donnie said quietly.

"Wish I was twenty-one," Gremlin added. "I'd go and get one."

"Me, too," Donnie added.

Gremlin nudged me. "You get a chance, dance with her today."

"Only if you want my foot in your balls," Amanda snarled.

And Mullie didn't say a thing.

Meanwhile, I thought that, three years from now, I could come back to this town, go into the Palomino, and watch my stepmom caress her tits, bend over, and show off her cooch.

That was both hot as hell and incredibly sick and twisted, all at the same time.

I need to get a fake ID. Now.

As Lilly got to the altar, Gremlin sang, quietly, "Sit on my face, and tell me that you love me. I'll sit on your face and tell you I love you too."

That made all us guys laugh. I bit my bottom lip hard, trying to keep it in. Donnie and Mullie were trying their hardest to keep it quiet. It didn't work. Everyone looked our way. Dad looked at us, took a finger, and made the throat-slitting motion. We stopped, but man, that was hard to do.

The minister quickly began the ceremony. Once I quit laughing, I was never more jealous of Dad, all while never being more proud of him. I mean, the dude got a trophy wife!

No disrespect toward Mom, I guessed she was pretty, or something like that, but this was like trading in a Chevy for a Ferrari. I paid hardly any attention to whatever it was the minister said, although I heard Dad and Lilly's vows clearly. My eyes were fixed on Lilly's tight, heart-shaped ass. Oh, and the dude leading the ceremony wasn't talking very loud anyway.

ℰ✄ℰ✄

Me and the band set up our gear while a bunch of stuff went on around us. Workers in white outfits and white paper chef's hats prepared the buffet. A bartender in a white tuxedo shirt, black bow tie, and black vest poured drinks for everybody. In the center of the room was a table with the wedding cake and a bowl of punch on it. A DJ played crappy disco and dance music.

Earlier, he played "Sister Christian" by Night Ranger. Dad played air guitar. I wanted to die.

Amanda stood next to me as I tuned the Stratocaster. She looked bored.

Gremlin ran in front of me. "Let's commit some crime. Let's spike the punch and drink it!"

"Dude," I calmly said, a wide smile on my face. "This is my dad's wedding reception. Trust me, the punch is already spiked."

Donnie plugged his guitar into his amp. "I thought you didn't drink?" he asked Gremlin.

"I do now."

"Since when?" Donnie asked.

"Since spring break in Havasu. Drinking expands the pool of potential one-night stands like you wouldn't believe."

And while me, Donnie, and Mullie laughed, Gremlin said, "There's nothing like a ten at two who becomes a two at ten."

Amanda stormed off while we laughed.

"Hey," I yelled, concerned. "Where you going?"

"To the bathroom," she snapped.

I sighed and went back to tuning my guitar while the laughter died down. "It's gonna be a long night."

"Relax," Mullie said. "Just don't ignore her, and you'll be all right."

I grinned and nodded. "Yeah, you're right, bro. Better keep my eyes from roaming. How'm I supposed to enjoy this fuckin' thing anyway?"

Gremlin tuned his kick drum. "Yeah, I so do not envy you."

Amanda returned a few minutes later, but she was not enjoying herself. She seemed disgusted by the entire atmosphere, even though it was, as Gremlin said, pretty lame.

"Where's the table dancing?" Gremlin asked. "I wanna see drunk chicks feelin' themselves up. We're in a room full of Vegas strippers, and somehow Havasu was wilder than this."

Either these women were way more mellow than the stereotype we had of them, or they just weren't drunk enough yet. Still, they were out there dancing, with each other and the guys Dad knew from the gym. The cabbies were shit outta luck.

And so were we. Shitty music being played. Strippers dancing with their clothes on. The appetizers were good, but the goddamn punch was *not* spiked! How the hell did that happen? And we had to sit at our table for over an hour, pretty much bored out of our minds. Even the sight of my dad channeling his inner *Saturday Night Fever* during the 1970s disco the DJ played couldn't even make the night interesting. It did, however, almost cause me to hide under the tablecloth.

But before I did that, Dad tapped me on the shoulder. "Hey."

I turned around. "Hey, Dad. Having fun?"

He held a glass of red wine. His breath smelled like a vineyard. "Yeah. Nice looking broads in here, huh? Bet I can get ya a blow job from one of them." He elbowed me in the ribs, totally forgetting Amanda stood right next to me.

I thought fast. "I got the best-looking girl right here." I put my arm around her waist.

She shoved me and jumped up. She got in my dad's face. "How dare you say something like that to him, in front of me, on your wedding day?" she said with intensity, but still holding back.

Dad was taken by surprise by what she said to him, and he clearly didn't like it. I saw that look he had on his face many times before. It usually was followed with "I brought you into this world, I can take you out of it." But he didn't go that route this time. Instead, he turned on that charm he had when he wanted to use it, put a hand on her shoulder, and said, with a used-car salesman smile, "Hey, it's cool. I was just being funny, that's all."

"Well, don't quit your day job. And get your filthy hands off me, you pervert." Amanda stormed off. A few nearby guests started to watch the drama, lured by Amanda's rising voice.

Dad laughed and watched her walk away. "Wooeee. Spitfire!" he said. I saw him wiggle his tongue as she stormed off. Then he touched my shoulder and said, "Get your band ready to play, son. I can't wait to hear how you guys sound and what you're gonna play for me."

CHAPTER 35

*S*trippers, fat guys, and buff guys. One outta three ain't bad. Never figured I'd be playing for fatsos and bodybuilders when me and Donnie started this band in junior high.

And Dad, just married to a stripper I'd love to meet backstage? Right in front? Showing shapely leg and tight cleavage? Weird.

Amanda was in a corner in the back of the room. What was her friggin' problem? I told her the songs we were gonna play were a *practical joke* on my dad. *Sure, I've thought about Lilly here and there during...shall we say?...those private moments, but that's my business, not hers. Like she doesn't think about other guys when she's frigging herself.*

Gremlin was right. I should not have let her sit in on our practices of the two songs we played at the reception.

Another thing I didn't understand about Dad and Lilly getting married—she's more in tune with me. She convinced Dad that we probably wouldn't be all that excited to play something real old, so she talked him into letting us play a song that we chose.

"But none of that heavy metal, 'I love dykes' Jewish Priests stuff," Dad said. He never had been able to pronounce Judas Priest right.

None of that mattered when everyone gathered around where we set up our instruments. Thanks to my dad's crude remarks in front of Amanda, I had to get myself back into a mood to play fun songs. He'd pissed me off. It'd be fine if we were playing something angry and aggressive, but that was not the two songs of our set. So our debut in front of about sixty people or so, the largest crowd we had ever played in front of, had to wait while I brought myself back from wanting to punch my stupid father in the face.

I tried something I heard a couple of people in the record store talk about: meditation. My back was to all the guests, and I faced Gremlin's drum set. I closed my eyes, thought of nothing but breathing. I thought about my anger leaving my body, and goodness coming in. In my mind, the anger was black smoke. Calm was clear air. Not sure how long I did it, but I was calm soon, although it seemed like an eternity because everyone was waiting. Of course, I could've used more time, but leave it to Dad to put the spotlight on him.

"Hey," he said through my microphone. "This is my boy right here on guitar." He put his tanned, muscular arm around my neck, like a headlock and pulled me toward him. I nearly fell backward. All the calm left. Now it was fear of being pulled down. I regained my footing, focused on my breathing, but with my eyes open, facing everyone, trying to maintain my cool. And I wasn't nervous anymore. I just wanted this damn thing over with. For one thing, I had listened to and played the two song we were gonna perform so damn much that we were totally sick of them. My dad's obnoxious behavior made me want to just leave this damn hotel and go anywhere he wasn't.

"This is my son's band," Dad announced. "This guy here is Donnie. And this guy is…" Dad pointed at our bass player, who I said was Mullie. Then dad looked at the guy behind the drums, a guy with a slicked down red mohawk, seventies tux shirt and jacket, and plaid bow tie. "And you are…" Dad paused, unsure what else to say. "Just what the *fuck* are you, anyway?"

"That's our drummer," I said into the microphone. "Gremlin, the lounge lizard."

Then Gremlin yelled, "I'm going commando! I'm runnin' free!"

Too bad he had a microphone at that moment. I smiled. So did Donnie. Couldn't see Mullie. A few of Lilly's friends laughed. Someone whistled.

Dad closed his eyes and shook his head. He turned to face the crowd. "Well, my son's band is gonna play a couple songs for us. What's your guy's name?"

"The Subterraneans," I said into the mic.

Dad returned to Lilly's side, just a few feet away from me. I counted to four, and Donnie launched into our first song, "Turning Japanese." The strippers shouted, and several of them began dancing. Lilly was one of them. Dad stood still. It was the perfect song to play at this reception, since not only did Dad hate it, but it was about jacking off. Of course, me, Donnie, and Mullie didn't know that until Gremlin told us.

"It's about the way your face looks when you're whacking your pud," he said.

And, suddenly, the song made a hell of a lot more sense than it did when we first heard it in fifth grade.

As I began singing, I made sure I ignored everybody in the crowd. "Look out at the crowd," Dad once told me, "but never *at* any of them." It was the best advice he ever gave.

We were on. Gremlin and Mullie were locked in to the rhythm. Donnie played the fast, power-chord-based simple song perfectly. It was as if none of us were nervous. I fed off the energy we played with. I felt the passion in everybody's playing. I sang with more confidence than I ever felt.

At times, I had experienced this feeling of truly connecting with the guitar, with the guys in the band. But every time that happened in the past, I recognized it and suddenly that connection was lost. I could still play the part I was playing, but not *feel* it. And then I'd be sad because that feeling was so uplifting. What I felt during those few seconds was as close as I came to that spirituality thing Amanda talked about.

And it wasn't until we finished the song that I realized I'd prolonged that feeling.

We got a loud ovation from the girls and several of Dad's gym buddies, and polite applause from the middle-aged cabbies. Right in front of me, Lilly had an arm around Amanda's shoulders. Both were smiling. Amanda clapped. Lilly shouted, "That was great," and gave me a thumbs up. I didn't even bother checking to see what Dad thought.

I wanted to savor the moment, but I knew we had to begin playing again. I leaned into the microphone and said, to the band, "You guys ready?" When I got a collective "yeah," I counted to four, and we launched into *Pictures of Lilly*.

That feeling of being locked in musically was still there. Suddenly, there was no crowd in front of me, just a blur that looked like the shapes of people. I was aware of the audience, but able to focus on singing a song that tested my singing since it was in a higher register than what I was used to. Then there were the harmony vocals during the chorus on the words "Pictures of Lilly." Me and Donnie had a hard time getting into harmony, but we got it at the reception. And after we sang those words, I heard a loud roar come up from almost every woman in the joint.

Then, almost as quickly as it started, it was over. Me and Donnie sang the title one last time, and right at the end of the vocals, the band stopped too. The ovation was mixed. Lilly's friends were loud. Amanda smirked. It seemed like she suddenly understood why I wanted to play those songs. Lilly was laughing and clapping. She knew what the song was about and clearly felt flattered.

CHAPTER 36

Me and Dad walked outside the conference room and into a hallway that had some of the tackiest green jungle-patterned carpeting ever. *Who chose that? Do hotels everywhere have that kind of horrible carpeting, or was that just in Vegas?*

Then Dad stood in front of me. He had that look I'd seen whenever he was drunk and wanted to kick my ass to prove to his own shallow, pathetic mind that he was a tough guy.

But I wasn't afraid. What was he gonna do? Start a fight on his wedding day? I'd call the cops, and he'd spend his wedding night in jail. Instead of getting some from Lilly, he might end up somebody's bitch. I'd *love* to see that. *C'mon, Dad, try something. I ain't ten years old anymore. In a few months, if I wanted to, I could follow War into the military. Yeah, it might be father and son, but it's now man to man. It'll be a fight. He might be more muscular, stronger, but I'll unleash a shitload of rage on the fucker. Try something, Dad. I dare you.*

"Well?" I asked confidently, knowing I had the edge.

"You think you're funny, don't you?"

"Yeah."

Dad scowled and pointed at me. "I don't know who you think you are. You don't pull that shit on me. You're supposed to respect and obey me."

I shook my head and laughed loudly. "Man, listen to you. Making a big-ass deal about respect, when you've never respected me. You never respected Mom, did you? All those time you hit her, you call that respect? And you used to tell me when I was little, 'you gotta give respect to get it'." I got pissed. I yelled. "You been disrespectin' me as long as I can remember, and now you're wonderin' why I'm not treatin' you with respect?"

"This ain't about me, it's about you."

"Bullshit," I yelled. "This *is* about you. You oughta like that, being as selfish as you are. And yes, you do disrespect me."

"I don't disrespect you, but I—"

"You don't get it, do you? Okay, first off, you didn't say what songs *to* play and *not* to play, all right, so don't go gettin' on me for playin' that song." Dad was about to start up again, but I cut him off and pointed at him. My voice got louder. "Lemme finish, all right? For once, *you* listen."

He had a habit of always interrupting in an argument. Wonder if Lilly knew about that when she said, "I do"?

Dad pointed at me, making sure to shove his finger into my chest. He spoke slowly. "I respect you, goddammit."

I stared at a face that was a mask of anger. In the past, that look terrified me, but not today. "No you don't," I said quietly. I did it on purpose, to show that I was in control. "And you don't respect Amanda either. I saw what you did when she walked away, wagging your tongue. She's half your age, Dad."

I must've shocked him. He looked startled. I felt something inside. Not nerves, no fear, no tension, just numb. Numb to his attitude, numb to his threats, numb to him in general. "Ever since I was a kid, I've never been good enough for you. Never." I wanted to yell at him, but I held back. Rather than unleash my rage, I always felt a need to hold back. My voice seethed. "I was never good enough for you with other kids. I was never good enough for you with music. I was never good enough for you that one year I played Little League. All you ever did was put me down."

"I was trying to motivate you to get better. And this has nothing to do with—"

I snapped, "*Yes, it does, goddammit!*"

I didn't care if anyone inside the room heard me. *Come out. Everybody come out. See what a scum bag this guy is. Come see the guy that, in junior high, I referred to as sperm donor when I mentioned him around my friends. Come out and see how he really is, not that smiling, joking, guy you love who stuffs dollar bills into your garter.*

I continued, but quieter. "Remember when I was invited to try out for the all-star team and there were fourteen spots and fifteen kids trying out? And after I was the one player who got cut, you said you knew I'd get cut? Remember that?"

Dad sighed again. "I was trying to motivate you to practice more so you'd get better and make the team the next year," he said angrily. "And this has nothing to do with that shit you just pulled. Who the fuck do you think you are, embarrassing me like that? I brought you into this world—"

"'I can take you out of it.' I get it. Oh, and, just so you know, after you said you'd know I'd get cut, I never picked up my glove again. Remember? After we moved here, every time you asked if I wanted to play Little League, or try out for Pop Warner, I said no."

He sighed. He shook his head, looking more annoyed than apologetic. "Look, I'm sorry you didn't like what I said, but what the hell does that have to do with anything?"

"It has to do with everything."

"So, what, you decided to be a smart ass because you didn't like what I said after you got cut? Jesus, you're worse than a fuckin' little bitch."

"Nice talk, you sexist pig." That was the first time those two words ever came out of my mouth. "And our performance wasn't just about what happened *that* day. Yeah, we thought we were funny. Yeah, we chose those songs on

purpose, and yeah, *I* made the decision for us to do it because not only do I not respect you, I don't love you. Do
you understand? *I don't love you!*"

Dad said nothing. It seemed his life was being drained
from him. He was always so loud, the life of the party. He
always made sure he was the center of attention. And for
once, it wasn't for his sense of humor. This was for his dark
side.

"You don't love me?" he said with some agitation.

I thought about it for a second. "Let's put it this way. If
you were on life support, and it were up to me to continue
treatment or pull the plug, I'd pull the plug—and I'd say
'now, we're even.' And since you're wondering if this was
all about the Little League comment, no. This is about a
lifetime of you trying to control me, trying to control Mom,
and you deciding to beat us up whenever you didn't get
your way, and whenever one of us would try and address
this with you, you'd try to change the subject."

And Dad just didn't seem to listen. He had to stay on his
topic no matter what anyone else said. "What does any of
this have to do with your little smart-ass thing you did?" He
tried sounding angry, but his tone changed. I was getting to
him, granted, slower than I wanted, but I was reaching him.
We stared at each other. He wanted to see if I'd give up, so
he could talk about his agenda, but he forgot that I was just
as stubborn as he is.

"Listen to somebody else for once, will ya?"

"All right," he sarcastically said. "Go right ahead."

"School," I said. "You never gave a *fuck* about how I did.
I'd bring home a report card with all As and Bs and all
you'd focus on, let's see, in Brooklyn it was all about how I
wasn't a good enough athlete, and then we move here, and
it was always how the teachers would give me bad marks
for not being able to get along with other students. And now
it's all about how I'm not doing as good as I used to. As if
you ever gave a shit about how good I did in the first
place."

Was I starting to reach him? After almost eighteen years, it looked like I might be. He wasn't standing with his arms out, trying to show off his muscles. His shoulders slumped. His hands were in his pockets. His face, soft. His tough-guy front was gone. Everything he did wrong was being thrown back at him, and I didn't give him a chance to talk his way out of it.

I had to go for his jugular. "Oh, and, just so you know, I overheard every time you started beating up Mom, pulling her hair, calling her shit like a worthless cunt." Somehow I stayed calm. "Remember that shit? Remember all those times she complained about your gambling losses and how drunk you were, and you said you'd kill her and that pathetic little waste of cum? Remember that? And you wonder why when you told me that you and Mom were getting divorced, all I said was 'good.' Well, now you know. I don't respect you because you never treated me or Mom with any. When I needed someone to soothe me, you were a hard ass. When I was afraid, you called me a chicken shit."

He turned away. I heard him sniffle. This was taking a toll on me too. My neck was tense, and my heart raced. I breathed deep, but slow. But despite all that junk that was now out in the open, despite ruining his wedding day, I didn't feel any better. I wanted to hit him. Right in the face. I didn't care if he was muscular. I wanted to take his ass on. My rage still wasn't purged. I didn't think it ever would be purged.

"And to think, you still wonder why Mom threw you out after we—yes, her and I—caught *you* fucking that cocktail waitress on the couch? I wondered why she didn't leave your sorry ass years earlier. And yeah, I told Mom that. And you know what she said? She said she didn't know either."

His back was to me. "And I have to go around the rest of my life with your name," I quietly sneered.

I heard him sniffle again. He tilted his head back. I couldn't see his face, but I knew what was going on. He was probably crying. I never saw him do it, but I assumed the whole thing was just an act.

I was still furious, but for a different reason. I realized that I cursed a lot because he did. And it made me sick. Out of all his despicable habits, I had picked up on one of them. Sure, it wasn't as awful as hitting women and children, or manipulating people, but cursing was awful. And in that moment, I vowed to myself to try and stop cursing.

"Oh, my god," Dad said. "I've completely failed, haven't I?"

"Yeah, pretty much," I said, and if he called me a smart ass at that moment, he would've been right.

Okay, maybe his crying was legit. Maybe I made him realize what a lousy father he was. And to think, I didn't even bring up the fact that he married someone who he stuffed dollar bills into a garter on her thigh.

He turned around and faced me. "You really hate me?" he asked through a waterfall of tears.

I sighed. "All right, maybe hate's a bit strong. But I don't have a lot of love for you."

"You know, son, I've always tried to treat you like a friend. I mean, you know, joking with you and stuff."

"I'm not your friend, all right? I'm your son."

That caught Dad off guard. He was stunned. And I decided that the conversation was over. I turned to go back to the reception. Lilly opened the door as I turned around.

"Is everything okay?" she asked.

"Yeah, everything's fine. Oh, and, by the way, I hope he treats you better than he does me. Too bad the bar's so low that an ant can't limbo under it."

I walked through the door. Before I closed it, I said to Dad, "Take your Strat home tonight. I don't need it anymore."

CHAPTER 37

Yeah, it's a tad cliché to say it, but it's true: everything changed.

No really, it's true.

No one believed that I gave the Strat back to my dad. In fact, no one knew it was actually his guitar. With the way I treated that thing, talked about it, knew about its history, took care of it—always wiping the fingerprints off the body and pickguard, cleaning the strings after I was done playing it—everybody swore that it was my guitar. And I think Dad meant for it to be my guitar, which is why it *had* to go back to him. I had to show him that I was no longer his "friend" or whatever the hell he thought of me as. You could say it was like leaving home, only I didn't go anywhere. I was now my own man, even if I still had a few months before I legally became one at eighteen.

The best part of that whole deal was that I didn't have to rely on him to get another guitar. I went without one for about ten days, or until the next payday at the record store, and then took that cash, and the other money I stashed away in my room, and went to the pawn shop in Northtown—where Mom and my late Uncle Mickey used to work at—to buy another one. One that would truly be *mine*. But the trip there was more than asserting freedom. It was my first journey into stupid adult worries.

Every time we went to that pawn shop before, I thought nothing of the neighborhood. Yeah, it was older than ours. Yeah, the parking lot abounded with cracked and bumpy pavement, with weeds sprouting up here and there. Of course, both my parents insisted that Northtown wasn't the best part of Vegas, and there were blacks and Mexicans walking around, when no one walked the sidewalks in our neighborhood, but so what? I liked going into that dark store, crammed full of all sorts of stuff people got rid of, stuff like lamps, TVs, stereos, speakers, jewelry, guns, and other assorted crap, but for me, it was always about the musical instruments, especially the guitars and basses.

All sorts of old guitars hung from the ceiling, many of them with sunburst finishes, that captured my attention. Dad's too. He'd look at the guitars, commenting on their finish, their manufacturer, telling whatever anecdotes he knew about the make, and he didn't care if anyone was listening. Sometimes he'd grab 'em to look at them closer. "High action," he might say about the strings on a cheap guitar. If it was one of the models he'd rave about, he'd hold it, pick a few notes, then talk about how smooth the action was and how much he'd love to plug it in. He also proved to be the only person, I think, who could perfectly segue from "I saw her standing there," by the Beatles to "In a Gadda Da Vida" without missing a note. And just when he was entering guitar heaven, Mom would have to reel him in.

So when I got my new guitar, Amanda was my mom. She even shared my anxiety about someone stealing the Duster. Showed we watched too much damn TV news. But she didn't have to reel me in that much. Most of the guitars Al Jay's had were too expensive, and I couldn't put it on layaway since I was under eighteen and didn't have a co-signer. I wasn't about to buy a total beater with high action.

After about an hour, I settled on a red Fender Mustang with a white pickguard. It had two pickups instead of three like the Strat, and it still had a tremolo arm, not like I'd ever use it. I liked that it pretty much looked like a Strat. It had the same double cutaways near the neck and a similar body shape. The headstock's shape was identical as well. Instead of a maple neck, it had one made of rosewood, which sucked, because I loved the way the maple looked. Playing it, it didn't feel quite the same, and it didn't sound as good through my amp as Dad's Strat. It sounded worse. But given the direction our music was taking, it actually sounded better. Yeah, go figure. The Mustang even came with a case. As for the color, let's just say I'd always wanted to play with a redhead, at least since Dad met Lilly.

"Think this is it," I told Amanda.

"Yeah? Looks nice."

"Well, let's see what kinda deal I can get." I wasn't sure if the guy I spoke to worked with Mom and Uncle Mickey or not. I never noticed who else worked at the place.

"You want one-fifty for this?"

"Yup." The guy behind the counter, who didn't look familiar, never looked up from the jewelry he was polishing."

"I'll give ya a hundred."

He chuckled. "Forget it, kid."

"It's a fair price."

"It's what I paid for the thing."

"Okay. One-twenty-five."

"Nope. Price as marked."

"C'mon, I'm a senior at Fremont. I'm buying this with money I earned working, and my mom and uncle used to work here. Can we lower the price some?"

"I don't give a shit if your mom and uncle are the mayor. You want that, you pay one-fifty. Besides, it includes a case."

I caved. Left me with next to nothing, but I got the guitar, it was mine, and Dad wouldn't be able to hold the Strat over my head if he wanted to. And I really needed to get better at negotiations, or let someone else do them.

✑✑✑

Life settled into a routine. School, work, a weekly visit
to Chris at the county jail, some time somewhere with
Amanda—usually around her parents—and hanging out at
the record store when I wasn't working. Actually, work
wasn't really work. Sure, we had stuff to do, but since
somebody else from the band was usually hanging out, we
split the duties. Gave us more time to hang out, listen to
records, and work on songs.

Reclamation Records became our hangout. Donnie and I
would show up with our guitars, Mullie with his bass, and
Gremlin with his drumsticks, and we'd work out arrangements. The guitars weren't plugged in, and Gremlin hit any
surface that sounded like a certain type of drum, but otherwise, it was the perfect rehearsal space. We got tighter as a
band, and it showed during the few times we actually were
able to plug in and kick out the jams. And the owner was
cool with everything as long as work got done and customers were taken care of. It certainly didn't hurt that he got
free labor out of the deal.

The storeroom in the back became the perfect spot for
those of us with girlfriends to get laid. Sometimes it would
just happen when Amanda or Roxie walked in. Sometimes
it would happen when we'd be in the back doing—are you
ready for this?—homework.

Yes, Donnie, Mullie, and myself began paying more attention to our homework. We'd do it more, put a little more
effort in. It still sucked doing it, but we got to hang out together, try to figure out things like chemistry or government
as one, and get tutored either by Amanda, Roxie, or Gremlin, especially with government.

Gradually, we truly developed a take-no-shit attitude.
Me and Donnie always had one, most of the time, but there
were times when we took shit from other people. Maybe it
was a false sense of authority, or, in the case of the jocks,
being outnumbered. And no episode epitomized our truly
take-no-shit attitude than one gorgeous spring Sunday.

All four of us were at the store. Gremlin and I were both working, Donnie and Mullie came by to hang out. We had *Zen Arcade* by Husker Du on the turntable, and the store actually had a few customers browsing. Business was finally picking up. Outside the store, an old guy who we'd seen quite a bit walked by. It wasn't unusual to see that. Only this time, he stopped. Maybe it was because the door was open, but instead of going to the frozen yogurt shop next door, he came inside the store.

"What da hell do ya think ya doin'?" he yelled to be heard over the music, and he succeeded. All the customers looked our way. And there was no mistaking that accent: New Jersey. Heard it whenever we went to Montclair to visit Grandma before she died.

"Is there a problem, sir?" Gremlin politely asked.

"Hell, yeah there's a problem," the guy yelled. "This shit ya playin'. I'm tryin' ta run a fam'ly business next door, and you guys are in 'ere blastin' out this garbage."

"I'm sorry, sir," I politely interjected. "But this is the volume we keep the stereo at. It's the same as any other—"

"How da hell am I supposed to draw families with these fuckin' weirdos screamin' about what's goin' on in their head? If you animals were actually decent people, you might undastand."

"We're sorry you feel that way, sir—" Gremlin added, only to be interrupted again. I think he was on the same wavelength as me. We were gonna kill him with kindness, using our excellent customer service skills as a front to, in effect, tell him to fuck off without having to actually curse.

"You're gonna be sorry when I get dis store closed. You hoodlums are a disgrace to this shopping centa." And he stormed out of our store to go next door and dispense frozen yogurt to the hordes of Sin City moral prudes and their fine, upstanding children, at least until we destroyed their lives by playing something from our inventory. Now they were hoodlums!

"Where did that come from?" Mullie asked.

"He's havin' a rotten day." Gremlin took the needle off the record.

I scoffed. "And we were *polite* to that jerk."

"I'd say we handled that really good," Donnie added.

"Absolutely." Gremlin put the record back in its sleeve. "Can one of you guys see if we have *Damaged* by Black Flag?"

Donnie went to look for it. "Do you wanna do what I think you wanna do?" I asked.

Gremlin smiled. "It'd be a great chance for us to work on vocals."

Donnie quickly found the record, and Gremlin put it on the turntable to the first track on side one: "Rise Above." As the song started, he told us, "We're singing along with the chorus, right at him," he said, pointing to the wall.

And when the chorus came around, all four of us screamed at the wall separating our two stores about how we were tired of his abuse and that it was no use to try to stop us. And we did it every time the chorus came up. And as the song wound down, we screamed at the wall about how we were going to rise above—over and over.

It was one thing to have a take-no-shit passive-aggressive attitude through a store wall. The real test was yet to come.

CHAPTER 38

The downside of us spending so much of our money on stuff like amps, albums, and, in Donnie's case, rent, was that we had to stay on Fremont's campus for lunch. No drifting off to Jack-in-the-Box for tacos or Mad Dogs for chili cheese fries to get something to eat in the middle of the day. We had to eat in the school cafeteria, the dining equivalent of a cat box.

"Hey, Nick," Donnie, Roxie, and Mullie said when Amanda and I sat at the circular brown Formica-topped table they'd grabbed. "What'd you get?" Mullie asked.

"Cardboard topped by a cheese-like substance, red circular meat by-product, orangey grease, and sauce loaded with food coloring," I replied. "It's gonna be tasty!"

Everyone laughed.

"And you insist that Jack-in-the-Box tacos are gourmet food," Mullie replied.

"Hell, yeah," I replied. "You don't know the story behind that, do you?"

"No."

"I haven't heard it," Amanda said.

Donnie smiled as I recalled the tale. "Freshman year. Me, Donnie, Micah, and Chris were hanging out in my room listening to my dad's Led Zeppelin Two album, when he walked in my room. He says 'Hey.' We reply 'Hey.' He

asks, 'You guys like that album?' We said yes, and my dad
says, 'Yeah, that's a great album. Me and my band, we used
to listen to that album, smoke pot, and eat Jack-in-the-Box
tacos.'"

Mullie laughed. "Nice."

Amanda shook her head. "Oh my God," she said with a
tone that didn't sound amused. "He said that? You guys
were, what, fourteen years old?"

"Yeah, well, that's my dad."

The next voice we heard said, "The scuzzy one's gone,
but it still smells around you guys."

Owen. No mistaking that condescending, nasally tone.
And Jeff was with him, his smug smirk decorating his pim-
ply, pockmarked face.

I chuckled and shook my head. I stood up, walked over
to Owen. Looking him squarely in his brown eyes, close
enough to smell cardboard pizza on his breath, close enough
for him to realize that I was through putting up with his shit.

"Listen to you. Here we are, about to graduate high
school, and you're still acting the way you did in junior
high." Then I yelled, "Look at you! You're pathetic!"

A good chunk of the lunchroom went quiet and looked
our way. A couple of kids at some tables stood up, antici-
pating a fight. And I deliberately *didn't* curse. You can figure out why.

"You know, if you're his friend—" I pointed at Jeff. "—
you'd be thanking me for saving his life. If it weren't for
me, he would've ended up taking a bullet. He might've *died*
if not for me. And this is how you show your gratitude?" I
paused. "Some friend you are."

Owen stood, looking so confused, I wanted to laugh at
him but didn't. He had no comeback. Jeff had no comeback.
There they were, Owen, captain of the soccer team, and Jeff,
captain of the football team, self-appointed kings of
Fremont, bringing unlimited glory to our concrete box in
the form of brief items in the sports sections of the papers,

humiliated, in front of their subjects, by what they thought was among the lowest of the serfs.

"You gonna get outta of my face or you gonna stand there looking all silly?" I asked, my voice low, but confident.

Owen walked away, his face shrouded in a scowl. It was a victory, maybe the ultimate one. At that moment, it made up for Owen's pig dad covering for him and Jeff after the Calico Basin ambush. But, in truth, it didn't make up for that, for all the years of harassment, threats, and violence.

My friend—maybe my best friend, a true friend—was going to prison because of these guys, who would get to take the field at whatever college they were going to, and all their misdeeds would be covered up by coaches and the media. They'd be hailed for scoring the goal or touchdown that got State U the win over Whowazzit State and brought the Big Fuckin' Deal Tin Jock Stap Trophy back to campus for the first time since some Wall Street greedy fuck alumni was a trust-fund sophomore.

Chris was going to prison for attempted murder of a living person, but they were never going to go on trial for a slow assassination, one that went on for so long, that it took my friend's will to live. But that was okay. They could run a damn football and kick a soccer ball. Chris's life had been ruined by the shit they did. Mine had certainly been tarnished. Religious types told you to forgive, that it healed you. I supposed I could do that, but that wouldn't remove what they did.

And in that moment, I once again second-guessed myself for saving their lives.

So I was not in a great mood when I sat down at the table. My heart raced in its usual way after a confrontation with those guys. My jaw clenched. I had the urge to hit something. Hard. I stared at that cardboard grease concoction and slowly pushed it away, resisting the urge to throw it.

"You okay?" Amanda asked.

"Yeah."

Silence.

"No."

Amanda got out of her chair, wrapped her arms around my neck and head, but I gently pushed her away. I wanted a hug, needed a hug, and not just from her, but from Donnie and Mullie, but I couldn't admit that. Not here. Not in a place where a hug between guys automatically made them gay and subjected them to being called a faggot with as much ferocity as we got for having long hair and being unable to hit a goddamn curve ball. It all had to be kept in. Suppress your emotions, show no affection, unless it was sexual, toward the opposite sex, and a means to show how dominant you were over them.

Chris, it turned out, had traded one prison for another. Micah escaped. But did you have to die in order to be free?

Four years in this joint—

"Nick, are you okay?"

Now I noticed the brown paint on the walls above the faded tan lockers in the hallway. And I noticed just how alike everybody in this place looked—same haircuts. Same clothes. Same shirts. Pants. Blouses. Skirts. Bought at the same place in the mall. Same. All the same. Links in nationwide chains, homogenized clothes. *Express yourself by looking just like the person sitting next to you. It's all shared experience. We're all the same. Or are we?*

"Hello, Nick…"

High school. A caste system filled with flawed logic. It's not the content of your character that matters. It's how well you wear the mall-derived camouflage. And the mannequins in the mall have something stuck up their asses in the display window. Get the same haircut. Listen to the same music. So much for free will. Get a label. Jock. Preppie. Mod. Stoner. Geek. Whatever. Pigeonholed before any of the pigeons can even get to know who you really are.

"It's all a fraud."

"What is?"

Was that Donnie? "Our lives."

"Nick, what is going on?"

Amanda?

"Yeah, where the hell did you go?"

Roxie?

"Everything they're telling us is to make us believe in a shared fiction—"

"Shared fiction?" *Mullie?*

"—so that we can just go out and be a cog in some casino, sweeping up cigarette butts—"

"Nick, are you there?"

"—so that we believe the government looks out for us, and our vote matters—"

"Where is this coming from?"

"—our history teacher lied to us. Iron Maiden spoke the truth. Run to the Hills. Run for your life. That was manifest destiny. Not some divine—"

"Man, you've been hanging around Gremlin too much."

"—ly ordained fulfillment."

"Nick, we gotta go to class."

"We'll be eighteen, able to buy cigarettes and porn, be tried as an adult in court, ignore city curfews, no longer protected by child labor laws—"

"Let him be. We're gonna be late."

"—vote for the figurehead in the White House, enlist in the military and go kill whatever foreigner the government tells you too—but you can't play a slot machine or buy a beer."

"Nick, c'mon."

If only I could've convinced Chris that things would get better.

They couldn't get much worse.

If only I could've reached Micah before Sonny made the lethal injection.

If only...

CHAPTER 39

Anyone stepping into Mad Dogs when we were there got a true glimpse of the insecurity of teenage romance. Six people congregated in a booth that maybe, at best, could hold just that many. Only it was supposed to be three on one side, three on the other. Not the imbalance we showed. Somehow, me, Amanda, Donnie, and Roxie insisted on being Siamese twins. The four of us crowded into one side of the booth.

Yes indeed, we had to sit together! The communal unspoken thought between these two pairs was: we're a couple, and dammit, we sit together, not apart! We would never even so much as think about sitting across from each other. Not when either one guy would sit with two girls or two guys sit with one girl. Too many sexual overtones there, even if all we were doing was getting chili cheese fries and sodas. And even then, there were unspoken sexual insecurities involved.

Roxie and Amanda had to sit next to each other, Donnie was almost squished against the wall, while I had half my ass and one leg actually stuck out of the booth. That imaginary sexual situation—the two girls squished together—was okay with me and Donnie's perverse sexism. No way we would let ourselves be that damn close together. That would not be manly! But it was okay for girls to be that close together. Hell, I'd even heard them refer to female friends as girlfriends. If a guy referred to another male as a boyfriend, he was either gay, or, worse, one of those NAMBLA pervs.

And while all this needless unspoken drama played itself out on our side of the table, Mullie and Gremlin comfortably sat across from us, looking amused as our insecurities led us to be human shoehorns.

Gremlin never took his eyes off us as he put the silver ghetto blaster on the table. The thing was large, not quite as gigantic as the boomboxes you saw in rap videos, but big enough lengthwise to go across the table, so much so that Donnie now had no room for a plate or soda in front of him. And now there was no point in reaching for the salt and pepper, ketchup, and mustard, or even napkins. That boombox functioned as a Berlin Wall.

The middle-aged waitress brought three orders of chili-cheese fries and six sodas and arranged them on our table, ignoring the ghetto blaster, even though Run-DMC was playing on the jukebox. *Ignore it*, she probably thought, *and maybe there won't be a fight over the music.* But she did notice our uncomfortable seating arrangement. "Would you like me to bring you a chair?" she asked.

"I'm good," I said, with a smile that showed I was worried about my Speed Stick holding up in such tight quarters.

"Quit elbowing me," Amanda said, to whom I wasn't sure.

"Okay, I got two questions," Gremlin said as everyone else began to eat. "One, you guys wanna put on our demo, and two, are we changing our name to Cramped and the Sardines?"

"Yes on the first, and no on the second," I replied.

"I don't know. I kinda like that new band name," Mullie said.

"Me too. Very sixties garage," Gremlin added.

"Like trying to fit a 'sixty-nine Impala into a one-car garage."

"Exactly."

"Ho, ho, very jolly. Ha, ha. It is to laugh," I said, channeling a favorite Daffy Duck line. "Put on the demo, will ya?"

"You know, next time I get all depressed about having to jack off because I don't have a girlfriend, I'm gonna think back to this moment and how stupid you all look."

I gave Gremlin the stare of death, eyes lowered, head tilted slightly forward.

"All right, all right, I'll put the tape on."

I knew from experience this demo was gonna sound awful. Little did Donnie, Chris, or War know it, but I recorded us jamming a couple of times, and it was a loud, distorted mess. I'd never set foot in a recording studio, but it didn't take long to figure out that albums were not recorded on a cassette through a department store tape player with a record button. Hell, when I was a kid I listened to reel-to-reel tapes of my dad's band, Krishna Karma—lousy band names ran in the family—and they didn't sound all that great. Maybe it was because they were playing some hippie crap. But I knew from experience that the only good you could get from a cheap tape recorder was recording a riff on guitar.

Our "recording" session was last night at Donnie and Gremlin's. Put the ghetto blaster in the corner of the room, stick in a blank cassette, hit play, and record, and jam on our original tunes. Since this recording was made without the cassette player being hidden behind some furniture, maybe it would sound better.

It did, but only in that the sound wasn't muffled. But what it had in clarity was obliterated by sheer volume. My god! The furniture acted as a sort of volume control, but with that gone, it was a mess of distortion, drums, and screaming. Screaming? Is that what I was doing? I thought I was singing. Okay, not singing, but I didn't think I was screaming. Was I that desperate to be heard over this mishmash of music-based noise?

"Your drums sound good, dude" Mullie enthusiastically told Gremlin.

I nodded in agreement. "Well, they are the loudest thing on there."

"Dude," added Donnie, "our guitars sound like a mess."

"I can't hear my bass," Mullie said.

I finished a sip of Mountain Dew. "That's weird. Heard you clearly last night."

"What song're you guys playing?" Amanda asked.

"The new one I wrote," I said. "Fallen."

We sat for about a minute, listening to the raw noise. I wasn't sure what to think of it.

"You know, it really doesn't sound all that good," Mullie said in his usual deadpan manner.

There was a lot of laughter, but one person didn't join in the fun.

"You know what. I don't like this music you're making," said Roxie, who was at our cheap-ass recording session. "I mean, seriously, who wants to listen to stuff like that. I mean, playing Metallica was bad enough, but this stuff, what is it?"

"Would you prefer we play 'Nothin' But a Good Time?" I asked calmly. I knew she'd react the way she did to the stuff her boyfriend was being forced to play by that "Noo Yawk wise ass and that skirt-wearing freak." Her words, not mine.

"Well, yeah!" she said, drawing out the last syllable as long as possible. "Life sucks as it is. Do we have to be reminded of it with music? I want music that's gonna make me feel good, wanna party. I'm sorry, Nick, I think you're cool, but I just don't like this music. And stop playing that song about not wearing underwear! My god, it's gross."

"Would it make you feel better if I started wearing a garter belt and thigh-high fishnets with my 'plaid skirt'?" Gremlin asked.

"Ewww," Roxie replied. "You're weird."

"Says the girl who wants us to cover songs by a bunch of guys with chick hair and makeup."

"I gotta agree with him," Mullie said. "Poison sucks. All the freshman pukes wear their T-shirts."

In the past, I would've gotten pissed off, but now, I knew not to take it personally. I knew the music I was writing now was not what was popular, and it wasn't being played on KOMP, but I was writing from within. My music was now honest. And so was Gremlin's "Going Commando," or so he said. No one was lining up to verify that.

"You know, you guys're really starting to piss me off," Donnie said. "First, quit pickin' on Roxie—"

I cut him off. "We're not pickin' on Roxie. We're just having—"

"Yes, you guys are."

Our table fell into thirty seconds of silence before Donnie continued. "And you know what? I'm kinda frustrated with our music now. I don't even get to solo anymore."

"Is there some federal law requiring guitar solos on every song?" Gremlin asked.

Donnie squeezed an arm out of its cramped surroundings and pointed. "You know, you just waltz on in here, and just cuz you're a hot-shit drummer, think you own this band now?"

"I don't. I thought we were working together on our music, coming up with ideas and arrangements. I mean, everything seemed fine with us, until now."

"It just seems like everything did a complete one-eighty the minute you get in here. Nick gets all gaga over punk and everything changes."

"I thought you were okay with everything?" I asked.

"No, I'm not."

I could've asked what it would take to make him feel better about our music, but I knew what his answer would be. And I was sick of solos that were just there and didn't do anything to take the song somewhere. Or maybe I realized that our leaner sound could work just fine with one guitarist.

"So quit."

"What?" Amanda asked.

I got up. "If you don't like it, you can leave."

"Nick, what the hell's wrong with you?" Amanda asked, her face, along with everyone else's, was a mask of pure bewilderment.

"So it's your way or no way?" Donnie angrily asked.

I paused for a moment to think about what he said. While I did this, I heard Donnie say "Let's go, Roxie."

"Donnie, wait, man. It isn't my way or no way. I want this to be a communal effort, with everyone contributing, and if we have disagreements, we work them out. I don't wanna be a dictator. All I was saying is if you're that unhappy, you might as well go."

Donnie's face showed his anger. "You honestly want me to go?"

I shook my head. "No. We've been through too much." I sighed. "I can't just let you go. But if you have ideas, spit 'em out."

"I wanna have solos in our songs."

I saw Gremlin roll his eyes.

"Dude, I gotta be honest with you. You're just not that great a shredder. I mean, you're better than I am, which ain't sayin' much, but you're just not that good."

Donnie and the girls sat in stunned silence, as if I had committed some ultimate act of blasphemy. "Member all those times we played *'Master of Puppets'*? You really didn't nail the solo."

Donnie chuckled. "Or that time I swore to you, War, and Micah that I nailed 'Eruption.'"

"Yeah, that was…um…pretty bad. We just didn't have the balls to tell you that."

We fell into silence again.

"Well, if I can't solo, and if all I'm doing is playing the same part as you, I guess I oughta leave."

"We can come up with a separate guitar part," I quickly replied.

Donnie nodded. "Yeah, I guess so. But solos are out, I s'pose."

"Not entirely," said an unlikely source: Gremlin. "Husker Du has them, but they're not that play-every-note-you-know, hold the guitar like it's your weenie, with a final high-speed flourish up the neck. You'll have to listen to it, I can't explain it."

Donnie nodded.

"You still in?" I asked.

"You want me in?"

"Yeah."

"Then I'm in."

Then our table seemed to loosen up, with the exception of Roxie. I think she was hoping Donnie would quit. We ate our now-cold chili-cheese fries and drank our sodas, talking about anything other than business. But that respite lasted only a short time.

"So what're we gonna do with this demo?" I asked.

"We might as well trash it," Gremlin replied, "since we're gonna be rearranging our songs. And once we do, if we're gonna get a label interested, we have to book time in a recording studio. Make a quality-sounding demo. And that means we better save our money."

"No more chili cheese fries?" Donnie asked. "That sucks."

"I think we can make an allowance for chili cheese fries," Mullie added.

"What label's gonna put out your kind of stuff—" Roxie asked.

Gremlin cut her off. "An independent label. One that puts out underground stuff."

It was becoming clear that when we did go into a studio that a hard and fast rule had to be created and enforced: No girlfriends allowed.

"Actually, Donnie, I hate to tell you this, but we're really gonna have to save our money," I said. "Not only do we need to get into a studio, but I think we should save up some dough to get outta town."

"Lemme guess," Donnie said. "You're not thinking of LA."

"Well, Amanda is thinking of going to the University of Washington, and it's in Seattle."

"Yeah, Amanda said it's really cool, and the University of Washington is a really good school," Roxie said. "I think I'm gonna go there too. Amanda sold me on the place."

"It's really cool," Amanda said.

"Aren't they a bunch of lumberjacks up there or something?" Donnie asked.

"Yes, they are," Gremlin said. "A bunch of flannel-shirt-wearing guys who cut down trees, they eat their lunch, they go to the lavatory. A bunch of lumberjacks who write music that you'll totally hate, Roxie, because it sounds nothing like Poison, but they're okay."

"What? No way!"

"Yes, way."

"How do you know?" asked Mullie.

"We got some records from up there at the station. Bands with great names like Cat Butt and The Thrown Ups. Cat Butt's a personal favorite of mine, and not just because of the awesome name. That and the Butthole Surfers, but they're from Texas."

The others at the table laughed.

"I'm thinking that's where we should go," I said. "But we should go check it out."

"Well, this calls for one thing," Gremlin said. "Road trip to Seattle."

"I'm off next weekend," I said. "And it's right after payday, so we'll have money for gas."

Donnie wiped chili off his face with a napkin and threw it on the table. "I gotta work next Saturday. Gotta make the rent." He didn't sound upset, however.

"I gotta work too," Mullie added. "Saturday and Sunday."

"I'm off next weekend," Gremlin said.

I smiled, because if there was one thing I loved more than anything, it was hitting the pavement, getting out of town, and seeing and experiencing somewhere new. "Then let's hit the road and check that place out."

CHAPTER 40

Twenty-three straight hours on the road. A case of Mountain Dew to keep us alert as we drove through the Nevada desert, the Sierra Nevadas, then up I-5 through northern California, Oregon and into Washington state. Five bags of Doritos to keep the stomachs from grumbling. About a dozen homemade cassette mixtapes to keep us occupied, and they'd all been listened to twice already.

One big-time lie to my mom and her husband: That I was staying at Donnie and Gremlin's for the weekend. At least ten trucker bombs were flung out the Duster's windows, since we only stopped for gas and to take a shit. After all that, we arrived in Seattle as the sun rose behind a gray blanket sky.

Ironically, "Everything Turns Gray" by Agent Orange was blaring from the stereo as we passed the big green sign that said *Entering Seattle*.

It wasn't the greatest first impression, pulling in from the suburbs south of the city. On the driver's side was an airport. To the right was a green, tree-filled hillside. Then we passed a bunch of industrial buildings, but the Kingdome and the skyscrapers of downtown lurked in the distance. We could make out the Space Needle, which was pretty small from where we were on the Interstate at that moment.

"Thar she blows!" bellowed Gremlin when downtown came into view.

"She does? Excellent! I need a blow job."

"I ain't givin' you one."

"Don't want one from you."

"You sure? I have nice legs." Gremlin began hiking his skirt, sorry, kilt, to show off some leg. Great incentive to keep my eyes on the road.

"I thought you said all those Doritos were going right to your thighs."

"And my hips." Gremlin quickly switched topics. "So, mister ex-Noo Yawk boy, seeing those skyscrapers give you flashbacks?"

"A bit. But that don't compare to Manhattan. Whole island's like that."

"Never been there."

"I loved it. 'Course, didn't see much more than Brooklyn, Brighton Beach mostly. Couple times my dad took me to see the Yankees or the Mets, and sometimes we'd go through Manhattan to visit Mom's family in Jersey, but it was across the north end of the island, going across the George Washington Bridge."

I thought about how after we moved to Vegas, I cut out pictures of New York from the newspaper and any magazines my parents brought home and stuck them on the wall of my bedroom closet, just to remember home. I even tore pictures out of books from the school library of things like the Empire State Building, the Twin Towers, even Coney Island, or any pictures of the Yankees or Mets that were in the sports section, and taped them up.

I'd steal a flashlight from Dad's tool box and, when I was supposed to be sleeping, I'd look at those pictures. I'd want to cry, but held it in as much as I could. If anything, I tried to make it as quiet as I could. Getting caught was not an option. I didn't need the lecture about how the city was falling apart, all the violence, especially after the riots that broke out the night I turned seven and the power went off. I just didn't want to hear it. I didn't care. It was home, in a way Vegas never was, or would ever, be. And to make sure my parents didn't see my little shrine, which I took down during fifth grade, I'd put all my Star Wars toys against the wall. They thought I was such a neat and organized kid who always cleaned his room.

"Feels weird," I said, "Seeing tall buildings without bright flashing lights all over them, up and down, and all that neon and shit."

"Welcome to the rest of America."

"Think it all looks like this?" I asked, and got no reply.

We navigated I-5 through downtown, which was not an easy task with all these lanes that went off in screwy directions and lanes that suddenly ended. We just narrowly avoided going off to some place called Bellevue or West Seattle or some street that we did not want to drive on. Our main task was to find a park called Green Lake, near the University of Washington, according to the city map Amanda loaned us.

Even though we were excited about finally arriving, we needed sleep. This Mountain Dew buzz would wear off soon, and we would be in no condition to maneuver a muscle car through city traffic. So we desperately needed slumber. And we were prepared for it. We brought pillows, blankets, and even took turns behind the wheel so one of us could get at least a catnap during our marathon up the western spine of the country. And that was all either one of us got, for reasons that were best saved for a confessional.

We easily found Green Lake. Didn't even get lost. And unlike the cliché about men, yes, we looked at the map. So we found a parking spot in a gravel lot and backed the Duster up against some trees, in a lame attempt to get more darkness, even though the sky stayed gray. I put my cardboard auto shade in the windshield to try and get more darkness.

An hour or so of cramped tossing and turning ensued, with me in the back seat and Gremlin up front. No way was

there gonna be any sleep, not with cars going by, a few dogs
barking, and the creepy feeling that someone was gonna call
the cops on this vehicle with the Nevada plates with these
two leather jacket-wearing bums in there trying to sleep,
and, "good God, Officer, one of them's in drag! I just finished my jog, walked by and saw right up this guy's skirt!
Didn't see anything, but still, Officer, these slime are drug
addicts!"

"Nick."

"What."

"I can't sleep."

"Try shuttin' up first."

"I did, and now I'm gonna keep your ass up too."

"Fuck you."

"Only if you've got Crisco and don't stick it in too far."

And once you laughed like I did, there was no way in
hell you could go back to sleep. So we went off to play
tourist. Driving around it was clear that this place was not
Vegas. First off, what kind of people lived here, that they
didn't have six-foot-tall gray cinderblock walls surrounding
their backyards? Why weren't the houses all stucco and
Spanish tile? Why were even the main roads just two lanes,
and why weren't there separate turn lanes for those making
left turns? And what the hell was going on with these people walking around, using sidewalks? Didn't they know
they were just there to emphasize that no one used them?

"You know, we really oughta park this hunk of Mopar
shit and walk around," Gremlin said.

"What? Are you kidding? We're Las Vegans, dammit!
We don't walk around unless we have to."

"Get a grip on yourself! We absolutely *have* to walk
around, if this trip is to have any meaning. And I don't
wanna max out my credit card on gas before we even have
the chance to get stranded in some bumfuck little Oregon
town on the way back."

"Why the hell are we talking like this?"

"We're delirious."

"We're going mad."

"I think we need a soda. Find a place to park."

From there, we spent the day exploring the part of the city we were in. We got a proper meal, at least by the low standards of our trip, at a drive-in burger joint called Dick's. We walked, noticed the differences between there and Vegas, got a feel for the place, and endured what in Vegas would be a torrential rain storm. The rest of the world called it drizzle.

After a while we stumbled on the music scene we began hearing about. We walked into a record store called Cellophane Square, and it made Reclamation Records look pathetic. Their selection of stuff outside the usual top forty and popular poodle rockers like Poison, to put it mildly, blew our store away. Of course, we had to carry that mainstream stuff—we gotta make money somehow—but my god, there was probably more stuff there that I *hadn't* heard of than stuff that I was aware of. But I had a distraction: A newspaper called *The Rocket* that led to me reading more than I had in years. It was nothing but articles about local bands, clubs, upcoming shows, record reviews, gossip.

"What're you reading?" Gremlin asked.

"The Bible."

"You at the passage that says 'Thou shalt not exaggerate?"

"No. I'm reading Skin Yard, chapter four, verse seven," I sarcastically replied in reference to an article on a local band that further proved Gremlin was right about one thing: the Seattle bands had the best names. "This is a whole newspaper devoted to music, and all this shit's is what's going on in town."

"You serious?"

"Everything's in here."

I handed him the paper. He scanned through it while I walked around the store, checking out the music, posters, and T-shirt selection, wishing I had some extra cash. A couple of minutes later, he handed it back to me, after he had went and got a couple of copies. "Wait'll Donnie and Mullie see this. If this doesn't convince them that we need to come up here, nothing will. I mean, we'd never get this kinda support from the *R-J* or the *Sun*."

"We'd have to become a lounge act." Then I realized what Gremlin was really saying. "Wait, you wanna move here? We've only been here a coupla hours."

"Nick, I've been playing some of these bands that are in this very magazine at the station for six months now. It's happening here. Vegas is nowhere. The guys in our scene, like Bobby Barfo, they're all in their mid-twenties now. Their time is done, over. And nothing came of it. I know Donnie wants to go to LA, because he likes Motley Crue and that shit, and he thinks LA is pretty much the only option, but that scene is slowly dying too. Amanda's right. We *belong* here."

I agreed but was reluctant to do so openly. And it was only because of the reasons he said. I, too, thought LA was the only option. And, besides, it was the closest option. As it was, we had to drive across the Nevada desert for eight boring hours, across endless sagebrush, brown barren mountains, endless sand, straightaways that went on for miles across empty valleys, and that was just to reach Reno. Then we had to cross two mountain ranges just to get into Oregon. And then it was another twelve hours from there. Compared to the insane trip to get here, and the amount of money we spent on gas, LA was a trip to the corner store to get M&M'S.

"I don't know, Gremlin. We're gonna have a serious sales job on our hands."

"That's why I grabbed these newspapers. In fact, anything pertaining to the music scene here that's free, take it. Newspapers, show fliers, free records, take it. We need to overwhelm Donnie and Mullie. And while you're at it, steal that Lubricated Goat album."

"I ain't stealing it, you steal it," I whispered.

"Good. 'Cause I can't bail your ass out. I'd leave you in there to rot, steal your car, then trade that Dustpan for a new pair of retreads for the Deathmobile. I'd cruise the Strip in even less style than I already have."

"You cheap, two-bit bastard. You only wanted me to steal it so you wouldn't get caught and raped in jail for wearing that skirt. You'd be butt-fucked so much that when you went before the judge your shower nickname'll be Lubricated Goat."

And then we both laughed. For what seemed like a really long time, and it probably was, but it didn't matter. We didn't get any strange or dirty looks from anyone, like we would back home. And that was good. We were delirious. We were on the brink of insanity from a winning combination of sleep deprivation, crap food, soda withdrawal, and the seemingly endless road we took to get here.

When we regained composure, I went back to looking at *The Rocket* when I noticed an ad. "Hey, bunk muffin, come 'ere."

I pointed at an ad for a place called the Central Tavern. It was hosting a show that night, and the headliners were a band whose name sounded familiar. "Soundgarden. Where have I heard that name before?" I asked.

"I played them on KREB here and there. They're okay. A bit metal for my tastes, but the rest of you guys would probably like them."

"Really?" I asked. "Some band called Nirvana is opening. Sounds like a song title my dad's shitty hippie band would've played."

"Let's go," Gremlin said.

"What?"

"Let's go."

"To the show?"

"Yeah."

"It's twenty-one and over. Look at the ad."

"So?" Gremlin asked.

"I'm not doing it."

ᏋᎠᏋᎠ

"How the hell did you talk me into this?"

Gremlin smiled but didn't respond. We were at the back end of a short line to get into the Central Tavern. It was located in a part of the city called Pioneer Square that was teeming with people walking around. It seemed like everyone here was going to bars, clubs, and restaurants, all of which were housed in older brick buildings. Plenty of cars drove by as well, and all of them were playing different kinds of music. It blended with the sounds of talking and music coming from the establishments to create a noisy, but beautiful mix of sound. Indeed, everyone seemed to be laid back and having a good time, but there were plenty of jock types cruising around. You couldn't miss them. They were the loudmouths who were insulting people as they drove or walked by and were playing the same kind of crap the jocks back home listened to.

Despite the laid-back vibe, I was nervous. Gremlin, however, looked calm.

I leaned in to talk to him. "First, the ad in *The Rocket* said it, and now the sign up there says it: it's a twenty-one and over show. I don't know if I mentioned this earlier, but I don't have a fake ID."

"You didn't say anything. And it's all right. I don't have a fake ID either."

"Then what the hell we doin' here?"

"Maybe they won't check," Gremlin said. "You never know."

"They're gonna check."

"Be cool. They might not check. It's happened before."

"Yeah, right," I sarcastically replied.

When we got to the front of the line, we ran into Mr. Clean. Seriously. The guy blocking the door was kinda muscular, had on a white T-shirt, a bald head, a hoop earring, and even stood with his arms folded just like the dude

on those cleaning products Mom uses. I didn't know if I
should ask for an autograph or break out my driver's license.
But he set the agenda when he asked, "Can I see some ID?"

I froze. *Should I break out my license? Maybe flash it in
front of him real fast and walk in. Keep moving. Try to trick
him. It's the only way, since I'm seventeen.* But Gremlin
broke out his wallet and handed the guy something while I
stood like a totem pole.

The bouncer looked at the card and quickly gave it back
to Gremlin. "This is a college ID. Got anything with your
age on it?"

"It's a college ID. I'm old enough."

"Gimmie some real ID." Then he asked me, "What about
you?"

I was caught but didn't want to admit it. Gremlin butted
in. "Sir, the truth is we're from a college radio station.
KREB-FM. University of Nevada, Las Vegas. We're here
to scout for talent to bring to Las Vegas to play a show at
the student union, and we're thinking about bringing these
two excellent bands to town."

Mr. Clean folded his arms in front of his chest. He
moved to block the way into the club. I was waiting for him
to grab us by our necks, carry us to a garbage can, and toss
us in head first. "Get the out of here," he said.

"You're not going to let us in?" Gremlin asked.

I tapped him on the shoulder. "Dude, forget it."

"No. We need to—"

I yanked Gremlin's jacket, and we stepped out of the line.
I dragged him onto the sidewalk, letting him go just before I
hit a newspaper rack. People walked all around us. Gremlin
turned toward the bouncer and yelled, "You swine! You'll
never get away with this! I'm the program director of this
nation's number one—"

I grabbed Gremlin's jacket by its collar and dragged him
toward me. He stumbled and nearly fell.

"You friggin' idiot," I said. "Quit yellin' at the guy. You're gonna get our asses locked up in a fuckin' mental ward."

Gremlin regained his balance. He shoved my hand away. "That club is engaged in age discrimination. They have no right to keep us out! If I were a lawyer, I'd sue."

"It's a club, you goddamn moron. They serve booze in there. The law lets them do that. And if you were a lawyer, you wouldn't have any damn clients, except for maybe drag queens with bushy Fu Manchus."

"Yeah, well, at least I tried to get in. I didn't just give up like you did."

"Give up?" I yelled. "I don't have a fake ID, remember? And what if you got in, huh? Leave my ass out here? Alone, in some drizzly-ass place where I have no clue where I'm at."

"Oh, relax, will you? What're you complaining about? You have the car keys."

I sighed, took a deep breath to calm down. "So now what?"

Gremlin smirked. "We crash the party."

CHAPTER 41

Last time I was in an alley so dark, damp, and narrow, I saw a drug deal. Life in New York. You saw it, looked away, kept walking, said nothing to nobody, and hoped no one would give you shit for seeing it in the first place. Still, this place seemed a lot less menacing. I didn't even see any garbage. Come to think of it, I hadn't seen any litter anywhere in Seattle. Weird.

But even a clean alley still had a hint of menace, and it was only because of what we were trying to do.

I asked, "You sure about this?"

Gremlin walked with his hands in the pockets of his leather jacket. "I've done it before," he said. "Quite a few shows, actually."

"Sure you have."

"I have."

The back door of The Central was surrounded by brick buildings. Garbage bags were everywhere. Three vans, their back doors open, were parked.

I slapped Gremlin's jacket with the back of my hand. "Can we get busted for doing this?"

He stopped walking. "Worst they can do is throw us out."

"You sure?"

"That's what happened in Vegas whenever I got caught."

"This ain't Vegas."

"Relax, Nick. If we get thrown out, we'll go somewhere else."

"Yeah, like jail."

Gremlin grabbed my jacket. "Look. It's simple. Walk in there and act like you own the place. We get past the door, we're fine. We're in. Got it?"

"Hope you're right."

Long-haired musicians hauled instruments inside a door guarded by a metal gate. A cinderblock held it open. Gremlin whispered, "Okay, just walk in behind those guys. Do *not* hesitate. Got it?" I nodded.

A guy with long, straight black hair and a thick beard carried a guitar case inside. We followed. I was behind Gremlin. We hit dark stairs. We walked up, hearing music and talking.

The club was dark and rectangular, smoky, smelling of cigarettes, cloves, and beer. It had a tall ceiling and brick walls covered with posters. There were a few wooden support beams. The bar was toward the front door. People were everywhere, smoking, talking, smiling, drinking beer and other booze. Some sat at scratched tables. They had long hair, short hair, punker hair. Some wore flannels, others wore leather or jean jackets. Jeans and T-shirts were standard. Sounded like Green River was playing. We shoved our way through the crowd so we could get a decent view of the stage.

"What did I tell you," Gremlin yelled. "We got in, we're fine."

I smiled, nodded, and leaned toward his ear so he could hear me. "All right, all right. Let's not do anything to get anybody suspicious."

"Just avoid the bar."

"You want me to avoid the bar?" I yelled. "Fuckin' Nazi."

It seemed like forever that we waited for the first band. The floor was hard, as if it was concrete. Made my feet hurt.

Wearing steel-toed combat boots didn't help. The first two bands were boring. Would Soundgarden suck? A band that sounded like shit live could you turn you off to them for a long time.

We tried talking between bands, but it was too loud in there to have a conversation. Too many people talking.

Four scruffy-looking dudes took the stage. They wore jeans and had long, straight hair. The bass player, who had long, brown hair and a thick beard, was friggin' tall. Combine that with being on that elevated stage, and the dude looked like an anorexic giant.

The singer played a Fender Mustang guitar, just like mine, only he was left-handed. His guitar was turned upside-down, the way Hendrix played his Stratocasters. The guy had long, straight, greasy-looking blonde hair, had a bunch of holes in his jeans and wore a gray sweater that had moth holes in it. He looked like he was stoned.

"We're Nirvana," he mumbled into the microphone. "This song's called 'About a Girl.'"

He started playing a simple, catchy two-chord progression, the only distortion coming from the amps, not an effects pedal. E minor to G fifth. He played those chords until the other three guys in the band came in. I was amazed that four guys who made me and Donnie and Mullie look like preppies could make such melodic music. And the singer's voice had a rasp and a whine. How he did that was beyond me. Amazing.

Nirvana's music got more aggressive. I tried staying next to Gremlin. Impossible. The club became a mosh pit. It was like being in a full-contact hockey game with too many players on the ice and no one in pads. I moved in whatever direction I was forced to. I kept my forearms in front of my chest and elbows tucked in so I wouldn't get hurt, just like everyone else. I gazed between taller heads and saw people climbing on stage and diving into the crowd. Raised hands pushed them.

The crowd was polite. If someone slammed into me hard, they'd apologize and smile. What was up with that? In Vegas, nobody said they were sorry. They just acted like a bad ass.

The last song Nirvana played was "Negative Creep." Pure distorted aggression. The singer kept screaming lyrics half the time, not even distracted by his long hair getting stuck in the sides of his mouth.

I was covered in sweat, as wet as if I mowed the lawn on a Vegas summer morning. So was everybody else, it seemed. I had on my leather jacket and flannel. It was stuffy in there. When I was shoved near the stage, a guy in jeans, a flannel with long hair stage dived. I put my arms up, got his shoulders, and pushed him away.

Where the hell did Gremlin go? Where was he in this mess? Good thing I had the car keys.

Then Nirvana's set ended. The mosh pit died, and the crowd loudly cheered. Nirvana was intense, full of angst, yet melodic. Wasn't pure punk. Wasn't metal either. Their image would've gotten them labeled stoners at Fremont, but there was something different about them. They were raw, but they showed they could be polished, yet still have an edge. It was what I wanted for the band.

I got shoved from behind. Gremlin yelled, "What did you think?" His face was drenched.

"Dude," I yelled, "That was *intense*."

"You liked it, didn't you?"

"Fuckin' loved it. We gotta work on getting that kinda sound, man. It's perfect for us."

"That's cool with me."

We then traded punches to the shoulder.

A half hour later, Soundgarden came on. The guitar player was the guy we were behind as we snuck in. The singer looked like Jesus. Same long, curly hair and mustache. The bass player looked Chinese. All of them were dressed like they could've easily been in the crowd.

The mosh pit started again. I got shoved into a wooden beam by Gremlin. Wasn't his fault. Pain in my ribs. The mosh pushed me toward the bar.

Somehow, me and Gremlin didn't get separated. Soundgarden was as intense as Nirvana. People stage dived throughout the set. The singer was amazing. Such a powerful voice. It cut through the music and set itself right in your bones.

Toward the end of the night, Soundgarden played "Entering," a song I knew from Gremlin's show on KREB. Me and him were right at the front of the stage when the song started.

"C'mon," Gremlin yelled in my ear, "let's stage dive."

He dragged me by my jacket. Gremlin got up on that stage, at least three-and-a-half feet above the floor. I climbed up too. I stared into the swirling crowd. It looked violent.

Gremlin yelled, "C'mon Nick."

He jumped into the crowd, back first. He was caught in mid-flight. I followed, trusting a bunch of people I didn't know. I saw the black ceiling high above me when I felt hands catch me and pass me along. It was like floating on water. I hoped nobody would steal my wallet.

"Nick," Gremlin yelled. "Is this a fuckin' blast or what?"

I saw right up his kilt. Going commando was not just a song he wrote. Neither was his claim about a three-inch dick. Good to know he wasn't BS-ing about those things I didn't wanna know.

"Yeah, it is," I yelled, but I doubt he heard me. Didn't matter.

The show was incredible, better than any concert I'd seen at the Thomas & Mack Center. There, we were separate from the bands on stage. Here, it seemed like the bands weren't any different than us. And the people at the show weren't any different than us. We weren't treated rude, like we were all over Vegas, even by the few people who looked and dressed like us. The music was the kind of stuff we were starting to play and listen too. It reminded me of New York. And Amanda was going to college here.

Move to LA? Please. My mind was made up. We had to be part of this scene. We were moving to Seattle.

CHAPTER 42

"Hey, Nick, Amanda. What's up?" Donnie looked confused as he let us in the house. "What brings you guys over?"

Normally, he wouldn't ask such a question if I came over. I was confused. "Gremlin told me to come by. Why?"

"Hey, Nick," Mullie called from the kitchen, where he had just grabbed a soda.

Normally, we'd all get together if we were going to jam. It was rare for all of us to hang out just for the sake of hanging out. Mullie was the most withdrawn out of all of us, and he was more of the type to hang out with one person, not a group.

"What're you doin' here?" I asked.

"Same reason as you. Gremlin said to come by. Anybody know why?"

Roxie invited us to sit down, and we did. No one was sure why we were summoned to some sort of meeting.

"You think it's like something out of *The Godfather*?" Mullie asked.

"I don't know," replied Donnie. "Never seen it."

"You've *never* seen *The Godfather*?" Roxie was incredulous. "How can that be?"

I wasn't about to admit that I hadn't seen the entire movie either.

"Never got around to it?" Donnie said defensively.

Suddenly, brakes squealed. A loud, rumbly engine shut off.

"Sounds like a good driver," Mullie deadpanned.

Right at the same time the burning rubber smell hit us, Gremlin burst through the door. He breathed as if he was on the run from some CIA assassins. He slammed the door, even though there was no need to. He stood in place, wearing that damn skirt of his, bouncing up and down, almost like Tigger from *Winnie the Pooh*. He kept raising and lowering his arms, shaking them, like he was a TV preacher healing somebody. Or maybe he was having a seizure?

"Oh! Wow! Oh—man!" he shouted.

Three guys and two girls all asked, "What?" at the same time.

Gremlin then rapidly paced around the living room, shouting exclamations of excitement whenever he could. Then he tried to complete a sentence. "You guys—Wow, man. This is—This is the greatest fuckin' day of my life!"

"That's nice," Mullie said.

"No, you don't get it. This is the greatest night of all our lives!"

I stood up from the couch. "Oh, c'mon, Gremlin. What're you talkin' about? And by the way, it's three o'clock in the afternoon."

Gremlin approached me. He had that same passion and intensity he had the day I found him at the record store, and he was talking about Reagan and the Republicans. "Who cares what time it is? This is the greatest thing ever! I mean, at least for now. Man, I got the greatest news!"

"Then quit stalling and tell us."

Gremlin took a couple of deep breaths to supposedly calm himself down. Talk about milking it. But when he spoke, his voice was hyper and excited. It also climbed half an octave, as if he was at some teenybopper concert.

"I got us a gig in LA!"

CHAPTER 43

We were approaching Victorville doing a hundred miles an hour on the I-15 when the truth shattered the illusion.

"So what club're we playin' at?" Mullie screamed from the back of the Deathmobile, which was crammed full of guitars, drums, amplifiers, and he and Donnie. Mullie had to yell to be heard over the music and the sound of rushing wind, thanks to the windows being rolled down in a failed attempt to keep the interior cool.

"What?" Gremlin asked.

"He asked what club we're playin' at," I yelled.

"Oh, we're not playing a club," Gremlin yelled. "We're playing a gig in a warehouse."

"A warehouse?" Donnie asked.

"A warehouse?" I asked, startled and feeling like we'd been lied to.

"Yeah, a warehouse. It's all right. I know the promoter. We did a couple shows in Orange County when I was in Projectile Vomit. It's how I got us the gig. I just called the dude, told him about us and—"

I interrupted. "Wait a sec. Did you say Orange County?"

"Yeah."

"Are we goin' to LA or Orange County?"

"Huntington Beach."

"That ain't LA."

Gremlin looked at me. "That's very perceptive of you, dumb ass. Huntington Beach is in Orange County."

"What?" Donnie yelled from the back. "We're playin' fuckin' Disneyland?"

Gremlin slowly shook his head. "No, we are not playing fuckin' Disneyland."

Then Mullie yelled, "It's probably Knott's Berry Farm."

Gremlin looked behind him. "Jesus, are you guys that stupid? Neither of those places are in Huntington Beach."

"It's called sarcasm, Gremlin," I yelled. "They're being smart-asses."

Gremlin shut off the radio. "I don't know what you guys are complaining about. Orange County's a good gig. This guy's put on a lot of shows. He knows people."

"Oh yeah," Donnie said. "Name me one band that's come from that area."

Gremlin seemed to scoff at Donnie's question before answering. "You guys really don't know punk do you?" He turned to look behind him while aiming the hearse. "For starters, Suicidal Tendencies and Black Flag are from Orange County. And if I remember correctly, you kind of like Black Flag, don't you, Donnie."

I shoved Gremlin in the shoulder. "C'mon, man. Don't fuck with him, okay? This is all new for us. We ain't been around it the way you have."

Gremlin didn't reply. Just before he turned on the radio again, he said, "Sorry about that." He sounded like he meant it too.

For a second there, I felt shitty about the gig. A warehouse? But if Black Flag and Suicidal Tendencies came out of Orange County, maybe Gremlin knew what he was doing. Maybe he was telling us the truth about this promoter he knew. Not that he'd lied to us. If anything, the only thing he told us that wasn't a truth was that a particular band was good, but one or two or all three of us—being me, Donnie, and Mullie—thought they sucked. But that was just an opinion. That always happened in a band.

After Victorville, we went through the mountains and came out in a flat area filled with high tan grass. The air got cooler and noticeably more humid. We were approaching San Bernardino.

"Ha, ha, ha." A staccato rhythm came from Gremlin's mouth. "You guys ready?"

"For what?" I asked.

"The gridlock. The stuff that legends are born. This is the ultimate driving test, boys." Gremlin stared at a wide expanse of I-15 in front of us with a toothy grin that made his face look every bit as wicked as his adopted name. "Yes, from Berdoo to the coast, this is the test of one's patience."

We hit our first slowdown near an exit for Rancho Cucamonga. Suddenly, we were doing forty-five, and this was at two in the afternoon. I thought it was sort of strange that Gremlin wanted to hit the road so early to get down here for a gig that wouldn't start until nine. Me, Donnie, and Mullie were thinking we could walk around, play tourist a bit.

Traffic slowed even more as we passed more places. Ontario, Norco, Corona, and getting on the Riverside Freeway, heading west. Traffic slowed more when we hit Yorba Linda and Anaheim. Might as well have been driving on The Strip on a Friday night. This was a freeway? We were only going twenty.

But no one complained. We weren't even close to running late for the gig. That and there was too much to see. It was so unlike Vegas, with the hills and signs of grass and trees and feeling like the moisture that was sucked out of your skin by the vampire desert air was being replaced.

"Can you smell that?" Mullie asked. "The air. It smells like the ocean."

"Smells like car exhaust," I said.

"Still. It smells…incredible."

I turned around. "What the hell you talkin' about, Mullie?"

Mullie's face was a mask of wonderment. "This is just so amazing."

"It's a freeway," I said sarcastically. "We got these back in Vegas, remember?"

"Yeah, but I've never been out of Vegas before."

"So how do you know if the air smells like the ocean?" Donnie asked.

"I'm just guessing, that's all."

And right there, Mullie's excitement made sense. And I felt bad that he'd never been off that desert island.

Gremlin was right to have us leave so early. It took us about three hours to go from Vegas to San Bernardino, a distance of over two hundred miles. It took three more hours to go from Berdoo to Huntington Beach, a distance of about forty miles.

We cruised by the beach, parked the Deathmobile, and got out to gaze at the Pacific. An oil refinery was nearby, but that wasn't of interest to us. The water was. All four of us stood in front of the hearse, absorbing the scene, breathing the ocean air, feeling the cool breezes, occasionally checking out some tanned babes in bikinis. The beach was largely empty as the orange sun set in front of us, so I guess we weren't the only ones who thought the late spring air and the ocean breeze was cool. The scene was like something out of one of the best dreams anyone could ever have, and, at that moment, I felt more alive than I had in years, with the exception of the Seattle trip, of course.

"Can you believe it?" Mullie asked. "This beach has sand."

"That's cuz this ain't Boulder Beach and Lake Mead," I replied. "This is the real thing, bro."

"It's gorgeous."

Donnie sighed. "I wish Roxie was here."

"Amanda would love to be here with me right now."

"I hear ya," Gremlin said. "It sure would be nice to have a girl here."

And Mullie never said a thing about wanting a girl with him.

We took turns watching the Deathmobile while another duo went into the ocean. Donnie and Mullie went first. They took off their T-shirts, hi-tops, and socks, threw their wallets and keys onto the hearse hood, and ran to the water. They ran with all the enthusiasm we used to show whenever we went to Boulder Beach or Rogers Spring.

"Donnie ever been to the coast?" Gremlin asked.

"Don't know. Really don't."

"Not something you guys talk about?"

"Never."

Me and Gremlin sat on the hood of the Deathmobile and watched Donnie and Mullie splash each other. They only went in the water partway, but the waves splashed their jeans. They cringed whenever the other one of them would get them wet, or when the ocean hit them. They too were alive. I had seen Donnie act like that before, but not in several years. As for Mullie, his face was gonna be sore tomorrow. I know it was said that it took more muscles to frown than smile, but let's be honest—our frowning muscles were in much better shape, and Mullie was no exception. It might've been the first time I'd ever really seen him smile.

"That's amazing about Mullie," Gremlin said.

I asked him what he meant.

"That he's never been out of Vegas before." Gremlin exhaled and shook his head. "Feel bad for the guy."

I nodded and kept staring at the ocean, suddenly aware that life was now as open as the salt water in front of us, and the setting sun was our lives in Vegas.

"Can I tell you something?" I asked Gremlin.

"Go ahead."

"Never told anybody how I ended up in Vegas."

"Not even Amanda?"

"Nope."

"Go ahead," Gremlin said, staring into the sunset.

"For my seventh birthday, Dad took me to a Mets game. We were watching the game, then the lights went out. Everywhere. The stadium, the dumpy junkyards beyond the outfield, even Manhattan. All of them out. We stuck around until the umps called the game, and everything was still dark. We drove home, and we saw buildings on fire, heard gunshots. Then we got to our neighborhood, and people were breaking windows of stores. Dad always kept a crowbar on the front seat, and he drove the last few blocks holding on to it. We got home and he told me to run inside. He stood out there with the crowbar. When I got inside, Mom hugged me tighter than she ever hugged me. Our apartment was so hot. The fans didn't work, everything was dark. I couldn't even get to sleep that night with the sounds of sirens, the heat, the screaming, the smell of things on fire. Two weeks later, we were here, living in the motel with the glass pool on the Strip, and a coupla weeks after that, we moved into the house I'm in now."

"If I went through anything like that I'd never wanna set foot in that place again," Gremlin said, and, in that moment, so many things in my life made sense. And it raised more questions, but those would be pondered at some point in the future.

Donnie and Mullie came back to the car, both of them shivering, their hair partly wet. While they put on their T-shirts, me and Gremlin took off ours, threw our wallets and keys onto the hood, took off our shoes and socks, and ran like two drunken idiots toward the water. Our feet sank in the warm sand, slowing us, but we still ran fast. I felt my thighs and calves burn and grow tired from exertion. As we hit the ocean, we screamed about how cold the water was, but we kept going, my jeans getting soaked. We ran past the crashing waves, the splash hitting our bare upper bodies, the cold making us yell even more.

"Shit," Gremlin yelled. "I'm getting shrinkage!"

Finally, we dove into a wave, the cool Pacific swallowing our chests, backs, arms and shoulders. We were a good fifty yards out from shore, but our feet still touched the bottom, and our shoulders were out of the water. When the sea was calm, we could see the bottom and the ripples of sand. As we stood, letting the waves hit us, our feet sank into the sand.

Gremlin couldn't take much of it. His kilt drifted up to the surface. He kept fumbling to keep it around his waist, and every time he did, another wave smacked into his back and knocked him forward.

"I gotta go back," he yelled. "My dick's probably shrunk into a clit, and that damn sun's gonna fry me."

"Okay."

But I stayed in the water, body surfing with every wave that came by, some waves bigger and more powerful than others. I couldn't quit smiling. I even smiled when the water hit my lips, and licking them, I tasted the salt. It was like I was back at Coney Island, and I wanted the moment to last forever.

But it couldn't. Donnie, hands cupped around his mouth, yelled at me from the shore. "Nick, we gotta get going!"

I felt like a little kid whose dad was telling him it was time to go home. I felt bummed for a second, until I remembered we were here to play our first gig, and we'd take the stage in just a couple of hours.

Once we got the sand off our feet and got dressed, we went to a nearby In-N-Out Burger to eat something for the first time that day.

After eating our burger and fries, me, Donnie, and Mullie understood all those California wanna-bes at school who wore shirts from this burger joint, even the ones who wore the shirts that said, *In-N-Out Urge*.

All the tension of the drive down there was gone. Being at the beach changed all that.

This was turning out to be a great day, and we figured it would only get better. Gremlin suddenly seemed like a damn genius for getting us this gig. Nothing could spoil what we felt.

Then we got to the warehouse.

CHAPTER 44

What a dump. Graffiti, pallets everywhere. A metal roll-up door was up about halfway. Moths flew around a fluorescent light next to the door. The place reeked of garbage.

Mullie grabbed his bass out of the Deathmobile. "Nice place."

Me and Donnie chuckled sarcastically.

"Smells like Brooklyn," I said.

"It looks and smells like crap, but it's a great place to play," Gremlin replied. "The crowds here are really into it."

"What, garbage?" Donnie asked.

Me and Mullie laughed.

We got our gear and went in. It looked like a place the mafia would hang someone on a meat hook and beat them senseless. Concrete floor and walls looked like tin foil. Fluorescent lights hung from the ceiling. A big black curtain separated backstage from the crowd. Weird-haired musicians were crammed everywhere, tuning guitars, basses, drums, going over set lists.

Gremlin took off to find the promoter. Me, Donnie, and Mullie looked out of place, if only because of our hair and lack of holes in our bodies. None of us had any piercings, and everybody else there did, in the ears, nose, eyelids, lips and who knows where else. And as for the hair, well, Gremlin fit in. At least two other guys, ironically both drummers, had mohawks. A lot of the guys had spiky hair of different lengths. One guy had dreadlocks. And there was not a mustache to be found.

"Think we belong here?" Mullie asked.

"We'll be fine," I replied. "Don't worry about a thing."

A weak attempt at trying to keep him from getting any more anxious, yes, but I had to do it. Hell, *I* was wondering if we fit in. We were outcasts in a room full of outcasts.

Most of the other musicians wore faded, tight, torn jeans; sneakers; and old T-shirts like we did. No one wore a kilt. One stick-thin guy wore a black T-shirt that said *Arthurian Romance Potboiler* on it. What a sight. He had a bunch of braids on his hair, bead bracelets, thick eyeliner, and had on green man-tights. Three other guys also wore green man-tights. Must be in the same band. And I thought the kilt was disturbing.

Gremlin came back a few minutes later. "Hey, guys, we better get loose. We're the first band on."

He handed us fliers used to promote the show. The picture on it was the scene from *Dr. Strangelove* where a guy rode a bomb, waving a cowboy hat, only the smiling face belonged to President Reagan. Underneath, in all caps, the word "Jihad!" was scrawled.

I smiled and chuckled. "Nice. Fuckin' perfect."

Gremlin wore a grin. "Isn't it?"

"I thought Reagan wanted to nuke Commies, not Muslim terrorists?" Mullie asked, gazing at the flier.

"Reagan wants to nuke everybody who doesn't believe in Jesus and capitalism or wants gays dead of AIDS. Surprised we haven't nuked Central America back to the—"

"Let's get ready, guys," I interrupted.

The other three bands on the bill had strange names: Dave's Not Here, Left Turn At Albuquerque, and Arthurian Romance Potboiler, the band with the guys in the green man-tights.

I wondered if everyone else was as excited as I was. I was nervous about one thing—playing drums.

We decided the lyrics to "Going Commando" would have more punch if Gremlin pranced around the stage like Mick Jagger in a knee-length plaid skirt. I agreed to play the simple, fast drum part.

"So how long're we playing?" Donnie asked.

"Twenty minutes," Gremlin replied.

I was shocked. "Twenty minutes? We drove six fuckin' hours to play for twenty minutes?"

Gremlin tuned his snare. "Nick, that's all the material we have. And we're the opening act."

"Think someone's gonna yell 'get the hell off the stage'?" Mullie asked then chuckled.

Donnie laughed. "Oh, like Micah did when Great White opened for Whitesnake?"

"You guys went to see that shit?" Gremlin asked.

Me and Donnie both said, "Yeah."

Gremlin glanced around and whispered, "Well, don't say that too loud around here. This is absolutely *not* that kinda crowd."

Then Mullie asked, "So how much're we getting paid for tonight?"

"Fifty bucks," Gremlin said.

Donnie nodded. "That ain't bad."

"It's for all four of us."

And me, Donnie, and Mullie all yelled, "What?" at the same time.

"We're splitting it four ways."

"Fifty dollars?" I snapped.

"Yeah. Twelve fifty a person. C'mon, that ain't bad for twenty minutes. Takes about four hours at the record store to make that much."

Donnie set his guitar against his amp. "You mean to tell me we came all this way, cramped in the back of that damn hearse, for twelve fifty?"

Mullie sighed. "We're gonna put most of that money into the gas tank to get back home."

Gremlin sat with his jaw open. "What the fuck are you guys complaining about? I've played gigs in Vegas and Phoenix where we were lucky to get anything."

"He's got a point," I said. "My dad's told me a lot of the same stories. Goin' to a gig, gettin' stiffed, runnin' outta gas on the way home, flat broke and having to siphon gas. Besides, guys, what're we in this for anyway? Shit, we're gettin' paid to fuckin' jam."

Donnie and Mullie thought about what I said for a second, then they quietly went back to tuning their instruments and warming up their hands.

While we were getting ready, some guy came up to us and asked what we wanted to hear out of the monitors.

"Monitors?" I asked.

Gremlin stepped in, knowing that if I was left to my ignorance, we'd come across like the total amateurs we were. "Give me the bass feed," he told the guy, "and give the bass player the kick drum. Give the guitarists the standard feed, same for our singer, him."

The guy then walked away. And suddenly, as if he had no clue what he was getting into when he joined up with us, Gremlin came up to me and asked, "You mean to tell me you have no fuckin' clue what a monitor is?"

"No. None of us have," I replied.

He gazed around at the supposedly pro musicians in the room. He took a deep breath and let out a sigh. I thought he was about to pack his shit, get in the hearse, and leave us there while he went back to Vegas. Then he looked at us.

"Monitors are just speakers. They let you hear what everyone else is playing. That guy we just talked to, the sound tech, he mixes it so we can hear just certain things, instead of everything we play."

Me, Donnie, and Mullie were confused as hell. What did this mean? We were barely used to playing together as it was, and now to throw in monitors? So that was what those things were at the front of the stage at all those concerts we went to.

"So what's this mean?"

"Believe it or not, it'll make it easier," Gremlin said.

"You sure about that?" Donnie asked.

"Yeah. Just trust me."

So was he telling the truth or just trying to calm us? We'd soon find out.

A few minutes later we took the stage after setting up our gear. Nobody introduced us. We just walked onto the wooden stage. The place was crowded. People stood around talking to each other. It smelled like regular and clove cigarettes. There were people with mohawks, short spiky hair, dye jobs of all sorts of colors, but few longhairs in the crowd.

"Nice hair, Ronald McDonald," someone yelled.

Someone up front shouted, "Hey, where's your lipstick, pretty boy?"

I plugged in my Mustang, Donnie his Les Paul Junior, Mullie his bass. I hoped those smart-asses weren't getting to the guys. I tried not letting it bother me, but it did. Get teased enough, and every comment became a sword to the heart.

"Oooh, the roadies are gonna play," a voice shouted.

But there was no time to think about the heckling. We had to start playing before me, Donnie, and Mullie got down. I leaned toward the microphone, looking toward the back of the crowd. "We're The Subterraneans, from Las Vegas."

"Play some fuckin' Elvis," someone else yelled. A few people laughed.

We launched into "Fallen," which finally had lyrics. We sounded great, but the crowd was dead. Knew we should've started with a faster song. But one thing was going right. The monitors were helping. I actually could hear myself sing, something I had a hard time doing at every other time

I played in front of people. Things became so much clearer musically.

Luckily our next song was a faster, harder song. It was a new one I wrote about my dad, called "Namesake." I wrote it after the wedding.

And after that song was over, an intense performance, we got polite applause. A lot of people still talked. Most, especially at the front of the stage, stood with their arms folded, nasty looks on their faces. They looked like they wanted to kick our asses. I looked at a skinhead with a safety pin through his nose, and he flipped me off. I was about to give it back to that Nazi punk when I heard Gremlin yelling "Guys, c'mere."

He called us back to the drums. We huddled around him.

"Just ignore these assholes," he said. "Punkers are a bunch of hypocrites. They insist on looking different, but if you look different from them, they give you shit. They hate jocks and preppies, and they're just like them." Then he said, "Besides, people always act like this toward new bands. Let's just have some fun and kick some ass. We'll win 'em over."

We played the rest of our set with intensity and confidence. When I wasn't singing or screaming into the microphone, I gave myself whiplash, thrashing my head violently. It wasn't fake. I just let go, and that's what happened. Mullie at one point even jumped into the crowd and didn't miss a beat. Good thing the stage wasn't very high off the floor. Mullie's bass somehow never got unplugged. The heckling stopped. It was if the crowd saw that our music, our attitude, was honest and from our heart.

Our last song was "Going Commando." After leaning the Mustang against an amp, I sat behind Gremlin's drums, legs cramped because that short fuck kept his stool so low. I shouted the count-off and started in with the beat. After two bars of me kicking the bass drum and slamming the snare, Donnie and Mullie came in with the riff, and Gremlin began singing in that Iron Maiden meets Tom Jones style. And the crowd really came alive then. People moshed, did the pogo.

Near the end of the song, a bare-chested guy with a tall green mohawk jumped on stage, wearing a green tartan kilt, combat boots, holding his T-shirt in one hand. He grabbed the sides of his kilt, faced the audience, and lifted it up. A huge cheer followed. Then the guy turned to me and thrusted, making his dick flop around. Then he jumped back into the crowd. Me and Donnie laughed and somehow kept the song moving. Mullie smiled and nodded slowly. He didn't lose the rhythm. Neither did I—amazing, considering I got a porno dick wiggled at me.

We got a nice ovation when it was over. We won some of the crowd over. No one gave us shit. We quietly tore down our gear and carried it backstage. There wasn't much celebrating. We were tired and drenched after our performance. But I was happy, and I could tell everybody was pleased with how we did. We saw that we were legit as band and that we had a future together.

As we loaded the gear into the Deathmobile, Gremlin went to find the promoter to get our money. Then a bald, middle-aged guy approached me and asked, "Excuse me, can I talk to you for a moment?"

The man handed me a business card with a familiar logo: Geffen Records.

CHAPTER 45

Should I go talk with this guy? Was he really from a label? Should I get the other guys to come with? Were we really that good? No way. Was he for real? The card looked real.

I couldn't stop looking at it. Geffen Records?

"Excuse me," the guy yelled, sounding impatient, "Let's talk. You can look at my card later."

We walked down the alley a few feet while Donnie asked where I was going. "I'll be right back," I yelled.

The record company guy asked me my name. Then we quit walking, and he made his pitch. He began by pretty much forgetting my name. "Let me tell you, kid, you're beautiful. You've got the jawline of Jon Bon Jovi. You've got the looks to be huge. Huge!"

For a second, I wondered if that guy was gay.

"You're a natural on stage. You're…"

I quit listening. I thought about limos and chicks and booze and pot backstage and realized those were all clichés I learned from the bands I used to worship until I changed sects in my religion.

"…we can get you in the studio right away. Maybe I can get you to record a duet with a new pop singer I've discovered. Check her out."

The dude pulled out a picture of a chick who'd be pretty damn hot if her dark hair hadn't been stuck in a light socket. He handed me the picture and kept talking, fast. I gazed at the black and white pic of the singer, who went by the name "Nikki Sugar." Could they have put any more makeup on that broad? Just how many cans of hairspray did they use on her to get her hair to stand up and out that far? The fishnet stockings were all right. She had nice legs. And the leather teddy was pretty nice. Made her tits nice and round.

Then record company dude said, "Kid, she's gonna be the female Richard Marx."

What an insult. Record company guy wants me to duet with her? That was all I needed, to sing on a record my dad would've actually listened to while he cruised the Strip with his trophy wife.

And as that guy kept giving me his spin, I wondered if he was legit. I mean, he came to a punk show at a warehouse in Huntington Beach looking for someone to sing with an electroshock therapy chick? Not only that, he also never talked about anyone else in my band. It was all about me and how he wanted *me* to sound. This wasn't about what kind of music my band wanted to make. The last thing we were gonna do was some bullshit pop record full of lame-ass keyboards.

I had to cut him off to say anything. "So what about my band?"

He stuttered from being interrupted. "Wha—wha what'd you say?

"What about my band?"

"What about them?"

"Ain't you interested in us?"

The guy laughed. "Your bandmates? Gimmie a break. You got a guy who looks like Ichabod Crane meets Ronald McDonald on guitar, a bass player with bad teeth who doesn't know that musicians are supposed to stay on stage, and that midget drummer, good lord, what the hell's the deal with that skirt he wears?"

"So what do you think of Prince?" I asked.

"Prince? He's a musical genius. What's he got to do with anything?"

"Oh, I don't know. I don't exactly think of pouffy shirts with ruffles as being very macho either."

The guy pointed a finger at my chest and leaned in so close to me, I smelled his fishy breath. "Look, kid. Your band isn't very good. In fact, you guys are shit. You want a record deal, either go solo, take advantage of your looks, or your band needs to drop the pretentious name, grow your hair long, get it permed, put on some blush and mascara and start playing pop metal. All the companies are snagging up those bands right now."

"So you're saying we oughta start lookin' like women?"

"Hey, your drummer's already got the wardrobe."

I shook my head, not destroyed by any of his comments, but actually feeling sorry for this loser. He clearly didn't get what we were doing. In fact, it was sort of a compliment. I was proud that we were doing *our* thing, not everybody else's.

Besides, I suddenly thought the guy was a fake. Nothing about him seemed to add up.

But he did piss me off, talking about my friends the way he did. I could've started yelling at him, but figured the fewer words said, the better. I handed him the picture of Nikki Sugar, flicked his card in his face, and said, "Go fuck yourself."

CHAPTER 46

During senior year English, James Janninks's girl-friend, a tall, lean, tanned cheerleader named Tammy, acted like I didn't exist. She never turned my way, even to get out of her chair. Never said a thing to me or Amanda. Not that we cared. It was better to be ignored by someone from the high society than it was to be made fun of. And to think, in freshman year, I had a crush on that bitch.

It wasn't until I saw how stuck-up she was that I got over it. Then Micah got a crush on her, and he got rejected too. Only James shoved him into a locker and laughed about it. Tammy kissed him. Then James spit at me. She kissed him more. I hated her after that.

I never acted on my crush. I always assumed she'd laugh at me since I was a stoner and she came from a family with money to buy her new, fancy mall clothes. Then she got a brand new Acura for Christmas last year. She parked it in the paved parking lot in her own reserved space.

It wasn't until there were just two weeks to go in our sentence that I finally talked to my old crush. And I did it with Amanda sitting right next to me.

With the sound of several conversations from other students filling the room, Tammy sat at her desk and started crying. "I can't believe the best years of our lives are going to be over."

"So kill yourself," I said.

Tammy turned to me. Her jaws were open, tears still coming down her cheeks, smearing makeup she probably spent an hour putting on that morning. Her long, curly brown hair looked frizzy.

"What did you say?"

"Kill yourself. Right after graduation. Why bother goin' on." I heard Amanda chuckling.

"You cannot actually be, like, serious."

"I am, like, serious. You actually believe that high school's the best years of our lives? Please. We can't wear whatever we want. We hafta do whatever we're told to by a teacher or some principal or dean. I'm sorry, but the best years of my life are comin' after me and her and our friends get outta this school and outta this town and outta this state and have control of our lives."

Tammy wiped away a mix of tears and Maybeline from her tanned face and thick, red lips with a handkerchief she pulled out of her purse. Then, she yelled at me. "You are, like, such a negative creep."

I laughed sarcastically. I thought about the song I heard Nirvana play in Seattle. I wondered if that band's singer had this same experience.

"Lemme get this straight. For having an optimistic view of the future, for thinking that things are going to get better after we graduate, I'm a negative creep."

She immediately responded, "Yeah."

"Sure, Tammy. Whatever."

"My boyfriend won't take to kindly to you, like, making me cry."

"I didn't do it, you did it! You started crying. And your boyfriend, he's a little chicken shit wuss. The minute you stand up to him and his stupid-ass jock-itch buddies, they turn and run away." I shut up for a sec, to let my words sink in. "I know, 'cause it's happened. And James knows it."

Since the class bell rang, I turned and faced the chalk-board, where Mrs. Smith told us all about William Faulkner and how his writing so captured the "southern vernacular of the age."

Vernacular? Ain't that a sexually-transmitted disease?

Amanda tried reading the assignment and said it was pretty much unreadable. Then I opened the book and got two words into the first sentence when I agreed. So we didn't finish it. We read the Cliff's Notes instead. Actually, Amanda read them, I glanced at it here and there, just where I thought the answers to the multiple choice questions on the test would be. After all, the secret to school was getting rid of the wrong answers among A, B, C, and D before you filled in the bubble on the test form. Take psychology. In there, I learned that Sigmund Freud devised three parts of the human psyche: The ego, the superego, and the id. That I know. What each of them are and what they represent, I had no fuckin' clue. I just knew that the answer was D, all of the above.

After class was over, Mrs. Smith asked if she could talk to me. What, did she hear what I said to Tammy before class? What was she gonna do, demand I apologize? I wasn't doing that. If anything, she should've apologized to everybody I gave a shit about. Tammy should've apologized just for being herself.

Amanda was with me when I went to talk to Mrs. Smith.

"You have a band, don't you?" the teacher asked.

"Yeah."

"I'm part of the committee that's putting on the senior assembly on Friday. Would your band like to play at the assembly?"

CHAPTER 47

The thing about performing at the senior assembly was you didn't get to see it. "Don't worry about it, you guys aren't missing anything," said a voice who knew from last year, Gremlin. He said he was surprised we were invited. No one asked him to have Projectile Vomit play last year. "A bunch of preppies butchered a couple goddamn Journey songs," he said.

There was some Journey on the list Mrs. Smith gave me that were approved by the administrators. It was a nightmare of top forty radio. It had Mister, Mister; Bon Jovi; Wham!; and the male Nikki Sugar, Richard Marx, on it. There were a lot of forbidden tunes: "Fight For Your Right to Party;" "Cum on Feel the Noize," and everything by Motley Crue and Aerosmith. But there was an out. Like Dad's wedding, the list didn't say we what we *had* to play. It only said what was and was not certified safe.

We decided to play "Bastards of Young" by the Replacements. It was a song about being an income tax deduction after overhearing your dad, year after year, say that if it weren't for you, he'd owe the IRS money. And Gremlin was right, they were the spokesmen of our generation, at least our end of it. The lyrics just didn't seem relevant to the jocks or cheerleaders like Tammy. We also decided to play

"Rise Above" by Black Flag. It was a song that told off people like the jocks.

On the day of the assembly, the four of us, along with Amanda and Roxie, sat against the walls just outside the boys' locker room, waiting for our moment to perform in the basketball gym. The dance team was in there doing a routine to a Janet Jackson song.

Donnie and Mullie sat with their instruments, fiddling with them, getting their hands loose. Our amps were set up in the gym, as was Gremlin's drum kit. Amanda was next to me, hands wrapped around my right arm.

"You nervous?"

"No, actually. What about you guys?"

"I think this is totally cool," Mullie said.

Donnie kissed Roxie on the lips. "After our other two gigs, this is nothing."

Gremlin tapped his drumsticks against his knees. "You guys should be nervous."

"Why?" I asked.

Then he twirled a drum stick. "Because you guys got a lot at stake."

"What?" I asked. "Jocks gonna try and kick our asses for disgracing their sacred little basketball court?"

"The jocks aren't who you have to worry about. It's the administrators."

"Oh c'mon, Gremlin," Donnie said. "What're you talking about?"

"I'm a graduate. There's nothing they can do to me or her," he said, pointing at Joni, his new girlfriend. "But if the Nazis who run this dump don't like the songs we play, they'll ban you guys from the graduation ceremony. Wouldn't surprise me if they tried taking it out on Amanda and Roxie, just for hanging around us."

"Guilt by association," Roxie said.

"You got it," Gremlin replied.

"So what?" I asked.

"This is the kind of fascist tactics public schools do. Make you conform to what they want you to be, not what *you* want to be. School isn't just about trying to educate us, it's about socializing us, trying to get us to conform to society's expectations and norms and mores, to become homogeneous cogs in the national socioeconomic Judeo-Christian military-industrial complex—"

"Geez, bro. Chill out, will ya?" I said.

"Why do you think I didn't wear my kilt, eh? Because these idiots would have a fit if I showed up in what they'd call a skirt, and they'd take it out on you guys."

"I was wondering why you were wearing camouflage pants," Mullie said.

"Well, there you go. There's your answer."

I ran through a pentatonic scale on my Mustang, to warm up my fingers and hands. "Well, I don't care. I ain't afraid of anybody around here. Besides, graduation ceremonies are for parents."

"You don't want to show off to all those morons around here who doubted you that you could actually graduate? You don't wanna be able to rub it in the jocks and cheerleader's faces that you're graduating from the same school they are?"

I quit playing. "Gremlin, I don't need their validation anymore."

Donnie quit tuning a string. "Wow. Never heard you use a word that big before."

I slowly strummed an open G-major chord, letting all six perfectly tuned notes ring out. When the music faded, I smiled and said, "I ain't as dumb as I look, bro."

Amanda kissed my cheek. Then I said, "Besides, Gremlin, playing 'Rise Above,' we're gonna rub it in everybody's face."

Amazing how that drummer understood. His smile told me that.

Then I heard Mr. Markhart's deep voice. "Are you kids ready?"

We got up and began following Mr. Markhart and that's when it hit: This was a huge crowd. The entire senior class was packed onto one side of the gym. Six hundred students! It looked like a packed arena. I stopped walking and scanned the scene. Then I got nervous.

"Holy shit," Mullie whispered.

Gremlin's hand slammed down on my left shoulder. "Come on, guys. This is no time to be afraid. This is your moment."

How the hell did Gremlin know what to say at just the right time? I grinned and started walking again, Amanda holding my right arm. I walked faster and passed Gremlin and Donnie. It was my band. I figured I oughta lead them to the stage.

I plugged into my amp and turned it on. We set the levels before the assembly. Me and Donnie even put new batteries in our distortion pedals, just to be certain they wouldn't cut out on us in the middle of this gig. Amanda and Roxie leaned against the back of the amps. Mrs. Smith introduced us as The Subterraneans and told our classmates who we were.

No heckling from the jocks, and only a few scattered claps here and there as our lives of relative anonymity were about to end in a noisy, distorted way.

I counted to four and Donnie started in with the opening distorted riff. There were random cheers throughout the crowd. Then the rest of us came in.

We sounded great. In tune, in time with each other. I fed off Donnie's, Mullie's, and Gremlin's playing. I also fed off the vibe I picked up from some of the kids. Those who knew the song bobbed their heads, moved to the beat. I didn't look at anyone in particular. No one looked familiar, even though I saw people I knew. I thought of them not as individuals, just a group. I looked through them, not at them. I sang with a passion and intensity I hadn't done before. And I was perfecting the raspy vocal sound I wanted so badly, singing about how we were the sons of no one, the bastards of young.

The chorus was what concerned Gremlin. He thought it would give them a reason to stop us. Not that bastards was a bad word, but I didn't exactly think it was a word on the overlord-approved list. I expected someone to pull the plug on us. In a way, I wanted them to. But we were allowed to continue through another verse and another round on the chorus.

After one more go-round on the chorus, we came to the end of the song, where the structure broke down, and the playing was free of time signature and structure. I knew we nailed it. Not just the song, but our needed venting. I knew it was our best performance. I wanted to keep playing, turn this one-off show into a full-blown set. But there were speeches and other, more boring crap still on the program.

Then we stopped playing. I breathed like I sprinted down an alley. There was some, but not a lot of loud cheering. There was some fist pumping and bullshit polite applause from the bored. No surprise. Looking through the crowd, I saw who did what. The kids who were dressed grubbier or had longer or punker hair got it. The ones who didn't get it were easy to spot. They were the clones who bought into the Huey Lewis philosophy that it was "Hip to be Square," people like the jocks and Tammy.

After four years of them trying to make their point with us, conform to their norms, we gave part of our side of the story, but hardly anyone understood where we were coming from.

Then Gremlin started in with the drumbeat of "Rise Above," just as we planned. But when me and Donnie were supposed to come in with our guitar parts, we heard nothing. The jocks starting heckling us. Mrs. Smith ran toward us, and she looked worried.

CHAPTER 48

The door opened, and Dad said, "Hi, Barbara."

Of all the times and places for my parents to be in the same room together, why did it have to be the principal's office? Especially under these circumstances.

I didn't look at my parents. I sat next to Amanda and Donnie. Mullie and Roxie were also seated. Besides, the office was crowded. Mullie's mom was also there. It was clear where Mullie got his looks from—he looked like a male version of her. Same dark eyes, same sharp jaw, same tiny, rounded nose. Gremlin was there, as was Lilly. And now my mom and Rick crammed into whatever space was left in the office.

The room was so stuffed with bodies that it got hot in there, even with the AC going full blast. The air also felt humid, like a Brooklyn summer, thanks to everybody's breath.

"Hi, Nick," Mom said to my dad coldly. "Who's that?"

"That's my wife, Lilly."

Lilly said it was nice to meet Mom, but Mom couldn't seem to get past how young Lilly was. "That's your new *wife*?"

"Yeah, Barbara," Dad snapped. "That's my new wife."

I yelled, "Don't get into a damn argument, all right?"

Amanda hugged me. She knew I was in a rotten mood.

Last thing I needed was my parents fighting in the principal's office in front of all my friends.

The door opened again and in walked the school's very own Benito Mussolini. The principal excused himself, and everyone shuffled to let him walk through us and toward his huge desk. He got behind it but didn't sit down. Instead, he stood, leaning against the desk, probably trying to intimidate us. Didn't work. A short man, he had a gray comb-over, glasses, a brown suit and tie, and a sagging face. He reminded me of someone who'd send money to a TV preacher or vote for Ronald Reagan. Probably both.

This was the last step in trying to get us back in to graduation, not that I cared. I really didn't. But Amanda wanted me in the ceremony with her, and I knew my parents wanted me to take part. I'd do it for them. Especially after all the trouble they went to. Even Amanda's and Roxie's parents wrote letters to the papers, the school board, and principal Leonard. They called his office and talked to him. Finally, they demanded this conference.

He said in a deep voice, "What can I do for you?"

Dad spoke first, "I'd like to know why the fuck my son's banned from his graduation ceremony?"

Mom butted in. "Oh, that's really good, Nick. That kind of talk will get them to let Nicky back in the ceremony."

I put my hand into my face. When would they start calling me Nick, like everybody else in the damn world?

"Well, I can certainly see where this young man learned his ruffian behavior," Principal Leonard said before Dad could tell Mom off. All of us who were seated, meanwhile, looked at each other wondering what the hell the principal meant by ruffian. "Sir, this school and school district has rules, and what those three boys did at the senior assembly violated those rules."

"What rules?" I asked.

"The rules this school has against profanity," the principal said. "You sang an obscene song at an official school function."

"It's not an obscene song," Donnie said. "The album doesn't even have one of those warning stickers on it."

"It has the words 'bastards' in it," the principal coldly replied.

Gremlin laughed loudly. "Oh, c'mon. They can even say that on TV, and we couldn't play a song with that in the title?"

Gremlin wore his kilt and Minor Threat T-shirt. The principal stared at him for a long time before asking, "Excuse me, but who are you, anyway?"

"I'm this band's drummer and this guy's roommate," Gremlin patted Donnie on the shoulder. "You could say I'm his guardian, if that makes you feel better."

"You're his guardian?" There was no emotion in the principal's voice.

"Yes, I am. He got kicked out of his house, and if he wasn't staying with me, he'd be homeless and would've dropped out, even though he was so close to graduating. And this young man—"

The principal interrupted and slowly asked, "Why are you wearing that...thing?"

"Why are you wearing that thing?" Gremlin replied.

"Excuse me?"

"That hideous brown suit. I got news for you pal, Nixon resigned."

Everybody in the office, except for the principal, chuckled.

"That's enough!" the principal yelled, and everybody went quiet. "I think all of you should understand that this incident has generated a lot of unfavorable publicity toward this school. This school is one of the finest—"

Dad interrupted. "That's 'cause you're censoring freedom of speech."

Then Rick said, "Yeah. You ever heard of the First Amendment of the Constitution?"

"Sir, please speak to me respectfully."

"I would if you were being fair to these kids," Rick replied.

I wanted to mention about how "fairly" I was treated after the jocks jumped me in January, but I knew there were battles to fight and not to fight. This was one not worth fighting. I'd let everybody else state our case for us. Maybe he'd take parents and step-parents seriously. But I was also surprised at Rick. All the times he yelled at me for whatever it seemed like he wanted, and in this situation, he was on my side? Suddenly, I had a new reason to do whatever would be needed in order to get us reinstated. I also forgave Rick for his country music tapes, the way he talked about blacks and Mexicans, and forever yelling at me in the first place. Teamster truck drivers seemed a lot cooler at that point. Maybe there was more to him than I ever gave him credit for.

Mullie's mom calmly said, "Sir, my son showed me the list of songs his band was given to play. Nowhere on there did it say they couldn't play the song they chose." She handed the principal the list. "Take a look. It says what songs are approved and what songs are not allowed, and that song is nowhere on there. Nowhere on this list does it say they have to *only* play an approved song."

That's what we said, but we got ignored. It was why Dad called the media. Everyone knew we were getting screwed for having balls.

"Sir," Lilly said. "With all due respect, what you're doing to these boys is unfair. They clearly didn't violate any rules the school set out. And I agree that 'bastards' is not profanity. There's no good reason to keep these boys out of—"

Then Mom interrupted. "We are prepared to get a lawyer to help get our sons reinstated."

That was a surprise. I didn't think they'd go that far. Where would they get the money? Was Mom telling the truth or did Lilly surprise her? Was her claim legit or just another shot in her and Dad's ongoing game of one-upmanship?

"Sir," Mom calmly said, "These boys didn't mean any disrespect. They wanted to express themselves and did so the best way they could. Can't we just get this over with? The boys are sorry."

Maybe Donnie and Mullie were, but I wasn't. I really felt like we didn't do anything wrong. Hell, we *didn't* do anything wrong.

Principal Leonard appeared to be thinking about what everyone said. Then he asked, "Are you boys sorry for what you did?"

We looked at each other, and the silence told me no one felt bad for playing that song.

"I'm sorry," Mullie said convincingly.

"Me too, sir," added Donnie. "I'm sorry."

I looked into Principal Leonard's glasses and wanted to tell him no. I had to balance the anger I felt toward the principal, the jocks, and the school with the desire to not let my family or friends or Amanda down. If I didn't suck it up and give him what he wanted, that asshole might keep Donnie and Mullie out of the ceremony.

"Yeah, I'm sorry too."

Best acting I ever did.

CHAPTER 49

Amanda's house was the gathering place for graduation, at least for some of us. Gremlin and Donnie were at Roxie's. Mullie was with his mom and other relatives, including his long-gone father, at his place. My parents and stepparents were downstairs talking with Thomas and Vera. I could imagine the conversation that was taking place. *Wonder how Dad and Lilly would explain her job? Wonder if Jimmy's getting a little-boy crush on Lilly? Especially with the tight, short green dress she's wearing that has a very revealing V-neck.*

I was in the upstairs bathroom changing into clothes my parents bought me for the ceremony. They got me gray slacks, a pink dress shirt, and dark blue gargoyle socks. Amanda said they were called argyle socks. Whatever. Mom and Dad even got me a pink clip-on tie. Button all the buttons, clip on the noose, and presto! Instant sell out. Join Huey Lewis in the corporate board room. And the shoes, oh, man. They were shiny black lace-up dress shoes that were pointed in the front. They looked like the roach killers the Puerto Rican kids in Brooklyn used to wear.

Those clothes did not match the brown cap and gown I had to wear.

And that was a bone I had to pick. Why did both of Fremont's ugly school colors have to be in our graduation outfits? Couldn't we all wear one color, like black or something? Why did the guys have to wear brown caps and gowns and the chicks yellow ones?

Our school colors always made me think of sitting on the toilet.

Amanda waited for me in her room. She was already in her dress for the ceremony, a black and white one that buttoned up the front and went down to her knees. She had her hair curled, and just the right amount of makeup on. She was gorgeous. And I wanted to run my hand up her thigh and under that dress.

Amanda knocked on the bathroom door.

"Yeah," I said.

She walked in, put her chin on my shoulder and her arms around my waist. She smiled. "You look handsome."

I clipped on the tie. "I look like a goddamn preppie."

"There's nothing wrong with looking respectable every once in a while."

"Yeah, yeah, yeah," I said, wanting to change the topic. "Hey, guess what? I'm livin' up to one of our song titles."

"What do you mean?"

"I'm going commando."

Amanda smiled, but it was an amazed kind of grin, not a sly one. "You're kidding."

My poker face was improving. "No, I'm not."

"You're really gonna walk through the ceremony that way?"

I kissed Amanda's cheek. "Yeah. And Gremlin's wearing his kilt, in his usual way, of course."

She chuckled. "Do you really think Donnie and Mullie are going to do the same thing?"

"Well, we all said we were gonna go commando, but I ain't checkin'." I pointed at her and smiled. "Neither are you."

"Bummer." She giggled, and I gave her a fake dirty look.

I looked in the mirror and said, "This outfit's awful."

She patted my shoulder, left the bathroom, and returned with two gift-wrapped boxes. "I got you some presents," she said. "You get to unwrap a couple of others later tonight." We kissed and heard laughter downstairs.

I smiled. "I get to unwrap the other ones at Lone Mountain?"

"Maybe." Then she winked.

Amanda handed me a box. I unwrapped it and inside was a stylish long-sleeved black dress shirt and black and silver tie. Compared to what mom and dad got me, this was a lot more stylish. Granted, I hate wearing collared shirts, but still.

"Oh thank you so much, sweetie," I was happy to see I wouldn't have to wear something so ugly. "I'm putting this on right away."

"And don't worry about tying the tie," Amanda said. "I'll do it for you. I have to do it for Jimmy every Sunday before Mass. But before you do that, open this one."

I opened the other box and pulled out a new Ramones T-shirt, the exact same one I just changed out of a few minutes ago.

"Before you say anything, I know you have that shirt. I just wanted you to see that I got one too."

"You like the Ramones?"

"Being around you guys, I've really gotten to like them. They rock."

We kissed again. "I love you so much," I said.

"I love you too."

Amanda and her family went to graduation in the minivan. I rode to the ceremony with my parents and step-parents in Dad's Caddy. I was in the backseat between Mom and Lilly, and Rick was up front with Dad. The top was up, even though it was sunny. Thank goodness for air conditioning. It was a hundred and two that day, and if we rode with the top down, my hair would've been a wind-blown mess, and I would've sweat through my sellout outfit.

Get this: Mom and Dad both said they liked what Amanda got me better than the shirt and clip-on tie they got. Not that I was worried they'd get pissed at me or anything like that.

As we pulled out of the driveway, I thought about who I was riding with. Both my parents were still in their mid-thirties. Lilly was twenty-two. Four years ago, she was going through one of these. Meanwhile, Rick was ten years older than Mom.

So here I was riding in the back of my Dad's car next to my hot-ass stepmom, who was closer to my age than my dad's age, and who was young enough to be my stepfather's daughter. None of us looked like we belonged together. Rick wore a tan, long-sleeved dress shirt, bolo tie, jeans, and cowboy boots. Dad was once again dressed like a *Miami Vice* reject. Mom was in a white short-sleeved top and black knee-length skirt, and we all knew what Lilly was wearing. She looked like a hottie out of a video. I kept sneaking peeks at Lilly's legs. Goddamn, I wanted to cop a feel. This was fuckin' torture.

"Are you excited?" Mom asked,

I think you know what I was thinking, and wanted to say, but I knew what Mom was talking about. I played it straight. "Not really," I said.

"Are you nervous?" Lilly asked.

I shook my head. "Actually, no. Just wanna get this over with."

Mom chuckled. "You just want to hang out with your friends, don't you?"

I nodded.

Lilly jumped in. "Of course he does. That's all I wanted to do at my graduation."

"Me too," Mom said. "His father was the same way." She kissed my cheek. "I'm so proud of you." She hugged me. "I know I haven't said that enough, but you've really accomplished something big."

"Oh c'mon, Mom. They let everybody graduate."

"Nicky," Mom said, "With what you've been through this year, sometimes I'm amazed you're still alive."

I sighed. "Mom, don't call me Nicky. I *hate* that name."

Lilly shoved me. "That's your mother. She can call you whatever she wants."

Mom laughed. "Thank you, Lilly. He's been saying that since he was twelve."

"Yeah, but I've felt that way since I was six. I don't like it, all right?"

"Your dad's always going to be Nick, and you will always be Nicky to your parents," Lilly said. "There's nothing you can do about it."

"Well, what're you gonna call me?"

"Nicky."

"Damn you."

I was not going to win. Besides, I didn't want Mom getting all mushy about all the shit that happened. For me, graduation was not about looking back. It was the end and a new start. It was the death of Nicky, the end of that childish mentality, the meek kid who didn't stand up for himself enough, who let others walk all over him. This would be the true birth of Nick, a guy with balls, who would do his own thing, no matter what anybody else thought. He would be the guy who'd stick to what and who he believed in, no matter what.

When we got to the Convention Center, I tried getting away quickly so I could meet up with everybody, but Dad insisted on a hug. He grabbed me and held on for a long time, all while starting to cry. He told me he loved me and that he was so proud of me. I hugged him back. It just took me a while to do it. I didn't like hugging guys. I just wanted to get inside the Convention Center. It was too damn hot outside.

Rick kept things short. We shook hands. He looked me in the eye. "Congratulations, Nick."

I liked the way he did it. It was unsentimental on a day overflowing with gushy sentiment, something I was in no mood for. And he didn't call me Nicky. Bonus points for him.

But once I was inside the Convention Center with Amanda, Roxie, Donnie, and Mullie, we learned we couldn't sit together. We had to sit in alphabetical order, guys on one side of the aisle, girls on the other. What a pisser.

The ceremony was boring. We got to sit in uncomfortable folding chairs with some padding on it, listening to speeches from valedictorians, salutatorians, and Principal Leonard. There was also a politician or something like that, and listening to the school choir for what seemed like two hours. The choir even sang that "Time of my life" song from the movie *Dirty Dancing. Zzzzzzz.*

I just wanted to walk across the stage and get the hell out of there. I didn't wanna hear about our great accomplishment, the good times, the teachers, how much of a treasure we were to the community, and all that. And I really didn't believe that community treasure bullshit. Maybe most of my fellow graduates, but certainly not me.

Then, finally, us graduates got to walk across the stage and get our diplomas. One by one names were called, most unfamiliar, some recognizable, all to a steady strobe-like blast of flash bulbs. One-by-one, my friends' names were called, and they walked across the stage. The cheers of their families, and in Donnie's case, everybody else's families, could easily be heard. I cheered loudly as each of their names were announced.

"Amanda Bennett."

"Donald Clark."

"Roxanne Desiano."

"Michael Edwards-Mullin."

Then it was time for my row to go to the stage. The line seemed to move like an airport check-in counter. It gave me time to think. Think about everything that had gone on, good and bad and about what was next. One's true life accomplishments were not based on what was done in high school, but afterward.

My chance, Donnie's chance, Mullie's chance for redemption was coming. And I decided to never attend a Fremont High School Class of 1988 reunion.

Just before I walked across the stage. I looked to the roof, kissed my hand, and pointed skyward. It was my salute to Micah. I told him I loved him, although no one heard me since I didn't say anything. Then, just before my name was announced, I lowered my head and raised my right fist skyward. It was my salute to Chris "Scuzz" Scozzoli. I wished both he and Micah Knowles could be there, but it seemed like they had to be sacrificed for a reason. Me and Donnie had to learn from their mistakes in order to move forward in our lives, as painful as it was losing both of them in such a short period of time.

Then my name was called.

"Nick Karenka."

I walked to the center of the stage, got a handshake from Principal Leonard, who handed me what I thought was my diploma. His facial expression never changed. It was as if he didn't notice who I was. But I knew who he was. I stared into his four eyes and realized that this moment was my revenge. Maybe Mom was right. Maybe I had accomplished something special.

So I immediately opened up what I thought was my diploma. Inside was a certificate that said, "Congratulations, Graduate! You will receive your diploma in the mail within one to two weeks. Congratulations and good luck! Las Vegas Public Schools."

What a pisser. I thought I'd actually be walking out of there with that piece of paper. Instead, the damn thing was probably gonna arrive the same day as my car insurance bill. What a bullshit "right" of passage.

I walked off the stage arm-in-arm with some girl. I looked for my parents or Amanda's family and didn't see them, but I heard Dad. He shouted "Nicky" so damn loud. How embarrassing. Didn't he hear *my* name called?

I saw Jeff Day seated at the end of a row. I wanted to give him the finger. That was something Nicky would've done. Instead, I gave him the same icy glare I gave the principal. Jeff looked pissed, but there was nothing he could do about it. He was graduating from the same high school as me. He may have been heading to BYU on a football scholarship and I to Seattle to pursue music, but graduation proved that in the end, we were all equal. With that, I knew I had to let all my hatred toward him go. I assumed I'd never see him, Owen, James, or Tammy again.

Goodbye, good luck, good riddance.

When I got back to my aisle, I finally saw someone I recognized in the stands. In the front row was Gremlin. He had on that kilt and a Sex Pistols T-shirt, gave me a standing ovation and screamed as loud as he could.

Gremlin made the heavy metal devil horns sign and screamed, "I'm going commando!"

I was gonna yell back, "I'm runnin' free!" but he made me laugh. It was hard to imagine that a year ago, Gremlin, then known as Steve Portman, walked down this same aisle in a brown cap and gown, as a new Fremont High School graduate, just like everyone else in and around the band.

EPILOGUE

The view from Lone Mountain seemed brighter. Maybe it was because the darkness of growing up in Vegas was gone. The mid-September sun was down, but it was still over a hundred degrees. But the dry heat didn't matter. It was our last night in hell.

The band, Amanda, and Roxie sat on the tailgates of Donnie's truck and the Deathmobile. Mullie spent the whole summer showing no interest in getting a girlfriend or even getting laid. He sat on the Deathmobile's tailgate with Gremlin, who spent the whole summer trying to get laid, and maybe even a girlfriend, and getting more rejections than our demo tape.

Me and Amanda and Donnie and Roxie sat on the tailgate of the truck. Amanda sat in front of me, and I had my arms wrapped around her waist, my now stubbly cheek lightly touching hers.

In the morning, we'd leave for Seattle, where Amanda and Roxie were beginning their freshman year at the University of Washington as dorm roommates. They had no clue what they were gonna major in.

The Duster was gone. So was Mullie's Firebird. And those were two of the most painful decisions we ever had to do. We needed more gear for the gigs we played around Vegas and Southern California. Dad told us we'd need backup instruments in case a string broke during a song or the neck broke on the way to a show. Some of the cash helped get Donnie a new guitar, a funny-looking thing called a Humming Bird, made by some company called To-kai. The guitar was black and white and looked like something Johnny Ramone played, which was why Donnie bought it. Mullie got a beat-up faded red Fender Jazz Bass. It sounded great, stayed in tune, and became his main instrument.

I got another guitar and made the Mustang a backup since I couldn't keep the thing in tune. I got some weird sounds out of it, but it was damn annoying to always have to retune a string. So just after my eighteenth birthday in July, I went to a pawn shop and picked up a light blue Fender Jaguar. Like Donnie's Humming Bird, my Jaguar had a serious retro thing going on. But it was cheap and made a hell of a lot of noise when run through a distortion pedal.

"First, you buy a Mustang and now a Jaguar," Amanda said that day as we rode back from the pawn shop in the sauna-like Deathmobile with Gremlin. "Are those the cars you're gonna get when you guys are rich and famous?"

Me and Gremlin laughed. Then I replied, "I don't know about the Jaguar, but a Mustang, hell yeah. I'd love to get a 'sixty-nine with all the Shelby shit under the hood."

Then Gremlin added, "C'mon, Nick, get a brown 'seventy-four Mustang Two."

"Fuck that. That's what we had in Brooklyn. Thing was a piece of shit from the day Mom and Dad bought it. Dad said the only difference between that and a Pinto was that the Mustang didn't blow up if you kicked the rear bumper. Thing was always in the shop. That's why Dad always said Ford stood for 'Found On Road Dead.'"

"I thought it stood for 'Fix Or Repair Daily,'" Gremlin said, and we laughed.

Our look changed. Gremlin still looked like Gremlin, but Mullie grew his hair out. I did too, but unlike Mullie, I stopped getting my bangs trimmed. They were down to my lips, almost as long as it was in the back. But Donnie really changed. Tired of the Ronald McDonald wisecracks at every gig, Donnie showed up at the record store one day with short, spiky hair. Didn't even look like him. But it looked better. Roxie loved it. *That* surprised me. Hell, it surprised Donnie. He thought for sure she had some sort of Sampson complex and would dump his ass for getting sheared.

As for the music, I didn't know which way to go. I changed the lyrics to "Fallen" and "Namesake" and "Jock Itch" so much, it was like performing a new song every time we got together. Part of the problem was that, even though I took Gremlin's advice and poured my feelings into the lyrics, I thought each new set was like something out of an English class assignment, or worse, whining. Last thing I wanted was to be a damn crybaby. There had to be a way to express those emotions without giving birth to complaint rock.

The lyrics to "Marie Antoinette" were expanded upon, and the song had a variety of new titles, from "Ex" to "Ex-bitch" to "Now she's a bitch" to whatever else came into my head at the moment. "Going Commando" became a crowd favorite, the song we opened with, since it always got 'em going. And after a while, that song was my anthem too. Yes, I was running free. It was pretty convenient whenever me and Amanda wanted to have a quickie.

Me and Gremlin wrote some goofy lyrics. We wrote a song that probably every band had written at one time or another: "Let's get drunk." Then there were the words Gremlin said he started writing at the Jaycee State Fair one year, inspired by the surroundings. His song told the story about a guy getting all horny over the way a girl ate a corn dog, and how their love blossomed on the Tilt-A-Whirl before having a romp in a single-wide. When it was finished, it was called "White Trash Love Affair." Scary thing was, if it weren't for Amanda, that song might've been about me.

So two things happened with the lyrics. One set was deep and emotional and purged the pain, and the other set was goofy and retarded and hid the pain.

Mom and Dad wanted to send me to a counselor to deal with everything. I told them to forget it. Music was better.

The songs were largely the same. As we had talked about, guitar solos were gone, and Donnie was instead helping to put together guitar parts that weren't just parroting what I did. We began messing with guitar-led instrumental breaks, but now it was more about feedback and noise than playing every note imaginable at warp speed. And Donnie was actually pretty good at it. He really enjoyed those noisy interludes.

"It's like when I first got a guitar," he once told me.

Serving the song became our priority, being more like a group than letting our talent demand attention. Instead, we structured our songs so we could let our talent show as a group. That was what happened when you stayed up to four in the morning listening to old The Who albums.

Even then, I still tried coming up with chunky riffs. Even though I embraced punk and even some of what was now being called "classic rock," I still loved metal. I still listened to Maiden, Priest, Sabbath, Metallica, Megadeth, and Anthrax.

You can dye your hair any color you want, but the roots are eventually gonna show.

I even tried getting Gremlin into real metal. Metallica and Anthrax he sorta liked. Same for Guns 'n' Roses. Sabbath, forget it. Ditto AC/DC, although Gremlin loved their song "Big Balls." We sped it up and added it to our goofy set list.

Chris got twenty-five years. Bunch of crap. Too long a sentence. We urged him to appeal, but he was eligible for parole in ten, and he was resigned to take his chances. His defeated attitude made me wonder if he'd make it long enough to be eligible for parole, never mind the full sentence. He was sentenced to the state pen at Indian Springs, thirty miles north of town on the US-95 toward Reno. All four of us in the band went to visit him. I went every week. It provided inspiration for a song that I hadn't mentioned to anybody that I was working on—something about how the system was bullshit and full of cronyism. I tried writing the same kind of song only about our principal. I scribbled and scratched out lyrics and recorded riffs and rhythms on a portable tape player. And no matter how often I tried, I wasn't getting what I wanted to say in the way I wanted to say it. I also knew that I had to mention that we were taught lies in school about the way the system worked.

I didn't have a chip on my shoulder, I had a bag of them.

I told Chris to look me up in Seattle when he got out. A touring band needed a roadie. Everybody deserved a second chance. Too bad that second chance might have to wait until 2013. Then I thought about how damn far off that sounded. I remember that *movie 2001: A Space Odyssey.* That was the year, according to that movie, that we were supposed to have talking computers, a manned mission to Jupiter, and bases on the moon. And Chris would be getting out twelve *years* past that date. Jesus fuckin' Christ.

Yesterday was my last visit to see Chris. He had been in Indian Springs only a week when I drove up. The entire band and the girls drove up yesterday to meet with him one last time before we left. It was like a funeral procession— a series of mourners passing by the open coffin of the not-quite deceased.

He wasn't expecting me but was happy to get a visitor. "It'll probably be my last for years," he said.

"I'll visit every time we come back."

"And when will you come back?"

And I fell into a melancholic silence.

"Seriously, you think you'll be coming home for Christmas this year? Or any year?"

There was sadness and bitterness in his voice, and I couldn't blame him. But I didn't know how to console him. He was right. We wouldn't be back anytime soon. If we had car trouble on the way, it was conceivable we could end up being the entire rock scene in some backwater redneck shithole like Red Bluff, California. No gigs at the Central Tavern in Pioneer Square, no possible job at *The Rocket*, just stuck in Nowheresville,

❧

So here I was making all these plans for a ridiculously far off date when we'd be as old as our parents, and we didn't have shit. We were going to a strange city, and we really had no prospects. No record deal. No jobs. No connections within the music scene, the job market, or even a place to live. Four of us had made brief visits to the city, and Donnie and Mullie had no idea of what Seattle even looked like, aside from a few pictures from books Roxie borrowed from the neighborhood public library.

We had no idea of what was a good or bad neighborhood, how much rent would be, or even if we could find an affordable, but decent, place to rent. And where would we rehearse? I heard plenty of times that what we were doing was crazy. My parents would be so worried about me, and I guessed I couldn't blame them. I mean, no decent parent wanted their son to be homeless and unemployed.

But we believed in ourselves, believed in what we were doing, believed that it would somehow work out—and we're crazy enough to actually try it.

The plan was to take the truck and Deathmobile to Seattle, both loaded with all our gear, clothes, albums, tapes, and my dog, Boss, who had now taken on the role of band mascot. He even appeared in the group photos Amanda took of us. I wanted to take him along to gigs, but Amanda and Roxie talked me out of it. No point in making my little buddy deaf.

We planned to sell Donnie's Baja once we got there, and hoped we could live off that money until we could either get gigs or day jobs in record stores or both. We'd have one car—a hearse with *Deathmobile* spray-painted on the sides. As for Roxie and Amanda, Roxie had a car—a black late-model Ford Thunderbird, easily the nicest ride out of all of us—and they'd be riding up in it, with all their stuff shoved inside.

I was gonna try getting a job at that music newspaper, *The Rocket*. As for going to a community college, well, that had to wait at least a year.

But on our last night in the desert, with no music coming from either car, not everything revolved around moving to the northwest.

"Hey, Nick," Mullie asked. "You think War's gonna try out for the SEALs again?"

"Says he's gonna. I think he's insane if he does."

"What happened to him again?" Mullie asked.

"He was doin' the deep water swim, dove to about fifty feet, I think, and he blacked out. Had to be rescued and given CPR. They didn't find anything wrong with him, so he can try out again if he wants."

"Why does it seem like he has a death wish?" Donnie asked.

"Shit, I don't know."

"So what's he doing now?" Roxie asked.

"Got a letter from him yesterday. He said he's working as a hospital corpsman on base." I then told them the story he wrote about in the letter. It involved a female recruit, an enema, and a bedpan. It couldn't be true, I thought, but it was a hell of a story. When I was finished, the guys laughed like crazy, and the girls groaned about how "gross" the story was.

After the laughs died, Gremlin said, "Hey, maybe when he gets out of the navy we can make him a roadie."

"Yeah, really. Can you imagine that?" I asked. "I don't even wanna think about what he'd try on any of the groupies Mullie's gonna get."

Mullie smiled and shook his head. "I don't think so, guys."

And we just let that topic go.

For a while, everyone gazed at the lights, thinking their own thoughts.

This was the end. The end of ten years in the desert, hating every moment of it, longing to be back in New York or living in LA.

"You guys wanna hear something pretty weird?" I asked. "All of a sudden, I don't hate this place anymore."

Amanda turned around. "Wow. That's quite a change. What happened?"

I kissed her forehead. "Well, as much as things did suck, with Chris and Micah and the jocks and all the bullshit at Fremont, if I wasn't here, I never would've met any of you. Now I can't imagine my life without you. All of you."

Amanda smiled, then gave me a long, warm kiss.

But there was more to it than that. What I really wanted to say was that this place shaped who I was at that moment. It shaped my view of things, gave me a new appreciation for things I never even cared about before. I now found the barren desert to be beautiful in its own way. I even liked the dry climate, as long as it was below ninety degrees or after sundown. But somehow, instead, the other, far more mushy stuff—the stuff I really didn't want to reveal—came out. And now I was afraid to reveal how I felt about Vegas.

"You're so sweet, Nick," Roxie said.

Donnie, meanwhile, put an arm around my shoulder. "Feeling's mutual, bro."

"Yeah, I never thought I'd end up jamming with a bunch of high school metalheads," Gremlin said. "But, hey, you guys got some taste, and now we make killer music, eh?"

"Thanks to you and your influence, Gremlin," Donnie said.

"Dammit, Gremlin," I added. "Quit saying 'eh,' will ya?"

He smiled and yelled, "No, *eh*?" Everyone laughed.

"I never thought I'd be a bass player in a band," Mullie said in his low, deadpan manner when things quieted down. "Never thought I had it in me. I mean, the drawing and stuff was good, but I didn't think I was good enough to do anything with it, even though everybody told me I was. Still, I had no clue what I was gonna do after high school until I joined this band."

Few good things come out of crime. Even though Chris lost himself and his freedom, he helped Mullie determine his future. Mullie discovered he had musical talent and realized he was a good artist. He planned to take art classes at a community college.

Gremlin tapped Mullie on the shoulder. "We're glad to have you."

The rest of us agreed.

We sat quietly. Amanda leaned against my chest. I held her tight around her waist. The lights of Vegas glowed. I gently stroked Amanda's arm and kissed her softly on the earlobe.

"Think this is gonna work out?" I whispered.

"It better," she softly said.

I wasn't sure if I was talking about the band, the move north, or me and her, and I didn't think she quite knew either.

About the Author

John Santana grew up in Las Vegas, Nevada, and lived for a decade in post-grunge Seattle. A former award-winning newspaper reporter and columnist, today he is a college librarian who also teaches History of Rock Music at a small community college in New York's Hudson Valley. He is married with two children, two cats, two cats in dog suits, and four guitars. *Bastards of Young* is his first novel.